# SAVING SOPHIE

BOOK SEVEN IN THE *BODYGUARDS OF L.A. COUNTY* SERIES

# CATE BEAUMAN

# DEDICATION

To the courageous.

# CHAPTER ONE

March 2015
Bangor, Maine

SOPHIE'S HANDS SHOOK AS SHE CRUSHED THE WHITE PILL beneath the waxed paper. Heart pounding, she glanced at the elegant wall clock ticking away each precious second, knowing he would be home any minute. She had mere moments to get this right. If it didn't work...

She shook the thought away, taking three quick steps to the fridge, gasping when the front door opened. "Oh god." She grabbed the beer from the second shelf and moved back to the countertop, twisting off the top as his footsteps echoed down the hall.

"Hurry, Sophie. Hurry," she chanted in a desperate whisper, looking over her shoulder as she dumped the first few sips of amber liquid into the sink, then lifted the creased waxy paper, trying her best to steady her hands as she coaxed the powerful sleeping aid into the bottle with several gentle taps. Holding her thumb over the opening, she wiggled the chilled glass, making certain there were no traces of the powder left along the inside of the neck.

Crumpling the waxed paper, she shoved the small scrap into her pocket, wiping sweaty palms on her baggy pants as she darted glances around her workspace, searching for telltale signs of her deception, terrified he would somehow know and punish her the way he had last night. Her arms still throbbed where the bat had cracked against her skin.

"Where's my wine?" He strolled into the room, his long, lean frame towering over her five-foot-five stature as he pushed her body into the counter.

She swallowed, turning, careful not to spill on his Armani pinstripes. "Uh," she cleared her throat, her shoulders automatically tensing as she stared into his cool blue eyes. "I thought—I thought you might like this instead." She held up his favorite lager, handing it over with a small smile, praying he would drink instead of discipline her for making a decision without asking him first. "I—I bought lobster too." She licked her lips and smiled again, doing her best to ignore her pounding pulse. "A celebration," she continued, trying to gauge his measuring eyes. "Since today was my last day at work."

"I gave you permission to go to the store for a *nice* meal, and you picked out lobster and beer?"

She shrunk under his glare, waiting for the smash of the bottle against the wall or a nasty grab to the back of her neck. "I'm sorry. I thought you might—"

"That's what you get for thinking. Stupid." He shook his head. "You're so damn stupid."

"I'm—I'm sorry," she murmured for the second time. "I was going to make a salad. And I bought some of those butter rolls you like so much."

"That doesn't make you any less dumb."

"I know." She turned toward the sink, grabbing for the head of romaine she'd left on the counter, hoping he would go, but she was whirled around instead.

"Where's my money?"

"Right here." She groped behind her back for the receipt and dollar forty-two she hadn't spent.

He ripped the change from her hand, glancing at the paper slip he'd taken with it. "Ruthie checked you out?"

She nodded. "Yes."

"Who bagged you up?"

"I don't know her name. She's new." She'd waited in the longer line to make certain Robbie Winters didn't put her items in a bag. It didn't matter that Robbie was little more than seventeen and of no interest to her. Interactions with the opposite sex, no matter how harmless, were never worth the consequences.

"You were late getting home. I said five thirty. I checked the GPS. You pulled in at five thirty-four."

She clenched her stomach with the rush of dread. Last night's beating started with the same conversation. "The traffic was bad with the tourists heading into town. I didn't go anywhere but the grocery store."

"Twice in two days." He squeezed the welts on her forearms. "I guess I didn't make myself clear."

She struggled to suppress her whimper against his merciless grip. "No you did. I—"

"Good thing you'll be staying home from now on." He pressed harder on her bruised skin and shoved her away. "I won't have to listen to your foolish excuses."

She hated that he'd made her give up her job—her last piece of freedom. "Right."

"I expect dinner by six-thirty."

"Yes." She relaxed her shoulders a fraction when that appeared to be the end of his latest interrogation. "I thought we could eat out on the deck. It's so nice out tonight—an early tease of summer."

"You know all about teasing." He sipped the beer, stepping closer, backing her into the hard knobs jutting from the drawer. "I know how you like to flirt." He grabbed her hair. "Did you bat those witch's eyes and smile at all of the men walking by?"

"No. No of course not." She cringed, ready for the fist to the ribs as she darted a glance at the bottle he still held, wanting him to drink again and swallow every drop. "I—"

"I hate it when you lie."

"I'm not—"

"Yeah you are." He wrapped long ropes of blond around his hand, pulling her head back. "I know how you operate. Flirting is the only way you sell any of that ugly crap you make."

She said nothing for a moment, waiting for him to punish or release. "I—I have your cheese and crackers ready if you want me to bring them to you. I already turned the paper to the arts section."

He let her go, but not before the quick, cruel tug that made her gasp and him smile as he left for the living room.

She turned toward the counter, gripping the cool granite, already exhausted after one exchange. He'd only been home minutes, and the tension squeezing her muscles was unbearable. Letting loose a shuddering breath, she walked back to the fridge for the cheese, praying he would drink his beer faster than his miserly sips to his nightly glass of cabernet.

She reached in the cupboard for Eric's preferred selection of gourmet crackers, placing five wafers on a plate exactly two inches apart. Brie wedges in perfectly cut triangles followed, then green and purple grapes she scrutinized, making certain there were no imperfections among the fruit before she set them down. She glanced at the clock, stalling for as long as she dared, hoping the pill would start to kick in before she brought him food that might lessen the effects.

"Where are my cheese and crackers?" he hollered, his words slurring.

"I'll—I'll be right there." She bit her lip with a surge of hope, too afraid to let herself believe she might actually get away. "I'm coming," she added for good measure, waiting for his nasty reply.

Several more seconds passed, and she lifted the cobalt platter, making her way to the living room with her heart thundering in her ears, deafening, as she moved down the hall, peeking in at the man she feared. He lay in his La-Z-Boy with his eyes closed and his head resting against the butter-soft leather.

"Er—Eric," she whispered, her voice trembling as she walked closer. "Eric?" She crouched in front of him, touching her finger to his cheek, terrified he would open his eyes and make her stay. "Eric," she said louder, and he began to snore.

Her breath heaved in and out as tears—part terror, part relief—slid down her cheeks. This was real. This moment she'd dreamt of for months was truly happening. She stood on watery legs, grabbing the half-full beer bottle from his lap. "Eric," she said once more as she hurried from the room and dashed up the stairs, rushing into the master suite, looking over her shoulder the entire time, sure he was steps behind.

She closed herself in the bedroom, locking the door, and moved into the walk-in closet, yanking down the zipper on the enormous white bag holding her dreaded wedding gown. She fought with the endless layers of organza she hated but Eric had insisted on, and grabbed the business envelope she'd stuffed with cash and loosely secured in the bodice of the dress, then turned, crouching down, feeling around in the recesses of a small space behind her shoe rack, snatching out the framed picture of her and her mother smiling. Hustling into the bathroom next, she dumped the remaining contents of Eric's beer bottle down the sink and stood on the cushioned bench, reaching on top of the vanity for her mother's jewelers tools she wasn't supposed to have kept but couldn't bear to part with. She made her way back to the bed, shoving everything, including her purse, into her backpack.

Flinging the strap over her shoulder, she paused by the window, staring into the backyard at the mound of dirt packed over her beloved Cooper. "I'm so sorry, Coop. I'm so sorry." With one last glimpse she turned, tossing the four-carat diamond engagement ring she'd never wanted to the plush comforter and cautiously opened the door, listening, then booked it down the stairs when the house remained silent, making her way out the rear entrance.

The refreshing spring breeze tickled her face; the sun was sinking on the horizon. She yanked free Dylan's bike she'd hidden among the bushes along the side of the house, then glanced around at her neighbor's homes, making certain no one was looking out the windows, and mounted herself up on the seat, pedaling quickly, careful to keep her pace steady instead of frantic with the rush of adrenaline. Sweat dribbled down her temples as she pulled further away from the line of million-dollar homes, taking the path leading to town.

One mile quickly turned into two then three, barely straining her athletic body before she turned right toward the row of rundown apartments, stopping in front of the building where her one and only secret friend lived. She struggled to get the cumbersome mountain bike into the hallway and lock the chain in place, then dashed up two flights of stairs, pounding on the door marked 3B.

Dylan open the door dressed in short shorts and a cropped shirt, her long black hair tied back from her pretty pixy face. "Come in." She tugged on Sophie's arm, pulling her into the room.

She sucked in a sharp breath as Dylan's enthusiastic grip sent a deep ache along her tender bruises.

Dylan immediately dropped her hand. "I'm sorry. God, I'm sorry."

"It's okay." She stepped further inside the messy apartment.

"Let me see."

"We have to go." She looked out the window, certain the sleeping pill wouldn't last long enough for her to make her escape. "He didn't drink all of the beer. Most of it, but there was plenty left to pour down the sink. He might wake up."

Dylan shook her head. "That stuff hits hard. You have until morning. I can guarantee it. You'll be long gone by then."

Gone but not far enough. She would never be far enough away from Eric Winthrop.

"I want to go." She crossed her arms at her chest, uneasy standing idle. "I'm going to miss you so much, but I'm ready to leave."

"I'll miss you too, but I want you out of here...after the pictures. Now let me see so we can document this."

Sophie sighed, quickly pulling up her sleeves to Dylan's gasp as they both stared at the goose-egg-sized knots the wooden bat had left across her forearms.

"Sophie," Dylan whispered, tenderly brushing her fingers over the horrid wounds. "You're lucky he didn't break them."

The sound of the bat smacking against her bones echoed in her head. "It's all right."

11

She shook her head. "No it's not."

Dylan had seen dozens of her bruises—on her back, across her ribs, her arms and legs, but never ever her face. Eric always controlled his rage enough to keep her face free of the welts and dark purple bruises.

"It's not okay, Sophie."

"I know." Or she did somewhere deep down. She looked out the window again into the dark. "Let's just go."

"This will only take a minute. You need proof. All of the reading I've done says it's a good idea to keep everything documented."

"Okay," she said quietly, not meeting her friend's eyes. Somehow every snap of the camera was as demoralizing as each violent blow to her body.

The digital camera clicked four times before Dylan removed the memory card and pushed it into the slot on her laptop, pressing several buttons. "Take off your nun clothes," she said, pulling the thumb drive from her computer, and walked to a drawer, grabbing dark-wash skinny jeans and a breezy white long-sleeve top she'd bought for Sophie several weeks ago in preparation.

Sophie pulled off the bulky wool sweater and baggy cords she'd worn despite the mild temperatures and slid on the snug denim, hesitating as she stared at herself in the mirror. It had been over two years since she'd worn anything that actually fit. She put on the flowing, feminine shirt next, amazed at the sudden transformation.

"Oh, Sophie. You look so good. You're so pretty."

"Thank you." She continued to study herself, staring into her own weary violet eyes, overwhelmed and exhilarated by her first step toward liberation.

"Here." Dylan held out a hair tie and a shoulder-length black wig.

Sophie snagged both, twisting her long locks into a braid, making a flat bun at the back of her head, and settled the fake hair in place, fascinated by her fresh new look. "I don't even recognize myself."

"That's the point." Dylan went back to her drawer. "Here are the other clothes." She grabbed a black backpack. "And the new bag."

"Thank you." Sophie gathered her meager belongings from the bag she arrived with, tossed Eric's empty beer bottle she'd brought in the trash, and took the thumb drive Dylan still held. The shorts, second pair of jeans, and two tops went in along with her other items, then she tied a light gray sweatshirt around her tiny waist. "Let's go."

Dylan nodded, grabbing Sophie's hand, and they left the tiny studio apartment, stopping on the first floor.

"Hold on a second." Dylan knocked on apartment 1C's door.

Sophie turned away as the tall, muscled man answered. She walked to the small window, tensing, staring out at the parking lot, waiting for Eric to walk around the corner. He would charm the group of men and women smoking outside on the stoop with smiles and small talk then take her home and punish her within an inch of her life—if he didn't just kill her as he'd threatened to do hundreds of times.

"Thanks, Rod," Dylan said to the buff man leaning against the doorframe. "I'll have the car back by tomorrow morning."

"No prob."

Sophie snuck a peak at the college-aged kid, keeping herself turned, not wanting Rod to get a full-on look at her. The fewer people who saw her, the more likely Eric would never find her.

"Come on." Dylan took her hand again and they walked outside, around the back of the building to the rusted hatchback. "Let's get you out of here."

Sophie nodded, taking her seat among crumpled fast food bags and other trash.

Dylan started the car, and they made their way through Bangor.

Sophie glanced around one last time at the town she'd called home for more than twelve years as Dylan merged south on the onramp towards Brunswick, knowing she would never come back to the place where she and her mother had made their fresh start.

"Your train leaves at nine. We should make it in plenty of time."

"I've never traveled by train."

"Me neither." Dylan moved into the right lane, letting faster traffic pass. "Have you decided where you'll go?"

She shook her head, even though she'd thought of little else since she woke this morning, knowing today had to be the day. "Somewhere big. Somewhere where he can't find me." She swallowed. "He'll look. He'll never stop," she said, staring into the side mirror, waiting for the black Mercedes to rush up behind them and force them to pull over. "You have to be careful."

Dylan huffed out an amused laugh. "That bastard doesn't scare me."

She wished he didn't scare her either. "Be careful anyway."

"I will, but he's a coward."

"No more than me," she murmured, glancing down at the hints of bruised skin peeking out from under her sleeves.

Dylan tossed her a look. "Don't go there."

She sat back fully in her seat, unable to take her eyes off the mirror until Dylan eventually exited the interstate and drove toward the center of town, stopping in front of the Amtrak station as the train pulled up.

"Looks like you won't have to wait." She set the emergency brake and searched through her purse. "Here's my license." She handed over the Maine ID and paper ticket she'd bought and printed when Sophie gave her the green light from her kiosk at the mall. "We don't look all that different with your wig, so this should get you your next ticket in Boston."

"Thank you." Sophie leaned over and gave Dylan a big hug. "Thank you so much. I wouldn't have been able to do this without you."

"Don't look back, Sophie." Dylan eased away, squeezing her hand. "Get out of here and never look back. Here are the phone numbers for the Stowers house shelters in Baltimore and LA I told you about—just in case." She handed over the March copy of *Trendy* magazine with papers sticking out from the edges.

"Thanks. Please don't forget to put flowers on my mother's grave."

"I won't."

She nodded and hugged Dylan for the last time. "Bye."

"Bye. Take care of yourself."

"I will." Sophie got out, sliding her backpack on her shoulder as she made her way to the bored-eyed man at the ticket kiosk.

"Ticket and ID, Ma'am."

Sophie handed over both, holding her breath, waiting for her plan to fall apart.

"Safe trip." He gave them back.

"Thank you," she murmured, letting loose a shaky exhale as she turned and moved toward the train, wanting to run instead of walk. She boarded the first available car and stared out the window as she sat down, watching Dylan pull out of the lot in the rusty hatchback, already missing the only person she'd had a connection with. She bobbed her leg up and down, struggling to keep her fidgeting at bay. Minutes passed, feeling like hours, until finally the doors closed. The train jerked forward, moving toward Boston—the first stop on her journey to freedom.

# CHAPTER TWO

April
Los Angeles

SOPHIE SLID THE DUSTING CLOTH ALONG THE FRAMES OF the glossy photographs lining the long hall. She glanced at the cheap sports watch she'd picked up at the store, pleased she was slightly ahead of her own schedule. Now that she had a solid routine in place, she was able to clean each office suite in twenty minutes or less. If she streamlined her process even more, she'd be down to fifteen minutes in no time, easy.

She stopped at the next door, stuffing the edge of the rag into her jeans pocket as she entered the darkened room, grabbing and tying off the trash. She replaced the old bag with a new one and walked out, plopping the garbage into the cart she pulled behind her.

Cleaning offices certainly wasn't the dream job she'd envisioned on her journey west. She yearned to get back to jewelry making, but she couldn't complain. Every under-the-table paycheck was a step closer to her own car and apartment. She was incredibly grateful to the counselors at Stowers House for helping her secure employment, giving her the opportunity to earn a living.

She moved to the next picture frame, wiping away any dust that had settled since last night, then walked into another darkened room. She glanced up as she replaced the soiled trash bag by the desk, pausing to stare out at the massive skyscrapers lit in the night, and smiled, still amazed that she was here. Los Angeles was *huge*. It was easy to hide in an area that stretched out as far as the eye could see. Shaking her head, she focused on her work, reminding herself that she wasn't hiding. She was living her life and beginning again in the anonymity of a place that was home to millions.

For four blessed weeks she'd woken on her cot at the shelter without fear—or mostly. For the first time in too long she wore what she chose, ate what she wanted, and enjoyed the simple fact that she didn't have to walk on eggshells every blessed moment of every single day. But she still had to be careful. She pinned up her hair or braided it every day and wore a ball cap or hoodie whenever she left Stowers House, despite the relative safety of the city.

A door closed further down the hall, and a man walked by, moving toward the main lobby. He smiled. "Good night."

"Good night." She smiled back, remembering to meet his startlingly green eyes instead of look down and hunch her shoulders. If she wanted to blend in, she needed to behave like everyone else.

Alone again, she pulled her cloth free and moved to the last picture frame, wiping, peeking into the office where the man with almost shoulder-length, dark brown hair typed on his laptop. He was here often, at least twice a week, which meant that at least twice a week she waited until the last possible second to knock on his door. Nibbling her lip, she looked at the professional group picture she'd just cleaned, staring at the man's gorgeous face among more than a dozen other handsome men, then at his powerful shoulders as he stood like the rest of his co-workers with their muscular arms crossed at their chests. She took a deep breath, reminding herself that bodyguards didn't hurt people—they helped them—stepped forward again, swallowing, then raised her hand and knocked.

The man, Stone, she thought his name was, didn't bother to look up.

"I'm—I'm just going to grab your trash."

He grunted, his fingers never stopping on the keyboard as she hurried in, pulled out the full bag, replaced it, and left. She started back down the hall, relaxing her shoulders, glad the moment was over, trying to figure out why her frequent encounters with one of Ethan Cooke Security's agents always left her so frazzled. He barely paid her any attention. Other than the one time he'd said, "Yeah," in his deep voice, he responded in grunts. He'd never actually looked up from his laptop. He was just here a lot, which was oddly comforting...sort of...from a distance.

She walked into the final darkened office on her left, reaching for the trash bag, and stopped, staring as one of the men she recognized from the same picture held a black-haired beauty in an intense lip lock, chuckling as he nuzzled her neck and nipped at her ear before easing away.

"Hold on."

"Where you going, big guy?" the woman asked, pulling him back, then dropped her hands as her eyes met Sophie's. "Oh."

"I'm sorry." Sophie cleared her throat, backing from the room. "I'm sorry," she repeated.

"No. No. Excuse us," the woman said as she fixed her shirt. "We didn't know anyone was here."

"That's okay." Sophie automatically glanced down at her not-so-white Keds and looked up just as quickly, remembering her new rules on maintaining eye contact. "I was just—the trash." She stepped forward, grabbing the bag, pausing when she recognized the bodyguard's make-out partner as Abigail Harris. No, Abigail Quinn. The newspapers said she'd recently married.

"Don't let us get in your way."

"You're not." Was she actually in the same room as one of LA's top fashion designers and the visionary of Stowers House? Abigail Quinn was petite, powerful, and stunning. It was impossible to tell that she'd been through a horrifying ordeal not all that long ago.

"Sorry." The man skirted around Sophie, making his way to his desk. "We'll be out of here in a second."

"Oh, I'm—" She secured a clean bag in the trashcan. "I was leaving."

"You don't have to." Abigail moved forward, touching her arm. "Right, Jerrod?"

"Yeah. I forgot a file."

"Work, work, work." Abigail scoffed, rolling her eyes. "This guy thinks he's going to stare at his laptop on a Friday night instead of make out with his wife."

"I'm sure I can find time for both."

Abigail grinned, and Sophie relaxed as much as she could.

"I'm Abby."

"Nice to meet you." Sophie moved back to the door, unsure how to handle Abby's vivacious energy. She envied women who oozed such confidence. She'd always been shy and quiet. "I should get going. I still have a few offices to clean." Jerrod's trashcan was last on her list, but she didn't want to stay and chat. She didn't know how. "Good night."

Abby's smile dimmed. "Good night."

Sophie hurried down the hall to the supply closet,

dragging her cart behind her, taking her time putting her items away while she waited for Jerrod to close his door and for his and Abby's voices to fade.

The main office doors shut, and she sighed, remembering why she treasured the night shift so much. There was no chatting or questions asked in a mostly empty building. No one bothered her in the dark. She shouldered the bag she never let out of her sight and hurried down the hall past Stone's office, ready to enjoy her third full weekend in Los Angeles.

~~~~

"Good job, Aubrey. That looks great," Sophie encouraged as she helped the eight-year-old bead a necklace at the Saturday morning craft table. "Do you want pink next or purple?"

"Purple."

Sophie rifled through the large bucket of cheap plastic beads, looking for the desired color and shape as her eager student filled the pipe cleaner with the pattern they'd picked out only moments before.

"When will I be able to make bracelets like the kind you do?"

"Mmm, probably after you practice a little while longer." It had taken Sophie's mother an entire day to teach her how to twist and hammer metal into the intricate pattern that long-ago winter when she'd sprained her ankle. She touched the pretty sterling silver piece on her wrist, desperately missing mom's patience and sweet, quiet voice.

"Your mom teached you how to make real good stuff."

"Taught." Sophie corrected, smiling.

"She *taught* you how to make good stuff." Aubrey

smiled back.

"Thanks." Why was it so easy to relax around children when spending time with adults always tied her in knots? "Your mom's going to be excited. Maybe we should add a bracelet to go with it."

Aubrey nodded enthusiastically. "She'll have a surprise to wear when she comes back from her job interview."

"She'll love it."

"How do you know?"

"My mother always told me children's gifts are the best gifts of all."

"Did your dad hit your mom and make her cry?"

Sophie paused with her hand in the bucket, staring at the pretty little redhead at her side. Aubrey spoke so matter-of-factly about something no child should ever have to witness. "No. My dad always hugged and kissed me and my mother." Until he died and left them with a mess to clean up.

Aubrey stopped beading, meeting Sophie's eyes as if the concept couldn't possibly be true.

"What color should we make the bracelet?"

"The same as this." Aubrey pointed to her creation. "Mom can wear it when we get ice cream. She says we can have it, and that everything's going to be different now."

Sophie gave Aubrey a small smile as her heart broke for the sweet child. "I bet it will."

"My dad's never gonna lay a finger on either one of us again. He can't find us, so I don't have to be afraid anymore. My mom said so."

"That's good," she whispered, pressing a kiss to Aubrey's forehead. "That's really good, sweetie." She started rifling through the bucket again, glancing at the colorful clock on the wall, noting that her shift in the childcare room was almost over. Stowers House didn't ask for money in return for a bed and safe place to stay, just volunteer time.

"My mom says..."

Sophie no longer paid attention to Aubrey's endless chatter as she tuned into the cheerful, energetic voice across the room. She looked up, spotting Abigail Quinn talking to Lynn, the Director of Operations. Sophie watched Abigail's big blue eyes scan the bright, pretty space as she continued her conversation. Sophie clutched a handful of bead when Abby's gaze met hers, noting the immediate recognition and hint of surprise after their quick encounter last night.

"Sophie." Aubrey tugged on the sleeve of her shirt. "Sophie."

Sophie shook her head, fighting her way back into the moment. "Huh? Yes?"

"It's finished. See?" Aubrey held up her necklace with a triumphant grin.

"Nice." She shook her head again as the little girl's smile dimmed. "Beautiful. Very, very beautiful."

"I have to go to the bathroom, then we can start on the bracelet."

"Okay." She no longer thought of beads and pipe cleaners as her eyes locked on Abby's for the second time. Lynn tapped Abby's shoulder and Abby turned. Sophie took advantage of the moment, pushed back from the table, and headed upstairs. She slid the elastic tie she kept around her wrist into her hair, twisting the glossy blond into a tight bun, and pulled on her gray hoodie, covering her head. It was time to go.

Seeing Abby at Ethan Cooke Security was one thing, but now that she'd been discovered at the shelter too, Abigail Quinn could connect her place of employment and residence. The fashion designer's face was all over the newspapers and magazines now that her *Escape* line had taken off like wildfire. She was very much a well-known artist like Eric. They worked in different mediums, certainly, but what if they somehow knew each other? All it took was one question to the wrong person and her new life would be over before it had a chance to begin.

Someone knocked on her door, and she tensed.

"Sophie, are we gonna make my mom's bracelet?"

She turned, swamped with guilt as she stared at the petite redhead in her pretty black dress and purple striped tights. Crouching down, she took Aubrey's hands. "Sweetie, I have to leave."

"Can I come?"

She shook her head.

"Oh." Aubrey's face fell. "Okay."

Sophie raised her chin with a gentle finger. "You make beautiful jewelry. I taught you just the way my mom taught me. Go on down and finish up. I promise you your mother's going to love it."

"Are you coming back?"

She shook her head again, knowing Aubrey deserved the truth. "No, sweetie, I'm not."

Aubrey threw her arms around Sophie's neck. "But I'm going to miss you."

She closed her eyes, hugging the little girl tight. For the last three weeks Aubrey had been her shadow when her mother left the shelter to take the steps necessary to start a new life for herself and her daughter. "I'm going to miss you too. Here." She pulled off the bracelet she and her mom made over a decade ago. "I want you to have this."

Aubrey hesitated. "It's special."

Sophie nodded. "Yes it is, and so are you."

Aubrey put the jewelry on her small wrist. "Thank

you."

"You're welcome." She tapped Aubrey's nose. "Be a good girl."

"I will."

"Okay." She stood, shouldering the bag she never unpacked. "Bye, sweetie."

"Bye."

She did her best to ignore the tears on Aubrey's cheeks as she slid out the back entrance, making her way down the block to the Metro stop. It was time to find a new place to stay until she could figure out what she should do next.

# CHAPTER THREE

GRITTY ROCK N' ROLL POURED THROUGH HIGH DEFINITION speakers while Stone worked grout between the joints of his new marble tiling. Teasing the mixture into place, he made certain the air bubbles were gone before moving on to the next spot. He paused, wiping at the sweat dripping down his forehead despite the kerchief he wore on his head, and sat back on his heels, looking around his bathroom with a satisfied nod. The play of warm, sandy tones throughout the space had turned out exactly the way he'd envisioned. Another day or two and the first room in his new place would be completely finished.

The tiny fixer-upper across from the beach was just what he'd been looking for when he plunked down a good chunk of his savings late last September. With the addition well underway and new roof in place, by mid-summer he'd be living between the walls of his home instead of the camper parked outside, easy. He could technically live here now—there was running water and the kitchen was functional—but then he might rush, and he had nothing but time to make this place into exactly what he wanted.

He'd envisioned his beach house more than a few times while he sweated his ass off in the desert dodging gunfire. He'd scored big when he stepped off the plane and found this gem nestled on the hill overlooking the Pacific Coast Highway and ocean beyond. The structure had been little more than ruins, but the foundation had been good.

He glanced through the doorway toward the new windows in his soon-to-be bedroom, staring out at the cloudless blue sky and palm trees in the distance, content for the first time ever. This spot was his, and he was never leaving.

His cellphone rang on the waist of his grimy jeans, disturbing his moment of peace. He was tempted to let the call go to voicemail until he saw that it was Jerrod. Today was his day off, but that didn't mean work didn't need him. He set his trowel back in the thick paste and answered. "McCabe."

"Hey, Stone, it's Abby."

He closed his eyes with a deep sigh. The exhausting Abigail Quinn. The woman talked too much, and she was so damn chipper. But he liked her. It was impossible not to. Somehow she wore a body down until they couldn't help but adore her. She'd been through hell, yet she was a sweetheart. "Hey."

"I haven't seen you in awhile. How are you?"

"Good."

"Do go on, Stone."

He smiled.

"Have you been by the office lately?"

Abby asked but they both knew the answer. He'd ignored her and Jerrod last night when they came barreling down the hall, pawing at each other with their tongues shoved down each other's throats. "Yeah."

"Have you noticed the cleaning woman?"

"Sure." He'd noticed her all right. She was gorgeous, and she didn't say much, which worked just fine for him.

"Do you know her name?"

"Nope." He picked up his trowel, sliding more grout among the empty spaces where the new pedestal sink would eventually go.

"Well, what do you know about her?"

"Not much."

"Wow, two words. You actually said two words in a row. I think this might be a record."

He grinned. "What do you want, Abby?"

"Holy crap, a whole question. I'm going to pass out."

"I'm hanging up."

"No. Don't do that. Do you know what nights she works?"

"No."

Abby sighed in his ear.

"Monday through Friday, I guess. Why?"

"No reason. Just curiosity."

He narrowed his eyes. During the week he helped cover Abby's protection in Maryland, then the two days he'd had solo duty here in LA and one *long* damn plane ride with her to New York City, he learned that Abby had a million questions and a purpose for every one of them. "Bullshit. What's up?"

"I can't get into specifics, but I think she's had some trouble."

He shrugged off her concern. If the blond had problems, she could handle them. She was a big girl. "Okay."

"Stop with all the compassion."

He let Abby's frustrated comments slide off his back. He took care of himself unless he was paid to take care of someone else.

"Maybe if you see her—"

He already knew where this was going, and it was going to end here. "I'm on duty all this week."

"Yeah but—"

"I'll be in The Hills for the most part. I probably

won't see her."

"But if you do—"

"Abby."

"Just give her a once over and make sure she's okay."

He said nothing as he scooped up more grout.

"Can you do that? Stone?"

He huffed out a breath. "Yeah, I can do that."

"Promise?"

He didn't make promises to anyone. "If I see her I'll give her a once over."

"That's all I can ask."

"I'll talk to you later."

"You wanna come over for dinner?"

"No."

"I'll make that garlic chicken you liked."

"Who says I liked it?"

"You grunted and nodded your head."

He bit his cheek instead of chuckling. The last thing he needed to do was encourage her to keep talking.

"I guess I'll see you around."

"Bye." He hung up before she could say anything more and slid his phone away, then scooped up more grout, concentrating on his bathroom floor. He had no desire to worry about some cleaning woman with trouble on her hands.

~~~~

Stone stepped from the elevator and let himself into the Ethan Cooke Security Offices expecting to hear the vacuum humming in one of the rooms beyond, but there was only silence. Frowning, he checked his watch—eleven-thirty. The blond was usually finishing up right around now, which concluded with the hum of the Hoover somewhere in the distance.

He moved down the hall, certain he would see her gathering trash in the cart she pulled with her most nights or spot her putting the buckets and vacuum back in the supply closet, but she wasn't there. He shrugged, turning, ready to head home. It had been a long damn day with his ten-hour duty, but he said he would check on Abby's mysterious cleaning woman. Now he could tell her he'd tried.

The blond probably quit. She always wore jeans and a simple t-shirt to change the trashes and chase away the dust, but he knew high-end when he saw it. Whoever she was, she wasn't used to swabbing toilets to earn a few bucks. With a shake of his head, he moved toward the bathrooms in the dim light, catching an armful of woman as she rushed from the men's room, crashing into him.

Screaming, she tried to jerk away.

"Whoa." He dropped his hands from surprisingly firm arms. "Take it easy."

"Sorry," she shuddered out, swiping at her long braid with trembling fingers.

He took a step back. "I didn't think anyone was here."

"I got a late start." She swallowed as she met his eyes, looked down, then glanced up just as quickly. "I just finished with the bathrooms."

He grunted, studying her. Was she always this jumpy? He'd never paid much attention other than when she bent down to grab the trash bag next to his desk. She had an excellent ass.

"I'm going to—I have to put my stuff away." She picked up the bucket she'd dropped.

He made a noise in his throat again, staring. She

was a stunner—blonde hair, blue-eyes—or maybe gray, full, lush lips that didn't smile, all set in an oval face. Her skin was flawless and creamy, like the airbrushed models he kept away from the prying paparazzi. She definitely had the whole package.

"Sorry for bumping into you," she mumbled.

"Yeah."

"I've gotta go." She licked her lips. "Bye." She turned and booked it down the hall, taking her cleaning supplies with her.

He watched her open the closet door and lean her forehead against the wood as she pressed her hand to her heart. Interesting...but not his problem. He started toward the main lobby as the closet door closed, picking up his pace, not wanting to share an elevator with the jittery woman. He descended thirty floors and walked through the parking garage to his mint-condition 1966 Mustang, listening to the rain pound as he took his seat behind the wheel. The drive home was bound to suck in this downpour. He was probably looking at a good hour back to the Palisades. That's what happened when he played Good Samaritan. He should've been in his bed sleeping, but he'd driven himself into the city to check on the blond, because Abby's curiosity got the better of him.

Shaking his head, he turned over the engine and circled his way to the ground floor, taking a right out of the exit. He turned his wipers up to full blast as the woman walking on the desolate, dark sidewalk in the sheets of rain caught his eye. He squinted, recognizing her as Abby's new pal from upstairs, and swore. "Not your problem," he muttered to himself even as he slowed and pulled over to the curb. Leaning over to the passenger's seat, he rolled down the window. "You want a ride?"

The blond glanced his way, her clothes plastered to her short frame. "No thanks."

"You're soaking wet."

She stopped under the streetlight. "That's okay. I'm walking to the bus stop right over there." She pointed to the empty glass enclosure half a block up.

"If that's the way you want it."

"Yes, thanks. I should hurry. It's the last bus of the night." As she spoke, the bus slowed at the stop sign and drove off. Gasping, she ran after her ride. "Wait! Stop!" The bus was halfway down the block before she slowed, her shoulders slumping as she continued walking.

He sighed, pulling up next to her again instead of driving off the way he wanted to. "Just get in. I'll take you home."

She reached for the door handle, hesitating, as water streamed down her face.

"You're not getting any drier standing out there."

She opened the door and took her seat. "Thank you," she murmured through chattering teeth.

Stone cranked up the heat, wincing as she dripped all over the antique leather interior. "Where to?"

"Uh, East Sixth and Sanford Ave."

He stared at her. "East Sixth and Sanford Avenue?"

"Yes."

He shook his head and made a left, starting down Sixth Street. The rain slowed to a drizzle as they stopped for several lights. With each block he drove, the neighborhood grew more hopeless and the graffiti on the surrounding buildings increased. He passed bangers and addicts looking for their next score. Hookers waited for their Johns on the corners. Stone slid the pretty, classy blond a look as he turned on Sanford. "You're telling me you live down here?"

She held her hands clasped in her lap. "Yes."

"What the hell are you doing down in Skid Row?"

She shrugged. "It's that motel right there." She pointed to a rundown by-the-hour establishment.

"You've got to be kidding me."

"No."

He rolled to a stop, not daring to box himself in with the group of trouble standing at the corner watching him. He itched for the gun he wasn't carrying.

"Thank you." She reached for the handle.

"You're seriously getting out of this car?"

She licked her lips. "Yes. Thank you again." She stepped out and hurried toward the dilapidated building with the 'O' and 'L' glowing bright in the mostly burnt-out sign. The men at the corner whistled and hollered her way, wanting a piece of that, as she rushed up the stairs to the second floor, unlocked her door, and closed herself in.

He stared as the light blinked on behind dingy curtains in the window. "Unbelievable." He hesitated, then started back down the road, shrugging off his concern. Blondie was a big girl. If this was where she hung her hat, that was her problem.

~~~~

"I'm worried sick, Clyde." Eric sat in his La-Z-Boy with his feet up, flipping the ring he'd given Sophie between his thumb and index finger, blinking when the morning sun glinted off the diamonds and silver, accentuating the superior cut and quality of the gift she'd thrown in his face. Ungrateful. Stupid and ungrateful.

"I understand, Eric. I absolutely do. I can't even imagine what you're going through."

"You haven't heard anything? There's no news whatsoever?"

"I'm afraid not."

"It's been a month." His private investigator hadn't been able to come up with anything either. Somehow Sophie had managed to vanish.

"Her credit card and bank accounts haven't been touched and her purse is missing, but I still believe she left of her own accord. You found her ring on the bed. If foul play was involved, someone would've wanted that, I suspect. It's a beaut. It's apparent she was in a hurry to be gone with the way she closed up her shop."

He grit his teeth as he thought of the fool she'd made of him. Everyone was talking about Sophie Burke ditching him. For that alone he wanted her found. He'd expected the cops to bring her back the morning he woke from his stupor, but they'd had no luck. He'd kept the beer and whatever she'd drugged him with to himself. She'd make that up to him when the time came. "We're supposed to get married in eighteen days."

"And I feel real bad about that. Unfortunately there's not much I can do from a legal standpoint. There was no crime committed. It sounds like a case of cold feet. She'll come home, Eric. Just give her a little time."

Oh, Sophie would come home all right. She was too dumb to stay gone for long. And if he needed to help things along, he would. "I didn't want to bring this up. I hate to." He added a hint of anguish to his voice for the sake of Bangor's Chief of Police. "I checked my safe yesterday. There's about five thousand dollars missing."

"What? Are you sure?"

"Yeah." He smiled. "She broke my heart and stole from me, Clyde. I thought I knew her, and God knows why, I still love her. I still want to marry her."

"Do you want to press charges?"

He let his breath shudder into the phone. "I think—I think I have to. No. No, I can't." He grinned, trying hard not to chuckle. The good officer was eating it up.

"If you're sure she took it, you have every right to your money, son."

"I don't know..." She thought she'd outsmarted him when she slashed her prices and sold off all of her ugly jewelry the day she closed shop. And she'd been skimming from her books since early March. She owed him, just about five thousand dollars. Sophie wasn't allowed to have money. Everything she earned belonged to him.

Clyde sighed. "I'm going to encourage you to file charges. I sure hate to say that. Sophie's a sweetheart, but five thousand dollars is a decent chunk of change. Why don't you come on down to the station and we'll fill out a report?"

Five thousand was nothing. He demanded ten times that for his paintings, but paying Sophie back meant everything. She had almost five weeks to make up to him, and the humiliation he'd suffered, well, that was priceless. "I just want her to come home, Clyde. I need her. I miss her so much. I have the art show coming up next week in Boston. I wanted her with me."

"Hang in there. We'll get some posters hung and get her name in the system. We'll get this figured out."

"If you think that's best."

"I do."

"I'll come down soon."

"I'll see you when you get here."

"Thanks." He hung up and grabbed the photograph of Sophie's smiling face from the end table. "You think you can outsmart me?" He laughed at her stunning image and smashed the picture to the wood floor, splintering the glass. "You're too damn stupid to outsmart me. You're *nothing* without me." He stomped on her face with the heel of his shoe and made his way to the front door. He had a police report to file. Sophie would be coming home real soon.

# CHAPTER FOUR

SOPHIE LOOKED AT HER WATCH, HUFFING OUT A frustrated breath. She was just going to make it to the bus stop, and that was only if she hurried. No matter how she streamlined her routine, coming into the office later wasn't working. Making sure she avoided another run in with Abby Quinn was vital, but her work was suffering as a result—so was her paycheck.

She spritzed more Windex on the mirror, swiping quickly, then moved to the last sink, glancing at the time again with a shake of her head. She was losing an hour's pay each night, and her income was already meager at best. She'd redone her budget this afternoon while she snacked on the apple she'd designated as her lunch, and the new adjustments weren't pretty.

Now that she was staying at the motel, her financial situation had become even direr. The place was horrible. By day her room was disgusting at best, no matter how she scrubbed it. By night, room 22 was downright scary. Squeaking beds and prostitutes moaning through paper-thin walls competed with gunfire and police sirens. And the bugs skittering on the floor... She shuddered thinking of the roaches and trash bag in which she kept her belongings to keep them clean.

She needed more than this part-time job if she planned to get herself out of her current situation. If she ever wanted to open her own shop again, she was going to have to do better than this, but working under the table left her few options. She had no doubt that if she tried for something different, Eric's private investigator would find her the second her employer filed her W-2.

Going back to Stowers House was tempting, but she couldn't risk it. Abby had probably forgotten about the whole thing, but she wasn't willing to find out. Bugs and her by-the-hour neighbors were better than Eric's beatings. Even if she had to live in that motel for the rest of her life it would be better than seeing him again. He'd told her more than once that if she ever left he would kill her. Eric always meant what he said.

She scoured the sink until it shined, threw her rubber gloves in the trash, and pulled open the door, noting that Stone's light was on down the hall. He was here late for the second night in a row. She needed to pop her head in and thank him again for yesterday. He'd been kind to drive her home, and he'd actually spoken to her—not a conversation per se—but he'd done more than grunt. His voice was deep, and he smelled good, like expensive, sexy cologne. And his face. She'd finally gotten an up-close-and-personal, full-on look when they crashed into each other in the shadows. His longer hair and sharp cheekbones should've made him appear feminine somehow, but they didn't. They accentuated the guarded intensity in his brown eyes. And there was nothing wrong with his full, serious mouth and strong jaw with hints of dark stubble either. He was so tough and...*hot*, but that didn't matter. She had a bus to catch.

Focusing on what she needed to do, she put her cleaning bucket away and grabbed her hoodie, which was still damp after last night's soaking. She slid her bag on her shoulder, already bracing herself for another long night in the ghetto.

~~~~

Stone heard the closet door close and shut his laptop. He'd been pretending to type up a report for the last hour while Blondie hustled around doing whatever it was she did. He'd packed up his stuff twice, ready to leave, then pulled everything back out, trying to figure out why the hell he'd come in the first place. He didn't belong here. He was caught up on his work, and his living room walls were waiting to be patched and painted. He should've taken a right when he left his duty in The Hills, but he found himself on the 101 instead, heading downtown.

Blondie had been on his mind all day, no matter how hard he tried to shrug her off. Her haunted eyes and unbelievable living arrangements were impossible to forget. Even when he'd reminded himself that she wasn't his problem and he didn't really care, she kept sneaking back under his radar. She didn't belong down in that section of town. If she didn't smarten up, she wasn't going to live very long.

He slid his laptop in its case for the third time as she quickly walked his way, giving a quick knock on the doorframe.

"Um, hi."

He glanced up, taking in her smooth complexion and glossy hair slicked back in a tight braid. "Hey."

"I'm in a hurry, but I wanted to thank you again for the ride last night."

He zipped the case closed. "No problem."

"All right." She gave him a small, uncomfortable smile as she adjusted the backpack on her shoulder. "Well, thanks again." She spun away.

"Wait."

She stopped, hesitated, and turned back.

"You want another lift?"

"Oh, no thanks. I'll just take the bus."

He shrugged. Now what? "Suit yourself."

She nodded and left.

He hurried after her instead of avoiding her the way he'd tried to not even twenty-four hours ago. He couldn't let her go back there.

She tossed an uneasy look over her shoulder as the elevator doors opened and she stepped inside.

He slid in before they closed. "I'm on my way out."

She crossed her arms and hunched herself in the corner, looking down.

"You sure you don't want a ride?"

"No thanks."

"You still staying in the same place?"

She glanced up. "Yes."

He nodded and leaned back against the control panel, pressing the red button with his elbow, sending the car to a jerking stop.

Her eyes widened as her gaze flew to his. "What—what are you doing? I'm going to miss my bus," she hollered over the piercing alarm.

"You're putting me in a hell of a spot here, Blondie."

"What do you mean?" She swallowed, moving further back into the corner.

"You're living in a shit hole in an even shittier part of town. I'd hate to see that face of yours in the *Times*. The least you can do is let me take you home so I know you get there safe."

"I don't mind taking the bus."

He glanced at his watch, fairly certain she wouldn't be riding any buses tonight. "Have it your way." He pressed the red button, sending the car down.

"I don't understand," she said quietly. "Why do you care where I live?"

Hadn't he been asking himself the same thing all day? "I wish I knew."

The elevator stopped on the fourth floor. "You might as well get out with me."

"I'll be fine, thank you."

He shrugged. "Can't say I didn't try." He got out, watching the door close her inside, and turned toward the parking garage more than a little relieved she'd let him off the hook. He'd offered to help and she shot him down. There was nothing else he could do—or wanted to do. The doors opened again before he'd taken two steps.

"Wait."

Pausing, he looked over his shoulder.

"I'll—I'll take the ride. I'm pretty sure I missed my bus."

He nodded, trying to figure out why her acceptance annoyed him when he was the one who made her miss her bus in the first place. "Let's go." He pushed the door open, letting her into the garage ahead of him. "The Mustang right over there." He pointed to his black beauty.

"I remember."

He got in, leaned over, and unlocked her door.

She took her seat, mumbling her gratitude.

He grunted, turned over the engine, and pulled out of his spot as Staind's guitar riffs filled the car. He twisted down four stories and gunned it through the yellow light across from the entrance, glancing her way as she sat against the door, her hands clasped tight around the bag in her lap. She looked so stiff and uncomfortable. Taking a chance, he decided to try for a conversation. Her smooth, quiet voice wasn't exactly hard on the ears. "So, I'm curious, why East Sixth and Sanford?"

She shrugged. "It's by the bus stop."

He nodded, accelerating through the next green light. She'd summed it up easy enough. Points for her. There was nothing wrong with a woman who didn't feel the need to talk all the damn time. They cruised along the rough streets in silence as he made his way down block after block, finally turning on Sanford. Dozens of blue lights reflected off the rundown buildings the closer he got to the motel. "Looks like some action up at your place."

She slid him an uneasy glance as she clutched her bag tighter in her arms. "I guess so."

He stopped several feet from the police barricade, assessing the situation, watching CSI carry evidence bags out of the room next door to the one she'd closed herself in last night.

She reached for the handle. "Thank—"

"You're not getting out here."

She paused. "I have to."

"No you don't."

"This is where I live."

Was she *thick*? "You see that van right there?" He gestured to the white vehicle with the back doors open.

"Yes."

"That's the ME. This is a murder scene."

She swallowed as her gaze darted from the van to the motel. "Maybe—maybe they can give me a different room."

"Forget it," he said with more heat than he meant to.

She flinched, gripping the door handle tighter.

He frowned, surprised by her reaction. "Do you really expect me to leave you here while they roll a corpse out of the building? They're not going to let you anywhere near that place for hours."

She bit her lip as their eyes met.

"You're putting me in that bad spot again. Let me bring you to your sister's or mother's, girlfriend's or boyfriend's."

She stared down at the floor.

He steamed out a breath, realizing she had no place else to go. This just kept getting better and better. Why the hell didn't he just let her get out? Sighing, he ran a hand through his hair. "You got a name?"

"Sophie."

"Sophie." Classy and quiet. The name fit her well. "You can stay with me tonight." He smiled as her eyes darted to his. "I wasn't planning on sleeping with you. I have an extra bed, a cot in the place I'm renovating. You can figure something else out for tomorrow."

"I don't—"

He reversed before she could finish her refusal. He wasn't any more excited about tonight's arrangement than she was.

# CHAPTER FIVE

SOPHIE STARED OUT THE WINDSHIELD, TRYING TO CATCH glimpses of the ocean in the dark as Stone headed north on Highway One. For the last ten miles of their drive, she'd breathed in the salty scent she desperately missed. It had been too long since she heard the violent crash of water against the sand. Eric had broken her spirit the day he forbade her from going anywhere near the place she loved most.

Sighing quietly, she closed her eyes, listening, savoring, remembering her daily walks along the beach with her mother before mom's yearly checkup changed everything. They'd only gotten to the ocean once more after the devastating diagnosis. The cancer had moved quickly, eating away at the beautiful woman she'd adored.

She gripped her backpack, willing away memories of her mother's frail, sick body, concentrating instead on her turn of good luck. By some miracle, the tough, handsome stranger at her side had more or less rescued her from spending the night in that horrid motel room.

She slid him a glance, watching the warm breeze play with his hair as she caught another whiff of his cologne. She was sitting next to a virtual stranger in the dark while he drove her to some mysterious location. What in the world was she thinking, and why wasn't she afraid? Stone, last name still unknown, was gruff, direct, and more than a little rude, but he hadn't left her in the ghetto to fend for herself. She could only be grateful. "Thank you again."

"Yeah." He slowed and took a right, heading up a dirt road to the hills high above. The Mustang twisted and turned for a good quarter mile before finally making it to the top.

Sophie stared as Stone parked, taking in the tiny Airstream trailer, second car resting on blocks not far from a basketball hoop, and the small cottage in need of siding with its new windows reflecting the glow of the full moon.

"This is your house?"

"Yup."

"It's lovely." Or it could be. There was certainly potential.

"Not yet," he said, pulling his keys from the ignition.

Now what? She gripped her bag tighter, her stomach suddenly jumpy as her brain felt frozen and her cheeks hot, the way they always did when she didn't know what to do or say next. And somehow the wretched sensations were worse than usual. Stone made her nervous. Not the way Eric did; this was different. Stone's presence was so...primal and unapologetically sexy, which tied her up in knots. "I—I—"

"I'm tired."

She swiped at her hair. "You're tired?"

"Yeah." He rubbed his fingers over his forehead.

He didn't want to talk. Thank god. She let loose a quiet breath of relief. "If you'll just tell me where the cot is, I'm sure I can find it."

"I'll take you inside."

She wanted to tell him he didn't have to, but she nodded, fighting the need to stare at her bag as he held her gaze.

He got out and she followed, shouldering her backpack, standing next to him as he unlocked the door. She studied his face in the shadows, watching his long lashes brush his skin with every blink. Her gaze trailed over sharp cheekbones and powerful, tanned arms, darker in the play of light. She'd never thought a man beautiful before, until now.

He stepped inside and flipped a switch.

She walked in behind him, blinking against the shock of bright light pouring from the naked bulb hanging from the ceiling. She glanced around, taking everything in. The room was much bigger than it appeared from outside and smelled of sawdust. Drywall had been hung, framing large, gorgeous picture windows facing the ocean. If she listened closely, she could just hear the surf.

"Watch your step. I haven't gotten to the floors yet."

She looked down, realizing she was standing on plywood.

He walked away, down the unfinished hallway and into another room. He poked his head out. "You coming?"

"Oh." She moved in the direction he had, glancing over her shoulder at the tiny kitchen with dingy appliances. She passed two rooms along the way that were little more than two-by-fours and wiring, hurrying into the open space where Stone stood among more of the same. "This is nice."

He tossed her a baleful look.

She licked her lips as heat rushed to her cheeks, cursing herself for saying something so foolish. "I mean—"

"It will be." He threw a fitted sheet and two blankets on the cot's mattress. "I'm assuming you can make your own bed."

"Yes." It was hard to relax under his penetrating stare. He was so *big*. Not as tall as Eric, but Stone had her by a good seven inches. However, where Eric was long and lean, Stone was broad and powerful. Despite his brawn, he didn't invoke a heart-stopping fear the way the monster in Maine did.

Frowning, he took a step closer until they were standing almost toe-to-toe. "They're violet."

"Huh?" She stood perfectly still, waiting for him to give her some space.

"Your eyes. They're violet." He gripped her chin between his thumb and index finger, moving her face from side to side. "I thought they were blue, then gray, but they're violet."

She swallowed as his rough, calloused fingers pressed gently to her skin, sending her pulse scrambling. "Yes."

He let her go, stepping back. "Contacts?"

"No. The real deal."

"I've never seen anything like it."

"It's pretty rare. A genetic mutation." She shrugged, giving him a small smile. People had been commenting on her eye color for as long as she could remember but no one had ever touched her like that when they did.

"Huh. I'm going to bed."

She blinked at the abrupt change in subject. "Okay. Goodnight."

"Night." He walked from the room, stopped, and turned back. "The bathroom's through there." He pointed to the half-closed door down the hall to the left. "And there's some food in the kitchen."

"Thank you."

He turned and left.

The front door closed, and she set down her bag,

glancing around at the hammer, pliers, and other tools scattered about the skeleton of a house. She moved to the windows, opening them, breathing in the fresh air, smiling as she listened to the rush of waves several hundred yards in the distance—a welcome change from gunshots and moans. Stone's view had to be amazing.

She peeked her head in the small space that was probably going to be a closet, then moved to the next room across the hall, looking out another grouping of glass facing the driveway. She watched as Stone's tough frame filled the doorway of the camper before he shut the door behind him.

She went to her bed, slipped the fitted sheet in place, and fell back against the soft mattress, grinning. She was safe. For the first time in *years* she was actually *safe*. She laughed in delight, treasuring a sensation she hadn't felt in so long. She lay still, closing her eyes, listening to the waves. Tomorrow she would stare out at the mighty Pacific and sink her feet in the warm sand while seagulls cried and flew overhead.

Letting loose a huge sigh, she rolled to her side, looking at her backpack. She rushed to her feet, grabbing her plastic baggie full of travel toiletries, then pulled out the white t-shirt and sweat-shorts she'd taken from the donation bin at Stowers House, and made her way to the bathroom. Flipping on the light, she gaped.

"Wow," she whispered, stepping further in, instantly captivated by the intricate tile patterns covering the shower wall. The whole room was spectacular—a work of art—with the glass shower stall and multiple jets, beautiful marble flooring, and pretty pedestal sink. If this little piece of elegance was what Stone had in mind for his entire house, the place was going to be a masterpiece.

She undressed, turned on the shower, and stepped into the warm spray, reveling in the idea that she could stand here and not have to watch bugs crawl along the walls or keep one ear trained on the door, forever fearful someone would find a way to work their way past the chair she always wedged below the doorknob. She closed her eyes as water cascaded over her head, letting the tension release from her shoulders.

This was all hers. For one night she would sleep soundly. Eric wouldn't be searching for her here on Stone's cliff top. Tomorrow she would be forced to go back to the motel. Everything would go back to normal when the sun came up, but for now, she planned to savor every second of her reprieve. Who knew how long it would be before she had an opportunity like this again?

~~~~

Sophie opened her eyes, expecting to see water damage and filthy paint covering the motel ceiling. Frowning, she stared up at two-by-fours set in place every few feet instead. The rush of waves filled her ears as she turned her head slowly, stretching, waiting for the typical discomfort of a stiff neck and sore ribs after a night of rest on the three wooden chairs she lined up and slept on instead of the disgusting bed. She yawned huge, enjoying the serenity of her perfect Wednesday morning.

She'd planned to stay up and savor the sound of the ocean, but somehow she'd blinked and the sun was up again. She yawned for the second time and glanced at her watch, her eyes widening in surprise. *Eleven o'clock?* "Crap."

She jolted up and hurried out of bed, pulling the sheets she'd used off the mattress, and folded the two blankets. Stone was bound to think her a lush. She moved toward the kitchen, hating the idea of eating his food, but she hadn't had a real meal since breakfast at Stowers House on Saturday. Apples and peanut butter and jelly were getting old. She opened the fridge, spotting eggs, milk, beer and some unidentifiable black stuff she would stay far away from. Checking the date on the eggs and milk, she smiled. Scrambled eggs were a must.

The front door opened and she froze, guilty for getting caught helping herself, even though Stone had invited her to before he walked off last night.

He stumbled in, bare-chested, wearing ripped jeans he hadn't snapped. He was magnificent, looking like a model on a billboard with all those bumps and ropes of muscle. She'd never seen him in anything but slacks and a polo or the tuxedo he wore when he stood next to movie stars on the red carpet in the celebrity gossip magazines from time to time. She looked away, realizing she was staring. "Um, I was going to have a quick breakfast and get out of your way."

He grumbled something, his voice much deeper after sleep.

"I can go now if you'd rather." She glanced down wistfully at the egg carton in her hand and stepped right as he did, then left.

"*Move*, Blondie." He gripped her waist, picking her up in the small, crowded space.

Gasping, she clutched at his warm, firm shoulder, breathing him in as he turned with her in his arms, set her down, and made a beeline for the beat-up counter and coffee pot. She blinked as he grabbed the tin of coffee and scooped. Twice he'd touched her in a way no one ever had. Eric was always so proper unless he was beating her—then he was just plain vicious. She and Stone barely knew each other, and he'd put his hands on her again. Why did she want him to do it again? She cleared her throat, shocked by her own thoughts as he set a cup beneath the drip instead of the glass server.

"Milk," he said.

She frowned.

"I need the milk."

"Oh." She reached into the fridge, pulling out the half-gallon.

He snatched the container, pouring the two-percent in while the coffee still drizzled into the cup. He lifted the half-full mug, swallowing the contents down as he jammed the glass catcher in place.

She knew she stared, but she couldn't look away as he put his mug back under for the second time.

"What?"

"Nothing," she said with a start. "I just—I've never seen anyone drink coffee like that before."

He smiled. "Some people need crack. I need coffee."

She grinned. "I was going to make some eggs if that's okay."

He shrugged. "Whatever."

"Can I make you some too?" It was the least she could do.

"Sure."

"Do you have any bread?"

"Over there." He pointed to the dark, ugly paneled cupboard to her left. "You look different with your hair down."

She paused mid-reach as he slid a finger down a long strand.

"You're easy on the eyes, Blondie."

She set the eggs down before she dropped them, unsure of what to do. She didn't know how to handle casual touches and compliments.

"Uh, thanks." She opened the cupboards pulling out a wretched bright green bowl, and found the bread while he sat at the card table. She cracked eggs, attempting to think of something to say in the humming silence. "Can I make you another cup of coffee?"

"I won't turn it down."

She dumped out the sludge he made and started again, scooping the proper serving, adding the right amount of water. Moments later she set the steaming mug in front of him along with the milk container.

"You find another place to stay?"

"Yes, thank you." She turned back to the counter, not wanting to make eye contact as she whisked eggs and poured them into the heated pan. "The view is wonderful here. You have your own piece of paradise."

"Where are you staying?"

She pushed the eggs around, careful to prepare them just right. Eric would be angry if—she stopped. Eric wasn't here.

"You didn't answer my question."

"I've got it taken care of." There was no need for him to know that she would go back to the place he refused to drop her off. He'd been kind to let her stay here for the night. They would go their separate ways after breakfast, and he would be none the wiser.

"Good. I'll drop you off on my way into town."

"Oh, you don't have to," she said quickly. "I'll take the bus. I don't want to inconvenience you any more than I already have." She set the perfectly cooked eggs on a plate along with the toast, giving him her share as well. She wanted the golden, deliciously scented eggs desperately, but it was time to go. He was asking too many questions. "Here's your breakfast."

"Where's yours?"

"I'm not hungry." Her stomach growled as she said it. "Excuse me." Turning away from his penetrating stare, she ran warm water into the pan, and left the room. She went to the room she'd slept in and slid on a pair of jean shorts and a white tank top. Deodorant and a brush came next. She pulled her hair back in a bun and shouldered her pack, then walked out of the bedroom, hating that she had to leave a place that felt like home after so short a time. "I'm going to be on my way." She put a twenty-dollar bill on the table. "Thanks for the hot water and bed."

"Keep it."

She shook her head. "Your bathroom's beautiful by the way."

"Thanks. I'm going to get started on the living room today."

"You did that?"

"Yeah."

"You're very talented. I'm sure you'll make yourself a wonderful home. Thank you again, Stone." She'd never said his name before. "Bye."

"See ya."

She walked through the living room, savoring the comfort of safety, then stepped outside, back into the real world.

~~~~

Stone forked up the last bite of the best eggs he'd ever eaten as the door shut quietly. He glanced at the twenty-dollar bill sitting on the table and set down his silverware. She didn't have anywhere to stay. Blondie could make a mean breakfast, but she couldn't lie for shit. He sat back in the folding chair, steaming out a breath. "Not your problem, McCabe. Don't make this your problem."

He stood and walked to the window, watching as she made her way down his drive. She had excellent legs—lean and muscular—athletic to go with her arms. He studied the tight bun coiled at the back of her head. She was even more beautiful with her hair down. Why the hell did she wrap all of that gorgeous, soft hair up when it looked better falling down to her waist? She'd been different in her pajamas, puttering around in his ugly kitchen. She'd seemed relaxed. Her face transformed when she smiled. She was nice. And shy. He opened the front door, cursing himself as he called to her. "Sophie."

She stopped, turned.

He walked to where she stood. "Are the cops looking for you?"

"What? *No.*"

She shook her head with such adamant denial he knew it was the truth. Blondie might not be running from the law, but she was in some sort of trouble; Abby was right about that.

"You can stay here for a couple of days."

Hope filled those pretty violet eyes before she dropped her head and kicked the rock around with her sneakered foot. "That's very kind, but I really can't."

"Why?"

She met his gaze again. "Because I don't want to put you out. You're trying to build your home."

"If you get in my way, I'll let you know."

"You feel bad for me. I don't want to take advantage of that."

His brow rose. "Does it look like I let people take

advantage of me?"

"I—"

"Can you cook more than eggs?"

"Yes."

"You make a couple meals like the one you did this morning and keep this place clean and we'll call it even. There's a bus stop across the street. It'll take you an hour, maybe more to get downtown. You'll have to head into work earlier if you plan to get back here every night."

"This is nice, but—"

"Do you have a place to stay or not?"

She shook her head, not quite able to meet his eyes.

"This sounds like a pretty good deal to me. If you're smart you'll take it."

"I have to pay you."

She couldn't be making much. "I don't want your money."

"I need to give it to you."

He recognized pride and admired her for it. "Okay. What were you paying at the joint downtown?"

"Twenty-five a night."

"You'll need more money for bus fare, so we'll make it fifteen a day. You can use your rent to feed us and keep this place picked up."

She nibbled her lip as she looked toward the water. "Okay."

His shoulders relaxed when she accepted. He was still trying to figure out why he gave a damn one way or the other. Maybe it was her whole sweet, wounded deal. Damsels in distress weren't really his thing, but there was a first time for everything. Keeping an eye on her wouldn't be so bad if she fed him and did his laundry. He held out his hand.

Her brows furrowed.

"Do we have a deal or what? Last time I checked, good business ends with a handshake."

She took the hand he offered and smiled. "I guess it does."

# CHAPTER SIX

SOPHIE COATED THE JUMBO SHRIMP, PASTA, AND TOMATOES with the fresh pesto she'd prepared. Humming, she gently tossed the ingredients with a large serving spoon and pulled Cling Wrap from the drawer, securing the plastic in place. She set the container in the fridge and shut the door with a small bump of her hip. With half of the meal ready and an hour until the steaks had to go on the grill, she had plenty of time to get to the pair of earrings she'd been envisioning since she wandered back from the farmer's market down the road.

She glanced at the small pile of dishes soaking in the sink, took a step toward them, and turned away, walking to the card table where she and Stone ate and she created her jewelry in between meals. Eric always insisted that dishes be cleaned immediately. Messes of any kind were not permitted, but Stone didn't care one way or the other. She would get to the dishes after dinner, when *she* was ready to tidy the kitchen. To most, such a small rebellion was no big deal, but for her it was a huge step in the right direction. No one was in charge of her life anymore except for her. For the last several weeks she'd drilled the idea into her brain. Now she was starting to believe it.

She glanced toward the living room as Stone turned the buffing machine back on, listening to the quiet hum that had filled the house for much of the afternoon while he worked on the floor. Today was the second full day they'd had off together during the week and a half she'd been staying with him. It was nice having him here, watching him make progress on his home. He was definitely a busy man.

Living with Stone was far less complicated than she'd feared it might be. For the first couple of days she'd kept to her room or the kitchen, careful to stay out of his way, fearful she might upset him and be told to leave. But then he'd asked her what her problem was and that had been the end of that. Hiding and tiptoeing around the house wasn't something a young, confident woman in charge of her life would do. She so desperately wanted to be confident and in charge.

*Baby steps,* she reminded herself as she slid the pale blue Swarovski crystal on the headpin. Eventually she would feel like the Sophie she'd been before Mom got sick and she met Eric. She was making jewelry again, wasn't she? And she was following a routine that allowed her to be creative and productive without anyone else's directives.

Now she just needed to keep making her pieces and put her money away. She definitely couldn't stay here forever. Hopefully three square meals a day plus dessert and a spotless house would keep Stone in a generous mood until early fall. She bit her lip as she looped the wire around her pliers, wrapping the thin piece of sterling silver, hating the idea of leaving Stone's cliff-top home. She loved it here. It was highly unlikely that her own place would be close to the beach she loved to run on or have fresh fruit and vegetable stands just across the street the way Stone's did.

Heck, it was doubtful she would ever have a house as nice as this. Stone's home was a shamble—or had been before he bought the land and the shack on it, but Southern California property went for more than she would ever see. She thought of the trust she was likely never to inherit and shook her head as she set the wire-wrapped crystal on her beading mat.

Luckily her finances were improving. They weren't great, but they were certainly better now that she was here instead of the motel. The lean years she and Mom experienced after Dad died and Mom first opened her shop were beneficial to her now. She could feed herself and Stone well and pick up small things here and there to give his home a welcoming feel.

Two days ago she'd taken a risk and selected towels for the bathroom. She'd stood in the store aisle for almost an hour, agonizing over just the right shade—straight white or cream—sweating, terrified of making the wrong choice. Ultimately she'd chosen the cream, purchasing four Egyptian cotton sets, using the coupon she'd found online while taking advantage of the big one-day sale.

It had taken her most of yesterday morning to get up the courage to wash the new items and set them up perfectly on the racks. She'd worried herself sick, waiting for Stone to be angry with her for stupidly choosing wrong or for making the decision to purchase them without asking him first. When he'd taken his shower and walked out with the oversized towel draped around his waist and went back to his trailer without saying anything at all, she'd breathed a huge sigh of relief, realizing once and for all that Stone, like most men, was oblivious to such minor details.

This afternoon she'd gotten bold while running errands. She'd found a small bamboo hamper and candles on clearance at one of the department stores, then she'd gone to the Farmer's market and picked out three pretty plants, adding more touches to the bathroom, setting them about the beautifully tiled space, finishing the room with warm elegance.

The floor buffer shut off and the house was silent except for the waves in the distance.

"Blondie."

"Yeah?" She set down the clear crystal she was about to add to the next headpin.

"Can you come here for a minute?"

"Sure. Give me just a second." She went to the fridge, pulling out the pitcher of filtered water, pouring him a tall glass, adding a slice of lemon she kept at the ready. She walked to the doorway, stopping short, staring at the gorgeous glossy floors.

"Oh, Stone, this is amazing."

He grinned, his smile more devastating with his hair tucked beneath a kerchief. "You like it?"

"Yes. It's *beautiful*." She bent down, sliding her fingers over the smooth work.

"You can walk on it."

She stepped on the floor. "I can't get over how you've transformed this room in such a short time." He'd painted the walls a gray blue, playing nicely with the honey tone of the wood and white crown molding and baseboards. "This is—" She tripped over the buffer cord in her rush to stand at his side, losing her grip on the glass, gasping in horror as it shattered against the newly installed wood. She froze, staring down at the mess as the blood drained from her face. "I—I'm sorry," she shuddered out, rushing from the room for a towel as her heart pounded. Hurrying back, she bent down, sopping up the liquid with frantic presses to the freshly buffed finish. "I'm sorry," she said again. "I'm clumsy and stupid. This was a stupid mistake."

Stone stepped closer and she cringed, bracing herself, ready for the slap.

"Hey." He crouched next to her while she snatched up the shards of glass with trembling fingers.

"I'll have this cleaned up in just a second," she said in a rush, trying and failing to keep her breathing steady. "I—I can pay you for any damages." She hoped. The new floor had to have set him back a few grand.

"Hey." He grabbed her wrist.

She froze, darting him a glance as he frowned at her.

"Take it easy. You're going to cut yourself." He loosened his grip. "Why are you shaking?"

She felt the rush of heat move to her cheeks. "I—I don't know. I should've paid closer attention." She tried to break free of his hold. "I'll have this cleaned up in just a minute. I have money in my backpack to pay for the glass and the floor. I don't know why I'm so foolish." Her eyes filled.

"It's just a broken glass."

"And water. I spilled water all over your pretty floor."

He shrugged. "That's what the towel's for."

"I might've scratched the wood. I'm careless."

"The cord was in the way, and if one shattered glass scratches my floor I need to do a better job."

"I'm sorry. I just—"

"Stop saying that. It's no big deal."

"I'm sor—" She closed her eyes and took a deep breath. She was making a spectacle of herself. She looked at Stone again, measuring his curious eyes. "Let me get you another drink."

"Or you can go sit back down and finish the doo-dad you were making."

"But you must be thirsty."

"If I'm thirsty I'll get myself a drink. Staying here doesn't require you to wait on me."

She nodded. "You're probably getting hungry. I'll start the grill for the steaks."

61

"Did you hear what I just said?"

She nodded again, but she didn't know how *not* to wait on him. She was trying to break bad, unhealthy habits, but it was going to take longer than two months to do so.

"Go make your earrings or bracelet or whatever that thing is and I'll finish cleaning this up, then I'll get the grill started and make the steaks."

"But our agreement—"

"I'll take care of dinner, Blondie."

"There's—there's asparagus too," she mumbled.

"Huh?" He moved in closer.

"I said there's asparagus too. They'll need to be brushed with olive oil and dashed with kosher salt."

"Okay."

She swallowed, sliding several strands of hair behind her ear as she stared at his filthy sleeveless t-shirt instead of meet his gaze again. "Okay." She walked back to the kitchen on weak legs, taking her seat, breathing deep. Was that what it was like to make a mistake and not have to pay for it? And he was going to cook for her after she broke his dishes and got water all over his new floor? It had been so long since anyone had taken care of her in any way. She'd turned into Mom's full-time caregiver, then Eric's maid. Tonight, she was going to try her best to enjoy the idea of Stone helping her, even if it was just a steak and vegetables on the grill.

~~~~

Stone flipped the steaks, satisfied with the hearty sizzle of the t-bones Sophie had picked up at the market. He'd eaten like a king since she walked through his door. When he got home at night, the house smelled good, and there was always some sort of fancy, delicious meal tucked away in a Pyrex dish for him to throw in the microwave and heat up.

Initially he'd been relieved when she said she would stay, then he regretted offering her the room minutes after he proposed the idea, fearing he'd been duped by sad, violet eyes, but that had faded quickly. Now that Sophie was here he didn't have to worry about washing and ironing his clothes, and the bathroom looked great. She'd added towels, plants, and other little things he never would've thought of. And the kitchen for as ugly as it was, was homey with the fresh flowers in the vase and potted herbs sitting on the windowsill.

Having Sophie around was a damn good deal. She talked a lot more than the first few mornings they were home together, but it wasn't so bad. Intelligent, gorgeous women were tolerable, especially when they had a smile as pretty as hers. She did that more too. He liked making her weary eyes brighten and those luscious lips curve, but she was still troubled. At the strangest times she flinched or froze—like in the living room when she spilled the water. He frowned as he remembered the way she'd instantly gone pale and cleaned up, shaking as if breaking a damn glass was the end of the world. Her pulse had stuttered double time against his fingers as he held her wrist in his hand. She'd been terrified.

Sophie had secrets. He had his ideas as to what they were, but he didn't ask, although he was more curious than he wanted to admit. She wasn't interested in sharing, and he wasn't interested in prying. The classy, rich girl with a hint of northeast in her voice was a long way from home. If she wanted to let him in on the big mystery, she would when she was ready. Until then, they would go on as they were, which appeared to work well for both of them. The less he knew the better. Getting wrapped up in other people's problems didn't interest him. "We're about five, maybe six minutes from dinner," he called to her through the open screen door.

"Okay. The table's set and everything's ready."

He'd had little doubt it would be. He checked his watch as his phone rang. Sighing, he answered, not bothering to pay attention to the readout. "Yeah, McCabe."

"Hey, Stone. It's Abby."

He closed his eyes, wishing he'd taken the extra second to see who was calling. He didn't want to play twenty questions with Ms. Peppy. "Hey."

"How are you?"

"Fine."

"You wanna come for dinner? Jerrod and I are planning on a late meal. He's doing the benefit deal with Tatiana Livingston."

"No, I'm all set. I've got a steak on the grill."

"Oh. Okay."

"What's up?" Something was always up.

"Well, I was wondering if you had a chance to check in with the cleaning woman, Sophie."

"That's her name."

"I know. You told me. How's she doing?"

"As far as I know, good." He hadn't bothered to tell Abby about his new roommate.

"Good."

"Why are you so worried about her, anyway?" Maybe Abby had the answers he'd convinced himself he didn't care about.

"I'm not, I guess. She just seems nice and, I don't know, lonely."

He made a sound in his throat, knowing there was more to the story, but once again, it had nothing to do with him. He needed to remember that.

"Are you coming to Sarah's birthday party tomorrow?"

"No." He'd rather be shot.

"You're not going to your boss's wife's birthday party?"

"Nope."

"But everyone was invited. Everyone's going to be there. You should probably come for a little while."

He'd planned to get started on the room Sophie was using. If she was going to be here for a while, it might as well be more than plywood and two-by-fours, but maybe stopping in at Ethan's couldn't hurt. He typically didn't care if he slighted people, but the Cookes were good people, and his co-workers and their wives weren't bad. "I'll come for an hour." He glanced at Sophie setting a bowl in the center of the table. "I'm bringing someone."

"You are? Who?"

He didn't miss the hint of excitement. "Just someone I know."

"Okay. We'll see you tomorrow."

"Yeah." He hung up and took the steaks off the grill, bringing them inside. He put the smaller one on Sophie's plate and the monster-sized piece on his own.

"Thank you. These look great."

He studied the ugly card table set with his equally ugly dishes and the amazing pesto, shrimp deal in the center next to the plate of grilled asparagus. "Everything looks good," he agreed.

"Why don't you take your seat and I'll serve you." She made a grab for his dish.

What the hell was up with this serving crap? He

stopped her with a press of his hand on hers. "How about you sit down and serve yourself, and I'll plunk some food on my own plate."

She tensed, nodding, sitting and staring down at the table.

Maybe that came out a little gruffer than he'd meant. He sighed. "Look—"

Her shoulders tightened as she quickly met his eyes, then looked down again.

He didn't know how to handle the wounded woman across from him. He didn't do apologies, flowers, or gentle words. The women he was used to didn't put up with anybody's crap. He grabbed the serving spoon in the pasta salad and plunked a huge helping on her plate. "There."

She glanced up, staring at him.

"Your steaks gonna get cold."

She nodded and picked up her fork.

"We're going somewhere tomorrow," he said as he cut into his steak, cooked perfectly medium.

Her hand paused as she stabbed a noodle. "What?"

"Tomorrow there's a party."

"Oh, that's very nice of you to think of me, but I'll probably just stay here."

He shook his head. "If I have to go—and I do—I'm not suffering alone." In the almost two weeks she'd been here, he'd never heard her talk on the phone or make plans to meet up with anyone. It would be good for her to get out and get to know the women of Ethan Cooke Security. If anyone could make someone feel welcome it was that group. God knows they could talk, and they procreated like damn rabbits. Austin's kid was just born a month ago or something like that, and Jackson's wife, Alexa, was about to pop any day. And if all else failed, Abby would charm Sophie out of her shyness.

"I don't know..."

"I would consider it a favor." He knew that would turn the tide.

She pressed her lips firm as she clutched at her fork. "Where is it?"

"At a friend's house a few miles away in the Palisades."

She nodded. "Okay."

"It's a birthday party."

"A birthday? We have to bring a gift."

He stopped chewing. "No, we don't."

"Yes we do. It's rude not to."

"Well, hell." He swallowed and huffed out a breath.

She smiled. "Is this a child's birthday?"

"No, a woman."

Her smile brightened. "Consider her gift taken care of."

His spirits immediately lifted. He had no idea how to pick out cards and fancy crap for fancy women. "You sure?"

"Definitely."

He scooped up another forkful of delicious pasta salad. "This stuff's really good. You're a good cook, Sophie."

She blinked.

"You have to know you make excellent grub."

"Yes, I guess I do. I try to."

"Then why are you shocked that I'm giving you a compliment?"

"You just—" She shook her head. "It's silly." She shook her head again. "You never call me Sophie."

He thought of her as Sophie but always called her Blondie. Nicknames were less personal. "I guess I don't. You're a damn fine cook, Soph." They smiled at each other until he realized he had no idea what her last name was. He forked up more steak, glancing at the huge chip in the plate she was eating off of. "So, I was thinking about getting some new dishes."

She swallowed and wiped her mouth. "You were?"

"The kitchen's still a good few weeks away from demolition if not more, but this stuff in here's ugly."

She looked down at her mismatched orange and green plate and bowl. "It's certainly interesting—vintage flair. From the seventies."

He grinned, knowing she was trying not to hurt his feelings. "It's ugly as shit."

She smiled back. "Okay, yes. It's pretty awful."

"They were here when I moved in."

"What are you thinking of getting?"

He shrugged. "I was hoping you could help me out with that."

"Yes. Sure. I can try."

He pulled his wallet from his back pocket, grabbed a wad of cash, and tossed it on the table. "That should probably cover it. Let me know if it doesn't."

She toyed with a piece of shrimp as she stared at the money.

"What?"

"I don't know what you want. What are you hoping for exactly? A four-piece set or eight? Do you want glasses and silverware too or just plates and bowls?"

"Whatever you want. As long as it's doesn't look like this, I don't care."

She nibbled her lip. "You must have *some* ideas."

"Not really. The bathroom looks good with what you've done in there. I want you to do that to the kitchen."

She looked at him with stunned pleasure. What the hell was he supposed to do with that? He liked the plants and candles and the hamper deal. It wasn't that big of a thing.

"You could—you could really use new pots and pans."

"So get some."

"I saw a great set in the flyers I was looking through this morning." She pushed back from her seat, grabbed the stack of papers she spoke of, and walked over to him, leaning down for him to see. "These right here." She pointed. "They're top of the line—stainless steel. They're a little expensive but they'll last you forever, and I might be able to find a coupon to go with the sale."

He wanted to tell her he didn't give two shits; he never cooked, but then she would sit back down, and he liked the way she smelled and the way her soft hair brushed his arm. "Those are fine. What about those plates?" He tapped the black and white circular set, trying not to smile as she winced.

"If that's what you like, I can certainly pick them up for you."

"What do you like?"

She slid her finger to the pretty pale yellow set. "I was thinking of these, especially if you did stainless steel appliances and white cabinetry."

That's not what he'd had in mind, but he narrowed his eyes as he studied the tight space of his kitchen. He could see her vision and liked it a lot. "Okay."

"And it probably wouldn't hurt to pick up these serving dishes here and maybe some new silverware. There are a couple of patterns..." She searched for another flyer, fighting with the pages.

"Here." He took the stack and slid her plate to the space next to his. "We'll talk and eat at the same time."

"Sure. Let me grab a piece of paper and a pen."

"Can you snag my laptop too?"

She snatched up the pad she kept by her jewelry-making supplies and brought him the laptop off the counter, taking the seat at his side.

"Thanks." He opened up his computer and punched in his password.

"How do you feel about new glasses?"

"I feel like I should probably get you some more money."

She smiled. "I guess I'm getting a little carried away."

He liked her like this, when she forgot to be cautious. He liked sitting here with her planning out his new home. "I need everything you've mentioned, so you might as well get it." He accessed his home design files and called up the 3D plans of the kitchen. "Let me show you what I have in mind and you can decide how to fill it up. It'll be kind of like this." He turned the screen in her direction.

"That's going to be amazing." She beamed, her eyes full of excitement. "I love the glass-front cabinets you have incorporated into the design." She scooted closer. "It looks like you're thinking of this cherry toned wood."

"Maybe. I think I like the white idea better."

"The white seems like it would go well with your proximity to the water—kind of gives it a coastal, nautical feel. It'll also brighten up the space since it's not very big."

He agreed completely. "So white it is."

"All right. Let's finish supplying you with the basics. I think this drawer here by the stove would function well for linens." She pointed to the screen. "We should probably think about new dish towels, oven mitts, and trivets. I saw a couple of patterns." She turned to another page among the stack. "Right here."

His kitchen was coming to life before his eyes. "Those'll work."

She smiled again. "I thought they might."

"What else have you got?"

"How much money do you have?"

They both grinned. He couldn't get enough of her gentle voice and pretty smile. "Plenty to get this started."

"Well, I've got plenty of ideas. Let's look at a few of these appliances." She turned to yet another page and he leaned in close, more than content to spend the next little while looking at toasters and blenders in Sophie's company.

# CHAPTER SEVEN

SOPHIE SAT BY OLIVIA AND KYLEE AT THE KITCHEN TABLE, coloring while the girls chatted and on occasion asked her to pass a crayon. The kids were her saving grace at this party. She glanced at the beautiful women standing around the massive island in the spectacular kitchen wearing their pretty, fashionable clothes, chatting and laughing like a big, happy family. She didn't know how to do this—be around people, blend, converse, feel like she belonged.

She stole another peek at Wren, Morgan, Hailey, and the woman who looked so much like Abigail Quinn, Alexa. They were like gorgeous Madonnas, all holding their babies or, in Sarah and Alexa's cases, carrying their children in utero. And their husbands, many of whom she'd seen at the office, were no less striking.

She didn't belong here in her jeans and simple white top—the best she could do with her meager wardrobe options. She scanned the group of men standing around or sitting out on the deck, searching for Stone, who had long since disappeared. Sighing, she wondered where he'd gone and why hadn't he taken her with him.

"My mom's going to have Owen any day now. She's excited. She wants her feet to stop swelling."

Sophie looked at Olivia as the little girl colored a Disney princess, trying her best to stay in the lines— and mostly succeeding. "I'm sure you're excited to have a new brother on the way."

"Yeah."

Sophie picked up a pink crayon to color in the gown she was working on. "And your mom's having another baby too, Kylee. That's exciting."

"My mom throws up but just sometimes. Daddy said she won't throw up at all pretty soon."

"Oh." Sophie smiled, always surprised by what children were willing to share. "Well, I'm glad she's feeling better."

"Me too. Now I won't have to watch Emma in the playroom when she runs to the toilet."

"Mm, yes, I see."

There was a commotion in the hallway. Bear and Reece, the Cookes' enormous Mastiffs, and Mutt, Alexa and Jackson's lab, barked joyously as Abby's voice carried down the hall. Sophie stiffened as the woman she'd done her best to avoid made her way into the crowd, stopping to hand out hugs, with Jerrod following behind.

"Um, girls, I'll be right back," Sophie said, setting her crayon on the table. She should have known she would bump into Abby when Stone told her they were going to Ethan and Sarah Cooke's house. Why did she agree to come, especially when he vanished and left her alone in a houseful of strangers?

"Okay," the pretty blonds said in unison.

She scooted back from her chair and made her escape out the glass doors leading to the deck, smiling at Wren's husband as he looked her way. She had to get out of here. The Cooke Estate wasn't more than four or five miles from Stone's cliff. There had to be a bus stop down the road somewhere. She headed down a flight of stairs, coming to another deck. This place was huge—much bigger than Eric's house of horrors. How the heck did she get out of this maze?

She reached for the sliding door by the pool area and stepped into the coolest game room she had ever seen. "Wow," she whispered as she took in the arcade games and skee-ball machine settled among plush leather furnishings. The movie-theater-sized-screen on the back wall was insane. "Wow," she said again, hurrying for the nearest exit—she hoped. She opened the next door and found herself in yet another hallway. "Oh, come on." She started up the steps, recognizing the front entrance ahead, and walked out the door and around the corner closest to the driveway. Looking over her shoulder, she hurried down the path, making certain no one saw her, and crashed into something firm and unmovable. Gasping, she stumbled backwards, almost falling until Stone reached out and grabbed her.

"Going somewhere?" he asked, holding her against his chest, righting them both, dressed in simple dark-wash jeans and a black t-shirt.

"Um." She couldn't think when he looked at her like that, especially when their bodies were crushed together and they breathed each other's breath. "I—" She pushed at his shoulders.

"You abandoning ship, Soph?" He finally released her, taking a step away.

"You did," she said, surprised by the hint of heat in her own words. "You left me up there with all of those people while you came out here to hide."

He narrowed his eyes. "Are you giving me lip?"

She swallowed, stepping away, realizing she'd talked back and made him angry. But she was mad too. "No—Yes." She raised her chin, trying to find her courage. "Yes, I am. You invited me—"

"Good," he interrupted.

That was the last thing she'd expected him to say. "Good?"

"Yeah. *Good*. It's about damn time. It's nice to see there's a temper in there somewhere. You're too nice."

She frowned. "No I'm not."

"Yeah you are. There are a lot of assholes who like to take advantage of people like you.'"

People like her—weak and vulnerable. She didn't want him to think of her that way. For some reason it was vital that he thought of her as capable and powerful. "I—"

The front door opened. "There you are."

Sophie stiffened. Her back was to the house, but she recognized Abby's cheerful voice, desperately scanning for a way to escape.

"Hey, Abby," Stone said, holding Sophie's gaze, questioning her with his intense brown eyes.

Realizing there was nothing she could do but get through the moment, Sophie turned, watching surprise move over Abby's beautiful face.

"You're here." Abby beamed. "Stone, I had no idea."

Sophie frowned, confused.

"Stone said he was bringing someone." Abby held out her hand. "We met briefly a couple weeks ago at the office. I'm Abby Quinn."

"Yes." Sophie took Abby's outstretched hand. "Sophie."

"We're excited to have you with us."

"Actually I was just—"

"She was just coming to find me," Stone interjected. "We'll be up in a second."

Abby looked from Sophie to Stone. "Okay. I'll see you inside. I think cake is happening fairly soon."

Stone nodded as Abby started back up the steps. Seconds later, the door closed. "What's your deal?"

Sophie stared down at the grass. Stone didn't seem to miss much of anything. "I'm not sure... What do you mean?"

"You were a little cool with Ms. Peppy."

She had been and it wasn't right. Abby had been nothing but kind the two times they'd met. The almost-encounter at Stowers House was what worried her. What if Abby mentioned it in front of Stone or the others? Everyone knew the Stowers houses were refuges for abused women. She didn't want the moment in the childcare center to ruin everything she was building now. No one needed to know she'd let Eric hit her and turn her into a helpless victim. She was guilty of Stone's earlier observation. She'd let Eric take advantage, but not because she was too nice. She was weak and afraid—her own shameful secret. But that was in the past—if she let it be. If Abby would let it be. She loved where she lived and tolerated her work. It made living where she did possible. It made her fresh start a reality. "I didn't mean to be. I'll apologize."

He shrugged. "Don't apologize on my account. It was just an observation. Abby's a good lady—exhausting, but very nice. Kind."

She'd never heard Stone say anything complimentary about anyone. He didn't talk about other people. "Being rude is never right."

He shrugged again. "Am I taking you home or are you going back inside?"

There was a hint of challenge in his voice and eyes. It would've been easier to leave, but taking the easy route wasn't always right either. "I'm going back inside. Are you?" She lifted her brow.

He flashed her a quick grin. "I guess I'll follow you."

She turned and started up the steps, realizing he'd maneuvered her—but maybe she'd maneuvered him right back. There was nothing to do now but go in and get through the next little while.

~~~~

Stone stood back from the crowd with a beer in hand, watching Sophie sit with Olivia and Kylee while they ate their cake. She smiled when Kylee said something and responded, making the girls smile in return. She was relaxed and easy with the four-year-olds but not so much with the adults. She'd tried mingling. He'd kept his eye on her for most of the last hour, watching her struggle to converse about anything more than the weather or great California scenery.

Everyone had been kind to her. Hailey had let her hold Preston, and Morgan had handed over Jacob. They'd all tried to ask her questions about herself, but she'd deflected each one, always changing the subject to something about one of the kids or moms. Sophie was a closed book, and she seemed to be avoiding Abby like the plague, which was interesting.

Ethan blew on a party horn, quieting the group as he held their daughter Emma in one arm. "My lovely wife needs to open her presents before she falls asleep in what's left of her cake." He touched his hand to her pregnant belly, then clasped his fingers with hers as the room erupted with laughter.

Kylee and Olivia scrambled down, rushing over to the present pile. "We're your helpers, Mommy. Livy and I get to give you the presents."

"Okay, sweetie. You girls can take turns."

"I'll go first," Kylee declared.

Sarah raised her eyebrow at her daughter.

"Um, Livy, you can go first."

"That's very polite," Olivia said, hugging Kylee.

"You're my best friend because you're so polite."

Stone smiled, shaking his head as everyone laughed again. Both little blonds were hot tickets. The Cookes and Matthews had their hands full with their daughters.

Olivia contemplated the pile, nibbling on her index finger, then handed off the small gift bag Stone saw Sophie fuss over at the table earlier this morning. "Open this one, Sarah."

"Thank you." She smiled at Olivia and turned her attention to the fancy pink floral bag. "This is from Stone and Sophie." Sarah sent him a smile, then Sophie.

He had no idea what was in there. Sophie said she would handle the present, and he'd let her.

Sarah pulled a small white box free and opened it, gasping. "Oh my goodness. These are absolutely beautiful." She held up a pair of earrings, delicate twists of silver and pale blue crystal dangles. She reached her hand back in the bag and took out a second bigger box, opened it, and gasped again. "Stunning. This is absolutely stunning." Sarah looked at Stone as she held up a necklace in the same design.

He shrugged, pointing his beer bottle toward Sophie.

"Sophie, I've never seen anything so lovely. Where did you get these?"

"I made them."

All of the women started talking at once as they leaned in for a closer look.

"Dear *god*," Stone murmured, glancing at Jackson and Austin at his side. They sounded like a bunch of excited teenagers. Sophie made nice stuff. He'd given the earrings and necklaces and whatnot she created a glance more than once. She wasn't without her talents.

"Are you able to make more of these?" Wren asked.

"Yes. Definitely."

"I'd like to order a set if I could," Abby said as she stood next to Sarah, fingering the pretty jewelry.

"Me too," Morgan said. "And one for my mother if you can do something in a dark green."

"Sure." Sophie nodded.

"I'd love a bracelet and earrings," Hailey added. "But I have no idea what would work."

"I know just the thing," Sophie stood, stepping closer to the group of women. "We could do ambers or similar tones, something to play up your coloring."

Stone narrowed his eyes, studying his roommate. Her voice suddenly projected well. The shy woman had vanished. He stared at the confident beauty as the group fired off question after question, asking her for advice on how to select the pieces they wanted her to make. She answered each one, describing how each piece of jewelry could be, enticing her eager new customers with promises of Swarovski crystals, sterling silver, or gold. Why the hell was she wasting her time cleaning when she could do something like this? She'd make a killing.

"Do you think you could make me a dozen sets for my boutique?" Sarah's mother asked. "I think these would go in a snap."

"Uh, yes, sure. When would you want them by?"

"Is next week to soon?"

"No, no. I can do that."

"If they sell the way I think they're going to, I'll order more."

"I'd like to show this to Lily," Abby chimed in again. "Can you get me another set by Wednesday? It's her birthday."

"Yes, absolutely. I have other designs I can do as well—several, actually.

"Just make whatever you think would work best."

"I can do that. I'll be coming out with a catalog soon for anyone interested in hosting a home party. Hostesses get free gifts."

"I'll host a party," Hailey piped up.

"If you'd like to jot down your e-mail address I can send you some information as soon as I have it available."

"Great." Hailey turned in her chair. "Austin, do you have a pen?"

Stone pulled another sip from his beer, realizing there was a business shark beneath Sophie's quiet eyes and sweet smiles.

~~~~

Half an hour later, Sophie sat toward the back of the room making a list of all the orders she had to fulfill along with small notes about colors and design ideas that would work well for each of her new clients. In one day she'd managed to score requests for twenty-four beaded sets and a potential jewelry party. Hopefully her new customers would show off their pieces and their friends and families would want something too. If she could knock Sarah's mother's socks off, she might be able to get something steady going there.

Her juices started flowing as a mini business plan began taking shape. She was good at her craft and she'd been a semester away from her business degree before Mom's diagnosis. She'd planned to take Mom's small shop to another level when she graduated but that's not the way things worked out. She'd made her little booth at the mall work until she'd stupidly signed papers she barely paid attention to and unwittingly gave everything she and her mother had worked so hard for to the man who'd happily stolen it all away. With an order of this size, she was going to have to dip into the money she'd brought with her. The idea frightened her. Her emergency fund was meant for a quick escape and eventually her own place, but there was no way around it if she planned to fulfill two-dozen requests. She would easily recoup the loss with a decent profit, she reassured herself.

"Hi."

She attempted to relax her shoulders as Abby sat down in the chair next to hers. "Hi."

"Looks like you're going to be busy for a little while."

She tried a small smile, remembering her conversation with Stone. "Yes it does."

Abby tossed a glance over her shoulder. "I just thought I should take a moment and let you know that the goal of my company is to provide courageous women the chance to start their lives over again. I'm very proud of what Lily Brand and the *Escape* line have been able to accomplish so far. Anyone who passes through the doors of any of our Stowers House facilities has a right to their privacy. Everyone who comes and goes is bound by the same ethics: to protect each other's identities."

Sophie understood what Abby was getting at; she wouldn't say anything about seeing her at Stowers House. She nodded. "I appreciate that."

"I hope you'll come back and visit with all of us again. There's always some sort of party going on around here—wedding showers, baby showers, birthdays, holidays. You name it, it's happening."

"That's very nice. I'm glad Stone invited me. Everyone's so kind. Maybe we can throw a little party when he gets his house finished."

"That sounds fun. I don't mean to pry." She smiled. "Okay, maybe I do. Are you and Stone dating?"

Sophie's eyes popped wide. "No. *No.*" She chuckled at the idea. Surely Stone would too. He wasn't exactly her type, not that she actually knew what her type was. "He was kind enough to offer me a room in his home."

Abby's brows rose. "You live with Stone?"

"Temporarily. I pay rent, cook, and clean."

"Does he actually *talk* to you, like say words, or does he grunt?"

Sophie smiled. "No, he talks. Not a lot, but he does."

"I'll have to take your word for it. I know you're going to be busy, but would you like to have lunch sometime?"

Abby was offering an olive branch. She was offering her friendship. She hadn't had a friend since Dylan, and that had been more of a helper/helping relationship than a true friendship. What would it be like to live in the area and become part of this group? What would it be like to walk into the Cooke's home and fit in like everyone else did? She'd always wanted this, and Abby was giving her a chance. "Okay. I—I have to go downtown for some supplies tomorrow before I go to work. I could come early."

"Sure. We can meet at Yoshoris."

Yoshoris' dress code required something more upscale than the three outfits she had. "I don't think I can wear jeans there. That's all I have," she admitted, her cheeks flushing with her confession.

Stone walked over, stopping at her side. "You ready to go?"

The room was noisy as everyone talked and laughed around them. Oddly, she didn't want to leave. "Sure."

"Actually," Abby said. "I have to head downtown. I thought Sophie might like to come. I can show you where I work, and we can get to know each other better."

"Oh, uh, all right." She looked at Stone. "I guess I'm going with Abby."

Stone shrugged. "I guess I'll see you when I see you then."

She'd half expected him to tell her she couldn't go and remind her it was her job to make his dinner. She nodded, still trying to get used to the idea that her life was truly her own again. "I'll see you when I see you."

"Come on." Abby stood. "Let's go."

She got to her feet and grabbed her list, smiling, thrilled that for the first time in years she had impromptu plans.

# CHAPTER EIGHT

"SO HOW'S WORK?" ABBY ASKED AS SHE SPED DOWN Interstate Ten toward the Lily Brand offices.

"Good." Sophie unclasped her hands she gripped in her lap, commanding herself to relax. Abby had talked non-stop for the last forty minutes, bombarding her with question after question. She'd tried her best to answer instead of spin Abby's inquiries back at her—the new form of evasion she'd gotten very good at over the last couple of months.

"Jerrod told me his office looks great—very polished and clean."

Sophie smiled.

"I still can't get over how beautiful Sarah's new necklace set is. I can't wait to have one of my own." She wiggled her brows.

Sophie smiled again. "Thanks. I'm hoping to get back to jewelry making full-time as soon as possible."

"You made jewelry for a living?"

"Yes, my mother and I had a shop. Then I downsized a couple years ago and had my own booth at the mall." She swallowed, realizing that was the most she'd told anyone about herself in so long. Somehow it was easy to share little bits of who she was with Abby. Stone was right: Abby was extremely kind. Plus it didn't hurt that Abby had assured her she would keep her time at Stowers House a secret.

"You certainly have talent. Your creations are amazing. I'm sure you'll be back at it in no time at all."

She absorbed the quick thrill of Abby's compliment. Many people told her she made beautiful pieces, but coming from Abigail Quinn, fashion designer extraordinaire, that meant something. "Thank you. I hope so."

"I'm really glad we're getting this chance to get to know each other." Abby slid into the right lane and took her exit. "I hope you'll still have lunch with me tomorrow."

She didn't know how to *be* around a woman so different from herself. Abby was extroverted and sure of herself, but as she sat next to the energetic woman belting out the tune playing on the radio, she suddenly and desperately wanted this fledgling friendship to work. It would be so nice to have a real girlfriend, someone she could confide in and laugh with. "Do you still want to eat at Yoshoris?"

Abby nodded. "They have excellent food. It's an experience all in itself. I think we'll have fun."

She wasn't worried about fun. Abby was exciting enough for the both of them. Her lack of clothing options was what had her concerned. She slid a glance at Abby in her designer jeans and adorable lemon-colored chiffon flounce tank, envying her breezy style. "Do you have any suggestions on where I might be able to pick up a couple of new outfits for a reasonable price?"

"Absolutely." Abby pulled into a parking spot along the side of a huge building. "Right here."

"Oh," she said as she glanced at the sweeping Lily Brand Headquarters sign. Her idea of "reasonably priced" was clearly different than Abby's. Lily brand and the *Escape* line were high-end all the way.

"Come on." Abby unbuckled. "It's probably still pretty busy inside. Lily had a shoot today."

Sophie closed her door, hesitating on the sidewalk. "I don't want to be in the way."

"You won't be. I promise. Chaos reigned earlier this afternoon, *believe* me. That's why I was so late for Sarah's party. Let's go. I'll introduce you to some of my favorite people."

She nodded, less than thrilled that she was going to be walking around with one of the world's biggest fashion names in her tired clothing.

Abby moved up the steps, swiping them into the side entrance with her keycard. The door closed behind them as they started down the long carpeted hall. "Swinging by the office after a shoot is a great opportunity to snag some cool loot. Hey, Monique." Abby stopped to hug a tall, beautiful woman Sophie recognized from several magazine advertisements. "Monique, this is my friend Sophie. Monique is one of my models. I don't know what I would do without her."

"Aren't you sweet." Monique held out her hand. "Hi, Sophie."

Sophie smiled, taking the model's hand, praying her cheeks would stay cool and her tongue wouldn't go thick as she grew more uncomfortable in the unfamiliar setting. "Hi."

"I helped myself to a bunch of stuff." Monique held up a bulging Lily Brand bag. "I *love* the post-shoot grab. I really do. I'll see you next weekend." She hugged Abby again. "Nice to meet you, Sophie."

"You too."

Monique left and two women waved at Abby as they walked by with similar bags in their hands.

"See what I mean?"

"Where does all the stuff come from?"

"All over the place. When the makeup and hair companies get word that Lily's got something in the works, they send over all kinds of stuff—shampoo, conditioner, blusher, nail polish, hair dryers and curlers. The list goes on and on."

"Why?"

"Tit for tat. If they send stuff, our makeup artist and hairstylist might use it, then the magazines might give them a mention. It works well for everyone, and we send out the leftovers to the Stowers Houses. There's always plenty to share." Abby led her into a large hair and makeup room with a long row of vanity mirrors and salon chairs. "Do you want something?"

"Wow," she whispered, staring at the two huge tables jammed with every beauty product she could possibly think of. "*Look* at all of this." She laughed. "I've never seen anything like it."

Abby smiled. "Help yourself."

"I don't—I don't even know where to start."

"I'd start with a bag." Abby handed over one of the Lily Brand bags.

"Yes but look at all of these foundation options. There's powder or liquid, matte or original. And the blush colors and eyeliners. It's overwhelming."

"We can do a color test..." Abby trailed off as a pretty brown haired woman walked into the room carrying a large coffee. "Or we can ask the expert herself." Abby beamed. "Sophie, this is Jackie, Lily Brand's own hair and makeup genius." She hugged the woman. "Hey, Jacks."

"Hi, Abby." Jackie kissed Abby's cheek.

"Sophie and I were thinking about raiding the tables, but she's not sure what she should choose. Do you have any pointers?"

"You know I do." Jackie stepped closer to Sophie, sliding a finger along Sophie's cheek. "You have beautiful skin."

"Thank you." She gave Jackie a small smile. She wasn't used to people being so touchy feely. "Um, I don't wear a lot of makeup. None, actually. Usually just lip gloss." She hadn't even been able to wear that after she moved in with Eric.

Jackie tsked. "Well that's a shame, because your eyes are fascinating. You need to play them up. Violet. I've never seen it."

"All this stuff..." Sophie swept a hand toward the table. "It's pretty foreign to me." In high school, she'd been more interested in three-pointers and layups than mascara wands and blush. Mom tried to show her a couple of times, but she hadn't paid attention. Now that she was surrounded by so many beautiful people, she wished she had.

"It's time for an education. I can't let you leave without showing off those eyes. It would be a crime to my profession." Jackie took Sophie's hand. "Come on over to my chair and I'll show you how."

A tall man with a funky, slicked-back cap of black hair walked in.

"Marco." Abby hugged him. "Marco, god's gift to hair. I want you to meet my friend Sophie."

Sophie held out her hand. "Hi."

"Hey, nice to meet you." He slid his fingers through her hair. "Soft. Healthy. But too long."

She swallowed, unsure of what to say to Marco's critique.

"This doesn't do anything for that spectacular face of yours. Jackie gets to play with you. Can I play too?"

"Uh..." Never in her life had she met people like this before.

"I can see it now." He stepped behind the salon chair, talking to her as they looked at each other in the mirror. "We'll lose several inches, then I'm thinking a couple of light streaks right through here." He touched various strands of hair along the crown of her head.

She stared at the yards of pretty blonde she'd been growing for years. Marco wanted to cut it—*lots* of it. She digested the quick rush of fear. If Eric knew she was even contemplating the thought... He'd slapped her the day she'd come back from getting a trim, shouting that women were meant to have long hair. But Eric wasn't here anymore, and this was *her* hair. The idea of defying him was as liberating as it was frightening. "Okay. Yes. You can cut it. Do whatever you want," she said in a rush before she changed her mind.

Marco rubbed his hands together, grinning. "Let me go make up my color."

"Let's get a mani/pedi going while Marco takes care of your hair, then we'll get to the makeup," Jackie said as she rolled over a small cart.

"Oh, well, sure." Sophie glanced from Jackie to Abby. "Is this okay?"

"Absolutely. Marco and Jackie play with my hair and makeup all the time. I'm going to head down the hall for a few minutes."

"Okay."

"Have fun."

She was going to try, even if she was unsure. This is what women did with their girlfriends. They got their hair done and had manicures and pedicures. "I will."

Forty-five minutes later, Sophie's heart pounded while Marco dried her hair and Jackie brushed the wand over her lashes. She was trying her best to listen to Jackie's pointers on wiggling and sweeping from the base of the lash, but every time Marco slid the hairbrush through her hair, she couldn't help but notice his downward strokes stopped just below her shoulders. What had she *done,* and why had they insisted on turning her away from the mirror? They'd assured her more than once that she was going to love "the new her," but now that it was too late to change her mind she wasn't so certain.

Abby stepped back into the room, pushing a large cart with several dozen clothing items swaying on hangers. She stopped short, her eyes going wide.

Oh god. It was horrible. Sophie's heartbeat kicked up another notch as she gripped the armrest beneath her smock, struggling to keep herself from rushing from the chair. What if Marco had forgotten the original plan and she ended up with blue or pink streaks? She wasn't ultra trendy. She couldn't blend in with everyone else with pink hair.

Marco shut off the dryer, fluffed her ends, and stood in front of her, studying with his hand on his chin.

Jackie pushed the wand back in the tube of mascara, joining Abby and Marco as they all stared at her.

It was worse than she had imagined. They were trying to find a way to tell her. She swallowed, looking from Jackie to Abby to Marco. Why weren't they *saying* anything? She pressed a hand to her stomach. "I think I'm going to be sick."

Abby chuckled. "Let's put her out of her misery. Spin her around, guys."

"Yes, please. Please spin me around." She wiped her damp palms on her jeans and slammed her eyes shut as Jackie turned her toward the mirror. She opened one eye, then blinked in shock, staring at the stunning woman looking back at her. Marco hadn't turned her hair blue; he'd added barely noticeable streaks of bright blond, accentuating her natural color. She touched her fingertips to the blunt-cut, shoulder-length style. "I can't believe... Is that really *me*?"

Abby laughed.

Sophie stood, moving closer to the mirror, shocked that a slide of eyeliner and a few sweeps of mascara could make her eyes appear so huge.

"You look like you belong in a magazine, all sleek and polished." Abby stepped up next to her, wrapping an arm around her waist.

She *did*. "I can't possibly even..."

Jackie shoved a bag in her hand. "This is all the makeup we've talked about. And there's shampoo, conditioner, and other product Marco selected for you." Jackie hugged her. "You come back and visit us."

"I will." She embraced Marco next. "Thank you. Thank you both so much."

"Call me in six weeks for a trim. No one else touches your hair."

She nodded enthusiastically. "Okay."

Marco and Jackie's cell phones beeped at the same time. Jackie looked at her screen. "The boss lady's looking for us. We'll be back."

"See you soon." Abby clasped her hands below her chin, grinning as Marco and Jackie walked out. "Now it's *my* turn." She pulled the cart of clothes closer and grabbed a pair of jeans and a simple blue and white striped top from the pole. "Go ahead and try these on. I already know it's going to be perfect. I want to see that amazing figure of yours in the right clothes."

"Abby, I couldn't possibly. The hair and makeup..."

"Yes you can." Abby pushed her into the dressing room. "Don't ruin my fun." She closed the curtain with a playful smile.

She chuckled, hardly able to believe this was truly happening. Abby was her fairy godmother.

"How does it look?"

"Um, I don't know. I haven't tried it on yet."

"You're killing me with suspense."

"Okay. Hold on." She took off the clothes she'd arrived in and pulled on the snug jeans that accentuated her butt perfectly and made her waist appear tiny. She put on the light cotton top next, in awe that she was actually looking back at herself. In an hour's time she'd been transformed from dowdy to polished. She pulled the curtain aside, and Abby grinned.

"I *knew* it. Here." Abby handed her a brown leather belt. "Put this on." She got down on one knee and rolled Sophie's pant legs twice. "Go ahead and step into these too." She set brown leather sandals in front of her.

Sophie slid on the pretty, summery shoes that looked even better with her French manicured toenails.

Abby stood, looking Sophie up and down. "Yup. This is definitely right. Casual, classy, and fun."

She'd officially been transformed. For the first time ever, she felt beautiful. Somehow three strangers had known what she'd always wanted. She'd planned to remake her image after college to go along with her degree, but her vanity had taken a backseat to Mom's needs. "This is so great. Truly great."

"I'm glad—" Abby's phone rang. "Oh, just a second." She answered. "Hello." She smiled. "Yes. Not too long. You got it, big guy. I love you too." She hung up. "The hubs checking in to make sure I'm okay. He still gets a little nervous."

Sophie nodded, remembering that Abby had gone through an ordeal of her own.

Abby clasped her hands again. "So you like the outfit?"

"I love it." She glanced at her watch. Time had

flown by. "But I should probably get home."

"We need to bag up the rest of this stuff for you." She gestured to the cart full of clothing.

"But this is too much. I can't possibly take all of this. There must be a dozen outfits."

"Probably closer to two or three. And you can mix and match all of them, so really there's endless options."

"Abby, I can't—"

"Yes you can. I want you to. We give stuff away all the time. Our models grab stuff; you saw that for yourself."

She glanced at adorable skirts, tops, slacks, jeans, and numerous shoe options, loving everything Abby had picked. There were even a few lacey bra and panty sets. "I know I've said this a million times. Thank you."

"You're welcome. Now you can meet me at Yoshoris for lunch."

She smiled. "Yes I can." And she couldn't wait. "I'm going to catch the bus so you can get home to Jerrod."

"You're not taking the bus. You have too much stuff. I'm driving you."

Sophie shook her head. "It doesn't make any sense for you to drive all the way to the Palisades only to drive back down here."

"So we'll compromise and call a taxi."

She almost said no, but she knew Abby would insist on taking her. "Okay. A taxi it is."

Forty minutes later, Sophie sat in the back of the cab staring out the window, rehashing her awesome day—a party that had turned out to be fun, dozens of orders to make, and a new wardrobe, accessories, and beauty supplies. She'd been putting a few dollars away here and there to buy herself some new clothes, but now she didn't need to.

The cab rolled up to a stop at a set of lights next to one of her favorite department stores. She nibbled her lip, remembering the coffee maker she'd seen in the flyers last night. The thing was expensive, but it was a beauty and would be perfect for Stone. She wanted to get it for him, but the money... She crunched numbers in her head, figuring she could use the cash she hadn't spent on clothes plus the few extra dollars she hadn't spent at the grocery store yesterday. "Excuse me. Could you please pull in here and wait for me. I'll be quick."

"It's your dime, lady." The cabbie took the right, and she hustled into the store, making a beeline for the kitchen area. She searched the shelves, huffing out a breath when she noticed the shelf empty.

"Crap," she murmured and bent at the knees, noting the model she was looking for tucked back among one of the other brands. "*Yes.*" Grinning, she grabbed the last coffee maker in stock, wincing when she glanced at the price. This was good quality and state of the art *and* the least she could do for the man who was giving her a place to stay. Plus, it was twenty percent off, which made it worth it. She moved to the selection of coffees suggested for the machine she'd chosen, taking a variety package of pods, paid, and went back outside. "Thank you."

"Like I said. Your dime."

She bobbed her leg up and down, filled with excitement as the cab traveled down Highway One. She'd always loved doing this—surprising people with little gifts...or big gifts in this instance. At least, she *used* to love doing that.

Hopefully Stone would like it. They were about to find out.

She grinned, looking at the lights on in the house and Stone's car parked in its spot as the taxi pulled into the drive. She paid the driver and wrestled her huge bags inside, moving as quietly as she could, setting everything on the card table while Stone hammered away at something in one of the other rooms.

"Stone," she said quietly as she peeked down the hall, thrilled when he didn't respond. She pulled the present from the box, wanting to set up everything before he realized she was home.

~~~~

Stone double-checked his measurements and sent his knife through the panel of drywall. He tapped his pencil against the sheetrock in time with AC/DC's drummer, studying the two-by-fours he planned to cover with the piece he'd just cut. He sniffed the air, frowning when he caught a whiff of coffee. He sniffed again, figuring he was jonesing for a good cup, though he typically only craved his caffeine jolts when he first woke up.

Shaking his head, he picked up the slab of drywall and set it down just as quickly when he breathed deep again, certain the scent of fresh brew wasn't a figment of his imagination. He pulled the buds from his ears and started down the hall, listening as the refrigerator opened and closed. "Soph?"

"In here. I'm in the kitchen."

"What are you doing?" He glanced at his watch, wondering why the hell she was making coffee at almost seven thirty. She didn't drink the stuff, and he only guzzled two cups in the morning. He stepped into the room. "Why are you making—"

"Surprise!" She whirled, grinning, cradling one of his ugly mugs in her hands.

He stared at the stunningly *hot* woman smiling at

him. What did Abby *do* to her? Her hair was different—much shorter. And her eyes were so pretty and huge. She looked incredible.

"Do you like it?"

How could he not? Her clothes fit perfectly, showcasing her sirens body. Every inch of Sophie looked sensational. "Yeah. Definitely."

Her smile widened as she stepped closer to him, stopping almost toe-to-toe. "I was hoping you would. I saw it in the flyers last night. I wanted you to have it."

He frowned, unsure of what she meant, then realized she was talking about the coffee maker on the counter and steaming cup in her hands.

"It's top of the line. It's supposed to make some of the best brew on the market. Here." She handed him the mug. "I know it's getting late and you'll never sleep, but maybe you could just try a little."

He took the cup, holding her gaze, unable to look away from the hypnotic violet.

"Go ahead," she encouraged.

He sipped, groaning at the intensely robust flavor of excellent beans. "Damn, that's good."

She snagged her glossy bottom lip between her teeth. "Really?"

He sampled again. "Really. Taste for yourself." He held the cup to her lips.

She dutifully sampled and wrinkled her nose. "Strong." She shuddered. "Ugh, too strong."

He grinned. "Just the way I like it."

"I imagine someone has to."

He grabbed her chin, needing to touch her soft skin. "You and Abby were busy."

She gripped his wrist as they stared in each other's eyes. "Yes. She and a couple of her friends at Lily Brand gave me a makeover."

"I guess they did. You look good, Soph."

"Thanks."

He let her go, but he didn't want to. "Thanks for the coffee maker."

"You're welcome." She took a step away, sliding her hair behind her ear with a jerky swipe. "Do—do you want dinner? It's late but I could make something quick."

He'd made a sandwich an hour ago, but Sophie was bound to come up with something a hell of a lot better. And he wouldn't mind sitting next to her hearing about her makeover deal, especially if he could make her smile at him the way she had when he walked into the room. "I could eat."

"I was thinking of beef and broccoli."

"Sounds fine to me."

She nodded. "Let me put away my stuff and I'll get to it."

He looked at the piles of clothes, cosmetics, and shoes on the table. "Jesus. Did you buy out the stores?"

She smiled. "It certainly looks that way, but no."

"I guess I better get some closets built." He grabbed dozens of hangers poking through garment bags. "Let's find a place to hang this stuff in the meantime."

She snagged a bagful of hair and makeup supplies and another bulging with shoes. "You don't have to help."

He glanced over his shoulder as they made their way down to her bedroom. "I do if I want beef and broccoli sometime in the next century."

She flashed him another smile. "You do have a point."

They stepped into her room, and he hung everything on the now sagging rope he'd strung across a couple of the posts in the makeshift space. "God, I'll never understand why women have to have so much *stuff*."

She crouched down, taking the pairs of shoes out one by one—sandals, high heels, and boots—and set them by his feet in neat rows. "Because it makes us look nice."

He trailed his gaze over her pretty backside. "I guess I can't argue with you there." He grabbed some contraption from the makeup bag. The packaging said it was an eyelash curler. He set it down with a shake of his head. "I imagine that's where the whole 'beauty is pain' thing comes in, right?"

She laughed as she looked up at him. "Yes, I imagine so."

He offered his hand, realizing that was the first time he'd heard that light sound.

She took it, standing. "How about dinner?"

"Sounds good. I'll help."

"You don't have to."

He didn't, but he wanted to, which was new. Cooking wasn't his thing. He lifted her hand, studying her fancy nails. "I'll chop stuff. We don't want you ruining these."

She chuckled. "My hero."

"Come on. I'll save the day." He pulled her from the room, not bothering to let go of her hand along the way.

# CHAPTER NINE

SOPHIE'S NEW PHONE RANG, STARTLING HER OUT OF HER concentration. She set down the navy blue bead she'd been twisting among thin ropes of delicate silver and looked at the display, expecting Eric's name to pop up instead of Abby's. The kneejerk dread vanished and she smiled, remembering that she never had to answer Eric's hourly check-ins ever again.

Abby had convinced her that she could still be a part of the twenty-first century and stay anonymous with a pay-as-you-go phone, but having one made her uneasy. Eric's PI was relentless. It was highly unlikely he would track her down via a cell phone she could easily throw away, but if anyone could, it was his man. Dismissing the troubling thought, she answered, refusing to be a prisoner to the monster she fled. "Hello?"

"Hey, it's me again. Sorry to bother you."

Abby had called twice already this afternoon. The first time was just to chat and the second to invite her to Saturday night's monthly girls' get-together. She loved that Abby had thought to include her. For the first time in her life, she had an actual girlfriend. During most of her childhood she'd been too obsessed with basketball to worry over close friends. In high school and college, she'd concentrated on her education and need to bead when she wasn't busy scoring three-pointers for her team. She'd always been content to do her own thing—her crushing shyness had demanded it be so. And she'd always had her mother. Now she had Abby to talk to and hopefully the other women she desperately wanted to get to know. "You're not bothering me."

"Good. I actually only have a minute. I have a meeting with Lily in five, but there's been a little change in plans. Girls' night isn't going to be at Lex's after all. I talked her out of that crazy idea. Owen's due to arrive any second. The doctor told Lex and Jackson today that if my adorable new nephew doesn't decide to make his debut by Monday they're going to help things along."

"That's exciting." She fiddled with her chain-nose pliers as visions of a small gift for Alexa started taking shape.

"I'm pretty pumped."

"Do we need to reschedule?" She didn't want to be disappointed. She was trying not to be. Alexa was terribly uncomfortable, and Olivia was eagerly awaiting her new brother.

"Nah. Morgan's hosting instead."

She smiled. "Okay. Where does she live?"

"Just a couple miles from Ethan and Sarah. I'll swing by and give you a ride if you want."

This not having a car thing was becoming inconvenient. Now that she had a bit of a life, she needed to get places and not have it take an hour. She shrugged away her frustration. The bus would be her mode of transportation for a long time coming. "I appreciate the offer."

"Is six okay?"

"Yes. I'm still trying to decide what I should bring." She stood, walking to the cupboards, perusing the selection of baking supplies she had on hand.

"You don't have to bring anything."

"Yes, I do." She loved being creative in the kitchen. Now that she didn't have to worry about getting everything perfectly right and approved before she could shop or make it, she enjoyed cooking and baking again. Stone certainly didn't seem to mind.

"You're the boss."

She grinned at the idea. She *was* the boss of her own life. The utter thrill of being her own woman, of making her own choices and being able to come and go as any other adult could and did, made her giddy. "Then it's settled. I'll go for something sinful and chocolaty."

"*Now* you're talking. Oh, I've gotta go. I'll see you Saturday. Oh, Lily loves the jewelry by the way. She's wearing the necklace and earrings right now."

"*Really*?" Lily Thomas liked her work. An actual fashion mogul was wearing something *she* made.

"I wouldn't make it up. Okay, I really need to hang up. Bye."

"Bye." She ended the call on her way back to the card table, sighing, perfectly content. Rain fell in chilly sheets and the wind blew in nasty gusts, but that didn't dampen her spirits. She was in a warm, half-finished house doing the job she loved while beef stew simmered on the stove. She picked up the wire-wrapped bead she'd set down and attached the piece to the sterling silver fishhook, mentally rearranging tomorrow's schedule. She'd planned on a full day of work but now that she had weekend plans, she would have to finagle. She *loved* that she had to finagle.

She needed to get to the bead store for more supplies, stop off at the grocer's for ingredients for her chocolate mousse brownies, and run by the department store to pick up a few more items on her shrinking list of things for Stone's kitchen. She'd made a huge dent after her lunch date with Abby three days ago, but there was still more to see to, and she would get it done.

She set down the second fishhook wire, now swinging with a matching dangle, and slid up the sleeves on her stylish creamy blue cardigan. She was four days into her new, quietly sleek look and she adored every second of it. The frumpy woman who fled on a borrowed bike was gone for good; the confident, professional businesswoman, which was exactly what she intended to be, was here for the long haul. She no longer wore her hair in a bun or a hoodie to go out in public. Eric would no more recognize her dressed like this than he would if she wore a cap shoved low on her head.

She glanced at her to-do list and started tidying her ever-growing workspace, worrying a bit. Eventually she was going to have to apply for a license and deal with taxes. She had too many orders coming in to ignore her responsibilities in that regard, but the risks and complications that would come with establishing her place of business diminished her sense of peace, leaving her cold. Eric would find her, and he would come.

She shuddered out a breath, barely able to tolerate the thought. She wasn't ready to deal with him. She couldn't be sure she ever would be, but if she took the next step she would have to. She set her assorted pliers in the ancient cloth, rolling them up tight as she did every day, reassuring herself that waiting a while longer to deal with Uncle Sam and the state of California would be fine. Right now she was too busy to deal with the headaches anyway. Everything was happening so fast. Sarah's mother already sold the six sets she'd scrambled to put together Sunday night and Monday morning. Janice had requested a dozen more by tomorrow to have on hand for the weekend, and Hailey had reminded her via Abby that she was very interested in hosting a party at her house at the end of the month.

Business was officially hopping, as she'd hoped it would, which meant there was no way she could keep up with the demand and clean Ethan Cooke Security. That's why she'd stopped. Luckily when she called Cecilia Sunday evening to discuss giving up her night job, Cecilia had said she would let her go immediately. There was a woman at Stowers House desperate for the position. Sophie had happily handed off her responsibilities right then and there.

She gathered her supplies, and began stacking the Tupperware she was using to stay organized on the corner of the counter when a car pulled up in the drive. It instantly put her on alert, but she relaxed when she recognized the engine of Stone's Mustang. She took the cloth off the rolls that had been rising for the last couple hours and slid the cookie sheet into the oven as the front door opened and closed. "Supper will be ready in about fifteen minutes," she called.

Stone walked in, his hair and polo shirt soaked and dripping, carrying something squirming in a filthy once-white t-shirt. "Hey."

She frowned as the something yipped. "What do you have?"

He peeled back the shirt, exposing a shaking brown and black fur ball. "I found him about two miles back on the highway. I almost hit him."

She stepped away from the pathetic, whimpering pup as he shook in Stone's arms. "Is he hurt?"

"I don't know. I think he's got a few scratches, and he's cold. I didn't want to leave him, so I brought him home for you."

"For *me*?" She took another step away, thinking of

her beloved Cooper. "No. Why did you do that?"

"Because I just about creamed him. I thought you could keep an eye on him while he heals up."

Cooper's shocked cry echoed in her head. "I don't want him," she said as the dog let loose another round of mournful whimpers, tugging at her heart. "I *don't*." She turned away, closing her eyes, fisting her hands at her sides as she saw the bat come down, smashing into the side of her dog's head as he tried to protect her from Eric's vicious blows. Her sweet, wonderful Cooper had flown across the room, landing with a sickening thud. She'd rushed to him, her arms swollen and bruised, the pain unbearable, holding the love of her life as he took his last breath. Cooper had been all she'd had left of her mother. She'd brought Mom the adorable, silly mutt from the pound the day before she left for college, not wanting her mother to be alone. Cooper had been the best companion, and she'd let him down in the most awful of ways. She hadn't kept him safe.

"Fine. I'll just bring him to the shelter."

She whirled, glancing from the gorgeous soaking wet man to the sweet puppy with sad brown eyes. "Why—why can't you keep him?"

"Because I work all the time, and I can't take care of him."

She stared at the dog, loving him already, growing angry with Stone for putting her in this position. She didn't want to get attached to an animal she couldn't keep. She couldn't stay here forever. What if she had to go? But if Stone brought him to the pound, he would more than likely be euthanized.

"I'll take him down to the pound." Stone wrapped him back up in the filthy shirt. "Go ahead and eat without me."

"No." She walked to where he stood, her eyes filling with helpless tears. "Just give him to me."

He took a step back. "You just said you don't want him."

"He needs a bath and a meal." She seared Stone with a look, reaching forward, pulling the puppy and disgusting shirt out of his grip. "The rolls need to come out of the oven or they'll burn." She froze, realizing she'd snapped at him.

"Why are you pissed?"

"I don't...I..." That was it? There was no slap or shove for using a disrespectful tone? She raised her chin, trying to remember that not all men hit, and Stone didn't. It was okay to be upset and voice her frustrations. He *liked* it when she did. "For putting me in this position." She turned and walked to the bathroom with the shivering pup.

~~~~

Twenty minutes later, Stone stepped through his front door for the second time, carrying a bag full of supplies for the puppy. He set the items on the chair and walked to the stove, lifting the lid on the simmering stew, groaning as he breathed in the scent, more than ready for a huge bowl. He was freezing his ass off and hungry with it. Sophie's cooking would take care of the worst of both problems.

Her soft voice traveled from the bathroom as the water ran in the tub. He moved down the hall, grabbing a towel from the fresh pile of clean laundry, drying himself off several steps back from the doorway as he watched her gently scrub the malnourished, whimpering pup.

"We're almost finished. You're a filthy boy."

105

The pup lapped at her chin.

She smiled. "We'll warm you up with the hairdryer then get you some milk and send Stone out for your dinner." She gave the puppy a final rinse and grabbed one of the huge, soft towels. "Out you come."

She picked him up and snuggled him close, resting her cheek on top of his damp head as she moved to sit on the toilet. She was so pretty in her fancy, fitted jeans and sweater. He hadn't missed that she'd worn makeup and fixed her hair every day since her makeover or the way she hummed while she cleaned or worked at the table, making her jewelry almost non-stop.

Having her here definitely didn't suck. Hopefully her new four-legged friend would make her want to stick around for a while. If the thought had crossed his mind when he scooped the miserable puppy up off the side of the road, no one needed to know that but him. He probably hadn't needed to resort to slightly underhanded tactics; it seemed like she was going to stay. She certainly had a full closet, and Janice was calling her daily with new orders. And he'd seen the ideas she'd been fiddling around with for the catalog she was putting together for Hailey's party. If he had to guess, she had every intention of setting up shop right here in the LA-area, and he didn't hate the prospect.

But who the hell *was* she? He glanced into the half-finished room she slept in, trying to remember that it didn't matter as he eyed the backpack she kept tucked in the corner. She was settling in well enough; all of her belongings were stacked in a tidy way among the chaos of tools and sheets of drywall, but she had yet to unpack the navy blue bag. He looked back into the bathroom and walked into the bedroom as she turned on the hairdryer.

Sophie had been living in his house for almost

three weeks, and he knew nothing about her. She was starting to relax around him, but she never had anything to say about herself. Typically that worked for him. For the most part he didn't give a damn about other people, but he wanted to know something more about his roommate other than her age and birthdate. He only knew she was about to turn twenty-five on June first because he'd waited until she was too distracted to keep her guard up, then asked in his own roundabout way.

Sophie was very careful with everything she said. If she didn't want to spill, he would find the answers on his own. He tossed a glance over his shoulder as he crouched down next to her bag, hesitating before he unzipped the surprisingly heavy backpack. She had a right to her privacy, but he had a right to know who lived in his house. Or at least saying that made his conscious feel a bit justified.

He dug into the pack, recognizing the jeans and t-shirts she'd rolled tightly, then went straight to the bottom, grabbing hold of the thick, white business envelope, whistling through his teeth as he ran his thumb over the impressive stack of bills. He spotted the *Trendy* magazine featuring Abby on the cover and brushed his knuckles against something cool and hard. He lifted the silver frame, staring at Sophie smiling next to a stunning black-haired woman—her mother, maybe—as they both hugged the golden retriever mix nestled between them.

He frowned, wondering why she'd gotten so huffy about the puppy. Clearly she liked dogs. He slid the frame back in place as he spotted her purse, reaching for it as the dryer shut off. He quickly zipped the bag and left the room, hurrying down to the kitchen, making himself busy. He tossed the rolls back into the oven he'd forgotten to turn off when he grabbed them out the first time and took two new pale yellow bowls from the cupboard.

Sophie murmured to the pup in her arms as she stopped in the doorway.

He turned, battling with another wave of guilt as their eyes met. "I'll get us some food."

"There's a salad in the fridge," she said with a hint of cool.

He set down the bowls. "Look, I didn't realize bringing home a defenseless animal was going to put your back up. I said I would take him to the pound."

"He's not going to the pound. You and I both know what will happen to him there." She moved to the fridge, taking out the milk and a cereal bowl from the cupboard, pouring a small amount into the bottom. She microwaved the dish for fifteen seconds, stirred the milk with her finger, and set it on the floor along with the dog. "Here you go," she said in her soft voice as she crouched down next to the puppy's side.

The dog sniffed and started lapping greedily.

"He's starving. You poor thing," she cooed, petting him in long, gentle strokes.

He leaned back against the counter, watching Sophie's graceful fingers move along the brown and black fur. "So give him some more."

She shook her head, keeping her eyes glued to the dog. "Just a little at a time. We don't want to make him sick." She stood and put on an oven mitt, grabbing the homemade rolls she'd made at some point during the day.

"I didn't mean to make you mad. I thought you'd like having the company."

She met his gaze, letting loose a small sigh. "Murphy will have a good home here until I can find him a forever family."

"Murphy?"

"Yes." She looked down at the sleeping puppy, laughing as the exhausted dog lay by the bowl with his ear in what was left of the milk.

He stared at her, certain he would never get enough of that bright sound. "So how old do you think Murphy is?"

"Mmm. Maybe twelve or thirteen weeks. He's going to need an appointment with the vet."

"He's definitely not ugly. It looks like there's a bit of retriever and shepherd in him."

"Yes, I think you're right." She grabbed up the bowl and set it in the sink. "Your clothes are still soaked. I figured you would've changed."

"I went to the store." He gestured toward the bag on the chair."

"Thank you."

"Are you still mad?" He didn't want her to be. Sophie's quiet disapproval packed a nasty punch.

"A little." She sighed again. "Why don't you give me your shirt, and we'll throw it in the dryer."

He pulled off his top, setting it in her outstretched hand, then took hold of her fingers, tugging her closer. "I'm sorry."

Her eyes softened. "Thank you for your apology. It was kind of you to stop instead of leave him there. He probably wouldn't have lived long if you had. I'm sorry for snapping at you."

"I should've asked."

"He's here now. We'll take good care of him until we can find him a family."

He nodded, unable to look away from those enchanting violet eyes, wondering who the hell the sweet blond with the wad of cash was. "I'll get the salad, then I'll get a shirt."

"Okay." She smiled.

He let her go and turned toward the fridge, reminding himself that Sophie and her bagful of secrets had nothing to do with him.

~~~~

Eric hustled from his limo into the building, hurrying for the elevator before it closed. He pressed the button for the fifth floor, crossing his arms, careful to avoid wrinkles as he waited for the doors to open again. He counted down on his Rolex, growing impatient as the second hand started around the watch face for the second time. He was expected at the gallery, but David would be getting a visit first. They had an appointment tomorrow morning, but he wouldn't be kept waiting for one more moment.

Finally, the elevator came to a stop with a gentle ding and slide of the doors. He moved down the hall, more than ready to hear what his useless PI had to say. He was sick of the excuses and non-answers. David was lucky this trip to New York City had already been planned. He was a busy, important man. Taking impromptu trips didn't suit his schedule.

He pulled open the second door on the left and walked into the upscale waiting area decorated with ferns and dark leather furnishings.

"Hello, Mr. Winthrop." David's secretary greeted him with a polite smile.

He didn't bother to respond or wait for an invitation to go back to the office.

"Um, excuse me, Mr. Winthrop," the secretary called after him.

He moved down another hall and walked into a

meeting in session.

David and two other men stopped talking.

"I need to speak with you immediately."

David adjusted the glasses on his ugly pointed nose. "I'm in a meeting."

"Now you're not." Eric nodded at the men staring at him in their starchy pinstripes.

David stood, swiping at the top of his balding head. "If you'll excuse me for just a moment, gentlemen." He walked around his desk, taking Eric's arm as they moved into the hallway.

"Mr. Schmidt," the secretary came hustling up, her cheeks flushed. "I'm sorry."

"Don't worry about it. I'll take care of this. Go ahead and get back to work." He turned to Eric. "What the hell are you doing?"

"I think the better question here, David, is what the hell are *you* doing? I need answers and I need them now. Where the hell is Sophie?"

"I'm working on it. I run her license and social security number every day. I'm checking for bank and credit card activity. You know that. I send you my reports every night by five."

"It's not enough. I need her *back*. The wedding's Saturday, and she's going to be there." Sophie would be standing next to him at the altar he'd had hand-carved, so help him god.

"I don't know what else you want me to do."

"*Find* her, damn it."

"It's only a matter of time. The minute she makes a mistake, I'll have her. Have I ever let you down?"

David had been letting him down for the last two months. "There's a first time for everything."

"We're going to track her down."

"June first is right around the corner. You know

what's at stake. I won't lose out on that money." He glanced at his watch and straightened his tie. "I have to go to my show. I'm going to be late."

"Go sell your paintings and let me worry about Sophie."

"She should be here. She's making me look like a damn *fool*. Find her, David." He sailed back out as quickly as he'd come, hoping he'd made himself very clear.

# CHAPTER TEN

SOPHIE SAT WITH HER FOOT CURLED UNDER HER ON Morgan Phillips' couch, enjoying her glass of wine in her cute, pale-green, spaghetti-strap top and white shorts. She'd been nestled in her comfy seat for the last hour, talking and laughing, just being one of the girls. For the other six women this was a normal once-a-month gathering, but for her it was a special moment she would treasure forever. They'd welcomed her with open arms, letting her into their close-knit group because Abby had paved the way. Finally she belonged. She could never repay her new friend for opening up her world so completely.

Only months ago she'd been alone. Eric had slowly and effectively cut her off from anyone and everything until there had only been him. His life had been her entire focus.

She glanced at the pretty wall clock across the room and smiled into her glass as she took another sip of the sweet Riesling. It was ten o' clock in Maine, and she should have been Mrs. Eric Winthrop. By now she would have been dancing with her new husband in front of hundreds of stuffy guest she barely knew, but instead she was here, surrounded by fun, warm women. This right here was freedom. This was everything she'd ever wanted.

Murphy adjusted himself so his chin rested on her bare foot, and she smiled again, perfectly, wonderfully happy. Reaching down, she gave her new puppy a gentle rub between the ears. He hadn't left her side since Stone brought him home two days ago. He ran with her each morning and enjoyed his evening walks, trying desperately to catch seagulls. She'd tried her best not to get too attached, but she already was. Eventually she would have to find the sweet little mutt a family, but for now she and Murphy had each other. She stretched forward, taking a chocolate-covered strawberry from the tray on the coffee table, tuning into the conversation humming around her.

"Now that the business is officially back in the black, Tucker really wants to get started," Wren said as she forked up another bite of the mousse-topped brownies Sophie had brought along.

"So what are you waiting for?" Sarah asked. "The girls and their brother would love to welcome a cousin."

"Well, they might—" Wren paused with more brownie on her fork. "Are you and Ethan having a boy?"

"Yes." Sarah beamed. "We found out yesterday. He finally cooperated and faced the way we wanted him to."

"Aw, a nephew." Wren got up and walked over to Sarah, hugging her sister-in-law. "Congratulations. I'm going to have to swing by and give Ethan a hug."

"You know he would love it."

"Morgan, when are you and Hunter going to give Jacob a brother or sister?" Abby asked.

"Not for a while." Morgan set her plate on the small tray. "Jake's finally sleeping through the night. I want to enjoy that for a while. Besides, Hunter and I are happy practicing until we decide we're ready for round two."

Everyone chuckled.

"I finally decided to go for it," Hailey said as she switched Preston to her other breast.

"I'm sure Austin was okay with that," Abby said with a wiggle of her brows.

"I thought he was going to cry when I took his hand and led him to the bedroom." Hailey grinned. "God knows I made him wait long enough, but I just wasn't ready. He was sweet not to pressure me. I thought our first time after the baby was going to be slow and maybe romantic."

Morgan and Sarah chuckled at that notion.

Hailey grinned again. "Yeah, it ended up being a quickie. A really great, amazing quickie. We slowed down the second time around after we both blew off a little steam."

"Here's to seconds." Abby held up her glass with an exaggerated wink for Hailey.

"Hear, hear." Hailey said with her glass of lemon water.

"Forget sex." Alexa shifted uncomfortably in her chair. "At this point I'd agree to give it up for a year. I just want to have this baby."

Sarah nodded, squeezing Alexa's hand in sympathy.

"I'll be sweet enough to have a sweaty bought in your honor, big sis." Abby chuckled.

"Someday you'll know the discomfort of which I speak." Alexa smiled not so sweetly, with a bat of her lashes.

"Someday." Abby laughed. "But not tonight."

Sophie took another bite of her sinful strawberry, wondering what all the fuss was about. She hated sex. If she never had it again, it wouldn't be the end of the world.

"You're quiet over there, Sophie." Wren said, picking up her merlot.

"Oh, I was just thinking about how much I hate sex." Her cheeks immediately burned crimson as she realized she'd actually said that out loud.

"Well," Wren set her wine down without drinking, "I guess that means you need to find yourself a decent partner. The right person makes all the difference."

"Like Tucker." Abby teased with a bump of her elbow to Wren's arm.

"Absolutely." Wren winked, grinning hugely.

"Maybe Stone would be willing to give you a hand." Hailey sent Sophie a slow smile. "I mean you do live together."

"I—I don't think so." Sophie set her glass down before she dropped it. "I mean, yes, we live together, but no on the sex."

"He's pretty hot," Hailey added.

Everyone agreed.

"Well, yes." She sat up straighter and cleared her throat as Stone's sexy chest and six-pack abs flashed through her mind.

"I bet he's amazing in bed," Morgan said with a bite into a white-chocolate strawberry. "The quiet, broody ones usually are. Hunter isn't exactly quiet, but he certainly can brood." She bit her lip with a knowing smile.

As if on cue, Hunter walked into the living room with a fussy baby.

"Well speak of the devil," Morgan said, getting to her feet.

Morgan's gorgeous golden husband with the insanely blue eyes frowned as he gently bounced his son in his powerful arms. "What?"

"Nothing." She pressed a playful kiss to his lips. "It looks like Jake's ready for a snack." She smiled at her husband and kissed him again as she took their son.

Hunter shook his head and started back down the hall as Morgan moved toward the stairs.

Preston filled his diaper with a loud explosion and let out a wail.

Hailey stood, following Morgan. "I'm going to need to use Jake's changing table."

"Come on up."

Wren's cell phone rang. She glanced at the readout. "Sorry, but I need to take this." She put the phone to her ear. "Patrick? Yes. No, the pale blue." She stood, held up a finger, and left the room.

"Well, I guess I'll refill the platter," Abby said. "Sophie, you wanna come with me?"

"Sure." She grabbed the tray of dirty dishes and followed Abby to the kitchen.

"Our gatherings are a little different now that we have so many babies joining the party."

"I think it's wonderful." She set down the tray and opened the dishwasher.

Abby took several Tupperware containers from the fridge, placing them on the counter. "I hope we didn't make you uncomfortable just now."

Sophie paused with a dirty plate in her hand. "What do you mean?"

"The sex talk. They were only teasing."

"No. It was fine." She liked that they'd felt comfortable enough to include her in the fun.

Abby stopped arranging strawberries on the platter and faced her. "This is none of my business, but I know—I know what it's like to hate sex. I also know what it's like to love it."

Sophie sighed, swiping her hair behind her ear and grabbed another dish, not quite able to meet Abby's eyes. "I'm not like other women."

Abby frowned. "Why do you say that?"

"There's something wrong with me." She'd never confessed one of her biggest secrets to anyone, not that there'd been anyone to tell.

"Sexually?"

She nodded, trying to remember that Abby was her friend. Girlfriends talked about sex. "I don't like sex. It doesn't excite me. *Ever.*"

"Okay."

"I'm dysfunctional. I don't have orgasms, and I don't look forward to the next time the way the rest of you do."

Abby grabbed one of the dirty dishes, placing the plate next to the one Sophie just put in. "Has it always been like that?"

She nodded again. "Eric says I'm a dead lay." She looked down, mortified. "He says I'm a disappointment."

"I'm sure that's not true." Abby rested a supportive hand on her shoulder. "What about your other partners?"

"There haven't been any."

"Eric, he's the only man you've been with?"

"Yes. I was always too busy with sports and my mother's business to get involved with boys. Eric and I were friends. He's older than me—thirty-seven. Then my mother got sick and things changed. I'm not sure I wanted them to, but it was such a horrible time and it just...did." She shrugged, remembering the wretched period in her life as if it were yesterday.

"You were vulnerable."

"Yes. I guess I was." And she hated that she'd been so weak.

"Were you attracted to him?"

"He was more my friend. I leaned on him a lot as my mother got worse."

"Can I ask you another question?"

As much as it was embarrassing to talk about, it

was also a relief. "Yes."

"Are you attracted to Stone?"

"I—uh, I don't know." She sighed, knowing that wasn't true. "Yes, I guess, perhaps I might be."

Abby smiled. "He's gorgeous and broody, Sophie. A dead woman would find him appealing."

Sophie grinned. "It's just that I live with him, and he's been kind to let me stay. It's not right—"

"It's exactly right. And normal. Have you ever thought that there might not be anything wrong with you and maybe you were just with the wrong man? I'll second what Wren said earlier—the right partner makes all the difference. Trust me. Trust us."

"I don't know how to be with a man. I don't *want* to be with one. Ever."

Abby nodded. "There's nothing wrong with that, but it's also okay to change your mind. After the rape, I didn't think I would ever be able to think about sex in a healthy way again. Then Jerrod came along. I wanted to be with him. I love being with him. When your partner cares about you and wants you to enjoy the experience as much as he does, everything's different. It's wonderful."

She wanted to believe Abby, but her two-year track record in bed spoke for itself. "Thank you."

"You're welcome."

She set the last dish in the dishwasher and closed the door. "It looks like we're all finished."

Abby secured the lid on the strawberries and put the containers back in the fridge. "Ready for some more fun?"

She smiled. "Definitely."

"Come on."

They went out to the living room. Sophie took her seat on the couch as Abby set down the tray and rushed to her sister's side.

"Lex, are you okay?"

Alexa breathed in and out slowly several times, nodding.

"Contraction?"

Alexa nodded again, smiling as she breathed normally. "A *real* contraction—about a minute long."

"It's time." Abby smiled, taking her sister's hand.

"*Finally.*" Alexa sighed, getting to her feet with her sister's help. "I know in a couple hours from now I won't be so excited to be in pain, but I'm loving it now. I need to call Jack."

"Alexa, I'm going to take you home," Sarah said. "I'll bring Livy back to my house with me so you and Jackson can head to the hospital when you're ready."

Alexa grabbed her purse from the entryway table. "That sounds good."

Abby opened the door for them. "I'll come by soon. Give me half an hour."

"Take your time. If you remember, this usually takes a while." She kissed Abby's cheek. "I'll see you soon. Bye, Sophie."

"Goodbye." She picked up Murphy. "I'm happy to call a cab if you want to go with your sister and Sarah."

Abby shook her head. "No. I brought you; I'll bring you home. Lex's house is only a couple miles from Stone's."

"Okay, but I'd like to go so you can."

Hunter came back into the room. "Everybody's leaving?"

"Lex just went into labor," Abby said. "Sarah's bringing her home. I'm taking Sophie home. I have no idea where Wren went. Morgan and Hailey are upstairs."

"I guess I'll see you guys around."

"Tell Morgan we said thanks and bye."

"Will do. Give Jackson and Alexa our best." He started toward the stairs. "We'll stop by the hospital and visit tomorrow."

"Thank Morgan for me," Sophie piped in.

"I will. See ya." He disappeared up the steps.

She and Abby hurried to the car despite Alexa's calm reassurance to take their time. Ten minutes later, Sophie got out in Stone's driveway. "Thank you again for including me."

"Thanks for the delicious treats."

"Tell Alexa and Jackson good luck for me."

"I will. We should do lunch this week."

"Definitely. Call me when you have a new nephew to hold."

"Will do. Bye."

"Bye." She waved as Abby backed up and drove away. Murphy cuddled closer, whimpering in her arms as she walked toward the house. As she approached, she could hear the blasting sounds of U-2 pouring through the open windows. "It's okay," she reassured, kissing the top of Murphy's head. "Stone must be working." She opened the door and went inside, stopping abruptly when she saw her cot, clothes, and shoes piled in the living room. "What in the world? Stone?"

She moved down the hall to the room she typically slept in, pausing in the doorway as Stone put some white concoction where boards met in the fully dry-walled room. He was shirtless and sheened in sweat, wearing his typical grubby work jeans while his arm muscles bunched and flexed with his steady movements. Swallowing, her gaze trailed over the bumps and ridges of his solid back.

He bent down, scooping up more of the goop in

the bucket, and turned, jumping. "Son of a bitch. You scared me." He walked over and clicked off his iPod in the dock, sending the room into silence.

"Sorry. I'm back," she said, licking her lips, suddenly nervous as her conversation with Abby played through her mind. He looked so *good* with the black kerchief wrapped around his head, accentuating his fierce eyes and strong cheekbones. She slid a glance over his pecs and abs. What would it be like to feel those hard muscles against her hands? What would it feel like to lie beneath Stone's powerful body?

*I bet he's amazing in bed.* Her breath shuddered out and she cleared her throat as her cheeks went hot. He was probably an amazing lover, but not for a woman like her. Stone undoubtedly took gorgeous, experienced women to bed all the time, women who actually knew what to do to please a man. "I—" She didn't have anything to say, but she needed to think of something instead of stare and think about sex with Stone McCabe. "I—uh..."

"What?"

"I just—I'm back."

"You said that already."

"Yes. Right." She shook her head. "Of course I did."

"Did you have too much to drink?"

"No. No, only one glass of wine—a half a glass."

They stared at each other, and he frowned.

She cleared her throat again. "The—the room looks great. Different."

He took a drink from his water bottle. "Actual walls."

"What are you doing with that white stuff?"

"Taping the seams."

"Oh. Is that some type of glue?"

"Mud—compound."

She set Murphy down and stepped closer as Stone turned and applied the white goop in quick, smooth movements. "You have to do this whole room?"

"Yup. I'm just getting started. I'll do the entire house eventually, but tonight I'm taking care of this."

She looked around at all the screws and tiny crevices in need of covering "Do you want help?"

He glanced over his shoulder. "Thanks, but it's gotta be done right or the walls will look like hell."

She tried not to be insulted that he automatically assumed she would make his walls look like hell. "I guess Murphy and I will get out of your way."

"Do you want to try? I can teach you."

She was always game for learning something new; she was usually too shy to ask. "Um, sure."

"Your hands are going to get a little messy."

"Good thing we have soap."

He smiled. "Come on over." He gestured with his head.

She walked up to his side.

"Basically, you scoop up some of this compound here with the compound knife and slide it over the seam." He demonstrated. "You want to keep your movements smooth."

She nodded, taking the handle from him, scooping up the mud the way he had and put it on the crack, but as she moved in the same motions Stone had, she made a mess. "It doesn't look like yours."

"It takes practice." He placed his hand over hers, moving in quick, sure strokes, cleaning up the bumps she'd left behind. "Ready to try taping?"

"Why not?" It was easy to relax and try something new when she didn't have the pressure of perfection and a punishment if she made a mistake.

"You're going to take a piece of this tape and put it

over the mud we just put down." He put the white tape over the joint.

"That looks simple enough." She did what he had, smiling when it looked like his piece.

"Now take the knife and move it like this." He demonstrated, making long down strokes on top of the tape. "We don't want any excess compound underneath or we'll have bumps."

She nodded, taking the tool and doing as he'd done.

"Not half bad." He put his hand over hers, moving up close behind her so that her back brushed his chest and her naked shoulders warmed from his hot skin. "But more pressure. We'll need more mud for the next step." He bent down as she did, his breath heating her neck, sending a rush of tingles and goosebumps down her back. "Now go over the tape with the compound like this." Their hands moved together as he pressed down and on occasion away to the left or right, his chin brushing the top of her head, as they made a long, smooth line of white. "There you go. You taped your first joint."

"You make it look easy," she said, letting loose a quiet shuddering breath, trying to pull herself together before she turned. For the first time ever her stomach was tied up in more knots than her tongue.

"It is when you've done it as many times as I have." He set the compound knife down and crossed his arms as he sat on the edge of the sawhorse. "Did you have fun tonight?"

"Yes. Alexa went into labor."

His eyebrows shot up. "Must've been some party."

She laughed, and her stomach relaxed.

He grinned. "Good for Alexa and Jackson."

"It's exciting."

"Another new baby in the crew."

She nodded. "Thanks for the lesson. The next time I have to drywall I'll know what to do."

He sent her another smile. "I need to get back to work. Go ahead and take Murphy to the trailer. You guys can sleep in there tonight. I won't be finished up in here for awhile."

"Okay. Can I get you anything? Maybe something to eat?"

"Nah."

"Goodnight then."

"Night." He walked over to the docking station, turned up his music, and got back to work.

She went to the bathroom, washed her hands, snagged her pajamas from the pile in the living room, and picked up Murphy, walking outside into the warm breeze, needing to clear her head. Stone had done nothing more than show her how to slap compound on a wall, and her insides had turned to mush. Her heart still beat fast from the brushes of his skin touching hers. Who knew dry walling could be so sexy?

She liked it when Stone touched her—and not just tonight, which was new for her. She'd never liked it when Eric put his hands on her—even before he'd started abusing her. Maybe there was something to what Abby said. The right person could make all the difference, but that didn't change the fact that she wasn't Stone's type. The swift wave of disappointment surprised her. It shouldn't have. She and Stone were very different people...and this was silly.

Sighing, she climbed the two stairs and opened the trailer door, breathing in his cologne. She glanced at the unmade bed she would be sleeping on, realizing that tonight was going to be a long night.

# Chapter Eleven

Stone took the last turn on his way up to the house, slowing to a stop when he spotted Sophie shooting the basketball into the hoop for a three-point swish. "Not bad," he muttered as she hustled forward in black athletic shorts and a white tank top, grabbing the ball, dribbling back to the line. Instead of firing up another shot, she moved toward the basket, sending the ball through in an easy layup.

His brows rose in surprise as she turned in a quick move, pivoting, putting the ball up again effortlessly. Sophie could play—extremely damn well. He shifted the car into first with a small stirring of excitement and drove ahead, stopping with plenty of space between his Mustang and the half-court he'd had poured when he moved in. "You've got moves, Soph," he called out the window. He got out, shutting the door.

"Hi." Her cheeks were flushed and unframed with her hair pulled back in a ponytail.

"Why didn't you tell me?"

She shrugged, dribbling with the ease of experience.

"Give me two seconds and we'll play."

"Okay."

He hurried into the trailer, toeing off his dress shoes and socks, beyond excited that he was about to play a game of pickup with a woman he had no idea could shoot. He took off his collared shirt and black slacks and slid on a pair of shorts, low-cut sweat socks, and his basketball shoes, snagging a bandana on his way back outside. "Play to ten," he said as he secured the red kerchief around his head.

"Only ten?" She passed the ball between her legs to the other hand as challenge heated her eyes. "Tough day at work?"

He grinned, liking this sassy side he'd never seen. "Twenty then."

"Go." She tossed the ball to him for him to send back, then without looking, she let the ball sail, landing her shot.

He snagged the ball on the first bounce, sending it back to her. "Lucky shot. Let's go, Soph." He lunged in, stealing the ball only for her to take it back seconds later, pivot, and send it up for another point.

"Two-zero, McCabe," she smirked. "And I haven't played in almost three years."

"Shit-talker, huh?" He was loving this more and more as he took a defensive stance and moved in, snatching the ball away, scoring his first point. "Looks like we're just about tied up."

"Almost." She dribbled between her legs, turned, trying to get around him, but he had moves of his own and he was about to show her. He waited for her to shoot, taking advantage of her miss, and reached for the rebound before she could, fired and missed.

"Shit."

Sophie grabbed the ball inches from the line, twisting, shooting, stumbling, watching her swish on the way to the concrete.

He hustled to where she sat. "You okay?" He held out his hand.

She grabbed hold and he pulled. "Yes." Winded, she took off her tank top, tossing it aside, standing in her exercise bra. She made a motion for him to give her the ball as sweat dribbled down her toned stomach.

He bounced it to her.

"Come get me." She rushed by him, dribbling on her way for a layup. He had her by a good seven inches but her excellent evasive moves allowed her to sneak by and score her next point. "Three-one." She raised her eyebrow at him.

"You smirking?"

"No, just kicking your butt." She bounced the ball to him. "I hope this isn't your A-game."

He chuckled, trying to figure out where the shy beauty went. She sure as hell wasn't here on this court. Sophie was handing him his ass, but he wasn't about to let her know that. He dribbled, holding her intense gaze. "I'm just giving you a chance to score a couple points. It's bad form to let your opponent walk off the court with a goose egg." He tossed the ball up, making his basket, wiggling his brows as he grinned.

She ran after the ball. "Let's see if you can do that again." She sent the ball back to him with more force than necessary.

"I've got plenty more where that came from." He rushed off the line and to her right, beating her to the basket. "Where were you? You're not going to beat me like that."

The verbal sparring, brushes and rubs of drenched skin, and the occasional elbow check went on for thirty more minutes. They both panted as sweat dripped down their faces.

"Nineteen, nineteen," Stone said, out of breath. "Care to put any bets on the next point?"

"I never bet and play." She wiped at her forehead with her forearm.

"That's a damn shame. I was going to make you dinner when I win."

She crouched down as he dribbled, her eyes locked on his. "Can you even cook?"

"No."

She chuckled. "A bet should be worth winning."

He grinned, enjoying the hell out of this feisty she-cat. "Touché."

She lunged in and he deflected, spinning, moving toward the hoop. She swooped in, her shoulder crashing into his chest as she grabbed the ball and fired, winning the cutthroat game. "Yes! *Yes!*"

"Damn." He settled his hands on his hip, breathing deep.

"Guess that's that." She slapped her palms together as if dusting him off, her eyes playful as she smiled.

"Careful there, Soph." He hooked his arm around her waist, pulling her tight against him, and spun her around. "I'm still bigger than you."

She gasped, stiffening, and laughed as she clutched at his arm.

The scent of her hair filled his nose as he listened to her bright peal of laughter, sending her around once, twice. He set her down and she turned, grinning.

"Is that my prize—being dizzy?"

He couldn't remember the last time he'd enjoyed forty-five minutes more. He didn't know many women who could play ball. None of them played on the same level as Sophie. "Nah, let's go grab a burger."

"What about Murphy?"

They both looked at the pup asleep on his back in the late afternoon sunshine.

"Bring him along."

She smiled. "Okay. Give me ten minutes. I need to shower first."

"Yeah you do." He gave her a pained look.

She laughed, swatting at his arm. "I don't smell that

bad."

He chuckled. She didn't smell bad at all. Every time she'd brushed against him during the game, he'd caught a whiff of her perfume. "We both need a shower. I'll rinse off in the trailer. Meet you in ten."

"Ten it is. Come on, Murph."

He took the two steps up to the trailer, glancing over his shoulder as Sophie and the puppy walked into the house. He was looking forward to burgers. Dinner out had the potential to be as much fun as their impromptu basketball game. He was going to make sure it was.

~~~~

Van Morrison played through the Mustang's speakers while Sophie stared out the window, wondering where Stone was taking her as he forked right on the mountain road. The wind tossed her damp hair as she breathed in the greasy fries and burgers in the bag at her feet. She closed her eyes, savoring the peace of good music and the satisfaction of another great day. She'd completed her orders for the boutique and sent off her online catalog to Hailey, who'd written back ten minutes later, enthused about the upcoming party. So far there were twenty-five people who'd RSVP'd and fifteen invitations were still out. If half of Hailey's guests ordered something, she'd be that much closer to having her down payment for a car.

But that wasn't the best part. Her pickup game with Stone had been ridiculously fun, and now, dinner out on some mysterious mountain road on a warm, starlit night. This trumped any stuffy fine-dining meal Eric had insisted on.

"So, this isn't exactly up there with the view at

Griffith Observatory, but it doesn't suck."

She frowned as she looked around, seeing nothing but trees. "Uh..."

He forked right again, and the city shined bright.

She gasped. "It's *beautiful*."

"It's definitely not bad." He pulled off to the side, reversed, and parked the car in the middle of the desolate road.

She stared out at the endless lights of Los Angeles, still in awe that any one place could be so big.

"This is even better than the observatory." She smiled at him.

"Have you been?"

"Well, no but... I'm glad I'm here," she finished lamely.

He smiled. "I've been a few times, and I happen to agree with you one hundred percent."

"It's so quiet. I love the way everything twinkles— the lights, the stars. It's...magical."

He looked out as she did. "I've never thought about it like that, but I guess it is." He opened his door. "You wanna eat out here?"

She unbuckled her seatbelt. "Yeah. Sure." She stared down at Murphy sleeping at her side. "I guess I'll leave him here for now since the windows are down." She picked up the bag as Stone went to the trunk and grabbed a blanket. She got out, looking around at the brush everywhere, and turned, wondering where Stone thought they were going to sit, unless he planned to picnic in the road.

He draped his hood with the huge quilt. "Hop up."

She hesitated. The Mustang was his baby. "Are you sure?"

"Go for it." He gestured with his head.

She nibbled her lip. "I'm afraid I'll scratch the

paint."

He settled his hands on the hips of her denim short shorts, sitting her on top of the blanket. "There. Problem solved."

She watched him walk around the hood in mouthwatering jeans and a white Ethan Cooke Security t-shirt that accentuated his broad shoulders. He slid a leg up, settling himself on the driver's side. "How about one of those cheeseburgers."

"Sure. I'm starved." She handed off his meal and leaned back against the windshield the way Stone did, relaxing, listening to the music still playing quietly from the car.

"Is this your first Malcom's burger?" He unwrapped his enormous sandwich.

"Yes."

"Let me proudly introduce you to the best quarter pound of beef around. You've never had anything like it." He held his burger up to her mouth. "Go for it."

Holding his gaze, she took a huge bite, rolled her eyes, and moaned as charbroiled beef, ketchup, and pickle melded on her tongue. "Oh my god," she said over her mouthful, giggling as she covered her mouth with her hand. "It's so *good*."

"Damn right." He nodded and bit in, groaning. "Man, this never gets old."

She picked up three of her French fries, eyeing his huge box of onion rings. "I'll trade you for an onion ring."

"Deal." He snagged the thick potatoes from her fingers with his teeth, his lips brushing her skin as he pulled back.

The heat of his touch sent tingles straight to her belly, much like the warmth of his breath had Saturday night when he taught her how to tape drywall. She stared at him as he chewed, then bit into his burger as if the intimate gesture had been no big deal...much like the way he'd appeared unaffected the other night. She sighed.

"You still want that onion ring?"

"Oh, yeah. Sure." She gave him a small smile.

"Another experience right here," he said as he handed it over.

She sampled fried onion covered in beer batter. "Wow," she said over a full mouth. "Where has Malcom's been all my life?"

He grinned. "I wondered the same thing. Ethan introduced me to heaven when I got here last year. I've been grateful ever since."

"You're not from LA?"

"Nah, Vegas."

"Las Vegas? Exciting."

He let loose a humorless laugh. "Vegas isn't all showgirls and gambling."

She wasn't sure what that meant exactly. "Does your family still live there?"

He shrugged. "I couldn't tell you."

She stared at him, nibbling a fry. "You don't know where your family is?"

"I have no idea who my father is, and my mother was a drunk who worked at gas stations when she could get her ass out of bed."

"Oh. I'm sorry." Her mother had always been so strong. She couldn't imagine growing up without her unwavering support.

He shrugged again. "I got by."

"But it must've been hard."

"Not all of it. I had my friend, Chuck. He and his family lived on the other side of the tracks. I stayed with them a lot—from middle school on. His father owned a construction company—taught me everything I know. He put me to work in the summers. Kept me out of trouble and in basketball shoes."

"That's nice that they gave you a home."

"I loved being there. They gave me a shot at something decent. Then Marilynn, Chuck's mom, was killed in a car accident, and everything changed."

"That's terrible." She touched his arm with the rush of sympathy.

"It was pretty tough. Marilynn was definitely the glue that held that family together. Chuck and Donald ended up moving to Virginia. I got lost and started doing stupid shit."

"How old were you?"

"Eighteen. Old enough to know better. Luckily I was smart enough to get my butt to class and graduate, but after school I was hanging around with the wrong crowd. One night a couple of my 'friends' decided to lift a truck. I was about to find my way into a squad car, but Chuck's uncle was a cop and recognized me. He pulled me aside and told me he was going to give me a choice: I could have his wife pick me up and get myself signed up for the service, or he would haul my ass off to the slammer and I could waste my life in prison. Joleen picked me up, and I joined the Coast Guard the next day."

She paused with another fry at her lips. "The Coast Guard?"

"Yeah. I thought I'd try something different. Everyone did the Marines and Navy. I decided on Maritime Enforcement for a while—basically a cop on the water, until I joined the Deployable Operations Group."

"What's that?"

"We did classified missions with the Navy."

"Oh. So you ended your service last year?"

He shook his head. "Two-thousand ten. A couple buddies of mine got out and joined a private contracting group over in the Middle East. They were making crazy bucks. I decided to join them."

"That's pretty dangerous, isn't it?"

He shrugged. "It had its moments." He crumpled up his wrapper. "But those days are over."

"So now you work for Ethan. Do you like it?"

He nodded. "The pay's good, the men I work with are the best in the business, and I don't have to worry about bullets buzzing over my head or getting blown up all the damn time, so I'd say I like it a lot." He grabbed the last onion ring and bit in. "So what about you?"

She stopped chewing her burger. "What do you mean?"

"What do you mean, 'what do I mean?' We live together and I don't even know your last name."

She swallowed and sipped at her soupy vanilla milkshake, debating whether or not to tell him. He'd shared some of his story. She could do the same. "Burke," she said, taking a huge risk.

"Sophie Burke." He nodded. "So where'd you learn your moves on the basketball court?"

"Camp after camp after camp." She smiled. "I was born obsessed."

"I take it you played in school."

She nodded. "Started in middle school, high school, and college."

He whistled through his teeth. "Division One or Two?"

"One."

He whistled again and she grinned.

"Don't leave me hanging. What school?"

She sipped her shake, growing uneasy with all the questions, but if she evaded he would know she was hiding something. "UConn."

"Yeah, that's Division One all right. Jesus, Soph, the court's been out there for weeks. I had no idea I was living with Ms. UConn."

"I've been busy." Today was the first time she'd picked up a basketball in years. She hadn't had time for it when mom was sick, then Eric hadn't allowed it. She didn't realize how much she'd missed the game.

"So you graduated three years ago?"

She shook her head. "I didn't graduate. I never finished school."

He frowned. "Why?"

"My mother got sick halfway through my senior year."

He grunted. "That's tough."

"She passed away a couple years ago. Cervical Cancer."

"I'm sorry."

"Me too. It was awful." She still remembered her mother's phone call to the dorm, telling her the news. "When we found out it was already too late."

"No good."

"No." She'd been lost ever since—until she found Abby and Stone.

"Any brothers or sisters?"

She shook her head, sipping at her shake, then extended the cup to him. "It's just me," she said as he helped himself to a deep swallow of her dessert.

"What about your dad?"

"He died when I was in middle school. He was a real estate attorney down in Boston, but he moved his practice up to Portland before I was born. A month after he passed away my mother and I found out he was involved in some pretty shady deals." She'd never told anyone that. The idea of her father being a thief was embarrassing but somehow she knew Stone didn't care.

"I guess every family has something."

"I guess. My father blew through his and my mom's savings and the massive inheritance his grandmother left him. He tried to gain access to my trust and cashed in the life insurance. My mother sold the house and we moved away."

"Sounds eventful."

She chuckled. "That's a word for it." Those were hard times, but her mom made them work.

"You gonna open your own shop?"

"I'd like to eventually." She passed the shake to him for the second time, deciding this wasn't so bad. Sharing little bits of herself didn't have to be a big deal.

"Why wait? You're doing all right."

"Mmm...it's complicated." She trusted him, but she wasn't ready to tell him everything. She probably wouldn't ever be.

"Complicated." He gave the drink back, holding her gaze.

"Yeah."

"There's always a way around complications."

"Not always." She thought of Eric and immediately dismissed him. She didn't want to think of anything but the view and sitting here next to Stone. "Do you want the rest of my fries?"

He snagged the box from her hand and leaned back again.

She did the same, surprisingly relaxed after telling him more than she'd ever planned to. "This is nice."

"It's a hell of a way to spend an evening." He crossed his ankles. "I'm going to the store tomorrow to order the stuff for the kitchen—the range, fridge, so on and so forth. I thought you could come give me a hand since you actually use the stuff."

"Yeah. Sure." She liked that he valued her thoughts. "I have a meeting with Janice at one, but I'm free after that."

"We'll go when you get back." He glanced at his watch.

"It's getting late. We should probably head home, huh?" She didn't want to. She wanted to stay here just like this for hours more.

He turned his head, his eyes meeting hers. "After you agree to a rematch."

She laughed. "Definitely."

He hopped down from the hood and held out his hand. "Come on over."

She took the hand he offered.

He pulled her to his side of the car, staring into her eyes as he gripped her hips the way he'd done earlier, and set her down.

She licked her lips, suddenly nervous as they stood toe to toe. If this were a date he would probably try to kiss her, but it wasn't. "Thanks—thanks for dinner and the amazing view."

"No problem. It's the least I could do for the reigning champ."

She smiled. "We'll have to do this again."

"Any time you want." He snagged the blanket and walked to the trunk, ending one of the best nights she could remember.

# CHAPTER TWELVE

SOPHIE RAN UP THE ROAD, HER HEART JITTERY WITH PANIC as she glanced at her watch for the millionth time. She was late—incredibly late. She'd told Stone she would be home by three. It was quarter to four. Her breath puffed out as she picked up her pace, even though she wanted to turn and run the other way. He was going to be angry. Even laidback men like Stone had their limits. He might have shrugged off five or even ten minutes, but not forty-five.

She'd worried herself sick on the bus ride home, watching the minutes tick by on her wrist, trying to figure out what he was going to do when he saw her. Eric would have slapped her without mercy, reminding her of her disrespect, until he threw her to the floor and added a few kicks for good measure. But what about Stone? He was so much stronger than Eric. He probably wouldn't hit her, but he might make her leave. And what about Murphy?

"Murphy," she whispered, sprinting up the steep incline, turning the corner as Seether blasted through the stereo speakers from inside the house.

She slowed when she spotted Stone under the hood of the blue-gray Hyundai Azera that now had wheels on the rims and Murphy lying at Stone's feet, sleeping on his back in the sun. A rush of shame flooded her as she realized she'd compared Stone to Eric again. Even after all these weeks and his unending kindness, she still kept waiting for the worst. Eric had been nice to her too at first—too nice, but Stone didn't try overly hard to impress her. He didn't try at all. She hated that she continued to put him on the same level as the smarmy creature she left behind. Stone and Eric were *nothing* alike.

Murphy heard her first and rolled to his tummy, gaining his feet, hurrying toward her.

She smiled as his tail wagged faster the closer he came. "Hi, baby boy." She scooped him up, laughing as he bathed her cheek with several kisses. "Did you have fun with Stone?"

Stone stood from under the hood and faced her. "Hey."

"I'm so sorry I'm late. The meeting ran way over," she explained as she walked closer. "Janice is such a nice woman, but she talks so much. I didn't catch the bus I'd planned on, which put me further behind," she rambled with the rush of nerves as he stared at her despite her personal reminder that he was not Eric.

"Does it look like I'm in any hurry?"

She studied his handsome face smeared with grease and his filthy white muscle shirt. "No, but I told you I thought I would be home by three."

"And you weren't." He shrugged.

"Which is rude. I tried calling your phone, but you didn't answer so—"

"I left it in the trailer. I didn't want work bugging me today."

"I hope Murphy wasn't any trouble." She hugged the healthy puppy closer. "I should have planned better."

"Shit happens. It's no big deal."

She blinked, realizing he truly could care less. How long would it be before she finally adjusted to the idea that mistakes and unmet timetables didn't have to be the end of the world? "Thank you for understanding."

"There's nothing to understand. I'm not your keeper. You had a meeting, now you don't."

She nodded. "I'm ready whenever you are."

"Can you crank the engine for me?"

"Oh, yeah, sure." She went to the driver's seat and sat behind the wheel, settling Murphy in her lap as she turned the key. The engine turned over nice and smooth. She smiled as he hollered for her to shut it down. She got out, handing off the keys. "Great work."

"Thanks." He slammed the hood closed and wiped his hands on the rag dangling from his front pocket.

"I had no idea you were so handy with vehicles too. Where'd you get this anyway?"

"I bought it a couple months ago, but I haven't had time to do anything with it. Some rich little punk ran the thing into the ground. Never changed the oil. The engine needed to be rebuilt, the tires changed, along with pretty much everything else." He shook his head. "Daddy wanted it off his books. He sold it cheap."

"It definitely sounds like you know what you're doing," she said, studying the car now that it wasn't on blocks. "Maybe you can come with me when I'm ready to purchase mine."

"I could do that."

"That'll take a load off—"

"Or you could just have this one."

Her gaze flew to his as his words sunk in. "Oh no." She took a step back. "No I couldn't. This is your car, Stone."

He shook his head. "*That's* my car." He pointed to his Mustang. "This is just something I thought I would play with and eventually sell."

"Then you should. It's beautiful—kinda sporty looking."

"So take it."

It was vital that she pay her own way. She'd relied on a man during some of the worst moments of her life, and it had gotten her nothing but trouble. "I can't. I don't have enough money yet."

"So rent to own."

"I don't know." She nibbled her lip as she dared to even consider the idea. The bus would be a thing of the past. She could come and go as she pleased. Stone was offering her another piece of freedom with terms she could live with. "I—I guess I could."

"I don't know why you wouldn't. The car's here and ready to be used."

She pressed her lips together with the rush of excitement. "You'll have to decide what you think a fair price is."

"We'll work out the details later."

"Are you sure you want to do this?"

"I wouldn't have brought it up if I didn't."

"Okay." She glanced at the sporty little car—*her* new car—then back at him, squealing as she rushed forward, giving him a huge hug, laughing. "I *love* it. Thank you."

"You're welcome." He smiled, returning her embrace as he looked into her eyes. "I'm going to get your pretty clothes dirty."

She liked the feel of his arms around her and his solid chest pressed to hers but stepped back, glancing down at her pale blue-and-white flower-print sundress. "I'm grease free."

"Let's keep you that way." He smiled again. "I'm going to grab a quick shower and we'll go."

She nodded. "Okay."

He started toward the house, stopped and turned. "Hey, Soph."

She looked at him.

He tossed her the keys. "You should probably drive."

She grinned.

~~~~

Stone watched from the living room windows as Sophie walked the beach with Murphy at her side. He should've been painting the bedroom walls, but stared at Sophie while she moved toward the waves, holding something in her hand. He squinted, trying to make out what it was, but she was too far away.

He'd expected her to come back when the thunder started rumbling several minutes ago, but she hadn't. Lightening had flashed in the distance, and she still hadn't returned. Despite the incoming weather she kept moving along the sand, stopping close to the surf. What was she doing, and why was he standing here thinking about her instead of working?

They'd had a good time on their trip to the appliance center. Sophie had a hell of an eye and practical sense when shopping for big-ticket items...except for when it came to stainless-steel double ovens and detached ranges. She'd gotten so excited about roasting turkeys and baking cookies that he'd gotten caught up in her enthusiasm. Before he knew what he was doing, he'd told the salesman to add them to his bill. She'd grinned and assured him he wouldn't be sorry after she made him her mother's famous prime rib.

He chuckled, shaking his head as he glanced toward the kitchen, trying to figure out what in the hell he'd been thinking. He was going to have to reconfigure the entire layout of the small space and more than likely knock out the back wall to accommodate the additional items, but it would only add value to his property by the time he was finished. And Sophie was happy...or she had been.

He looked out the window, remembering the way she'd gotten quiet as they walked the other aisles of the store on the hunt for the right dishwasher. The thirty-minute ride home had been silent as the sun disappeared behind the clouds and the waves grew violent, crashing against the shore. He'd expected to have some sort of conversation about the new loot he'd just bought, but she'd stared straight ahead, driving the car he'd been wanting to give her for the last couple of weeks. He liked listening to what she had to say in that gentle voice of hers. Like last night.

Their trip to the mountains had been perfect. He'd shared parts of himself he didn't tell anyone, and in return she'd trusted him enough to give him something back. But she was still a mystery. He couldn't help but wonder about the wad of cash in her backpack and the "complications" she'd skimmed over while they stared out at the view, but he had enough to go on for now. He'd gotten what he needed...or mostly. He'd been tempted to kiss her when he helped her down from the hood of his car and quell his curiosities about the taste of that pretty mouth of hers, but Sophie wasn't his typical type of woman. What he wanted wasn't what she needed, so he'd left it alone.

He frowned as she sat down in the sand, looking so small and alone. Turning away from the window, he moved to the door instead of heading toward the bedroom he should've been working on. He walked outside into the breezy, cool temperatures, making his way over the walking bridge crossing Highway One. Something was wrong, which wasn't his problem, but even as he told himself so he took off his shoes and socks and made his way through the warm, white sand to where Sophie stared off with a yellow tulip in her hand.

Murphy barked, running to him.

"Hey, boy," he bent down, scrubbing the top of the puppy's head as Sophie glanced over her shoulder, looking at him with sad eyes. She didn't bother to greet him before she turned her attention back to the waves. He sighed, hating that wounded look. He let loose another deep exhale and continued toward her, sitting next to her when it would've been easier to turn and go home. Seconds turned into minutes while he waited for her to say something. "You coming back to the house?"

"In a little while."

He strained to hear her over the surf. "Did I do something to upset you?"

"No." She captured her hair in one hand, twisting it into submission.

"What are you doing down here, Soph?"

"Today's my mother's birthday." She looked to the sky as it started to sprinkle. "She would've been forty-nine."

Suddenly everything made sense. "I'm sorry."

"She was so young. Too young."

He didn't know what to say as he rested his arms on his knees.

"She loved yellow tulips, and she loved the ocean." Her lips trembled before she pressed them into a firm line. "I almost forgot."

"That she liked yellow tulips?"

She shook her head, shuddering out a breath. "Everything's been so busy with the jewelry and starting over... This morning and afternoon were crazy. I didn't realize today was her day until we were at the store and I started talking about her famous prime rib." A tear slid down her cheek, and she quickly wiped it away.

Those miserable violet eyes of hers were ripping at him. "She would understand," he tried.

She shook her head again. "After my dad died things weren't easy, but she always made me her priority. Always. She was so special. She deserves to be remembered." She swiped at the next tear.

He steamed out a breath, hating that she was crying and trying so hard not to. Tears were his worst nightmare. He didn't have gentle words or know how to comfort others; he rarely cared enough to try. "Are you happy?"

She sniffled. "Yes, happier than I've been in a long time."

"Don't you think she would be glad to know you were so caught up in being happy and living your life that maybe she would be okay with you forgetting for a little while?"

She released a shuddering breath, sucked in another one, and exhaled sharply again. "I guess she would."

"Well, there you go."

She fiddled with the stem of the flower as she held his gaze. "You—you're not what I thought you were."

"What did you think I was?"

"Cool—a little rude."

"Maybe I am."

She shook her head. "No, Stone, you're not."

He shrugged. He was both of those things, but not with her. There was something about her that made him want to be gentle. She made him care no matter how hard he tried not to.

"I think that maybe under all those grunts and

shrugs there's a pretty sweet man."

He shifted, clearing his throat, uncomfortable with being called "sweet." "Cool" and "rude" worked just fine for him.

"She would've liked you—my mother." Sophie gave him a small smile as she leaned her shoulder into his. "She would've thanked you for helping her daughter. You've helped me so much, Stone. I can never thank you for all you've done for me."

"You don't need to thank me." He didn't need her acknowledgements or want her gratitude. He did what he wanted to for no other reason than it suited him.

Lightning flashed in the distance, followed by a long roll of thunder and the trickling rain turned into a downpour.

She rushed to her feet. "Go ahead back up. You're getting soaked. I'll be along to make dinner in a couple of minutes."

He stood, wanting to do just that, but he couldn't leave her here alone while she closed her eyes, kissed the flower, and tossed it into the waves.

"Happy birthday, Mom. I love you." She turned, facing him as tears mixed with rain on her cheeks.

He couldn't remember the last time he'd felt so helpless or wanted so badly to vanish someone else's pain. Maybe he never had. "You don't have to cook."

"Yes I do."

He shook his head. "I'm in the mood for a sandwich anyway." He was freezing as the rain poured cold drops and the wind blew. He wanted something hot to chase away the chill, but his cooking rarely produced decent results, so that wasn't happening tonight.

"Then I'll make us sandwiches."

"Or I can make them. Slapping some mayo and

meat on a piece of bread isn't that big of a deal." The rain pounded now. "We should get back, unless being wet and cold is your thing."

"If you make sandwiches, I'll heat up some soup."

"Sounds like a deal."

"Good." She gave him a wobbly smile.

"You gonna be okay?"

She nodded and picked up Murphy, snuggling the wet puppy close as they started toward the walking bridge. Even though she'd said she was fine, her eyes were still sad.

He hesitated then settled his arm around her shoulders, pulling her against him, wanting desperately for her to flash him one of those pretty smiles. "What kind of soup are you thinking about making?"

She paused mid-step, meeting his gaze. "Does chicken noodle work?"

"Sounds damn good right about now."

She slid her arm around his waist as they walked home. "I thought so too."

~~~~

Eric circled through the cemetery as he had several times throughout the day, certain Sophie would come. There was no way she would go three years without paying her respects to poor pathetic Christina, especially on a day Sophie had always thought so important. She'd asked to lay flowers on her mother's grave every May thirteenth, and he'd happily told her no for no other reason than he could.

He'd allowed her to give her mother a proper burial. What would the people of Bangor have thought if he'd done otherwise? But he'd forbidden her from visiting from that point forward. She'd protested at first, but the slap and shove down the flight of stairs had ended that quickly enough. He'd always found a secret thrill that she'd been afraid enough of his consequences to stay away from a place she desperately wanted to be.

Sophie had adored her mother, never leaving Christina's side during the last few weeks of her life. While Sophie held vigil over her dying mother, he'd enjoyed spending the money Christina had put aside for her useless daughter. By the time they'd sent mommy into the ground he'd blown through most of the inheritance, purchasing his new vehicle and completing the renovations on the downstairs bathrooms and addition of the new bar for entertaining. He didn't mind sending up a toast to the dearly departed every now and again. The smooth granite countertops and high-end stock of wines and scotches she'd paid for suited him quite well.

He slowed, noticing the rusty car parked along the side of the road close to Christina's marble stone cast in the shadows of dusk. He grinned, spotting the small figure crouching down, setting a bouquet of yellow tulips at the grave.

"You just couldn't stay away, stupid, *stupid* Sophie." He smacked his hand on the steering wheel in triumph, thinking of all she had to pay for: the humiliation of canceling the wedding alone would cost her dearly, as it had cost him his pride. He pulled over then back on the road just as quickly when the woman stood. He narrowed his eyes, noting her willowy build and long black hair, realizing it wasn't Sophie after all. He grit his teeth with the surge of anger. Where the hell *was* she, and who was this person setting flowers by Christina's headstone?

He continued down the winding road, pulling into

the diner across the way, waiting, ready to find out. He tapped his fingers in frustration, watching the green digits on the center clock change three times before the piece-of-crap vehicle turned right. He followed at a distance, making note of the license plate, trying to figure out where he'd seen the woman before. There was something very familiar about her.

She turned into the ratty apartment parking on Twelfth Street, and he continued on, dialing David's number, knowing somehow that the lady with the yellow tulips would be the key to finding Sophie and his last shot at the rest of Sophie's money.

# CHAPTER THIRTEEN

SOPHIE HURRIED INTO THE RESTAURANT, SEARCHING FOR Abby. She spotted her friend's bright lilac spaghetti-strap top among dozens of other lunch-hour patrons and walked quickly to the table as their waitress moved away in the opposite direction. "Hi." She set her purse and two gift bags on the table. "I'm so sorry I'm late. Aubrey wanted to try bending wire today. She almost had it. I couldn't leave until she did."

"Don't worry about it. My meeting ran over by a few minutes, so I'm just getting here myself. I ordered us salads."

"Okay." She sat down and crossed her legs, wearing fitted black capris and a sleeveless lime colored top. "Good."

"So how are things over at Stowers House this afternoon?"

She tried to volunteer one morning a week at the place that had given her a fresh start and somewhere safe to stay. "Busy. So busy, Abby. More and more women are coming."

She nodded. "That means more and more women are getting themselves out of bad situations."

"Yes they are. Thanks to you and Lily they can." She sipped her lemon water, parched after a hectic day.

"I feel like I haven't seen you in forever." Abby handed over her phone. "Take a look at these."

"Oh, he's *beautiful*. He looks just like Jackson." She grinned as she swiped her finger across the screen, looking at the pictures of Abby's sweet new nephew, Owen. "Olivia must be in heaven."

"Definitely." Abby smiled. "She and I take turns holding him when I visit, which is every chance I get."

"How's Alexa doing?"

"She and Jackson are over the moon. They have the family they've always wanted."

"It's so nice to hear about happy endings."

"Yes it is."

"I actually have something for Alexa and Olivia." Sophie slid the pretty gift bags over to Abby's side of the table. "It's just something small. I noticed that Olivia has her ears pierced, so I made them both a pair of earrings."

"That's so sweet."

"I hope you can deliver them the next time you stop by your sister's."

"Absolutely. Thank you," Abby said as the waitress set their grilled chicken salads in front of them.

"Thank you," Sophie said as well, handing back the phone to Abby as the waitress walked off.

Abby picked up her fork. "So how are things going on the home front? We haven't had much of a chance to talk over the last couple of days."

"I know. We're both so busy, but things are pretty good." She smiled thinking of Stone sliding his arm around her shoulders on their walk home in the rain three days ago. "Great actually."

"We'll take 'great,'" Abby said after swallowing her bite.

Sophie grinned, so full of happiness she didn't know how she could possibly contain it all. "Tuesday night I kicked Stone's butt on the basketball court." She chuckled, remembering the fun they'd had. "Okay, I won by one point. He treated me to a victory dinner.

We ate Malcom's burgers on this desolate mountain road with an amazing view, and Wednesday I helped him pick out the appliances for the kitchen."

"Sounds fun." Abby beamed.

"It was. But I think one of the best parts of my week was when he helped me through a rough patch on my mom's birthday. I didn't know he'd realized I was upset, but he did. He sat with me on the beach in the rain, then we went home and made soup and sandwiches together."

"Aw." Abby's big blue eyes softened. "He's a good guy."

"He really is. He's very sweet, even though I don't think he liked it much when I told him so."

Abby chuckled. "I'm sure he didn't."

"I have a new car," Sophie said in an excited rush.

Abby's eyes widened. "You do?"

She nodded, thrilled that she'd driven into the city this morning without having to wait on a bus. The traffic had been awful, but it had been awful while she sat in her very *own* vehicle. "It's a 2013 so it's not exactly new but it is to me. Stone gave it to me." She shook her head. "He fixed up the car that had been in his driveway, you know the one on the blocks? We're doing a rent-to-own deal."

"Interesting."

Sophie frowned as she chewed her first bite of amazing blackened chicken. "What's that supposed to mean?"

"Nothing." Abby grinned. "I'm just glad things are working out well for the both of you. I think you're as good for Mr. Dark, Buff, and Broody as he is for you. I think Stone's got a thing for you."

It was Sophie's turn to widen her eyes at the idea of Stone McCabe having any sort of "thing" for her. "Oh, I

153

don't think so. We just live together. We're friends."

"I don't know, Sophie. Dinner out with a view, shopping, confidants, cars. It all sounds good and friendly until you realize we're talking about Stone."

Sophie set down her fork and pressed a hand to her jittery stomach, afraid as much as she was intrigued. "Are you sure? I just can't... I don't know what to do." She wadded her napkin as she shook her head. "He's gorgeous and kind, and I don't know what to do."

"What do you *want* to do?"

She expelled a rush of air. "I'm attracted to him. I don't know how it's possible not to be, but everything with Eric... I've only been on my own for a couple of months. Things were really messed up. I really let him mess me up."

"Don't be so hard on yourself." Abby reached over and squeezed her hand.

"It's true. I'm mad at myself and at him for letting him treat me the way he did, but I'm still afraid. It's like I'm under some sort of spell where just one look at him somehow vanishes all of my power. Thinking of him right *now* makes me feel powerless. I automatically shrink, and I hate it."

"I can't say I understand what you went through exactly, but I have some idea."

"I know. I think that's why it's so easy to talk to you."

"Good," Abby said with a decisive nod. "That's what friends are for."

"Yes it is." She smiled. "I'm so glad we're friends. You're such a nice person."

Abby squeezed her hand again. "Thanks."

"So what do you think I should do about Stone?"

"Nothing."

She frowned. "*Nothing?*"

"Things are good the way they are right now, right?"

"Yes."

"So let them be. If both of you want something more you'll get there when the time is right. Stone seems like the kind of guy who goes after what he wants. Just follow his lead."

"If you think that's right." She huffed and rolled her eyes. "I'm almost twenty-five and I'm *clueless* when it comes to men and relationships. It's ridiculous and embarrassing. I wish I would've paid more attention to boys in school than a darn basketball."

"You're evolving."

"Evolving." She smiled. "I like that."

Abby chuckled. "So, I have something I want to talk to you about."

"Okay." She took another bite of her salad.

"The gift you made for Lily..."

"Mmhm," she said as she swallowed and picked up her glass of lemon water.

"She wants another set, something different—a little more bold."

She set down her glass with a small thud. "She does?"

"She does, and she wants to set up a meeting to talk about including some of your pieces in a couple of the upcoming fashion shows."

Sophie stared, trying to believe what she was hearing. "*What*?"

"Lily wants to use some of your work. This has the potential to take your business to a whole different level."

She shook her head. "Lily Thomas wants to use *my* jewelry on the runway?"

"Yup."

"Is this a good time to start hyperventilating, or should I just pass out?"

Abby laughed. "How about you say you'll meet with Lily on Monday to discuss the idea instead."

"Yes. Absolutely. Of course." She needed to call Stone and tell him the news. She set her napkin on the table and stood, walking over to Abby, giving her a hug. "This is so *exciting*." Her name was going to be everywhere; her picture would be in the papers. This was the exposure she needed—but couldn't accept. Her smile vanished as trickles of reality ruined the moment. Eric would see her. He would find her. She took her seat. "I can't."

Abby paused with a bite to her lips, her eyes full of surprise. "You can't?"

She shook her head. "No."

"Sophie, this is a once-in-a-lifetime opportunity."

"I know," she said quietly, looking down as she tried to settle her nerves. The idea of Eric finding her sent a rush of terror through her veins. "I can't. I'm sorry."

"But I thought—"

"I would love to, but it won't work." She gripped her hands tight in her lap, realizing she would never have a chance like this again.

"Can I ask why?"

"He'll find me." She met her friend's gaze. "He's powerful—very influential. He has connections—lot's of them. I just don't..." She gripped her arms with icy fingers.

"You don't have to say anything more."

"I'm sorry." Abby would never understand the level of her regret. This was what she'd dreamed of. This was where she'd always hoped to take Burke Jewelers, but that would never be a possibility on the run.

"Don't be."

She nodded.

"Let me just say one more thing and we'll drop this entire conversation. If you ever want to share or need to talk it all out, I'm here. I bet Stone would want to help too."

She shook her head. "I can't tell him about Eric. I want him—no, I *need* him to see me as normal. I'm sure that doesn't make sense—"

"Oh yes it does. I can promise you that." Abby held out her arm, showing off her watch. "This thing's fitted with a transmitter so Jerrod and Ethan can find me if I disappear. For the most part we think I'm safe..." She shrugged. "There's little about my situation that's normal, but Jerrod loves me for me. Sometimes it's hard, but we're both learning to roll with the way things are."

She studied the pretty watch on Abby's wrist, then looked at the petite yet powerful woman sitting across from her, feeling utter admiration. Abby had been through an unimaginable nightmare, yet she thrived. She had a successful business and healthy relationship with a man she loved who loved her in return. "How did you put it behind you?"

"I doubt I'll ever put it fully behind me, but time helps, and support and wanting to win by living a full, happy life. When we have people in our lives that care, they want to help if you'll let them."

She nodded, hearing and understanding Abby's message. "It's a wonderful feeling."

"There's a whole group of men and women who will rally around you. All you have to do is ask."

She had so much more than she ever thought she would. "And I'm so grateful."

"Right now you need to do what feels right for you.

Everything will fall into place after that."

She smiled. "Thank you."

"You're welcome."

~~~~

Sophie sat back on the comfy new cream-colored couch that had been delivered earlier in the evening, half listening to the murmurs from the television while she doodled bold new designs she would love to see featured on Lily Thomas' runway. She sighed her frustration as the pretty necklace came to life on the sketchpad she held in her lap, resenting Eric's latest victory. She'd run thousands of miles to get away from him, yet he still controlled her life. She swiped at her damp hair with a bad-tempered shove and stood in her pink-striped pajama shorts and tank top, too restless to be still.

She hadn't been able to stop thinking about her conversation with Abby and the ideas that had popped into her head on her drive home. Abby's new *Escape* line was a powerhouse in the markets. What if there was a *Freedom* line of jewelry available that complimented Abby's designs?

Burke Jewelry could be huge, and a chunk of the profits would help Abby and Lily fund more Stowers House locations. She'd almost called Abby while she drove down the Santa Monica Freeway as the excitement and possibilities gave her a rush of enthusiasm she hadn't felt in such a long time—but then she'd thought of what that would mean to her safe, quiet life and shoved her phone back in her purse.

She sat down with a huff, glancing out the curtain-less windows, realizing she'd been too distracted with her creations to focus on the ever-present willies that snuck up on her when she was home alone late at night. Stone's serene hilltop oasis turned downright creepy after the sun went down. Anyone could be out there on his stretch of land that faded into the canyons, and she would never know. Shuddering, she picked up the remote and turned up the romantic comedy she hadn't paid any attention to, finding comfort in the noise as she yawned, trying to decide whether to continue with her work or go to sleep.

Murphy stretched himself out on the floor, rolling to his back, and snored on. Clearly he wasn't bothered by the dark. Smiling, she glanced at the pretty wall clock she'd suggested to Stone when they'd been out and about a few days ago. One-thirty. "Definitely time for bed," she murmured, standing again as headlights cut across the living room window. Her shoulders automatically tensed and relaxed when she recognized the sound of Stone's Mustang rolling to a stop.

Seconds later, his car door slammed and he unlocked the front door, stepping inside.

"Good morning," she said before her smile vanished and she gasped, rushing to him, gently touching the nasty bruising along his cheekbone. "What *happened*?"

He evaded her fingers. "Rough night."

"I'd say." She winced, still staring at his cheek. "Come on." She took his hand, pulling him with her to the kitchen. "Let's get something cool on that. Go ahead and take a seat." She opened the freezer door, searching for a good substitute for an ice pack. She spotted the baggie of blueberries she had on hand for her smoothies. "I guess this will have to do." She pulled the package out and closed the door.

"It's just a bump." He rubbed at the back of his neck as he leaned against the counter in jeans and a black polo shirt.

"That's more than a bump. It's really swollen." She grabbed a fresh dishtowel from the drawer and wrapped it around the frozen bag of fruit. "Sit. Please," she added when he made no attempt to honor her request.

He sat down in the chair and leaned back, closing his eyes with a long sigh.

She crouched between his legs. "Here we go," she murmured, gently pressing the bag against his swollen cheek.

His eyes flew open.

She took his hand, settling it on his makeshift icepack. "Go ahead and hold this in place for a few minutes. Hopefully nothing's broken," she said, moving in closer, tsking as she scrutinized the tender skin surrounding the deep, dark bruising. "I'll get you a couple of Tylenol."

He snagged her wrist before she could stand. "I'm fine."

She glanced down at his hand holding her in place, noting his raw knuckles. Frowning, she pulled his hand up for a closer inspection in the dim kitchen light. "Look at you. What on earth happened tonight?"

"Bar brawl."

"Oh." She didn't know what to think of that.

"On the clock. Shane and I pulled duty for Skeeter and Joseph Sharpe, you know, the pop singers? We ended up in some seedy club over in West Hollywood. Things got a little ugly when a couple of guys didn't like their girlfriends posing for pictures and getting autographs."

"What's so bad about that?"

"The ladies thought Skeeter and Joseph should sign their boobs, then they proceeded to shove their tongues down Skeeter and Joseph's throats. All hell broke loose after that."

"Oh," she said again, blinking. "How often do your clients sign breasts?"

He grinned. "More often than you'd think."

She smiled. "Who knew?"

"You have no idea what goes on at some of those places."

"I don't think I want to."

He shook his head. "You definitely don't."

"Well then..." Her thoughts died away as she looked down, realizing they were still holding hands. She glanced up, meeting his intense gaze, swallowing as his thumb began to move against her skin. "I, uh...I should probably..."

"You curious, Soph?" he asked as his eyes darted to her mouth.

"I'm..." She swallowed again, her heart pounding as Stone set the bag of blueberries on the table and moved forward in his seat.

"I've been wondering," he said quietly, settling his hands around her waist, pulling her up to her knees, never breaking eye contact as he touched his lips to hers with gentle pressure.

She stiffened from the shock of heat, bunching her fists against the tops of his thighs with the rush of nerves. "Stone, I—"

"Relax," he murmured, holding her gaze, pressing his mouth to hers again. "Relax," he repeated, moving in for the third time, slowly coaxing her into following his lead.

Closing her eyes, surrendering, she leaned into his chest as his rough palms moved up and down the sides of her waist, teasing the skin of her back and stomach, intoxicating her with his potent flavor as he seduced her with the clever strokes of his skilled tongue.

His fingers traveled along her spine, leaving behind a trail of goosebumps as his hands moved into her hair.

She gripped the sides of his shirt when he eased slowly away, then came back for more. A small, helpless sound escaped her throat as he changed angles, plundering, then gradually broke their embrace, holding her gaze.

She licked her lips, savoring the dark taste of Stone while she stared into his eyes.

He slid the pad of his thumb along her jaw. "You pack a punch, Soph."

"You too." She shuddered out a trembling breath. She'd never been kissed like that before.

He smiled. "Thanks for the blueberries."

"You're welcome."

"I should probably head to the trailer." He stood, pulling her to her feet. "I have to catch my flight in a few hours."

"Okay." She cleared her throat and crossed her arms, trying to appear as relaxed as Stone seemed to be, even though her insides were a jittery, fabulous mess. "So you'll be back on Tuesday, right?"

"Should be if everything goes as planned. I'll have to see how my stop off in New York City goes and the couple other places I have to hit before I can head home. But I'll see you in the morning before I leave."

"Okay." She nodded.

"Thanks again." He held up the package of frozen fruit, smiling, and turned toward the living room.

"Oh, wait." She hurried after him. "I didn't get you any Tylenol."

He stopped, turning back. "I have some in the trailer."

"Okay then." She didn't want him to go. She

wanted him to kiss her again. "Good night."

"Night, Soph." He twisted the lock on the knob and shut the door behind him.

She pressed a hand to her hammering heart and blew out a long, slow breath, watching him head toward the trailer. "Holy crap," she sighed. Was this what the girls had been talking about at the get-together the other night? She finally understood what it felt like to want more. Stone was gentle yet demanding, and she craved another sample. Shivering, she remembered his work-rough hands teasing the sensitive skin below the hem of her shirt. She touched her lips and smiled, hoping he would try to kiss her tomorrow before he left her for two days.

# CHAPTER FOURTEEN

STONE SAT IN THE SMALL DINER, SIPPING HIS COFFEE AS HE looked at the notes he was typing into a report for Ethan on the Bangor Concert Center. The mid-summer, five-stop concert tour for Smash would be a mix of large and small venues with Bangor, Maine, being the final stop before the team and band headed back to Los Angeles. Over the last forty-eight hours, he'd been to Hartford, Boston, Manchester, Portland, and now Bangor in a whirlwind of meetings and site tours on behalf of Ethan Cooke Security. Now that the facilities had been looked over and preliminary safety concerns discussed, he wanted to go home; he wanted to see Sophie. Hesitating, he reached for his cellphone and dialed hers. It was only seven twenty in LA, but she would be up. He was just checking in on the house anyway.

"Hello?"

"Hey."

"Hi."

He turned his cup in its saucer, loving that her voice brightened when she heard his. "How are things on the home front?"

"Good. Great. The guy down at the appliance store called yesterday. Everything's on time for delivery next Friday."

"Sounds good. Thanks for handling that."

"Of course."

He settled back in his booth, draping his arm over

the top, relaxed for the first time since early Sunday morning. "What else is going on beside refrigerator deliveries?"

"Well, I have a lunch meeting with Janice this afternoon. She said something about needing more product again already." She laughed with a hint of disbelief. "*And* Janice has a girlfriend who's going to tag along to our luncheon. She wants to talk about putting some of my stuff in her store up in Monterey."

"Good for you."

"I'm still having a hard time wrapping my head around all of my good fortune."

"You deserve it." And she did. Sophie worked her ass off every single day.

"Thank you. How are you?"

"Ready to come home." Now that they were talking he couldn't get there fast enough.

"Do you think you'll be here for dinner?"

"Depends on what time you plan to eat. I should land right around five, but then I have to deal with rush hour."

"So I'll fix something for seven thirty. I have a surprise for you."

He frowned. "You do?"

"Mmhm." Murphy barked in the background. "Oh, Murphy's ready for his run. I should go."

"I'll see you tonight."

"Okay. Bye."

"Bye." He hung up and shook his head, smiling. Having someone to go home to was a pretty good deal. Sophie sounded happy, and he rarely saw that haunted look in those gorgeous eyes anymore. He hadn't stopped thinking about her since she picked up Murphy and waved the dog's paw at him while he drove down the driveway Sunday morning. He'd replayed their late night kiss in the kitchen countless times, wishing he'd given in to his need to do it again before he left, but he'd wanted time to think. Sophie had been shy and sweet, but he hadn't been kidding when he told her she packed a punch. He'd satisfied his curiosities; he'd gotten a taste of her mouth, but something that should have been simple was turning out to be anything but.

"You all set, honey?" the waitress asked as she stopped next to his table.

"Yeah."

"I'll get you your check."

"I'll just come up to the register and pay."

"Whatever you want, honey."

He tossed a ten-dollar bill on the table by his half-empty cup and slid his laptop back into its case, shouldering his bag and carryon, and walked to the cash register.

Rhoda punched his order for coffee, eggs, and bacon into the ancient machine. "Five-fifty."

He handed over another ten as he glanced at the announcements stuck on the pegboard and froze when he spotted the flyer with Sophie's picture on it, reading "Bangor Police Department" at the top of the sheet. He moved closer, trying to read the rest of the page, but it was covered by the information on the pancake breakfast and festivities at the local college. "You got a lot of crime around here?" He asked Rhonda, gesturing to the snapshot of Sophie's Maine license photo.

Rhoda looked to where he pointed. "Oh no, that's Sophie." She tsked with a shake of her head. "Poor girl got cold feet and took off with a pile of Eric's money. Runaway Bride Syndrome or whatnot."

He fought to listen as he flashed back to the wad of cash he'd seen at the bottom of her backpack.

"Eric's heartbroken." She shook her head again. "I always thought Sophie was a sweet one. She's so shy and quiet—always has been. Now I'm just not so sure."

He grunted, not so sure himself.

"Looks like there might be a touch of tart to go along with all of that sugar." Rhoda held four ones and two quarters out to him. "Your change, honey."

"Keep it."

"Sure thing. You have a nice day." She pocketed the money and turned toward the kitchen.

He glanced over his shoulder, yanking the paper off the board, and walked out the door, heading for the airport as he stared down at the woman he'd found himself tangled up with.

Ten hours later, Stone punched the gas, passing a vehicle a mile away from his house. He'd been sick all day, replaying his conversation with the waitress over and over. Sophie was engaged, but worse, she was a thief. He shook his throbbing head, letting loose a humorless laugh, trying to figure out how he'd fallen for her act.

Sophie Burke was a smooth one. He had to give her that. She'd done a hell of a job of hosing him over. Poor, shy Sophie with the sad eyes wasn't in trouble; she was a first class con artist.

He turned up the drive, spotting her car parked in its typical spot, then glanced at the bright light pouring from big panes of glass and pretty planters of white flowers she'd added around the space. He gripped the steering wheel tight, absorbing the rush of hurt and anger, hating her a little for making him want the illusion she'd painted.

How long had she planned to reel him in? How much longer did she plan to wait before she added to her thick envelope and ripped him off too? He'd be damned if she'd take a piece of his heart with her the way she had the poor sucker back in Maine. Swearing, he got out as he spotted her walking by the window in a pretty powder-blue sundress. He cursed her again, longing for her despite it all. It was time for Sophie Burke to move the hell on.

~~~~

Sophie rushed around the kitchen, pausing to fuss with the cloth napkins that were already perfectly folded and in place. She glanced at the clock for the hundredth time, eagerly awaiting Stone's arrival. He would be home any minute.

She took their wedge salads out of the fridge and set them at each of their settings on the brand-new table she'd had custom made for the space. The splurge had been mighty, but the light maple wood with its chunky masculine feel was perfect, even if the kitchen construction hadn't started yet. She knew Stone's plans and couldn't wait to surprise him with her gift.

She opened the oven, peeking in at her roasted prime rib, grinning with the rush of anticipation when she heard the Mustang pull up. "He's here," she said to Murphy. "Stone's home."

Murphy wagged his tail and rushed to the front door as she did. She smoothed down her strapless, mid-thigh sundress and stepped outside, standing under the pale light of the entryway, revved with an excitement she hadn't felt...ever.

Stone slammed his door and started her way in the dark.

Her heart beat faster as she studied his broad shoulders in his polo shirt and the tailored cut of his slacks. He wore professional clothing, but the clean lines of his outfit did nothing to lessen his bad-boy edge. "Welcome home," she called.

He didn't respond as he moved closer.

Her smile dimmed. "Did you have a bad trip?"

"I guess you could say that." He walked passed her and went into the living room, ignoring Murphy's yips for affection as he dropped his bag to the floor.

"Rough flight?" she asked, following him inside, growing uneasy, reading his tense body language.

"Not so much." He slid his hands in his pockets, clenching his jaw as he held her gaze.

She swallowed, growing more uncomfortable under his impenetrable stare. "The traffic then?"

He shrugged. "Pretty typical."

"Stone, what's the matter?"

He reached down and grabbed a sheet of paper from his laptop case, handing it up to her. "Look familiar?"

Her eyes popped wide as she studied her picture beneath the Bangor Police Department heading. A surge of icy cold tingles rushed through her veins as the breath backed up in her throat and the blood drained from her face. "What—where did you get this?"

"On my trip to Maine."

Her gaze darted to his. "You went to Maine?" She stared down at the photo of herself again. "The police—they're looking for me?"

"That's generally what happens when you steal a few grand."

She leaned against the wall for support as her hands trembled and she fought to breathe. "He said I—he said I stole from him?" She shook her head. "No. I didn't." Tears pooled and fell with the punch of panic. "I didn't."

"Save the waterworks," he said, his voice cool and

harsh.

"I didn't."

"Give me one reason why I shouldn't call you in."

Her legs buckled as she realized Stone didn't believe her. He was going to call the police, and Eric would find her. She bolted to her room, smacking her hip into one of the sawhorses along the way in her rush. She gasped with the sharp pain but kept going, grabbing her bag and purse, yanking them up. She had to go. She had to get out right now. Running back to the living room, she snatched up Murphy, sprinting out the door, glancing behind her, terrified Stone would try and stop her, but he just stood in the doorway, staring after her.

She got in the car and backed out of her spot with a squeal of tires, racing down the road, pulling into oncoming traffic. Horns blared and brakes squealed as she righted herself in her lane, shaking so badly she could hardly steer.

Murphy whined at her side as the first sob escaped her.

"It's—it's okay," she choked out. "It's going to be all right." But she cried harder, knowing it wasn't. She turned on Interstate Ten, sobbing as she hadn't since her mother told her goodbye and closed her eyes for the last time. An hour passed in a blur, and somehow she found herself in the elevator heading to Abby's condo, then banging frantically on Abby and Jerrod's door.

Jerrod swung the door open, frowning. "Sophie, are you okay?"

"No. No, I'm not. I need Abby. Where's Abby?"

Abby rushed into the room with a measuring tape draped around her shoulders, her eyes full of concern. "Sophie?"

"Abby." A fresh wave of tears fell as she stepped inside, pushing Murphy into her arms. "You need to find him a good home. Please promise me you'll find him a good family." She didn't want to leave her sweet new puppy, but she couldn't keep him. She turned her back as Murphy whimpered again. "I have to go." Saying so almost broke her as she started toward the door.

"Wait." Abby grabbed her arm. "What's going on? Where are you going?"

"I need to leave. I have to leave."

"No you don't."

"Yes." She freed herself from Abby's grip. "He says I stole but I didn't. I didn't. Stone's going to call the police, and Eric will find me. He'll kill me. He said he would kill me if I left him."

"Sophie take a deep breath."

She tried, but the terror and heartbreak left her chest heavy. "I can't. There are posters. But I didn't do it. He beat me and killed Cooper." She crouched down, opening her bag, handing over the thumb drive Dylan had made for her. "Keep this safe, please. I'll find a way to contact you if I need it. If anything happens to me make sure the police know it was Eric." She handed over Stone's car keys. "These aren't mine." She hugged Abby, gripping tight, and pet Murphy once more, kissing his head and ran out the door as Abby called after her. She yearned to turn back, but she couldn't. If she wanted to survive she had to leave everything behind.

# CHAPTER FIFTEEN

STONE'S CELL PHONE RANG AS HE SAT IN HIS LIVING ROOM, sipping a beer, breathing in the scent of the roasted meat he'd pulled from the oven almost an hour ago. He glanced at the readout on his phone's display and clenched his jaw, already knowing what this would be about. Might as well get it over with. "Yeah," he answered.

"What the hell's going on?" Jerrod demanded. "Sophie's in the living room more than half hysterical, saying something about stealing and you calling the cops and Abby needing to find Murphy a home."

He closed his eyes, trying not to care about Sophie's tears or the way she'd trembled as she stood in front of him, pale and terrified, professing her innocence. "I guess we've all got problems."

"What's that supposed to mean?"

Stone glanced toward the kitchen and the new table he could see from his seat—his surprise, he assumed—then at the candles and vases and other doodads Sophie had added around the living room, making his house a home. "She's a con artist and a thief," he reminded himself as he told Jerrod.

"What makes you say so?"

"The wanted poster I saw of her in Maine today." He rubbed at the back of his neck, trying to remember a time when he'd ever felt so...miserable and empty.

"There has to be—hold on," Jerrod said as Abby's alarmed cry for her husband echoed through the phone. "I've gotta call you back." The line went dead.

Stone sighed as he moved to take another sip from the bottle, pausing when he noticed he was half sitting on one of Sophie's cardigans she sometimes wore in the evenings. He pulled the lightweight sweater out from under him, catching a whiff of her familiar scent and tossed it away, rubbing at his forehead. "Damn you, Soph. Damn you to hell," he muttered as his phone rang again. He debated whether or not to answer through the first two rings, then pressed "talk." This wouldn't go away until he did. The faster he dealt with Abby and Jerrod, the quicker he could forget Sophie Burke had ever walked into his life. "Yeah."

"Jesus Christ, McCabe."

The shock in Jerrod's voice tightened his stomach. "What?"

"Either Sophie's a first-class con who's a genius with makeup, or her prince charming beat the living shit out of her on a regular basis."

He rushed to his feet, already knowing he'd been wrong. Sophie stealing and intentionally hurting someone didn't make sense; Sophie being abused did. "What are you talking about?"

Abby murmured something to Jerrod.

"Sophie gave Abby a thumb drive with a bunch of pictures on it for safe keeping—in case something happens to her."

She'd been some bastard's punching bag, and he'd accused her of being a liar. He thought of the way she used to flinch and her weary eyes, finally understanding what the 'complications' were she'd spoken of while they ate burgers on the hood of his car. If he could've been any more of an idiot... "Don't—don't let her leave, man." He grabbed his keys and sprinted out the door. "Keep her there."

"It's too late. She already left."

"Damn it. Why the hell did you let her go?"

"She refused to stay."

"How long ago?"

"About five minutes."

"Son of a bitch. Did she say where she was going?"

"No. She didn't tell Abby much of anything. She left the car keys and Murphy here and took off."

"Goddamn." He had to find her. He had a pretty good idea of where she was going. Hanging up, he took his seat behind the wheel and peeled out of the drive, needing to get downtown, hoping he made it to the bus station before she left for good.

~~~~

Sophie got off the bus at the Greyhound depot and walked across the street to the hole-in-the-wall restaurant, locking herself in the dingy bathroom. She glanced at her watch and shook her head with a shaky huff. The hour-long ride from South Grand Avenue had been endless as the bus made stop after stop. She needed to hurry if she wanted to catch the last departure of the night, and that was if it wasn't already full.

Grabbing a paper towel, she folded the piece twice, turning on the disgusting faucet, and rinsed her face with cool water, hoping to erase her blotchy eyes and pink nose after her bout of endless crying. No matter how she tried to stem her tears, she couldn't make them stop. She didn't want to go. She didn't want to leave Murphy and Abby...or Stone. She shook her head again as his cold, hard eyes flashed through her mind, then pulled another paper towel from the dispenser, patting her cheeks dry.

Somehow she'd let herself believe she wouldn't have to run again, and that she could dig roots and make herself a home, but here she was, in some filthy restroom getting ready to move on. She tied her hair back in a loose bun, unrolled a pair of jeans and the light-pink top she had arrived in, and put on the wig she'd hidden among the clothes. She adjusted the choppy bangs into place and changed from the pretty pale blue sundress she bought just for tonight and put on the familiar outfit, her running outfit. Sighing, she folded her dress, rolling it tight, and put it in her bag among her things.

With a final look at herself in the filthy mirror, she walked back outside and crossed the street, watchful for police cruisers. Surely Stone had called her in by now and they were searching. Her cell phone rang again, as it had several times during the ride across town, but she'd ignored it, even though Stone's number had popped up consistently, as it did now. Did he really expect her to answer? She'd been tempted the few times Abby had tried to reach her, but she left that alone as well. This wasn't her home anymore. The people she'd grown attached to were just a memory now. She glanced at the phone she'd made her own, her last connection with Los Angeles and the time she'd spent here, and tossed it in the trash barrel at the corner of the building.

She pulled open the door to the Greyhound station, perusing her option for tickets, her urgency to be gone only increasing now that there was nothing left for her here. She wanted to make her way east to Baltimore and stay at the Stowers House until she could figure out what else to do. Heading north was probably best, then she would go south, double back a couple states, and proceed to Maryland. With her heart heavy, she walked to the counter with Dylan's ID in hand.

"Where to?" the lady said as she smacked her gum.

"I'll—I'll take a ticket to Boise please."

The woman typed up a ticket and handed it over. "Enjoy your trip."

"Thank you." She sat in the ugly brown bucket seat farthest from the windows, mindful to stay reasonably close to the door, ready to run if need be. Her lip wobbled and her eyes filled, thinking of Stone's harsh stare. He believed that she'd stolen. He thought her a liar. She blinked back tears and glanced at her watch, trying to convince herself that it didn't matter. In thirty more minutes, she would be Boise bound.

She picked up the newspaper someone had left behind as she caught a movement out of the corner of her eye. Her heart clogged her throat when she saw him running toward the door. "Oh god," she whispered, unfolding the paper as casually as she could with trembling fingers, and held it up in front of her face. She had her wig. If she played it cool he wouldn't notice. She dropped the paper to eye level, peeking over the top as he hurried to the counter, muttering something to the attendant.

The gum-smacker shook her head, and he ran toward the bathrooms.

Sophie stood, setting down the newspaper as the door closed behind him in the men's room. The women's room door opened next, and Stone called her name. She walked outside just as Stone made his way back to the main lobby. Picking up her pace, she run-walked down the street, hurrying faster, turning the corner in the dark, desperate to get away before Stone turned her over to her worst nightmare.

~~~~

Stone searched the faces of the bored-looking men and women sitting around the lobby, swearing in frustration. He didn't see Sophie, but he'd been certain she would be here. Leaving the city by bus made the most sense; she knew the schedules and routes well. He stepped outside, his stomach sinking, realizing she was long gone as he pulled his cell phone free of its holder, dialing, trying hers once more, even though it was more than likely too late. She wouldn't want to talk.

A phone rang close by, catching his attention. He turned toward the trash, rushing to the receptacle, rifling through, grabbing hold of Sophie's phone. "Damn it." She'd been here, but she wasn't anymore.

He scanned the area, spotting the dark-haired woman walking quickly in the light of the streetlamp, wearing a familiar pink t-shirt. She turned the corner, vanishing from his sight.

"Shit." He sprinted ahead, following the direction she'd taken, rushing around the edge of the building as she ran down the alley. "Sophie!"

She looked over her shoulder and picked up her pace.

He booked it in a dead run. "Sophie!" He gained on her, catching up as she approached the street, snatching her arm. "Sophie."

"No," she panted, fighting to pull free of his grip. "Let me go."

"Hold on." He grabbed her other arm, keeping her in place.

She tried to yank away again. "Let me *go*."

"Stop." He held her tighter, winded. "Wait."

She stood perfectly still, staring at him with weary, guarded eyes, gasping now as her chest heaved with each unsteady breath while tears poured down her cheeks.

"I'm sorry. I was wrong. I'm so sorry."

"You didn't—you didn't believe me," she choked out. "You didn't believe me."

"Come here." He pulled her against him, pressing her forehead to his shoulder as she gripped the sides of his shirt, weeping. "I'm sorry," he said again, as her body shook with her quiet crying. "God, Soph. God." He took off her wig, needing to see the shiny blond as he rubbed his hand along her back, hating himself for hurting her this way. "I thought I'd lost you." He hugged her closer, closing his eyes, relieved she was still here. "I thought you were long gone. Let's go home and—"

"No." She pulled away, sniffling and shuddering.

"I'm not calling the cops. I never was. I just want to know what the hell's going on."

She studied him, scrutinizing, taking another step away, poised to run.

There was no trust here anymore, and he regretted it deeply. "At least let me take you to Abby and Jerrod's."

"How do I know you won't drive me to the precinct down the road?"

"I won't."

"I don't believe you." She took another step back.

And why should she? If the pictures on the thumb drive were even half as bad as Jerrod had made them out to be, she had every right to be wary of whatever he had to say—of what any man had to say. "I don't blame you."

"I'm going back into the bus station, and I'm leaving. You're going to walk away and let me go."

"I don't want to let you go. I want to help you." He spotted the nasty diner across the street. "Will you at least have coffee with me until the bus gets here?"

She shook her head.

"Please. I won't stop you from getting on your bus, but at least talk to me."

"There's nothing to talk about."

"There's a wanted poster with your picture on it. That's definitely a conversation piece."

"I didn't steal from him."

"I know you didn't. I was a dumbass for ever thinking you did."

Her eyes welled, spilling more tears.

She was weakening, and he was desperate enough to beg. "Please come to the diner with me."

She looked at her watch. "You've got eighteen minutes."

He nodded and walked with her into the junky place that smelled of stale fried food. Sophie took the seat closest to the door.

He studied her swollen, red-rimmed eyes and blotchy cheeks in the bright light, cursing himself again for being so damn stupid. "Two coffees," he said to the waitress as he sat down across from Sophie. "I want to apologize again."

She jerked her shoulders, slumped in defeat as she stared down at the table. "It doesn't matter," she murmured quietly.

"Yes, it does." He touched her hand, wanting her to look at him. "I hurt you and accused you of something I know you could never do."

Her lips wobbled, and she let out a shaky exhale.

Another chink in her armor gone. He needed to fix this before the damn bus came. "I'm a bastard, Soph. You surprise me with a brand new table and a meal, and I accuse you of stealing."

Her miserable gaze whipped up to his.

"I love it. I wish we were at home eating that hunk of beef you made instead of sitting here."

The waitress brought over the coffees.

"Thanks."

"Thank you," Sophie mumbled. "I can't go back there with you."

He was horribly afraid she wouldn't. "I made a mistake. Seeing the poster and knowing you're engaged—"

"I'm not engaged."

"But you were."

"Yes, I was, but not because I wanted to be. I left the ring behind."

"You have every right to tell me to kiss your ass, but will you tell me what's going on instead? Let me help you, Soph. I want to help you."

She stared at the table for so long he was certain she would tell him to go to hell and be done with him once and for all.

"Please, Soph. Please tell me."

"The money's mine. I had a shop at the Bangor Mall—a kiosk. I'd been skimming cash from the register, little bits here and there for several weeks, creating small discrepancies. Eric's accountants keep track of everything so I had to be careful. He told me I had to close my store, that I wasn't allowed to work anymore, so I sold off everything and took the entire day's profits the day I knew I was going to leave."

He sighed, taking her hand, but she pulled away.

"I met Eric a few months after my mother got sick. Her diagnosis and prognosis were absolutely devastating. One day she seemed perfectly healthy and we were planning our Christmas vacation, the next she's dying of cervical cancer." She cupped her hands around the ugly mug. "We were all each other had. She was determined to beat the odds, and she did okay for a little while. She responded well to treatment and kept busy with work, but then she had a couple of complications the next summer and went downhill fairly quickly. Before long I was trying to take care of her, supply and run our shop—basically be all things at twenty-two years old."

"Sounds tough."

She nodded. "It was. After a couple months we barely had any inventory left. I couldn't keep up. I decided we needed to sell the house or the business. Mom's medical bills were eating up money faster than I could make it. The savings accounts were gone. I was only getting into the store two or three days a week at most." She sipped the coffee, wrinkled her nose, and set the cup down. "A friend of ours, a realtor, did a quick sale on the house I'd grown up in to prevent bankruptcy and helped me secure a small one-bedroom apartment. I had to sell off so much of Mom's favorite stuff." Sophie sniffled, shaking her head. "That right there just about killed her."

He wanted to pull his chair close to hers and wrap his arm around her the way he had at the beach, but he sat where he was, knowing she wouldn't accept his attempt to comfort.

"It was around that time that I met Eric. Bangor's famous artist. He came strolling into the shop looking for a pair of earrings for his secretary's birthday. He wanted me to design something and make it. We ended up talking for a while. He was very charming. He seemed so understanding, and I was so scared. I started relying on him as the weeks passed and my mother got worse and worse. Christmas came around again, and I needed to sell the business; the rent on the space was killing us. That's when I got the idea to open the kiosk at the mall. It would keep a little income coming in, but it would free up some much-needed cash."

"Makes sense."

"Mom had signed everything over to me by that point so I could make decisions on her behalf. I was her medical and financial power of attorney." She pushed her coffee cup away. "Not long after New Years we found out there was nothing more the doctors could do. The day her oncologist told us the news Eric handed me a piece of paper his lawyer had drawn up. He told me he would help me with the sale of the business so I didn't have to worry about it. I felt like the world was caving in around me. I was so overwhelmed that I hugged him and thanked him and signed my name without even reading what he put in front of me." She closed her eyes and shook her head. "I was a business major for God's sake, and I just scribbled down my name. I'm still mad at myself for being so foolish."

He hated that Sophie had struggled with so much on her own. "You were a scared kid with too much on your plate."

She shrugged. "If I had taken the time to read the document, I would've realized I was signing over financial power of attorney to Eric. Our relationship changed quickly after that. He started belittling me and taking control, but I was so busy with mom I hardly noticed. I was just trying to get through each day and keep her as comfortable as possible. She hung on until March. When she died, my world stopped. I knew it was coming, but still... Eventually I realized I didn't have a nickel to my name. He'd spent my inheritance and tried to mess with my trust."

Anger sickened his stomach as he thought of the detestable Eric. "Trust?"

"I have a trust worth five million dollars."

Stone raised his brows and whistled through his teeth.

"It's basically useless. I can't draw from it unless I've been married for a year by my twenty-six birthday."

"What the hell kind of condition is that?"

She shrugged. "My great-grandmother Burke was old fashioned. She didn't believe a woman should handle money on her own."

"Is that even legal?"

"It was her trust, her money, her conditions. She could and did put in whatever contingencies she wanted."

"What happens to the money if you don't meet the deadline?"

"It goes to a nature conservatory in Boston."

He'd never heard of anything so stupid. "You've got to be kidding."

She shook her head, giving him a small smile. "I couldn't make that up."

He smiled back, hoping they were getting somewhere.

Her smile faded. "Eric expected me to marry him. The wedding was supposed to be a week and a half ago—some huge, awful, fancy ceremony where I wore an ugly dress I didn't even get to pick out. It was to be a garden-terrace affair with five hundred of his closest friends." She rolled her eyes. "He'd been planning it for two years, insisting that we be the first couple married at the brand new Bangor Country Club."

"Sounds like fun."

She let loose a humorless laugh. "*No*, it doesn't."

He thought of the pictures Jerrod had spoken of on the thumb drive. "Did he hurt you?"

Her gaze darted to the table, then back to his.

"Yes."

He closed his eyes, scrubbing his hand over his jaw. "What are you going to do? Keep running?"

"I don't know what else *to* do. He said he would kill me if I ever ran away."

"Bastard," he hissed. "I think we should go to the cops."

"No." The color left her face as she pushed back in her chair.

He snagged her wrist. "We won't. We don't have to."

"Eric is friends with several police officers. Have you—have you heard of Eric Winthrop?"

"The artist? Yeah."

"That's him."

"That's *him*?"

She nodded.

The guy was a genius with a paintbrush, but he was also a fucking string bean prick with a bad, cultured accent. "You don't have to go. We can help you figure this out—me and Abby, even Ethan."

"I don't know that there's anything anyone can do."

He didn't miss the stirrings of hope in her eyes. "There's always a solution; we just have to figure out what it is."

"He says I stole from him. I'm sure he and his accountant have made sure it looks like I did." The bus rolled up across the street. She shouldered her bag and stood. "That's my bus."

"Yeah." The heavy weight of panic settled on his shoulders. He'd been making headway, but she was going to leave. He got to his feet, tossing a few bills on the table.

"Thank you for giving me a place to stay over the last few weeks."

"You're welcome." He fought to stay cool when he wanted to drag her to the car and tell her she wasn't going anywhere but back home with him, where he knew she would be safe. "What about all of your stuff?"

"Donate it, except for my mother's tools."

"What do you want me to do with them?"

"Give them to Abby. I'll find a way to contact her. I left your car keys with her."

"What about Murphy?"

She shook her head as her eyes filled. "Abby's going to help me find him a family."

"*You're* his family."

"Please don't say that." She pushed open the door.

"Don't go, Soph. Please don't leave."

"Goodbye, Stone." She stepped out and walked away.

He hurried after her as a thought came to mind. "Marry me."

She stopped, turning. "*What*?"

"Marry me and take the money from your great-grandmother's trust."

She looked down.

"I don't want it." He rushed forward, stopping in front of her, lifting her chin. "I don't want a dime. We'll have a lawyer draw something up—a lawyer you pick that says it's yours."

"Why would you do this?"

"Because I want to help you. Because I don't want you to leave. You have a life here. Friends here. A dog waiting for you to pick him up. Clearing things up with the asshole in Maine might be a little easier when he realizes he's not just messing with you anymore."

She shook her head. "I can't ask you to do this."

"I'm offering." Marriage had never crossed his mind, or not seriously anyway. "It's a year."

"Exactly. What if you meet someone?"

The only person he was interested in was standing right here. "I won't."

"You could, then where does that leave us?"

"Twelve months in a lifetime is a blink of an eye."

"Stone—"

"You can think on it overnight. If you want to get on a bus tomorrow I'll drop you off myself." He held out his hand. "One more night, Soph." He'd try like hell to make sure one night turned into one more and another until she settled back in and learned to trust him again.

"One more night." She took the hand he held out and shook.

"Let's get Murphy and go home."

# Chapter Sixteen

Sophie snuggled Murphy in her lap while she sat in the Mustang's passenger seat, staring out the windshield the way she had the first night Stone brought her home, but tonight she didn't feel the sense of cautious relief she had all those weeks ago. The wind rushed through her window, bathing her skin in the warm breeze. Despite the salty air and muted rush of waves, her stomach was in knots.

She slid her fingers through Murphy's soft coat, trying her best to relax her shoulders, but the shock of wanted posters, bus tickets, and impromptu marriage proposals had been more than she could take in three short hours. Tonight had been a disaster. Nothing had gone as planned. She and Stone were supposed to have enjoyed the meal she'd prepared and maybe a walk on the beach. He was supposed to have kissed her again as she'd hoped he would Sunday morning before he left on his business trip.

She glanced at him as the wind tossed his hair about, still trying to take everything in. He'd hurt her with his accusations. His lack of faith in her had been more painful than any punch or kick Eric had thrown her way, but then he'd come running after her, hugging her close and listening, offering her a not-so-simple solution to her problems. Marriage. Millions of dollars and help with Eric, all for the bargain price of one year of their lives.

She closed her eyes, sighing with the ridiculousness

of it all. Stone was willing to give up so much to help. But why? He assured her he didn't have an interest in her trust fund. She looked his way again and couldn't help but believe him. He'd been kind to her before he knew anything about her inheritance. But money—lots of money—changed people and their intentions.

He flicked on his blinker, slowed, and took a right when they came to his road, catching her eye and giving her a small smile as he made his way up the hill. "We're home."

She stared straight ahead, not bothering to comment. *They* weren't home. Stone was home. This used to feel like her place, like she belonged, but that was when she'd let herself forget that she was a guest. God, this whole situation was a mess. She needed tonight to figure out what to do next.

Stone turned the last corner, and the house she adored came into view, so warm and cozy with the lights ablaze. *His* house with the pretty planters she'd filled with thriving blooms and the rooms she'd brought to life with a mix of both of their ideas. But none of this belonged to her. "What about the house?"

"What about it?"

"If we get married we have to split everything fifty-fifty."

"Do you want my house, Soph?"

She never wanted to leave this pretty spot of land. "It's not mine."

"There you go."

Was it really that simple? Could this whole situation be that cut and dry? "What about vows? You don't love me."

"I care about you."

She shook her head, trying to be content with that. "It's not the same thing."

"If we were doing this for the long-haul I'd think twice, but twelve months is twelve months."

"Yeah." It sounded so cold...and awful. Somehow this didn't seem any less empty than Eric's country club wedding.

He rolled to a stop and shut off the engine. "Look, Soph, you and I were getting along just fine before things went to shit tonight. We'll just keep doing what we were doing while we get some of this mess figured out."

"But you—you kissed me."

He steamed out a long breath as he held her gaze. "Yeah, I did."

"That complicates this."

"It doesn't have to."

*How could it not?* she wanted to ask, but as she stared into his eyes, she no longer needed to. Stone was gorgeous. He more than likely kissed women all the time. Their late-night embrace hadn't meant anything to him. He'd been curious. He'd told her so. She'd packed a punch, and he'd stolen a piece of her heart. End of story.

"All we have to do is go to the courthouse, say a few words, and be done with the whole thing. No big deal."

But it was a big deal. "We would be legally married."

"So?"

How could he shrug his shoulders? "We're not just talking about rent, groceries, and laundry anymore."

"It's business, just like the rent, groceries, and laundry."

She looked down, trying to ignore the quick stab of hurt. Why couldn't she look at this situation as casually as he did? She met his gaze again. "What about my warrant?"

"They don't check for warrants when issuing a marriage license, but we'll have Ethan take care of it anyway."

She frowned. "What does that mean?"

"It means I'll handle everything until we can handle Eric. Just trust me."

She held his gaze.

"Or at least try. I know I'm pretty high on your shit list—"

"I trust you. Maybe that's stupid, but I do. If I didn't I'd be sitting on a Greyhound on my way to Boise."

"Well, I guess that's something. Let's go in. It's late."

She got out of the car, carrying Murphy in her arms and her backpack on her shoulder, staring at the pretty cottage she thought she would never see again.

Stone unlocked the door, letting her in before him.

She breathed in the scent of her roast lingering in the air as she walked closer to the kitchen, looking in at the pretty settings and wilted lettuce on the table. Sighing, she set the puppy on the floor, catching sight of her picture on the Bangor Police Department flyer lying on the arm of the couch. She picked up the paper, glancing back at the table, to Stone, then to the sheet, no longer able to pretend her life was as simple as cozy dinners in a cliff-top home with a man who liked her enough to help her out. She shook her head, overwhelmingly confused and afraid for the first time in weeks. This was wrong. All of this was so incredibly wrong. Everything was different now, and soiled. The new life she'd built for herself had been tainted by Eric's poison. "What am I doing here? Why did I come back?"

Stone took the paper from her hand, folding it. "I'm going to handle this."

"I don't belong here. I thought I did; I thought I'd found my place, but I didn't." She swallowed over the tight ball clogging her throat.

"Yes you did."

She shook her head as her lips trembled. "I should've gone to Boise. I should've left and started over again."

"No." He slid several strands of hair behind her ear. "I messed this up, Soph. Everything was fine until I did. This is exactly where you should be."

On the verge of more tears, she nodded, even though she didn't agree.

"Go get some sleep."

She nodded again, stepping away from his gentle touch.

He closed the distance between them for the second time. "Are you going to be here when I wake up in the morning?"

"Yes."

He held her gaze. "I guess I'll see you in a few hours. We can figure out what you want to do from there."

"Okay."

"Good night."

"Night." She walked down the hall and closed herself in the room she'd fled mere hours ago.

~~~~

Stone sat on the couch in the dark, sipping another beer, waiting for the light under Sophie's door to switch off. She'd said she would be here in the morning when he woke, but he'd seen the uncertainty in her eyes as she wished him goodnight. He wasn't taking any chances that she might slip away.

Finally, her room went dark and he pulled the thumb drive Jerrod had slipped him out of his pocket and pushed it into the USB port, needing to see what Sophie had lived through. For weeks he'd assured himself he didn't care, that Sophie's problems were her own, but after tonight he figured out he'd been lying to himself for quite some time. With a few clicks of his mouse, he pulled up the file he wanted. Instantly, dozens of pictures filled his screen. He swore looking at nasty bruises and welts covering the delicate skin of Sophie's arms, thighs, ribs, and stomach. "Damn."

He scrolled down, stopping on a photo of three long, bright-red marks across her back that could only have been made by a belt, then moved to the last pictures taken in March, clenching his jaw, staring at huge purple goose eggs on her forearms. "You fucker," he whispered. "You fucking bastard." He shook his head, looking away, hating Eric Winthrop for what he'd done.

He glanced at the pictures again and shoved his hand through his hair, hardly able to stand it. He'd witnessed his fair share of brutality over the years, but this affected him more deeply than anything he'd seen overseas. This was Sophie, the woman down the hall. The woman he hadn't been able to let walk away.

He opened Google, typing in *Eric Winthrop*, finding several images of the pompous bastard with his arm draped around Sophie at numerous art gallery functions. She looked so different. Her hair was so long and her dresses baggy and ultra conservative as she smiled for the camera. But her eyes weren't bright and beautiful the way they were when she laughed with him.

He flipped back to the pictures of the bruises and stood, too disgusted to be still. "God. Son of a bitch." He paced the living room with a helpless feeling that left him ill. They were going to talk. He needed to convince her right here and now that she had to accept the help he was desperate to give. Walking down the hall, he opened her door. "Soph," he said quietly, peeking in.

Murphy stirred, waging his tail twice, then closed his eyes and fell back to sleep at Sophie's side.

Stone moved further into the room as she slept deeply, lying on her stomach. Sighing, he crouched down, staring at her beautiful face in the faint wash of moonlight filtering through the big windows. He glanced at her arm resting above the covers and slid his knuckles along her skin where the huge bump had once been. She was safe here; he planned to keep her that way. The deal was marriage for a year, but as he touched her and breathed in the familiar scent of Sophie, he knew he would easily sign on for five or even ten—whatever it took to make everything okay. He wanted to wake her and make her promise to stay, but she was exhausted. Tomorrow would have to be soon enough.

# Chapter Seventeen

Eric sat parked among the piece-of-crap cars in the lot outside the mystery woman's building, being blinded by the midmorning sun. Huffing out a breath, he shoved down his visor with a nasty swat, growing more impatient as thirty minutes turned into forty-five.

This wasn't the first time he'd sat here since his Wednesday night drive through the cemetery. He'd been back on several occasions, never catching sight of her again after her visit to Christina's grave. He glanced at the time on the dashboard, muttering a swear. For almost a week he'd been racking his brain, trying to figure out where he'd seen her before. The license plate number on the rust bucket vehicle she'd driven was registered to some jock's parents down in New Hampshire, which didn't help him worth a damn, so he'd been reduced to this—spending his precious free time stalking dirty parking lots in hopes of catching another glimpse of the willowy stranger—with no luck. Hopefully today would be the day. He glanced at the date on his Rolex, shaking his head. Today *needed* to be the day. Sophie's birthday was right around the corner. He had less than two weeks to find her before he lost out on five million dollars.

Once he brought Sophie back to Bangor—and he would bring her back—they would have no choice but to seek out a Justice of the Peace to officiate their marriage. There would be little time to put together another large event. Gritting his teeth, he thought of the country club and his missed opportunity to be the first to marry there. He was the pillar of this community. Someone of his standing should have received the press time, not Hodge Mosses and his lard-butt daughter with her low-class wedding last weekend. He deserved the best; he expected it, and Sophie had ruined everything.

He glanced at his watch again, growing angrier. He was late for a meeting at the gallery—the third time this week. And it was all her fault. Sophie caused him constant problems. She wasn't even *here*, and she was making his life a misery, as she had for the last two years. Now if the floozy inside would step out...

He came to attention when she appeared in the doorway, struggling to roll her bike down the stairs. "*Yes*." It was about time. Blowing out an impatient breath, he waited for her to pedal her way to the main road before he started his Mercedes and followed. He pulled off twice, once at the diner and again at the gas station, giving her plenty of space. Then she turned into the mall parking lot and he remembered—the little bimbo who sold fancy hair ties, wigs, and other crap next to Sophie's booth. She was the nosy woman who stood around Sophie's kiosk, giving him nasty looks.

What was the name of her business? He got out and went inside, smiling and waving to folks as he rushed ahead, stopping several feet from her booth by the cookie counter. *Hair Wonder.* He turned, grabbing his cellphone, pressing David's number as he made his way back toward the exit. Having his PI in New York was really damn inconvenient, but David was the best—or he used to be.

"Hello."

"I think I've got something. I want everything you

can find on the owner of *Hair Wonder* at the Bangor Mall."

"I take it that's the woman you saw putting flowers on Christina's grave."

"Of course it is. I want something within the hour, David. You get me something, because I'm just about out of time."

"I'm aware of your timeframe. I'll call you back soon."

"Fine. Bye." He pushed open the glass door as Tammy Stuben came through, smiling, her children at her side.

"Thank you, Eric."

He plastered on his best smile for his hygienist. "You're welcome." He winked at her brats. He hated kids—messy, dirty little things.

"How are you doing?"

He let his smile fade, knowing the busybody was asking about his personal life. "Okay."

"Any luck finding Sophie?"

He shook his head mournfully. "I keep hoping she'll come back. I want to work things out."

"Of course you do, honey, but you remember there are plenty of fish in the sea. Plenty who will treat you right."

But the other fish didn't come with a five-million-dollar trust. And he didn't owe the others what he owed Sophie. "Thanks, Tammy."

"All right. You take care."

"You too." He hurried back to his car, getting in and speeding off toward the gallery. The members of the art council were going to be unhappy, but they would have to deal with it. He was a busy man. Marlene was just going to have to make excuses and actually earn the wage he paid her. Important people were often pressed for time, and he was very important. He pulled into the gallery parking lot ten minutes later, stepping out of his car as Marlene pushed through the doorway.

"Eric, where have you been? You're over an hour late."

He tried his hardest to give her his best apologetic look when really he wanted to tell her to pack up her desk and get the hell out. How dare she speak to him in that terse tone? She was his *subordinate*. It wasn't her job to question, only to do as he said. He reined in his temper, remembering how important it was to keep the people of Bangor on his side. If one of them spotted Sophie they might be more apt to tell him. "I know. I couldn't—I couldn't get out of bed. I stayed up all night thinking of Sophie. I can't get her off my mind. I wish she would at least call. I just want to hear her voice and know she's okay."

Marlene's eyes softened. "I'm sorry, Eric." She rested her hand on his arm. "I know this is hard on you. Every day will get a little better. I bought the board breakfast. Sam rushed an order over from the diner."

"Thank you."

"Let's get you into work." She wrapped her arm around his waist as they started toward the door. "It'll help settle your mind."

He nodded. "I think you're right." His phone rang and he paused. "I have to take this."

"But the board—"

"I have to *take* this." He shoved her supportive arm away.

Surprise filled Marlene's eyes, and he sighed. "I'm sorry. I'm still a little raw."

"I'll get everyone another cup of coffee."

He nodded and turned, no longer concerned with anything but this call. "What do you have?"

"I'll have more shortly, but I'm off to an interesting start right here in her DMV records. Dylan Matthers, owner of *Hair Wonder,* filed for a new drivers license several weeks ago. She traveled extensively right around the same time. In fact, she left on an Amtrack from Brunswick to Boston the same night Sophie vanished. From there she went to Chicago. And just last night she bought a bus ticket from Los Angeles to Boise, Idaho."

"Interesting how she's in two places at once."

"Very. I'll call you back when I know more."

Eric grinned. "I want more within the hour."

"I'll call you back when I've got it."

Eric walked toward his building, chuckling. "Stupid, *stupid* Sophie. Your game's about to end."

~~~~

Sophie opened her eyes to the bright sunshine and turned her head, smiling at Murphy snoring by her side. She looked around the pretty room Stone had painted dark ecru and at the plywood floor that would soon be transformed with glossy hardwood and the custom-made closet doors leaning against the wall. With the right furnishings he was going to have a beautiful bedroom. She sighed, wondering if she would still be here when he finished it.

Sitting up, she listened to the rush of waves through the big windows, no less confused than she had been hours ago. If she agreed to marry Stone, she could wake up in this house for the next year, but what about after? By then the house would be completed and she would be more in love...with the cottage. Growing more attached and eventually leaving would break her heart, but staying would keep her safe. She sighed again, brushing her hand through her hair, still unsure of what to do. She'd planned to have a solid decision by sunrise, but somehow she'd fallen dead asleep despite the turmoil of the evening.

She glanced at Murphy as she gently pulled back her covers, leaving her puppy to his dreams, and walked down the hall, spotting Stone sitting on the couch in gray athletic shorts and no top, staring at his laptop. "Stone?"

He looked up, his eyes exhausted and his chin darker with the day's growth of beard. "Hey."

"What are you doing?"

He slid a hand through his hair. "I don't know. Thinking, I guess."

He looked awful. She sat down next to him, relieved that despite everything that happened last night, there didn't appear to be any awkwardness between them. "Are you feeling all right?"

"Yeah."

She glanced at his laptop screen, realizing he was looking at the pictures Dylan had taken. "Where did you—I didn't know you had that."

He didn't answer as she looked from the dark, nasty bruises covering the right side of her ribcage to the raw welts Eric had left along her back with the belt he'd chased her around with one horrifying night. She closed her eyes and her pulse accelerated with the memories of violence and pain.

"You went through hell," he said quietly, his voice rough with his lack of sleep.

She opened her eyes, meeting his. "Yes. I guess I did."

"There are months and months of pictures here, Soph."

"About six. It went on longer, but that's about

when I met Dylan and she insisted we start documenting." She took a deep breath, needing to give Stone more of her story. "He started hitting me the day after my mother's funeral. I wanted to go to the cemetery and sit by her grave. I desperately needed to feel close to her, but he said I couldn't. I told him I was going, and he grabbed me by the hair. He hollered about disrespect and how he made the rules, then he pushed me backwards down the stairs."

Stone swore as she traced the stripes on her shorts, ashamed she'd let Eric do that to her. "It got worse from that point forward. He would apologize at first, then he stopped. We both knew he wasn't sorry." She shook her head. "I should've left. I wanted to, but I was too afraid."

"What tipped the scales?"

"I'd been thinking about it for a long time, especially as the wedding date came closer, but then he killed Cooper." She darted him a shamed glance.

"Who's Cooper?"

"My mother's dog. I loved him so much. He was all I had left of her. I brought him home the day before I left for college. I didn't want her to be lonely." She swallowed, shaking her head. "He tried to protect me the night Eric used a bat." She pointed to the pictures of the massive goose eggs on the tops of her forearms. "Cooper bit him in the leg when I screamed, and Eric hit him across the head." She clenched her fists, remembering the moment before Cooper's whimpers quieted, and he closed his eyes for the last time. "It—it still breaks my heart." She sniffled. "I didn't protect him. I should have, but I didn't."

"Soph—"

She shook her head, knowing Stone was about to make excuses for her. "I was too weak." He opened his mouth to speak, so she rushed on. "After that I had no doubt I was next. It was only a matter of time. He wants my money, but he likes to hurt me more. He gets so angry and out of control." She frowned. "But he's in control all at the same time." How could she put into words his cold calculation? "He never hit me on my face or anywhere people would see. His image is very important to him."

"Never again." Stone set down the laptop and moved closer to her side, gently cupping her cheeks in his palms, staring into her eyes. "He will never touch you again. I'm promising you that."

She rested her hands on the tops of his, believing him, treasuring the warrior's light in his determined brown eyes and the safety she felt.

"I'm so damn sorry you went through all that." He pressed a tender kiss to her forehead. "I'm so sorry, Soph."

"Thank you." She squeezed his fingers.

Murphy ran down the hall from the bedroom, his tail wagging and tongue hanging out of his mouth.

Sophie eased away from Stone, looking down at the sweet puppy. "Good morning, sleepy boy. I see you've decided to get up."

His tail moved faster.

"Would you like to go outside?"

He barked.

"He's so smart. He knows exactly what I'm saying."

"You think so?"

She looked at Stone, relieved that he was smiling. "I do." She smiled back and returned her attention to Murphy. "Come on."

Murphy followed her to the door.

She let him out. "I'll be out to clean up after you in a minute." She turned back as Stone yawned. "Did you sleep at all?"

"Not much."

"Let me get you a cup of coffee."

"I don't need you to get me a cup of coffee."

"I want to." She moved to the kitchen, wincing at the wilted salads still out and spoiled meat sitting on the stovetop, then prepared the hot brew the way she knew Stone liked it. Moments later she started back to the couch. "Here you go." She handed off the steaming mug.

"Thanks." He sipped and hummed his gratitude. "Why doesn't it taste like this when I make it?"

She smiled, always delighted by his appreciation for the little things. "I don't know. You pop in the pod and the machine takes care of the rest."

"No. It's different—a hell of a lot better."

"Magic touch, I guess."

"I guess so." He sipped again. "So, did you have a chance to think about what we talked about last night?"

She glanced at the pictures of the bruises marring her skin, then at Stone, so handsome and strong. He didn't love her, and she wasn't exactly sure what she felt for the man sitting at her side, but he was kind and safe, and he could help her. He *wanted* to help her. She'd hoped to marry someday, to find a partner who would share a lifetime with her despite her great-grandmother's trust. The current scenario was far from ideal, but taking him up on his proposal gave her the opportunity to iron out several of her problems. "Yes."

"And?"

"I'll—I'll marry you if the offer's still on the table."

"You got it." He set down his mug.

She leaned forward, placing his cup on one of the pretty coasters she bought.

"You know once we file our license he's going to come."

*You belong to me. You'll die before I let you get away.* She swallowed sheer terror and nodded, remembering Stone's vow that Eric would never touch her again. "Are you sure—are you sure you want to do this?"

"I'm sure I want to help you."

"If you decide you've changed your mind at any point, we'll annul our arrangement immediately."

"I won't."

"But if you do—"

"I won't, Soph."

"Okay."

"Give me a couple hours to work a few things out with Ethan and we'll find an attorney to draw up a prenup."

Stone was willing to give up so much for her. He was more than entitled to fifty percent of her trust. "I don't need an attorney."

"Yes, you do."

She shook her head. "This house is yours. Everything on this property belongs to you. And I don't need that much money."

"I don't want your money, Sophie."

"And I don't want an attorney."

He nodded. "I'll talk to Ethan and we'll go down to the courthouse."

"Okay."

# CHAPTER EIGHTEEN

STONE SAT NEXT TO SOPHIE IN THE UNCOMFORTABLE courthouse chairs while they waited for their turn in front of the judge. The morning had been a whirlwind of phone calls and e-mails while Ethan worked his magic, pulling strings so he and Sophie could apply for their marriage license, get married, and have a copy of the certificate in hand for her new social security card today. Eventually she would need a California driver's license, but that could wait. The next couple of hours would officially start the ball rolling to get Eric Winthrop the hell out of her life.

Thinking of the pictures he hadn't been able to erase from his mind, he slid a glance Sophie's way, looking at her smooth, toned arms, remembering her forearms covered in nasty bruises. She was strong—stronger than she knew—yet delicate and vulnerable all at the same time.

She met his gaze, and he sent her a small smile. She was so pretty in her pale pink sundress with all of that shiny blond hair curled in loose ringlets. Her eyes lit up as she smiled back, and he could only be thankful she was here instead of in Boise, Idaho. He'd had several bad moments throughout the morning, replaying the events of last night. If he hadn't looked up as she turned the corner at the bus depot... Everything could have worked out so differently. He might not have—

Sophie nudged him.

"Hmm."

"They're calling us. It's our turn."

"Oh." He got to his feet, wearing black slacks and a white polo. "Let's go."

"Wait." She grabbed his hand as she stood. "I want to be sure you're—this is so much to ask."

"I'm ready if you are." He wanted his name next to hers on a marriage certificate—the sooner the better. Eric the asshole would lose most of his thunder when he realized he was no longer in the running for Sophie's money.

"Yes, I guess I am."

"Then let's go." He held out his arm, and she locked hers through his, walking with him to the waiting judge and clerk. He glanced from the tall, friendly man with horn-rims to his bride to be. Never had he pictured himself here. If anyone had suggested he'd be getting himself hitched to some gorgeous blond in a mess of trouble, he would have laughed his ass off, but here he was.

"Stone and Sophie," the judge said.

"Yes," they both replied at the same time.

The judge started into his spiel about promises, permanency, and exclusivity. "Stone, do you take Sophie to be your lawfully wedded wife? Will you forsake all others, love, honor, and cherish her in sickness and in health, in good times and in bad?"

"I will."

"Sophie, do you take Stone to be your lawfully wedded husband? Will you forsake all others, love, honor, and cherish him in sickness and in health, in good times and in bad?"

She nodded, swallowing. "Yes, I will."

"Now for the rings."

Stone stared at Sophie, realizing they'd forgotten to buy them.

"A wedding ring is a symbol that has no beginning or end," the judge continued. "Let your rings remind you of your solemn promises and keep you faithful for all the days of your lives. Stone—"

"Uh." He looked from the judge to Sophie. "We don't—"

"Yes we do." Sophie unfolded her palm, holding two simple silver wire-wrapped rings. "I made them while you were talking to Ethan," she murmured.

He'd been busy, jumping through hoops, making certain the legalities were in place, and Sophie had been making him a ring. He studied the plain band and couldn't help but smile as he stared into her eyes.

She smiled back.

"Stone, place the ring on Sophie's finger and repeat after me."

He took the smaller of the two identical rings from Sophie's palm and slid the piece of silver on her finger. "Sophie, take this ring as a sign of my love and fidelity," he said after the judge.

"Sophie, place the ring on Stone and repeat after me."

Sophie slid on the ring. "Stone, take this ring as a sign of my love and fidelity."

"Now join hands."

They clasped hands.

"By the power vested in me and the State of California, I now pronounce you husband and wife. You may kiss the bride."

Stone pressed his lips to Sophie's, far more chastely than he had early Sunday morning.

"Thank you," she whispered, touching his cheek as the judge congratulated them and signed off on the paperwork the clerk handed him.

He eased away, looking into her kind eyes, wishing

the moment had somehow been more special. He and Sophie had married for nothing more than an arrangement and affection at most, but he could have at least gotten her a bouquet of flowers or something. The entire deal had been so generic and cold. "You're welcome."

The clerk took the paper back from the judge. "Mr. and Mrs. McCabe, if you'll follow me we'll get this filed right away."

He blinked with the quick jolt as the clerk called Sophie "Mrs. McCabe." He, the self-proclaimed bachelor for life, actually had a wife.

Sophie held his gaze a moment longer before they followed the woman to her office.

~~~~

"Just tell Stone to head over," Abby said.

"Okay. We'll be there in a few minutes." Sophie juggled her phone, purse, and verification forms as she slid on her sunglasses while she and Stone walked to the Mustang from the Social Security office.

"See you soon."

"Bye." She hung up. "Abby wants us to stop by Ethan Cooke Security before we grab my car."

"Why?" he asked wearily, unlocking his door.

She shrugged. "She said she has something for us."

He stared her way through the lenses of dark shades. "I wanted to get started on the kitchen. I should be able to get the countertops and cabinetry ripped out if we're home by one."

I-dos and kitchen demolition all in one day. She twisted the ring he'd put on her finger more than an hour ago. This definitely wasn't the wedding day she'd envisioned as a little girl. "How about I take the bus to the office? Abby can give me a ride back to her condo so I can get my car."

He glanced at his watch. "No, I'll take you."

"I'm perfectly capable of taking the bus downtown." Why was his rush to get home and destroy the kitchen irritating her? He just did her a life-altering favor. He'd married her for heaven's sake, and she was getting huffy because he had things to do on his day off.

"Now that you've got that ring on your finger you're not going to turn into one of those nagging, bitchy wives are you?"

His smile faded as she shook her head and turned, making her way toward the bus stop across the parking lot.

Her marriage was a farce. They'd stood in front of the judge, stared into each other's eyes, and lied. They'd sealed a business deal with a kiss instead of their usual handshake. The whole thing was absolutely absurd. Why couldn't she laugh off the situation the way Stone was? Today was just any other day.

"Hey. Wait." He hurried after her, taking her arm. "Don't get pissy, Soph. I'm kidding. I said I'd take you."

"There's no need." She exhaled slowly, trying to relax. "I'm sorry. I'm a little out of sorts. Go home and get started on the kitchen."

"I will...after we see what Abby wants." He held out his hand.

She took it and walked back to the car with him. "We'll keep it quick."

"Nothing's quick when you and Abby get together."

"Okay, I promise I'll *try* to make it quick." She smiled, smoothing his collar. "Let's give being social a try."

"We're not social people."

She was trying to be, although she was content to spend days without leaving the oasis of his cliff. "We are today. I don't want to ruin Abby's fun."

"We wouldn't want to do that." He opened her door.

"You're a good friend," she said, ignoring his sarcasm as she got into the Mustang.

"The best," he murmured before he shut her door and moved around to his side.

Twenty minutes later the elevator slid open on the thirty-fourth floor. They walked down the hall to the Ethan Cooke Security offices, stepping into the lobby. More than a dozen people—Stone's co-workers and their wives—stood around in casual attire, chatting among ivory balloons, flowers, and a tower of prettily iced cupcakes.

"What the hell is this?" Stone muttered close to her ear as everyone in the room stopped and looked at them.

"I—I don't know."

"You made it," Abby beamed, rushing toward them. "Come on in, guys, and congratulations." She hugged Sophie, then Stone. "We wanted to do something special for you on your big day."

Sophie swallowed, giving her friend an uneasy smile. Didn't Abby understand that this wasn't a special day? "Thank you," she said to Abby, extending her gratitude to everyone.

"We've got a delicious pasta bar set up in the conference room. Come on, bride and groom, let's get you some lunch." Abby took both of their hands, pulling them through the crowd.

"Um, Abby." Sophie stopped as they neared the empty corner in the large space. "This is so sweet, but—"

"Congratulations," Austin came over, holding his son in his arms.

"Thanks." Sophie smiled. "How's Preston?" She slid her palm over his soft cap of peach fuzz, staring into a beautiful face identical to his father's, except his eyes, which were so much like Hailey's.

"Growing like a weed."

"He's certainly bigger than the last time I saw him."

Preston started fussing and sucking at his fist.

"Looks like he's ready for lunch. I better go find Hailey."

"Thanks for..." What should she say? Thanks for stopping by? He *worked* here. She glanced at the pretty secretary speaking into her headset at the front desk as business carried on around the party. "Thanks."

"Here." Stone walked over to her side, his eyes unreadable, handing her a plate. "Grab some food so we can get this over with."

She nodded, starting through the line, selecting salad greens, shrimp, and a small portion of fettuccini with alfredo sauce. She ate her meal sitting next to Stone at their designated spot for two, struggling not to feel awkward. "I'm sorry," she said pushing the pasta around on her dish.

He shrugged. "It is what it is."

"I had no idea." Everyone had been so sweet to put this luncheon together for them. If she had known Abby had this in mind, she would've waited until tonight to call her and tell her what she and Stone planned to do instead of chat while she created two wedding rings. She hated being the center of attention, especially under false pretenses.

"I know you didn't."

Hunter, Jackson, and Tucker came over, surrounding the small table with their muscular frames.

"Congratulations." Hunter bent down and kissed Sophie's cheek. "We've got to head out."

"Thank you." She accepted kisses from Jackson and Tucker next before the men exchanged handshakes with Stone.

Shane walked over next, crouching down at her side. "Congratulations, crazy kids."

She smiled, staring into his startlingly green eyes set in his handsome face. She'd never seen eyes so bold and bright before. "Thanks."

"I hate to eat and run, but I've got a meeting in less than twenty. You ready for Sunday?" he asked Stone.

"I'm counting down the minutes with anticipation. Three hundred of Hollywood's biggest and brightest all together for one big night."

Shane grinned. "Should be memorable." He kissed Sophie's cheek. "Welcome to the family." He glanced around at the Ethan Cooke Security crew.

She was happy to be a part of this wonderful group of people, but there was a time limit to her belonging. "Thanks."

Most everyone had cleared out by the time Sophie finished her cupcake. She looked over at Stone as he spoke to Ethan's assistant, checking his watch for the umpteenth time. She took her plate to the tray where a woman from the catering service gathered dirty dishes. "Thank you. Lunch was delicious."

"Let me box up the rest of the cupcakes for you, sweetie."

She wanted to refuse, but that would be rude. "That would be lovely." She glanced around at the mess on the conference table and the men on cellphones while they tried to work and support their coworker at the same time. Today's gesture had been amazingly kind, yet the rushed, impromptu luncheon somehow accentuated the farce of her and Stone's arrangement. She looked down at the simple knot among the twists of metal on her finger and at Stone standing across the room staring at her. Her heart beat faster as their eyes held. The gorgeous man across the room was her husband.

He walked her way. "You ready to head out?"

"Sure. Why don't I take the bus to Abby's and grab the car. I'll only be a few minutes behind you. You can get started on the countertop."

"I think the kitchen's going to have to wait until next week."

"But your appliances—what about the delivery next Friday?"

"I'll push it back."

"I'm sorry."

"It's not your fault, and it's not a big deal."

She knew how badly he wanted to get to the kitchen. "I could help you when I get home."

He looked at his watch. "It's a pretty big mess. Once we start we can't stop. You can handle the crowbar on my day off next Wednesday if you want."

"All right." She would make sure she was available to help.

"Okay. Shoot," Abby said as she walked passed them while she spoke on her cell phone. "Let me call you back when I figure something out."

"What's wrong?" Sophie asked.

"Lily borrowed my car this afternoon. Apparently it decided to die a block away from the office."

"Borrow my car."

"No, I couldn't."

"Sure you can. I'll go home with Stone. I'll drive in with him tomorrow and pick it up then."

"Are you sure?"

She grabbed the keys from her purse, twisting the car key from the ring. "Absolutely."

"This is great." She gave Sophie a big hug. "Jerrod just left, so this is a life saver."

"I'm glad I can help. Thank you so much for putting this together. It was wonderful." She hugged her friend again.

"You're welcome. Don't forget your gifts."

"Gifts?" She couldn't accept presents. "I don't think—"

"They're right over there on the table. I've gotta go. I have a meeting in an hour. Wren said she'd take me to my office. Now she just needs to bring me a couple of blocks. Call me later."

"Okay."

"See ya, Stone."

"Bye." He shook his head as Abby hurried out the door. "Christ, she's exhausting."

"She's wonderful."

"And exhausting. Let's grab the stuff and get out of here."

She didn't feel right taking the presents, but she said nothing and followed behind Stone as he put the envelopes on top of the prettily wrapped box and opened the door for her.

An hour later they pulled into the drive after a quiet ride home. Neither had said much as the miles passed them by. This wasn't the way she wanted things to be. Stone had assured her everything would stay the same, but they were already different.

He turned off the car and stared out the window.

"Are you sure you don't want to get started on the kitchen?"

He shook his head. "Next week."

She nodded and opened her door, more than ready to escape the undercurrents of tension. "I guess I'll get some work finished up before I start dinner." She got out, carrying the box of cupcakes, not bothering to grab the items they put in the trunk. She didn't want to deal with cards and well wishes. Work was what she needed. It would help her settle, and maybe she could squeeze in a walk on the beach with Murphy before she started supper.

"Hey, Soph." Stone walked up behind her, grabbing her hand.

She wanted to tug free and keep going, but she turned, looking into Stone's dark glasses.

"I think newlyweds should definitely play to twenty on their wedding day."

"You do?"

"I do." He smiled, lifting his shades.

She grinned as she studied the challenging light in his eyes. Suddenly everything was okay. "Five minutes to change. First one out to the court gets the ball."

"You're on."

She rushed to the front door, laughing, relaxed for the first time in hours.

# CHAPTER NINETEEN

SOPHIE FORKED UP ANOTHER BITE OF HER SALAD, STARING at the band circling Stone's ring finger. He picked up his third fajita, bit in, then shook his head with a short groan.

"Damn, this is good. I think you should give up the jewelry thing and open a restaurant instead."

She gave him a small smile, glancing at his left hand again as the silver glint caught in the harsh light from the ceiling.

He paused with the next bite at his lips. "What?"

"I was just looking at your ring."

He grunted, sinking his teeth in for more green pepper, onion, steak, and cheese wrapped in the soft flour shell.

She twisted her own band round and round her finger. "You don't have to wear that."

He frowned. "Why wouldn't I?"

She jerked her shoulders. "I don't know. I guess it's kind of silly if you think about it."

"Did you marry me today?"

"Yes, but it isn't real."

He wiped his mouth and set down his napkin. "It's real for the next year. I said I would do this, so I will. I'm all in." He swiped at his hair, still damp from his after-game shower. "I guess the better question is are you?"

"Yes. Yes. It's just—" She set down her fork. "This morning when we woke up we were Stone and

Sophie—roommates. Now we're Mr. and Mrs. McCabe."

"So it's a little weird. We'll get used to it. Kind of like you'll get used to me kicking your butt on the court the way I did today."

She narrowed her eyes. "By two points." She'd fought to the end, but his last minute steal and excellent shooting skills made him the winner of their grueling, late-afternoon game.

He shrugged. "Two points is two points. *Winning* points."

"Anyone can win when they travel more than dribble."

"Bullshit. What about your elbow to my stomach? That was a technical—easy."

"I don't know what you're talking about," she answered primly, avoiding eye contact as she fibbed.

He grinned. "Dirty pool, Soph."

She laughed. "Maybe."

"Definitely."

She stacked her bowl on her plate, chuckling, feeling easier after their banter. "Do you want one of the cupcakes the caterer sent home with us?"

"Not yet. I want you to open the gifts." He gestured to the box and envelopes on the counter.

She nibbled her lip with the small wave of guilt. "I don't know—"

"They did this for us. We can't give them back."

"I just feel like we're lying."

"We're not *lying*, Soph. We've got a marriage certificate and rings to prove it."

Technicalities, but she sighed, relenting. "You're right."

"I know I am." He reached over, tipping in his chair, and grabbed the items, setting them in front of her.

"You open the card from the office."

"All right." He took the envelope from the small pile and tore it along the top crease, whistling through his teeth as he held up the gift certificate. "Looks like you and I will be dining in style at Domain. I hear the food is excellent."

"That was very kind."

"I say after we rip up the kitchen next week we go out for dinner."

She smiled, liking the idea. "It's a date."

"Your turn. Go ahead and open the box from Abby." He pushed it closer.

Nodding, she ripped the pretty paper. "Abby told me she had something for me a couple days ago. At this point I don't think I'll ever have to buy clothes again."

"She definitely keeps your closet full."

"You're telling me. I told her I have plenty—*more* than plenty, but she assures me I'm fun to dress." Chuckling, she lifted the lid, pulling the beautiful apricot-colored satin and lace slip from the tissue paper.

Stone raised his brows as their eyes met.

"Uh, I don't think—" She shoved the gorgeous nighty back into the box, certain her cheeks were bright red. "I—"

"Not bad."

"Yes, but—" She cleared her throat. "I don't think she meant to—I'm sure she wasn't suggesting—I can't wear this—"

"Relax, Soph. Sexy nighties don't obligate you to a roll in the sheets."

She swallowed with the rush of heat, glancing at his mouth, remembering the way his lips had moved against hers while his rough, calloused hands teased her skin. Her new sleepwear didn't force her into a roll in the sheets, but it reminded her that she was more than a little curious. "Right."

He opened the last couple of cards, holding up more gift certificates, this time for her favorite department store. "Our friends got us some nice stuff."

"Yes, they did."

He leaned in, resting his arms on the table. "So, what's up with the sad eyes?"

She held his gaze, still surprised he could read her so easily—that he cared enough to try and figure her out. "I'm not sad. I think uneasy is a better word. I'm so glad Ethan was able to help us get the license filed today, and the certificate. And it's a relief knowing the social security card is on the way, but now I'm on the radar again. I can't stop wondering how long it'll be before Eric's private investigator figures it out. He'll come." Her breath shuddered out on a rush of fear. "Eric will come as soon as he knows."

"And we'll be ready. Or we can put ourselves out of our misery and head up to Maine."

"No." She pushed back in her chair, ready to end the conversation.

"Easy, Soph." He hooked his ankles around the legs of her chair, pulling her back in. "You and I both know the best defense is a good offense. We'll lawyer up, get the charges dropped, and make Eric disappear. We have more control over the situation if we act first."

Everything Stone said was right, but the thought of seeing Eric again, of knowing what was in store if their plan didn't work, was almost too much. "I'm afraid," she admitted.

"I know." He touched her hand. "I'm not. We're officially in this together now. Let's take this asshole down."

"I just..." She huffed, hardly able to believe she was actually considering going back. "When would—when would we leave?"

"Ethan said he can give me until Sunday. We could catch the first flight out tomorrow. Maybe Murphy can stay with the Cookes, or Abby can keep an eye on him. We can deal with the bullshit and catch the redeye back."

"We could come home tomorrow?"

"It'll be a long day. We'll pack a bag just in case, but I don't see why we shouldn't be able to. You didn't do anything wrong, Soph."

Being in the same zip code as Eric for any amount of time was too long, but Stone would be with her.

"I'll contact the attorney Ethan suggested when I spoke to him at the reception deal Abby put together for us, and we'll see what he wants us to do."

She couldn't truly move on with her life until she put Eric and her warrant behind her. She nodded, still hesitant. "Okay. I guess it doesn't hurt for us to hear what he has to say."

"I'll call him right now."

She nodded, knowing that once they got the ball rolling there was no turning back.

~~~~

"Sounds great. Thanks, Jeremiah." Stone hung up. He'd been on the phone with the lawyer for nearly two hours. He walked down the hall from the living room to Sophie's bedroom and knocked on the doorframe.

"Come on in." She set down her book and sat up. The skimpy pink tank top she wore accentuated her small, perky breasts, driving him crazy. She'd twisted her hair into a loose bun, exposing more of her soft skin.

"Sorry that took so long."

"That's all right." She pulled back her covers, revealing shapely legs in her striped pajama bottoms.

"Don't get up."

"Okay." She settled herself so she leaned against the wall. "What did he say?"

He sat on the edge of the cot. "That we're all set. The police in Bangor have been contacted. They've agreed to suspend the warrant until we can get there and straighten this out."

She bunched her hands in her lap. "The attorney doesn't think we can handle things from here?

He didn't miss the nervous gesture or the way her voice tightened. He hated that the bastard made her so afraid. "Jeremiah is strongly encouraging us to come. It shows the police that you're fully willing to cooperate and have nothing to hide. Plus, it's easier to clear things up in person."

"What if they don't believe me? What if they put me in jail and release me to Eric?"

"They'll believe you because you're telling the truth. They have no proof otherwise. If worse comes to worst and they do put you in jail, which is incredibly unlikely, they'll release you to me because I'm your husband."

"I'm liking this marriage thing more and more." She gave him a small smile as she looked at him with worry in her eyes.

"This is going to work out, Soph. They've got nothing but his word over yours."

"His accountants can make it look like I took the money. Clearly they already have."

"But you didn't."

She shook her head. "No I didn't, but I—I drugged

220

him."

His brows winged high. "What?"

She licked her lips nervously, staring at the bed, plucking at her sheets. "I put sleeping pills in the beer I gave him so I could get away." She flicked him a guilty glance.

What the hell was he supposed to do with that? "You might've wanted to tell me that before now."

"I know. I'm sorry." She hooked her arms around her knees, wrapping herself in a tight ball. "My car was fitted with a tracking device. So was my cell phone. I had a strict schedule. He called me every hour. If I didn't answer by the second ring, I got in trouble. It was impossible to make a move he didn't know about. I didn't know what else to do. I was desperate..." She sighed. "It wasn't right."

"You did what you had to do." He gripped her ankle, giving a gentle shake. "We'll keep that to ourselves unless they bring it up."

She nodded.

"Is there anything else I should know about?"

She shook her head. "I don't think so. I can't think of anything."

"Let me know if you do."

"Okay."

"I booked us the first flight out—seven ten. We'll drop Murphy off at Ethan's. Bear and Reece will run heard over him until we get back."

"What time are we coming home?"

He held her gaze, already knowing she wasn't going to like his answer. "I didn't book our return flight yet."

She frowned. "Why?"

"We need to see how things go."

"What does that mean?"

"It means we have to see what Officer Abney has to say."

"*Clyde*? Eric's *buddy*?" She rushed to her feet and let out an exasperated laugh. "I can't do this. I can't go to Maine." She moved to the window, staring out.

"Soph." He stood, sighing as he walked to her. They had to go. They had to get this resolved.

"You have no idea what you're asking of me." She glanced over her shoulder, her eyes hot and miserable.

He settled his hands on her tense arms. "I don't exactly, but I can try to imagine. I'm going to be there with you."

"The idea of being there at all makes me ill. Being able to tell myself it's only for a couple hours makes the whole thing slightly tolerable. I need a timeframe. I need to know I get to come back to Los Angeles and the life I've started here."

"You will."

"You don't know that," she murmured, looking straight ahead.

Hesitating, he wrapped his arms around her, settling his cheek against her temple, needing to give the comfort she hadn't allowed him to last night. "Yes I do, because the lawyer we just put on retainer is supposed to be one of the best in Maine, and I'm not coming back here without you."

Her body relaxed as she settled her hands on his forearms.

"We're going to get through this." He pulled her tighter against him, breathing in her scent, feeling the softness of her skin pressed to his. "Together."

She slid her palms to his wrists, holding on. "How do I thank you for all that you've done and are doing?"

"You don't."

She turned, facing him, pressing a kiss to his cheek.

"Thank you anyway," she said quietly, smiling

He wanted to pull her mouth to his and draw out the tenderness, but he smiled instead, tucking the hair escaping her bun behind her ear. He'd never been like this with anyone. No one had ever caught him up the way Sophie did. It was so easy to be gentle and soothe. "You're welcome. Try to get some sleep. I'll see you soon."

She nodded and walked to the cot, pulling her covers back.

"We need to do better than that."

"What?"

"The cot." He gestured with his head.

"Oh, I don't mind. It's actually comfortable. But now that your room is almost finished we should probably think about me moving to the trailer so you can buy yourself a bedroom set."

As he stared at his pretty wife in the dim light, he had no intentions of buying anything until he knew he wouldn't have to sleep in here without her. "Let's worry about that after we get home."

"Okay." She settled herself under the covers. "Good night."

"Night." He walked out when he wished he could stay.

~~~~

Eric lay in bed, reading through David's latest report, swearing at the lack of anything new. Their lead on Sophie had fizzled. Dylan Matther's ID hadn't been used again after the purchase of the bus ticket in Los Angeles. If David didn't come up with something in the next day or two he was going to be forced to board a plane and fly west. Searching for Sophie on foot was bound to warrant more results than the useless crap David had produced. He crumpled the papers into a tight ball and threw it across the room.

"Damn it." This was getting him *nowhere*. Where the hell *was* she? His phone rang at his side, and he frowned when Bangor Police Department popped up on the screen. "Hello?"

"Hello, Eric, this is Clyde."

"Clyde?" He smoothed out his voice. "What can I do for you?"

"I'm sorry to be calling so late."

"No, you're fine. I was looking over a couple of documents for the gallery." He glanced at the wads of paper on his floor.

"Look." He sighed. "I shouldn't be telling you this. I could lose my job, but I'm going to anyway." He sighed again. "Sophie's coming to town tomorrow."

"*What*?" He jolted up, ripping his covers back, rushing to his feet. "How—"

"She's got herself an attorney. She's coming to fight the charges against her. Hold on." Clyde murmured something to someone.

How did Clyde expect him to hang on? Sophie was coming.

"Eric, I've gotta go."

"No, wait. I—"

"I have to go. I thought I owed you the courtesy after all you've done for the department. I can't say anything more."

The phone went dead in his ear. "Clyde? Hello?" How dare Clyde hang up? He tossed the phone on the bed, laughing through the disbelief. She was coming. Tomorrow Sophie would be back, and she would pay. "Stupid, *stupid*, Sophie. You should have stayed away."

# CHAPTER TWENTY

SOPHIE WALKED INTO THE POLICE STATION WITH STONE and Jeremiah Trombley at her side. She let loose a shaky breath as nerves ate at her stomach. She was deathly afraid, despite Stone's steady support and her powerhouse attorney leading the way. She breathed in the scent of stale coffee, glancing around at familiar faces as the soles of her sandals slapped against the linoleum floor. Now that she was here she wanted desperately to turn and run out the door.

"I'm going to let Officer Abney know we've arrived," Jeremiah said as he moved to the left in his suit, carrying his thick briefcase in his hand.

"Guess this is a good time to hit the bathrooms. You coming, Soph?" Stone held out his hand in his short-sleeve, navy-blue polo and dark-wash jeans, his simple outfit emphasizing his broad, muscular build.

"No, I think..." Her eyes locked with Joe Burlington's, who sat at his desk across the room. They'd known each other since high school. He'd been a regular customer of hers, buying jewelry for his wife year after year, yet his cool stare made it clear he thought she was a thief. "Yes." She took Stone's hand and they walked down the long corridor, turning into the small, quiet lobby separating the men's and women's rooms from the rest of the station.

"I'll be right back," Stone said, closing himself behind the door.

She nodded, crossing her arms over the white

spaghetti-strap tank she'd paired with a navy-blue striped maxi dress, brushing her palms against her chilled skin, trying to chase away the goosebumps. The early-summer temperatures were more than comfortable, yet she'd been cold ever since she and Stone boarded the plane this morning.

She glanced over her shoulder, unable to relax, moving closer to the plaques on the wall as she studied commendations various Bangor officers had received over the years. Hopefully their meeting with Clyde would be as painless as Jeremiah had assured her it would be. She just wanted this over with as quickly as possible. Blinking tired, weary eyes, she rubbed at the deep ache clenching her neck muscles. The day had been endless with long flights and torturous layovers, and it was far from over. Home. That's what she desperately needed—to be on Stone's cliffs with Murphy, maybe playing a pickup game or cooking something for an early dinner. Anything but this.

"Welcome back."

Her heart stopped as the prim, schooled voice brought a rush of wild fear. Whirling, she faced Eric.

"Look at you," he sneered, his gaze traveling up her body. "I barely recognized you. Nothing but a streetwalker." He sniffed the air. "You smell like one too."

Her breath rushed in and out in hot waves as she stared into his mean blue eyes.

He shook his head on a disgusted laugh. "This is exactly why I tell you what to wear."

"Leave me alone," she whispered, fisting her hands at her sides, paralyzed by the primal terror he invoked.

"Talking back?" He grabbed her arms.

She flinched, gasping from the painful bite of his fingers into her skin.

"Since when do you talk back to *me*?" He gave her a nasty shake, his cheeks pinking, his eyes growing more hostile with his ragged breathing.

She cringed, waiting for the fist or kick that was surely coming any second.

"Two months, Sophie." He gave her another brutal shake, yanking her against him. "I owe you for two long months. Did you think I wouldn't know the moment you walked through this door? You've *humiliated* me." He gripped her tighter, making her whimper from the throbbing pain. "I've been keeping track of all that you owe me, and it's a hell of a lot more than five million dollars." He shoved her towards the women's bathroom. "I told you what would happen if you left. You're going to—"

The men's door opened with a rough yank. Before Sophie could blink, Stone rushed forward, gripping Eric's collar, slamming him against the wall with a nasty thud.

"Get your hands off—"

"Shut up." He pressed his muscled forearm into Eric's throat, making Eric gasp. "You listen to me, asshole," he said through clenched teeth. "Don't you *ever* fucking touch her again. Don't look at her or even breathe in her direction. You got it?"

Eric's eyes were huge as he fought to breath, trying to push Stone's arm away.

Stone pressed harder. "I asked you if you understand."

Eric nodded frantically.

"Good." Stone loosened his grip.

Eric coughed violently, yanking at his tie and collar. "Who—who the hell are *you*?"

"Sophie's husband. Consider this your one and only warning." He let Eric go and turned, his eyes still fierce as he looked at her. "Are you okay?"

She swallowed, gripping her arms across her chest, trying to stop trembling as she glanced from Stone to Eric.

Stone took the two steps separating them, standing toe to toe, brushing gentle hands down her arms, caressing the bright-red marks Eric left on her biceps. "Are you all right, Soph?"

She'd never seen that side of Stone—the shocking capacity for violence, yet he touched her as if she were fragile. "Yes. I'm just a little shaken up."

He slid the hair back from her cheeks, tucking several strands behind her ears. "Should we go?"

"Yes."

"Come on." He took her hand, eyeing Eric as they moved around the corner and walked down the hall.

"I'm sorry," she murmured. "I should've been able to handle that."

"Don't worry about it. I just did."

"But—"

He slowed, hooking his arm around her shoulders. "It's okay, Soph."

No it wasn't. *None* of this was all right. She glanced up into the security mirror in the corner by the ceiling, shuddering, watching Eric stare after her. "I—I don't want you saying anything about what just happened."

"Of course I'm going to say something. He left marks—"

"*No*," she cut him off, her skin crawling as she looked at Eric again. If the incident was brought up, it would only complicate everything and keep her here longer. If there was even the remotest of chances she could be on the next flight home, that was all she cared about.

"Soph—"

She pulled away from him. "I want you to drop it."

Jeremiah stepped out of Clyde's office with the portly, fifty-something officer at his side, ending their conversation. "We're ready for you."

Sophie took a deep breath and walked in, taking one of the padded chairs in front of Clyde's desk.

Stone sat in the seat next to her, snagging her hand, giving her a subtle nod.

She squeezed his fingers, grateful for his strength and support and his willingness to respect her wishes.

"Welcome home, Sophie," Clyde said as he took his seat behind his desk, his gaze wandering over her and Stone's clasped hands. "It sounds like we've got a bit of a situation we need to clear up."

"Yes," she replied quietly, remembering to look him in the eye instead of stare at her lap the way she wanted to. "I didn't steal Eric's money."

"That's what Attorney Trombley says."

"That's what *I* say. The money I left Maine with was from the inventory I sold during my last day in business at the mall. "

Clyde nodded. "And that's where the problem lies. According to the documents I've seen, Eric owns full partnership of Burke Jewelers."

"Clyde," Jeremiah addressed the officer, "Sophie didn't take the funds from Burke Jewelers with malicious intent. She's more than willing to return the full amount Mr. Winthrop feels is owed to him to end this matter."

"I guess I'm wondering why you left the way you did, Sophie. You and Eric had a strong, committed relationship. You were weeks away from getting married."

"Things may have appeared fine, but they weren't." She held the officer's stare.

Clyde sighed, folding his hands on his desk. "Attorney Trombley has shared some very serious accusations you're making against Eric."

"No less serious or damaging than the allegations Mr. Winthrop has made against Sophie," Jeremiah added. "But we're willing to let that go."

"I see you've married," Clyde glanced at the ring on her finger as her hand lay folded loosely in Stone's.

"Yes."

"What does that have to do with anything?" Stone asked.

Jeremiah sent Stone a warning glance. "Sophie would like the charges against her dropped," Jeremiah said. "This entire situation is nothing more than a huge misunderstanding."

Clyde puffed up his flabby chest. "But Eric's accountants are able to show us a five-thousand-dollar deficit in his books, which *does* make these charges stick."

"Which Sophie has explained to you she believed to be hers," Jeremiah interjected. "The inventory she sold was made with her own hands."

"Sophie turned the business over to Eric when Christina was ill," Clyde argued.

"I did," she admitted. "Which I regret every single day."

"And one might be able to argue that Sophie signed the legal documentation Mr. Winthrop presented her to gain control of the business under emotional duress," Jeremiah suggested. "But that's an entirely different can of worms. Let's get back to the here and now." Jeremiah scooted up in his chair. "Mr. Winthrop's accountants should be able to show that Sophie is entitled to some sort of compensation for providing product to his company and for being his employee, which she did not receive."

Clyde chewed on the inside of his cheek. "I'll have to see how Eric would like to proceed."

"Let's cut through all the bullshit here," Stone said sitting up, ignoring Jeremiah's not so subtle clearing of his throat. "Eric can waste his time, the court's time, and ours, but we all know these charges aren't going to stick once we get in front of the judge. Sophie's set to inherit five million dollars next year. Why would she risk a criminal record over five grand? This whole thing's a bunch of crap, and you know it."

Clyde sat back in his chair, holding Stone's intense stare.

"I'd really like to give the money back, Clyde, and go home," Sophie added, hoping to relax some of the tension in the room.

Stone squeezed her fingers. "Even though it's yours."

"Let me talk to Eric," Clyde said.

"You make sure to tell him to stay away from Sophie," Stone added.

"I can't make guarantees on Eric's behalf."

"I'm still trying to figure out how he knew she was here."

It was Clyde's turn to shift in his seat as he cleared his throat.

"We want this entire matter to go away," Jeremiah said. "Sophie has agreed to leave the past in the past if we can find a resolution to our current problem."

"If you're speaking of her allegations of abuse, Jeremiah, you know I can't go around issuing warrants for domestic violence without proof. Now with all due respect, Sophie, you know Eric loves you—"

"Hold the hell up," Stone interjected. "I just peeled your *pal* off of my *wife* back by the bathrooms—"

"I don't care about that or any of the rest," Sophie said in a rush, flicking a glance toward Stone's unreadable gaze. "I just want the warrant for my arrest to go away."

"We'll let you speak to Mr. Winthrop or his attorney." Jeremiah closed his briefcase. "You can give me a call when you know how he would like to proceed."

"Ms. Burke, or Mrs. McCabe, I guess it is now, is not free to leave the state," Clyde said as he stood.

She glanced toward the window, hating the idea of being stuck here for even one more minute.

"We'll be at the hotel over by the airport," Stone added as he and Sophie got to their feet.

"Thanks for your cooperation in this matter, Clyde," Jeremiah shook his hand, and they walked out.

She stepped from the room, pausing when she spotted Eric speaking to Joe.

Stone took her hand. "Come on. Let's get out of here." He tightened his grip, and they left as quickly as they'd arrived.

~~~~

Stone sat across from Sophie, watching her push her food around her plate, as she'd done for the last several minutes. He'd hoped the quaint Italian place with its classic checkered tablecloths and squat candle burning in the center of the table might relax her, but that clearly wasn't the case. He polished off the remains of his perfectly prepared rib eye and set down his silverware. "How's the piccata?"

She continued sliding her bite among the pasta and spears of grilled asparagus, staring into the flame.

"Soph." He brushed his finger over her knuckles.

Her eyes darted to his. "Hmm?"

"How's the food?"

"Good."

"Yeah?"

"Yes." She sat up further in her seat. "Very delicious."

"I haven't seen you take a bite yet."

Sighing, she looked at her plate. "I'm not hungry."

He stood, abandoning his side of the table, and slid into the booth next to her. "You should eat." He took the fork and stabbed the piece of golden chicken, bringing it to her lips.

She took the bite and chewed.

"Good?"

She nodded.

He wrapped his arm around her shoulders, wanting to erase the troubled look that had been in her eyes since last night. Their trip to her mother's grave and walk along her favorite local beach had brought her little comfort. Nothing seemed to help. "How you doing?" he murmured against her soft hair.

She leaned further into him, resting her head in the crook of his neck. "Okay." She touched his wedding band, twisting the silver on his finger. "I hate it here. This was my home for so many years, but now I want to leave so badly and never come back."

He thought of Eric's nasty murmurs through the bathroom door and the way the asshole had grabbed Sophie's arms, shoving her toward the women's room as he opened the door. He'd wanted to kill the bastard. He'd wanted to squeeze the fucker's windpipe until his heart stopped. "We'll be out of here soon," he said, struggling to force the sickening memory away.

"I can't settle. I keep waiting to turn around and see Clyde coming at me with a pair of handcuffs."

He pulled her closer against him. "I don't think that's going to happen."

She twisted his ring faster. "I'm not so sure. He and Eric are such good friends. Eric does a lot for the department—scholarships for the officers' children, family barbeques, art nights for the spouses, not to mention he and Clyde are golf buddies." She stopped fiddling with his finger. "I feel like everyone's looking at me, like this whole town is against me. He has them all fooled."

He glanced around the busy restaurant, noting the looks they were getting. "Screw them." He held up his hand as the waitress walked by. "Check please."

"Sure thing." The woman eyed Sophie as she turned away.

"I just want to go back to Los Angeles."

"Hopefully tomorrow."

She nodded.

The waitress brought the bill over. "Thanks for coming in. It was good to see you again, Sophie. You look so different."

She smiled. "Thanks, Liza."

Stone jotted down a tip and signed the merchant's copy. "Let's get out of here." He took her hand, and they walked outside into the cooling evening. He scanned their surroundings in the dim streetlights, pulling her close to him, for warmth but also because he'd spotted the familiar black Mercedes parallel parked halfway down the block. Eric was here. He'd followed them at a distance for most of the day. Eric Winthrop could paint, and he had a knack for beating defenseless women, but he sure as hell wasn't stealthy by any means. Calling the cops to report harassment wasn't an option. Clyde and his crew clearly weren't on Sophie's side, so he'd done his best to ignore Eric's presence. Sophie hadn't seemed to notice the intrusion, which worked just fine for him. "I don't know about you, but I'm ready for bed," he said as they crossed the street. He opened the door to the hotel lobby, letting her in before him.

"I'm too restless."

He punched the button for the elevator. "What if you try a shower?"

She shrugged as they stepped inside. "I guess."

Within moments the door opened on the fifth floor. They walked to their room and he let them in.

"I guess it doesn't hurt to give the shower a try."

"Go for it." He grabbed the remote and turned on the TV as she unzipped her carryon, pulling her clothes from the bag, heading toward the bathroom.

Stone stripped down himself, changing into basketball shorts, stretching out on the bed. For the first time since they landed, he was able to let his guard down. He pressed the buttons on the remote, flipping through the unfamiliar channel lineup while he waited for Sophie. Several minutes later she came out, among a plume of steam, in her usual tank top and shorts, her face free of makeup and her hair damp from the shower.

"Better?"

"Mmm. Much."

"Good."

She put her clothes away and wandered to the window, her shoulders set and rigid as they had been for hours.

He glanced at the Dodgers' highlights and at Sophie as she moved toward the small table, nibbling her lip then started back toward the window. "You gonna sit down, Soph, or wear out the carpet?"

She paused, touching the glass. "I'm sorry. I can't

seem to settle. I keep telling myself I just have to make it through tonight, then we get to go home, but it doesn't help." She licked her lips, swiping wisps of hair behind her ear. "His house is over there among that grouping of lights." She shuddered, crossing her arms. "I know it's miles away, but still." She huffed. "I keep replaying the way he grabbed me at the police station. I hate that I let him touch me. I hate that he scares me."

She was tying herself up in more knots. He sat up. "Come here." He patted the space next to him on the bed.

She glanced over her shoulder, turned, and walked his way, sitting at his side.

"Watch TV with me." He hooked his arm around her waist, pulling her down with him, settling her against him. "Romantic comedy, right?"

"You pick. I'm too distracted to pay attention."

He nudged her rigid body closer, wanting desperately for her to relax. "Let's give it a try anyway." He flipped through stations, stopping on a Matthew McConaughey and Kate Hudson flick already playing. "How about this?"

"Sure."

He settled back on the pillow, rubbing his thumb in gentle circles against her arm. As the minutes passed her body relaxed, and eventually she uncurled her fist lying on his chest. He glanced down at her wedding ring close to his heart, staring at her pretty fingers touching his skin.

She chuckled, then all-out laughed while the couple on TV bantered back and forth.

He smiled. This was exactly what he wanted. He tuned into the movie himself, content with Sophie in his arms, and found himself chuckling right along with her before the movie cut to a commercial break.

She looked up at him. "I forgot how funny this is."

"It's not too bad."

She grinned. "I'm pretty sure I heard you laughing."

He smiled. "Chick flicks aren't really my deal."

"What do you like?"

"The clichéd manly movies. The more stuff that blows up, the better." He smiled as she did.

Her gaze flicked to his mouth, then met his.

She smelled amazing, as always; her skin was warm against his as he trailed his fingers along her jaw, down her neck and arm. "You thinking about kissing me, Soph?" he asked quietly.

Her breath shuddered in and out as she touched his cheek. "Yes."

"Kiss me," he whispered.

She moved in hesitantly, capturing his mouth slowly, chastely.

"That's a nice start." He stopped her from easing away with his hand on the back of her neck. "Kiss me again."

She came back for more, holding his gaze as he parted his lips, sliding his tongue against the silk of hers. Following his lead, she copied him stroke for stroke, running her fingers through his hair, far less shy than she had been in his kitchen. He took her deeper, savoring her taste, pulling her on top of him, brushing his palms down her ribs, to her waist and the hem of her shirt, sliding up the cotton as he traveled back. Her breathing came faster as he tore his lips from hers, staring into her eyes, rolling until she lay against the pillow and he settled himself at her side. But all he wanted was to feel her beneath him. "Is this okay?"

She nodded, her cheeks flushed, the violet of her eyes shades darker.

He took her mouth again, more urgently, nibbling

her bottom lip, tugging gently, wanting it all, needing it. Feathering kisses along her temples and cheekbones, he moved to the rapid pulse point in her neck, then her collarbone, groaning when her hesitant hands trailed up his arms to his shoulders and down his back. Her touch was so timid and teasing, her gaze so shy as she held his.

God he could eat her alive. He pushed at the loose straps of her top, exposing her beautiful breasts, her pink nipples already hard. He touched her with the tips of his fingers, and she arched. Leaning in, he bathed her sensitive peak, tracing the point as she clutched at his waist, her hips rocking as she whimpered. He sampled her other breast, watching her stomach shudder with each shaky breath. She was so responsive. He wanted her. He could have her right now, but not here and not like this. He kissed her again, regretting the crappy timing, and eased away, caressing her cheek. "I think your movie's back on."

Her brows furrowed slightly, and she licked her swollen lips. "Huh?"

"Your movie."

"But—"

"You're missing your show."

Confusion moved through her eyes before she looked away as if she'd done something wrong.

"Hey." He gripped her chin, holding her gaze. "Not here," he murmured, kissing her again, fixing her shirt. "Not here, Soph. Not when you're thinking about him."

She nodded, touching his cheek.

His cell phone started ringing on the side table. "I need to get that." He leaned over her, reaching for the phone. "Yeah. Hello."

"Stone, it's Jeremiah."

"Hey, what's going on?" He sat up, and Sophie

followed.

"It looks like Eric is willing to drop the charges as long as Sophie gives up the money."

He clenched his jaw. The bastard had balls, that was for sure. "But it's hers." He didn't give a damn what the legalities were. That money belonged to Sophie, and everyone knew it.

"That may be so. We can make this easy or we can drag it out."

He looked at Sophie staring at him, her eyes weary again, her cheeks, flushed just moments ago, now pale. He wanted her to file charges against Eric for the marks he left on her today and the hell he'd put her though over the last couple of years. He deserved to rot in jail. "So he gets the money, and he's going to stay away."

"That's what he says."

"I want it in writing."

"I'm already a step ahead of you. I drafted something up when I got back to the office. Eric's supposed to be meeting up with his lawyer right now. They'll be faxing me the paperwork within the hour. If you want I can stop by the hotel in the morning and grab the money. You and Sophie should be good to head home."

"And that'll wrap this up?"

"That'll end it."

He'd already looked at potential flights out while Sophie sat by her mother's grave. They weren't going anywhere until eleven. "We'll see you around eight if that works for you."

"I'll see you then."

"Thanks for all your help."

"I'm glad I could. Bye."

"Bye." He hung up.

"So?" She swallowed, clutching her hands in her

lap.

"It's over."

"It's over," she repeated cautiously.

"Eric wants the cash, but he's signing something Jeremiah drew up saying he'll leave you alone."

"He's going to leave me alone."

"Yeah." But he knew that was a bunch of bullshit. Someone who'd gone to the lengths Eric had wouldn't just walk away.

"And he has to?"

"If he doesn't want to end up in court."

"Okay." She stood. "Okay," she said again on a shaky laugh. "Do we need to take the money to the police?" She hurried to her bag.

It bothered him that she didn't seem to care about what happened today or the fact that she was handing over the cash she'd earned. "Jeremiah will meet us here in the morning."

"I can't believe this is over," she said again walking to him, hugging him.

He pulled her to his side, holding her closer, sliding his hand down her back. "Are you sure you don't want to file charges for the abuse?"

"I'm sure."

"But we have the thumb drive. You have proof."

She shook her head. "I don't care about the money. I don't care about the past or what happened at the police station a few hours ago. I just want to get on a plane, go home, and move on with my life." She drew back, her arms around his waist. "This is such good news."

It was good news if Eric stuck to his end of the deal, but that was doubtful. He gave her a small smile. "We should head to bed."

"I might actually be able to sleep. Maybe." She

crawled across the mattress and slid under the covers. "I can't wait to see Murphy. I miss him so much."

He picked up his laptop and lay on the bed next to her. "Let's see if we can get a flight out of here." He wanted them back in LA as much as Sophie wanted to go. The more miles they had between themselves and Eric Winthrop, the better.

~~~~

Eric sat back in his home office, staring at the paperwork his attorney had urged him to sign—for cooperation's sake, of course. He'd argued the point for almost an hour, loathing the fact that Sophie had maneuvered the entire situation to her advantage, but somehow the stupid bitch had done just that.

She was here in Maine, just miles away. She was afraid, but more, she was *married*. David confirmed Sophie and her new husband had filed their license in Los Angeles yesterday. He'd followed the happy couple around Bangor and the surrounding area, yet he still couldn't believe it. Everything was *ruined*. The five million dollars he'd rightfully earned now belonged to that muscled goon who manhandled him in the police station.

He picked up the crystal glass on his desk, his hand shaking, his breath heaving as he swirled his top-shelf whiskey. "Stupid, *stupid* Sophie," he murmured. But this time she'd been smart. He chucked his glass, letting it fly against the wall, waiting for the satisfaction his random bouts of destruction brought, but the sensation was irritatingly absent. Sophie Burke—or *McCabe*—won this round, but she had to know he never came in last.

# Chapter Twenty-one

Sophie sat sandwiched between Stone and Abby in the noisy restaurant, swallowing the last sip of her strawberry daiquiri. The music was loud, the food good, the company even better. She'd never been on a double date before, but now that she was, she couldn't wait for the next one. Abby had picked the spot, insisting they kick off the first-ever Sophie McCabe birthday eve celebration. She'd been content to spend a quiet evening at home with Stone, but this was a great alternative.

"Do you want another one?" Abby gestured to her empty glass.

"No thanks. One is good for me."

"Jerrod and I are going to dance." Abby wiggled her brows as her husband gave her a pained look. "You guys wanna join us?"

"*No*," Stone answered for Sophie.

"Aw, party poopers."

"I'll dance with you." Sophie smiled.

Abby beamed. "Great. Come on." She took her hand, walking with her to the busy dance floor in the center of the dining area.

"I'm not really much of a dancer."

"That's okay. Just have fun." Abby raised her hands above her head, moving her hips to the beat in her slinky red dress.

Sophie did her best to copy in her black mid-thigh length skirt and white, clinging crocheted racer-back top. She swayed left and right, laughing, surprised to realize she actually had rhythm.

"Awesome!" Abby took her hand again and they both spun around. "Your hair looks amazing tonight, by the way."

She smiled, brushing back the glossy locks she'd curled at the ends. "Thanks. Marco sent me a bottle of some shine stuff and a new curling iron, along with detailed instructions."

"Well, he didn't do you wrong."

"He certainly didn't. I'll have to swing by Lily Brand this week and thank him for thinking of me."

"I happen to know firsthand that Marco is smitten with you."

She blinked her surprise. "He is?"

"He thinks you're 'a gentle beauty with great hair.' And that's a direct quote."

"Oh." She didn't know what to think of that. "I don't want to take advantage of—"

"He's gay, Sophie." Abby grinned. "He just really likes you."

"Oh." She smiled her relief. "Okay. I feel much better about that."

She looked over to where Stone and Jerrod sat, talking and watching. Stone wore a simple white Ethan Cooke Security t-shirt with blue jeans and one of those kerchiefs that tucked back his hair—and made her mouth water.

He motioned for her to come to him with a crook of his finger. Grinning, she shook her head, pointing to the spot next to her. He shook his head in response and she shrugged, turning back to Abby. "I don't think they're coming."

"Sure they are." She grinned mischievously, winking. "I know for a fact Jerrod can only hold out for so long. He can't keep his hands off me."

As if on cue, Jerrod stood and made his way over.

"See?"

She laughed. "I guess so."

"I'm going to have to cut in," Jerrod said, pulling Abby against him, wrapping her up tight as a cute man sporting a charming smile and crew cut took Sophie's hand.

"Looking lovely tonight, hottie." He tugged her further into the crowd. "Let's dance."

"Uh... I don't know."

"Come on." He turned up the wattage on his grin. "It'll be fun."

"I—"

Stone appeared, tapping the guy's shoulder. "Beat it."

Frowning, Mr. Crew Cut opened his mouth to protest.

"That's my wife. Go find your own."

"Thanks anyway," Sophie called as the man walked off, secretly thrilled Stone had come.

He clutched her hips, tugging her close. "I'm still new to this whole marriage thing, but I'm pretty sure flaunting other men in your spouse's face is bad form."

Grinning, she laced her hands behind his neck as they moved slowly, despite the upbeat tempo. "That's what I've heard, but you're here dancing with me, so it all worked out."

"Smooth operator, huh?"

She chuckled. "Perhaps."

He smiled. "You feeling any older?"

She shook her head. "I'm not twenty-five yet."

He glanced at his watch. "Another couple hours."

"That's two more hours to treasure my early twenties."

He raised his brow. "I've heard that thirty is the new eighty."

She laughed. "I realize you've come to terms with your ripe old age since you're mere months from transitioning to the big three-oh, but I'm still adjusting."

"I see."

She smiled, absolutely, perfectly happy now that Stone was home from his week-and-a-half of impromptu travel. From the moment their flight from Maine touched down at LAX until late last night he'd been gone. First, the star-studded Hollywood gala kept him away, then the last-second, weeklong trip to London. He'd kissed her good and long when he stumbled through the door at two o' clock this morning, gave Murphy a quick tummy rub, and disappeared into the trailer until Abby's afternoon phone call woke him. "Are you tired?"

He shook his head. "Not too bad."

"Thanks for coming out with us. I know you would rather be home."

"I wouldn't mind being home." He held her gaze, his meaning perfectly clear. They both wanted to pick up where they'd left off in the hotel.

Her stomach tightened with the rush of nervous anticipation. For days she'd thought of the way he'd touched her and made her feel. Stone kept gifting her new experiences. Tonight she hoped he would give her the rest. Snagging her lip, she looked down, wondering how to tell him she wanted him to make her his lover.

"Or we can stay right here. This works for me too."

He was giving her the option, ultimately letting her decide how the rest of the evening would go. She met his gaze. "We—we could go."

He took her hand, pressing his lips to her knuckles,

sending a cascade of heat along her skin with the promise in his eyes. "We should say goodnight to Abby and Jerrod."

"I—yes." She swallowed. "Okay."

They walked over to where Abby and Jerrod snuggled together, laughing.

"Um, we're going to go."

"Oh." Abby freed herself from Jerrod's arms. "Are you sure?"

She nodded, holding Abby's gaze, knowing the moment her friend understood.

"All right then." Abby hugged her tight. "Take care and enjoy the rest of your evening."

"I will."

"Call me tomorrow."

"Definitely." She hugged Jerrod. "Thanks for the fun."

"You're welcome. Happy birthday."

"Thanks."

Stone exchanged a hug with Abby and a handshake with Jerrod. "Ready?"

"Yes."

He took her hand as they made their way to the Mustang. "You wanna stop and walk the beach first?"

She shook her head. "I'm ready to go home." She wanted him to put her out of her misery and take her to bed.

He opened her door, closed her in, and walked around to his side. Minutes later, they took the quick right onto Ocean Ave, merging onto Highway One. He grabbed her hand, holding it as he got up to speed among the busy flow of traffic.

She sent him a smile. "I was thinking—" Her phone rang—her new phone Stone had convinced her to get with a service plan instead of the pay-as-you-go, now that she didn't have to worry about hiding. "I'm going to ignore that."

"Go ahead and answer. There aren't many people who have your number. If someone's calling, there's a reason."

"That's true." Regretfully, she withdrew her hand from his and dug into her purse, pulling out the phone. "Hello?"

"Sophie, it's Lily."

She pressed a hand to her ear, trying to hear over the wind blowing in through the open windows. "Lily?"

Stone raised his brows.

"Happy birthday."

"Thank—thank you."

"Listen, I'll keep this short. Abby said you had dinner plans tonight."

"Oh, that's okay. We just left, actually."

"I'll keep it short anyway. I want your jewelry for the next fashion show. Abby shared your idea for a *Freedom* line. I've seen your work. I like the whole concept. I'd like to meet with you tomorrow at eleven to discuss terms and get a contract worked up."

Her eyes grew huge as she swatted at Stone's arm. "Uh, yes. Yes. I can do that."

"Great. I'll see you then. Bring samples."

"Okay." The line disconnected in her ear. "Hello?" Frowning, she pulled the phone back. Lily didn't mess around. She put the phone away, trying to digest the conversation she'd just had. "Holy cow. Holy *cow*."

"What? You're killing me here, Soph."

"I just got off the phone with Lily Thomas."

"I know."

"The same Lily Thomas who wants to sit down and talk a contract tomorrow for my own *jewelry* line." She laughed. "I can't *believe* this." She squealed, doing a quick boogie in her seat. "I really can't believe this."

He grinned. "That's freaking awesome."

"Yeah, it is." Sighing her contentment, she stared out her window, looking up to the stars, stunned by the changes her life had taken in so short a time—home, marriage, friends, the career she'd always dreamed of.

Stone slowed, taking the turn toward the cliffs, traveling to the top of his road, and stopped in his spot in the driveway. "What are you thinking about?"

"About how lucky I am." She looked at him. "I'm so lucky, Stone."

"You deserve a little luck."

She shrugged. "I guess."

"Are you getting out?" He gestured to the door.

"Yeah." She got out, meeting him at the front bumper.

He pulled her into a hug. "Congratulations, Soph."

She closed her eyes, holding on. "Thanks."

"You deserve this."

"Thank you." She pressed her lips to his, once, twice, too excited to be shy.

He locked his hands around her waist. "I guess we're going to have to schedule another celebration. Do you want to call Abby?"

The only thing she wanted to think about right now was him. "I'll talk to her tomorrow."

"I can get behind that." He kissed her, pulling an inch away, and came back, sliding his tongue along her bottom lip. "Mmm. Strawberry."

"The daiquiri."

"Tastes good," he murmured, sampling again, molding her hips with his hands, wandering to her butt, pulling them heat to heat.

She hummed with the whippy, rushing thrill.

"Come on, Soph," he said against her mouth.

She nodded, walking with him to the house.

He pulled her against him again when they reached the entrance, pressing her to the solid wood of the door.

She locked her arms around the back of his neck. "Thanks for tonight."

"You're welcome."

"Dinner was incredible."

"I don't want to talk about food."

"Right." She licked her lips as her nerves came back.

"I want to show you something."

She was certain he was going to show her all kinds of things. "Okay."

He let them into the house, and Murphy ran out, peed, and came back in.

"Hi, baby boy." She crouched down, rubbing her sweet puppy as his tail wagged frantically. "You're a good boy. Yes you are."

Murphy licked her cheek.

"Aw, thanks. Go lay back down and get some sleep." She stood as Murphy wandered over to the bed she'd bought him.

"You finished?"

"Yes."

"Good." He snagged her hand, walking with her down the hallway, and flipped on the light switch.

She gasped, staring at the big oak sleigh bed and matching furnishings set up around the half-finished space. "Stone, this is beautiful."

"I still have work to do in here." He drew her further into the room. "We'll have to pull all of this out when I get ready to do the floor, but I wanted you to have this in the meantime—a real place to sleep."

She took in the pretty ivory and pale-green

wedding ring quilt, brushed nickel lamps on the bedside tables, and flourishing plants tucked in beautifully glazed pots by the window. "I *love* it."

"Wren helped me pick out everything."

"You two did an excellent job."

"You're sure you like it?"

She nodded, making her way to the bed, touching the soft fabric of the blankets. "Definitely. It's perfect."

He walked to her, sliding the hair back from her shoulders. "Happy birthday, Soph."

"Thank you." She snagged her lip, unsure of what to do as he stared in her eyes.

He cupped her face in his hands, kissing her in the dim light of the new lamps, drawing out their tender embrace until she thought she might melt right there.

She slipped out of her sandals and eased back, pulling off her shirt, and made a grab for the front clasp of her bra.

He pressed his hand over hers, halting her movements. "What are you doing?"

"I'm—I'm getting undressed."

"There's no rush."

There was always a rush. He was supposed to be naked by now and she lying on the bed ready to receive him. "I just thought—"

"I want to do this." He kissed her chin. "I want to peel off your clothes." He brushed his lips along her jaw while he slid his palms over the fabric of her bra.

Closing her eyes, she let loose a shaky breath as her nipples responded to his teasing thumbs.

"I'm going to touch you." He pulled at the clasp, catching her breasts as they fell. "And taste." He brought his mouth to sensitive skin, lapping, nibbling, suckling.

She moaned, settling her hands on his hips,

absorbing the flickers of delicious sensations while he pressed kisses to her neck and unzipped her skirt, sending it to the floor. She tipped her heavy head to the side as his tongue trailed a hot line along her collarbone and he clutched at her butt, over her panties, then under.

"God, Soph," he groaned. "You're so soft."

Kissing him, she went after the snap on his jeans.

He pulled back. "Not yet."

They should be finished by now. There were never soft kisses and gentle touches. This wasn't the way she knew. "I'm—I'm not—when?"

"When we're ready."

She looked down at the bulge in his jeans. "I want you to be satisfied."

He took her hand, pressing it against him. "Does that feel like I'm unsatisfied?"

He felt hard, and big, and ready. "No."

He pulled off his shirt and kicked off his shoes. "Come lay down with me."

She nodded, knowing it was finally time.

He eased her down, joining her, lying at her side the way he had in the hotel. "How's this?"

She licked her lips. "Good."

He kissed her until she relaxed enough to touch his cheek and pull the kerchief from his head so she could run her fingers through his hair.

He adjusted his position, lying on top of her, pressing her into the mattress with his weight.

She arched, eager to feel his chest against her breasts.

He captured her lips again, hungrily, as his whispering touch slid down her waist. His mouth eventually followed, stopping at her breasts, nipping and licking until she whimpered and clutched at his shoulders.

Continuing his journey, he paused at her bellybutton and her hips, spreading her thighs further open. "Soph." He traced the edges of her panties, making her whimper with the teasing touch. His thumb rubbed over her and she moaned, experiencing the delicious sensations of true desire for the first time.

He slid the silk barrier aside, exploring with curious fingers, his gaze holding hers as he stroked and dipped.

She rocked her hips, whimpering, desperate for him to keep going.

He tugged at her underwear, tossing them to the floor, and pulled her closer, his breath warming her skin, his tongue bathing her with moist, feathery strokes.

Moaning, she reached down, clutching at his hair as he continued relentlessly. She gasped, tensing, as unbelievable sensations built. "Stone—Stone, I—" She bit her lip, fighting the deep ache growing with his ceaseless teasing.

He grabbed her hands, lacing their fingers, carrying on with his devastating work, suckling and pulling until heat engulfed her and she exploded on a long, loud moan.

She gripped his hands as he slowed his rhythm, bringing her down easy and started his journey back up her body, going after her mouth with fevered intensity.

"I need you, Soph." He pulled at his pants, freeing himself of the rest of his clothing. "God, I need you."

She stared into his eyes as he hovered above her, working himself inside her, pushing deep. Bowing back, she shivered, still sensitive as he moved, pumping slowly, kissing her endlessly until his breathing grew labored.

She shuddered, her fingernails biting into his waist as the newly familiar ache started again. "Stone. Stone," she whispered, lost in pleasure.

He kissed her as she went over for the second time and nestled his head in the crook of her neck, shoving himself deeper, groaning next to her ear, once, twice, three times, stiffening as he emptied himself inside her.

She lay still, fighting for air as he lifted his head, brushing her lips. "It's midnight, Soph. Happy birthday."

She smiled, feeling like a woman for the first time in twenty-five years. "Thank you."

~~~~

The alarm beeped on the side table. Stone opened one eye, glancing toward the clock. How was it eight already? Slapping at the snooze button, he smiled as Sophie groaned at his side. He rolled back, pulling her closer against him, kissing her shoulder. He liked this, waking up with her. It didn't hurt that she was naked either. He planned to start each day like this as often as possible. And ending his nights the way they did worked just fine too. "I guess it's time to get up."

"I don't want to," she said sleepily.

"You have your meeting with Lily—"

"That's right." She sprang up, throwing the covers back, inching her way toward the edge of the bed. "I have to—"

"Easy there." He snagged her around the waist, tugging her back, pulling her down. "You've got plenty of time."

She looked at the clock. "Not really. I have to take Murphy for his run, and shower. Traffic's probably going to be a mess." She swiped at her hair.

He rolled, settling her on top of him. "This is a good thing, so relax."

"I can't." She rested her arms on his chest. "In three hours I have a meeting with one of the world's top designers. I don't have samples picked out. I don't even have a name for my company. I can't be Burke Jewelers anymore. Eric owns the name."

He traced his fingers up her spine, loving the feel of her soft skin. "We can work on getting it back."

She shook her head. "I don't want it anymore. It's...ruined."

"I guess that leaves coming up with something different."

"That was ours—mine and my mother's. Our name."

"So use McCabe."

She shook her head again, looking away, nibbling her lip. "I can't."

He frowned. "Why?"

"Because next year..." She met his gaze. "What about next year?"

He didn't want to think about next year. "You can keep my name, Soph." He tucked her hair behind her ear, staring into her eyes, wanting the world to know she was his. Now that they lay here like this, he wanted their arrangement to stay exactly the way it was.

"The *Freedom* line by Sophie McCabe of McCabe Jewelry."

He nodded his approval. "Doesn't sound half bad."

She smiled. "I like it." She kissed him once, twice. "This is all so *wonderful*. I've never had anything so amazing happen before."

"Uh, didn't we sleep together last night?"

Her eyes went huge. "Yes. No. That was amazing—"

He laughed. "Soph, I'm kidding."

"I'm not." She touched his cheek. "That was... I loved it. I loved being with you."

He wrapped his arms around her waist, unable to get close enough. "I loved it too."

"I've never had sex like that before. The way you...you know...did everything. Abby told me it could be amazing. Now I can tell her I absolutely agree. And the whole oral sex thing..."

His satisfied smile vanished into a frown. "What about it?"

She shrugged. "I've never felt anything like that. It was incredible."

"You've never had oral sex?"

She shook her head.

He stared at her in disbelief. "No one's ever gone *down* on you?"

"Nope."

"Why the hell not?"

She shrugged. "He didn't do that. Usually we undressed ourselves, he would do his thing, take a shower, and fall asleep."

Now he understood why she had been in such a rush. "Was it like that all the time?"

"Yes."

"*Every* time?"

She nodded.

Eric Winthrop was a dumbass. "I can promise you that won't be happening around here."

"Thank goodness. I want to have more orgasms." She smiled.

"That was a first too?"

Her cheeks pinked up as she wrinkled her nose. "Yeah."

Sex had never been about her before. He glanced at the clock again, needing to get ready for work, but that could wait. "Have you ever had shower sex?"

"No."

He grinned, looking forward to showing her how it could be. He rolled her off of him and sat up, scooping her into his arms. "Sophie McCabe, let me introduce you to sex in the shower."

She smiled. "I think I'm going to like this."

"Oh, I can promise you you're going to love it. And I wouldn't feel right about walking into this deal without offering you at least a three orgasm guarantee." He nipped at her neck, making her laugh as he carried her to the bathroom.

before the light turned red, accelerating on Highway One.

Why had she been fighting so hard to save something that wasn't real? Why was she just now realizing she should have let Stone go from the beginning? She'd been so selfish, holding him back from his life. Great sex and a promise to help didn't obligate him to forever or even the year he'd offered. Somewhere along the way she'd confused a complicated friendship with something that didn't exist. He didn't love her. He wasn't interested in "'til death do us part." She was the one who'd hoped for more, but it was time to stop. It was time to let Stone move on.

*What if you meet someone?*

*I won't.*

*You could, then where does that leave us?"*

Exactly where they were right now, because he had. Amber and Stone were always together—at the office, at Ethan and Sarah's, and today at Smitty's. Why hadn't she figured that out sooner?

She pressed a trembling hand to her lips, her breath heaving, sure her heart would stop beating. Never had she felt so empty, not even after mom died. Her phone started ringing, and she jumped, shaking her head, unable to keep her tears from falling.

"God. God." She listened to the incessant ringtone, knowing who waited for her to answer. She didn't want him to call. He didn't have to pretend anymore. There was no need for him to be "all in." Tomorrow morning she would fix the mess she'd made.

She slowed and turned right, heading to the cliffs, pulling into the driveway. Tonight she didn't admire the big, cheery blossoms in the pretty pots or watch the waves as she and Murphy made their way to the house.

Letting herself in, she set the Malcom's bag and soupy shake on the coffee table and walked to the bedroom, pulling the suitcases Abby had given her from under the bed. She moved to her drawers, transferring tops and jeans to the luggage, then grabbed the hanging items and her shoes from the closet. She started toward the bathroom as the front door opened and closed.

"Soph?"

She paused, her heart breaking impossibly more, and kept going, reminding herself that she needed to leave.

"Hey." He followed her down the hall. "Hey." He snagged her arm as they entered the bathroom.

"Please don't." She pulled free, staring straight ahead as she stood in front of the pretty cabinetry, opening her drawers, taking out her cosmetics.

"Didn't you see me at Smitty's? I called your name then I called your phone, but you didn't answer."

She closed her eyes. "I know."

"You got us Malcom's."

"Yes."

"Soph, why won't you look at me?" He captured her chin between his fingers, turning her head, giving her no choice but to meet his eyes. "Why are you crying?"

"I'm not."

He raised his brow.

"I'm fine." Her lips wobbled and she swallowed, dying to clear the choking lump of emotion.

"Let's go to the mountain." He slid his thumb along her cheek, killing her slowly with every gentle slide along her skin. "We can have a picnic and you can tell me what's wrong."

She shook her head, dislodging herself from his hold, and turned away, setting her items in a bag. "I can't."

"Why? What are you doing?"

She took a deep breath, knowing that this was truly the end. "I'm leaving."

He frowned in the reflection of the mirror. "You're leaving? For what, business? I didn't realize you were going to have to travel—"

"For good," she interrupted. "I'm leaving for good."

"*What*?" He spun her around. "I don't—"

"I can't do this, Stone." Her voice broke. "I can't do this anymore."

"Soph." He slid his palms down her arms, taking her hands. "What are you talking about?"

"Our marriage. It's not working. This entire thing isn't working."

"Yes it is." He gave her fingers a gentle squeeze.

"No."

"You can't leave. Where will you go?"

"The apartment over my shop." She sniffled, attempting to collect herself. "I haven't rented it out yet. I haven't had a chance to do anything to it, actually. I'm going to file for an annulment or divorce or whatever it is that I need to do."

"No." He shook his head, pulling her closer, his eyes desperate as they held hers. "No, Soph. What about the money?"

"I don't want it."

"Of course you do. Yes, you do."

She shook her head again. "No."

"But—"

"I'm tired." She sucked in a deep breath as more tears fell. "I'm so tired of the fighting. I'm so tired of arguing about something that will never change." She looked down, unable to stare into his confused gaze.

"Eric?"

She nodded. "He's never going away. He'll never

leave me alone because he wants me to pay. Fighting him is a useless battle."

"So I'll stop. I'll let it go."

She shook her head, so tempted to say okay, but she remembered the way he smiled at Amber. "I've known." She met his eyes again as she gave him the truth. "I'd hoped it could be different, but I knew all along because I know him. I've been terribly unfair. I can't ask you to put your life on hold any longer. It was wrong to walk into this marriage in the first place."

"Soph." He pressed his forehead to hers. "*Please* let me help you."

"You have." She touched his cheeks. "You're such a good man. You've been so good to me."

"Soph." He captured her mouth in a desperate kiss. "Soph," he whispered, moving in again.

Helplessly, she followed, sliding her tongue against his, clinging as he cupped the back of her neck.

"No." She pulled away, already knowing how this would end if she didn't stop them. They would go to bed and solve nothing. He didn't ask her to stay for love; he asked her to stay out of a sense of obligation. "I'm doing us both a favor. I'm doing what I should have from the start."

"Sophie, please—"

"This is the way I want it. This is what I want," she repeated, even though it wasn't, but this was what was right. "Goodbye, Stone." She kissed his cheek and hurried to the bedroom, grabbing her bags. "Come on, Murph. We have to go."

She walked out again, not daring to look back as she left behind everything she'd ever wanted.

~~~~

Stone sat in his window seat at thirty thousand feet, clenching his jaw, staring at the envelope the sheriff handed him just as he was about to get in his car and head to the airport. He flicked the pointed edge of the sealed packet with his thumb, replaying last night's conversation with Sophie, trying to figure out what in the hell went *wrong*. She'd bought them dinner— Malcom's—then she'd ripped his heart out and walked away. There'd been no warning. She was just leaving, and they were over.

He scrubbed a hand over the scruff on his face, picking up the envelope, and set it back down. Not even twenty-four hours and she had him served. She didn't even give him a chance to try to fix things. He'd been counting on a couple of weeks—or at least one— to let her cool off, then he'd planned to convince her to change her mind, but clearly she was in a hurry to be finished with him.

*Why*? Why was she doing this? He'd stopped himself more than a dozen times from driving over to her new place to demand answers and tell her he *loved* her. He'd never loved anyone the way he did Sophie. They had their problems but nothing they couldn't overcome. They had something. From the moment they met there had been a connection. And last night when she kissed him back, she'd been as desperate to hang on as he was.

Swallowing, he ripped open the envelope and pulled out the papers, scanning the legal jargon, noting that Sophie was waiving her rights to fifty percent of his assets.

*Do you want my house, Soph?*

*It isn't mine.*

But it was. That house was as much hers as his. Together they'd made it a home, and now she was gone. He shook his head, flipping to the next page, unable to take his eyes off of her looping signature petitioning the court for a simple dissolution of marriage. Sophie McCabe, his wife. But she didn't want to be anymore.

*This is the way I want it. This is what I want.*

But he didn't. He'd started out wanting to help; now he needed to build a life with her.

*I can't do this anymore. Our marriage. It's not working. This entire thing isn't working.*

He pulled a pen from his laptop case, pressing the tip to the paper, ready to give Sophie what she clearly needed. But then he closed his eyes and saw her pretty violet eyes staring into his in the steamy shower.

*Nothing else matters when we're together like this.*

So why did it now? What changed so quickly? How could she just throw it all away? "Damn it." He set the pen down and shoved the papers away, closing his eyes again, resting his forehead in his hands, drowning in angry despair. How the hell was he supposed to do this? How the hell was he supposed to let her go?

# Chapter Twenty-eight

Sophie stood among the chaos in her small shop, wearing the fitted, strapless black mini-dress Lily had personally made her, smiling for her guests, though all she wanted was to go upstairs and hide. The evening was going off without a hitch. The fashion show had been amazing. Jackie had done her makeup and Marco her hair. He'd done some sleek pullback that left her neck and shoulders bare, showcasing the jewelry she'd created for her walk down the catwalk, hand-in-hand with Abby, while dozens of camera bulbs flashed.

The caterers were doing an excellent job; she'd sold out of her inventory in presales and had thousands of dollars' of orders waiting for her and Carolyn to create, yet she wanted to cry. She glanced at the door as she had throughout the night, hoping Stone might walk in.

"You're kicking butt," Abby said, strolling over, wrapping her arm around Sophie.

She turned up the wattage on her smile. "It's amazing. I'm thrilled."

Abby raised her brow. "I'm pretty sure that's the fiftieth 'I'm thrilled,' 'it's great,' and 'I couldn't be happier,' I've heard tonight."

Her smile vanished. "Don't. Not now," she warned, praying Abby wouldn't push too hard, or she would lose it right here in front of the crowd.

"Then after we're finished. Oh, crap."

"What?" She looked around.

"Toni Terrell's heading our way."

Sophie tracked the blond with the dark tan walking toward them, growing uncomfortable as Abby tightened her grip around her waist. The nasty little weasel had almost cost Abby her life earlier this year.

"Mrs. McCabe—" Toni moved closer.

"Lily's handling the questions tonight," Abby interrupted.

"I've already spoken with Lily." Toni tossed her hair over her shoulder. "My photographer just needs a picture."

Lily stepped up next to them. "How's everything going? Toni, I've already answered your questions."

"I need a picture."

"Well, let's give *The Times* what they want." Lily slipped her arm around Sophie's waist.

Sophie draped her arm around Abby and Lily's shoulders, smiling as Toni's photographer snapped the camera four times, looked at his screen, and nodded.

"See you later," Toni said with a smirk.

"I hate her beady little eyes. I always get the feeling she's up to something." Abby took Sophie's hand. "Now come upstairs and talk to me."

"I can't—"

"Five minutes isn't going to kill anyone. Lily will hold down the fort."

"I can certainly do that," the silver-haired powerhouse said with a regal nod.

"See? Now come on." Abby pulled her toward the back office and up the stairs, where Murphy greeted them with the frantic wag of his tail.

"Hi, sweet boy." Sophie crouched down, petting him as Abby closed the door.

"Excuse us, Murph." Abby took Sophie's hand again. "Your mom and I have an appointment on the couch." Abby sat down, patting the next cushion over.

Sighing, Sophie sat, readying herself for another barrage of questions.

"So," Abby crossed her legs in her daring red dress, "how ya holding up?"

"Fine." She nodded as her bottom lip wobbled. "I'm really just fine." A tear fell and she turned away, muffling a sob.

"Aw, Sophie." Abby pulled her into a hug.

She closed her eyes and held on, sucking in several shaky breaths. "I'm sorry." She sniffled.

"Don't be."

She pulled a tissue from the box she kept close to her makeshift bed. Crying well into the night seemed to be part of her new routine. "I'm just a little emotional these days." She'd been a mess for over a week. "My chest is so heavy. I think my heart actually hurts. It's awful."

Abby stared at her with sympathy in her blue eyes. "Have you talked to him?"

She shook her head, blowing her nose. "I thought—I was hoping he might come tonight. I don't know why he would. I mean, we're not together." But she'd still hoped.

"He's out of town. Jerrod said he's been volunteering for all kinds of duties. He's hurting too, Sophie."

Standing, turning away from her friend, she shook her head again, having a hard time believing Stone could be anything but relieved. The charade was over; he could get back to his life. "Ending our marriage was for the best. We were arguing all the time. I couldn't give him what he wanted. He wouldn't let the stuff with Eric go."

"He's right about that."

She whirled, surprised by the lack of support. "No

he's not. I don't want to deal with Eric anymore."

"Eric won't go away until you do something about him. You can run and hide, but you won't be able to move on with your life until you tell him to go to hell. Trust me on that one."

She crossed her arms at her chest, holding herself tightly. "I'm afraid."

"I understand that too."

"I'll have to think on it." But she didn't want to.

"Call Stone, Sophie, or better yet, go see him. He should be back tomorrow afternoon. He took Jerrod's San Francisco duty yesterday."

"I can't." Her eyes watered again.

"*Why*?"

"Because I love him." She sat back on the couch as tears fell.

"Which is exactly why you need to go see him."

She stared down at the hardwood floor. "He doesn't love me." Saying so hurt.

"How can you say that?"

She met Abby's gaze. "Stone sees me as a friend— someone he feels responsible for. I don't want to be his obligation."

She frowned. "I thought you said you guys have amazing sex."

She nodded. "We do—did," she corrected. "When we were together we had this...connection. I've never felt so close to anyone. It's so intense, yet comforting. The way he touched me and looked into my eyes..." She would never have that again.

"That's not friend sex, Sophie. That's love sex."

"But Stone and Amber..." She swallowed. "I think he's interested in her. I'm not going to use five million dollars and Eric as an excuse to stand in the way of what he wants. I don't have the right to."

"Amber?" Abby shook her head. "Who's Amber?"

"You know, Ethan's secretary."

Abby closed her eyes, sighing. "Sophie, I love you, but you're an idiot."

She blinked her surprise, trying not to be insulted. "Thanks."

"Sophie." Abby took her hand. "Stone *loves* you."

He'd never told her so. She stood again, too restless to be still. "I don't know." She couldn't let herself believe what Abby said. Abby hadn't seen the way Stone and Amber looked at each other at Smitty's. "I'm not so sure." She huffed out a breath, pressing her hands to her face. "Everything's a mess. My life is such a mess."

"So take a little time to figure everything out."

"That's the plan." She glanced out the window, sighing as she spotted David across the way in the alley with his camera. She started to turn away but stopped. *He's never going to leave you alone until you stand up to him.* Stone's deep voice echoed in her head. She stared down at the wedding ring she hadn't been able to take off, swallowing her fear, afraid but ready to take the first step.

"I'm going to head downstairs."

"I'll be right there. I need—I need to make a call."

"Okay." Abby hugged her. "Everything's going to work out." She kissed her cheek. "Promise."

Nothing would work out if she didn't try. "Thank you." Picking up her phone, she pressed her lips together, waiting for Abby to shut the door, then selected Jeremiah's number with shaking fingers.

"Jeremiah Trombley."

"Jeremiah, this is Sophie McCabe."

"Hi, Sophie. How are things going?"

"They're all right."

"Good. I hope Kevin was able to help you get things settled out there in California."

"Yes. Thank you again." She'd called Jeremiah last week, immediately after she left Stone's house. He'd given her a local attorney's number, and he'd helped her expedite her request for a dissolution of marriage. "Kevin's been very kind."

"Good."

"Um—" She cleared her throat, more than half sick. "I would—I would like to take action against Eric for violating the terms of the agreement he signed." She pressed her fingers to her lips, glancing out the window. "His private investigator is still following me. I'm not sure what I need to do."

"Is the PI there now?"

She followed David with her eyes as he moved toward his vehicle. "He's getting in his car."

"The white Toyota?"

"Yes."

"Where are you?"

"I'm at my shop on Rodeo Drive."

"Okay. I'll get the ball rolling on this end. It'll take a little time, but we're going to get this taken care of."

"Thank you." She hung up, letting out a shuddering breath, terrified of the consequences of provoking Eric. She twisted her ring around her finger, knowing it would only be a matter of time before he retaliated.

~~~~

Stone typed down his final thoughts on the assessment report he was working on for Monday morning's meeting and glanced at his watch—twenty minutes until he needed to head to the airport. Stretching, he leaned back in the uncomfortable hotel chair, rubbing at his tired eyes, trying to figure out what in the hell he was going to do with himself when he landed in LA later this afternoon. He'd found a way to be gone since last Wednesday—Atlanta for Jackson, Toronto for five days for Tucker, and now San Francisco for Jerrod, but after he hopped this flight he wouldn't have to be on the road again for awhile.

He had yet to be home since Sophie walked out; he didn't want to be there without her, but today he would have to head to the cliffs on his own. This would be the first time since they'd met that she wouldn't be there waiting for him to walk through the door with a pretty smile on her face and a cute puppy wagging his tail at her feet. Steaming out a breath, he stood and took off his basketball shorts, replacing them with kaki slacks. At some point he was going to have to finish the kitchen—her kitchen—and lay down the flooring in their bedroom, then maybe he would take care of the last couple of rooms and put the damn place on the market.

Somewhere over the past few weeks he'd imagined the second bedroom as an eventual nursery and had given thought to adding on an office for Sophie for the days she wanted to work from the house, but now there wasn't much point in any of it. She had her apartment in the city, and they wouldn't be making any babies.

He slid on the green polo he'd been forced to purchase in the hotel store when he realized he was out of clean clothes and sat back down to put on his socks and shoes, stopping when his wedding band caught his attention. She had her show last night. He looked at the laptop then at the sock he had yet to put on and pulled the computer closer, clicking out of his document. He typed in the *Times*, even though he'd promised himself he wouldn't. There was sure to be something about the fashion show and after-event at McCabe Jewelry. Lily and Abby's names were too big not to get a mention.

The website popped up, and he clenched his jaw, looking into gorgeous violet eyes on the front page. There she was, with Lily on her left and Abby on her right, standing among the elegant flowers and pristine glass cases of her shop beneath the bold headline *Lily Brand Catches Its Next Rising Star*.

He read the article about the addition of the new *Freedom* line and the benefits both Sophie and Abby's contributions would make on the Stowers House projects. Three new locations would be opening in Miami, Houston, and Seattle over the next six months.

He scrolled down, taking in the last two pictures, one where Sophie walked the runway in a mouthwatering short black dress, hand in hand with Abby, and the next where she stood by herself, grinning triumphantly next to the McCabe Jewelry sign she'd agonized over for days before finally selecting the stylish black font. "Good for you, Soph," he murmured, staring at her stunning face before closing the lid on his computer.

Looking down at his ring again, he swallowed, missing the hell out of his wife. Sophie had what she'd been working toward. Her dreams were coming true. He wanted to be pissed at her for making him live without her—and maybe deep down he was—but he wanted her to be happy. She deserved all the happiness she could get.

He pulled the divorce papers from his bag, hesitating, then scribbled his signature on the line that would officially end their marriage. She didn't want what he did. Her life didn't include him anymore. What the hell right did he have to stand in her way? He folded them back up and shoved them away, ready to get the dreaded experience of going home alone over with.

# Chapter Twenty-nine

"Thank you," Sophie said, handing off one of the silver-frosted shopping bags she'd ordered for the store. They complemented the silver-toned jewelry boxes well. "I hope you'll come again."

"Honey, try and keep me away."

She smiled at the sleek, pampered forty-something...or maybe she was seventy. It was hard to tell in this town. "I'll look forward to seeing you back."

"Probably next week if not before." She winked. "Especially if you had something like that—" she pointed to the gold spiral link and cobalt beaded necklace on display— "in a burnt orange."

"I could make that happen."

"By Tuesday?"

She nibbled her lip. It would be tight with her backlog, but she nodded, not wanting to tell a potentially loyal customer no. As of late she craved the extra demands. Keeping her mind busy with catch-up work and new design ideas soothed, distracting her while the lonely late night hours ticked into morning. "Let me get your name and number."

The woman handed over a business card. Althea Oliver, CEO and Investment Broker at the Oliver Firm. "I want that design exactly but with the burnt orange beads."

"Okay." Sophie made notes on a custom-order sheet.

"I'll see you Tuesday."

"I'll look forward to it." She stapled the business card to the paper, studying her trendy client with a sharp eye. Althea had burned up her credit card on three necklace sets and two bracelets. If she made earrings and a bracelet to complement the new order, she had no doubt the CEO would take them off her hands in a heartbeat, and she could easily charge double while making the woman happy. It was win-win.

"I'll be telling my friends about this place." She pushed open the door.

"I appreciate it." Althea left, and Sophie's smile vanished, her shoulders sagging as she leaned against the glass case. Pasting on smiles and pretending everything was great for anyone who walked through the door was exhausting. Letting loose a deep breath, she glanced around her pretty shop, then at the credit card slip she held, worth more than a grand. This should have made her happy. She and mom had dreamed of something like this for years. Now she had it. But she didn't have Stone.

Shaking her head, she twisted her wedding ring round and round, knowing she needed to take it off. She set down the slip of paper and pulled the simple silver band halfway off, remembering Stone sliding it into place as he made promises neither of them intended to keep. Then she remembered his gaze holding hers as he tenderly kissed her knuckles the last time they were together in the shower. *That's not friend sex, Sophie. That's love sex.*

Sighing, she shoved the band back in place. "Tomorrow." She told herself that yesterday...and the day before. "God." Enough was enough. Standing up straight, she began to file the receipt when her phone rang. She glanced at the readout, and her stomach automatically tied itself in knots. Jeremiah. With fumbling hands she picked up her cell phone. "Hello?"

"Hi, Sophie, I'm sorry I'm just getting back to you. I've been in court all week."

"Oh, no that's okay." She'd been driving herself insane waiting for news. Jeremiah had called her while she stood with Lily and Abby thirty minutes after he'd "gotten the ball rolling" last Thursday night. He'd let her know that David had been arrested with several memory cards filled with pictures of her and even some with Stone. He'd assured her he would start proceedings for a restraining order Friday morning in the LA courts. Then Jeremiah's secretary called Monday afternoon, letting her know both David and Eric had been served with temporary restraining orders earlier that morning. Three days had passed without any more contact.

"I got the paperwork for the civil suit filed yesterday. I just heard back from the state police. Eric was served again today—about an hour ago—for violating our original agreement. The clerk told me we're looking at three to six weeks before we get our day in court. Things are pretty backed up right now."

"Do I—do I have to appear?" She bunched her fist, hardly able to stand the thought of going back to Maine. The possibility of facing Eric again left her nauseous, especially when she would have to do so on her own. Seeing him when she'd had Stone at her side had been hard enough.

"I'm going to try my best to make sure that doesn't have to happen, but we are the petitioning party."

"Yes, of course. If you could just let me know as soon as you do." She would need every second to prepare herself.

"Sure. Definitely."

"Thanks. Thank you so much for all of your help."

"I'm glad I was able to. I'll call you when I know more."

"Um, I have another question." She tucked several strands of hair behind her ear, growing more jittery.

"Shoot."

"Okay." She swallowed. "I know you're not handling my divorce, but when would I hear back—about how long does it typically take to get word back that paperwork has officially been filed with the Superior Court?"

"It really depends. I take it you're still waiting."

She nibbled her lip. "Yeah."

"You should give Kevin a call."

She had, leaving messages yesterday and Monday as well, but he hadn't returned her calls. She didn't want to be a bother. He'd helped her so much already. "I'll do that. Thanks again for everything."

"I'll talk to you later."

"Bye." She hung up, pressing her phone to her chin, debating what to do. Not having the answers where Stone was concerned was just as agonizing as her problems with Eric. Taking a deep breath, she dialed Kevin's direct line, bypassing his secretary altogether.

"Kevin McCall."

"Hi, Kevin. This is Sophie McCabe."

"Ah, Sophie. Shoot. I have you on my list of calls to make today."

"I'm really sorry to bother you."

"No, you're not."

"Okay, good. I was just wondering if you'd had a chance to file the paperwork with the clerk yet."

"Honestly, I haven't heard one way or the other. Typically my paralegal handles that. She left on maternity leave right around the time you initially contacted me. Our fill-in is still finding her rhythm a bit."

"Oh." She recognized the distraction in his voice as papers crinkled in the background. "Well, I'm sure everything's all set. I don't want you worrying about it." He'd been kind enough to meet with her the night she left Stone and draft up the necessary documents right then. It didn't make a whole lot of difference if she knew right now or in a day or two; the result was the same. She and Stone were no longer together. She just needed to hear that everything was settled so she could start the process of moving on. "Maybe after you and your new paralegal get into a routine she can give me a call and let me know that we're all set."

"I'm making a note right now, but I'm pretty sure Stone sent everything back in, so you should be good."

Her heart sank. "Thank you."

"Bye."

"Bye." She set down her phone, staring into the glass case as her eyes welled. Kevin was fairly certain they were good to go. She had her confirmation that she and Stone were through. This was a good thing...for Stone. He was free to move on, which had been the point. She breathed in a quaking breath, thankful no one else had come in to browse and that Carolyn had left early to take her son to baseball practice. Her marriage was over, and Eric was probably crazy with rage. The week couldn't get any better.

She sat on the stool she kept by the cash register, rubbing her forehead. Her relationship with Stone was now behind her, and her problems with Eric just beginning. Two subpoenas in less than four days. It wouldn't be long before he lashed out, making certain she knew she'd crossed the line. Restraining orders and lawsuits wouldn't hold him back—like she'd known all along.

Shaking her head, she stared out at the pretty palms and flowers lining the street. Why had she started this? What good could possibly come from it? For days she'd wondered if Eric would come himself or send his message through a stranger. She stood on unsteady legs, tempted to lock her door, but moved to the back room instead, picking up the piece she'd been working on when Althea walked in. Sitting around waiting made her feel powerless. She needed to focus on what little she could control, like her jewelry, while her life fell apart around her.

~~~~

"We're through here, Eric," David informed him. "Find someone else to handle your problems. Don't call me again."

"Bastard." Eric slammed down the phone and sat back in his office chair, gritting his teeth as he stared at the latest round of papers the State Police had delivered him. First the temporary restraining order Sophie and her attorney had filed against him, now a civil lawsuit for violating their original agreement. A mere four months in LA and Sophie had forgotten who was in charge. He would have to remedy that and make sure she remembered for a good long time that crossing him was dangerous. "Stupid, *stupid* Sophie." She hadn't gotten any smarter since March.

He crumpled the papers the officer had handed him an hour ago, winging the wad across the room. She was trying to *ruin* him. Monday he'd just stepped down from the podium, addressing the Bangor Women For The Arts Society, when a cop in full dress walked up, handing off the temporary restraining order in front of

Missy Zimmerman, one of the town's biggest busybodies and members of the Bangor Art Council. By Wednesday, rumors were flying around the community, and he was kissing Missy's ass, along with Todd Copper's and the other members of the local board, after Missy dug her nosy butt into the harassment and abuse accusations Sophie was claiming against him. No amount of schmoozing had discouraged them from temporarily suspending him as director until they could look further into "such a serious and troubling matter."

Missy and Todd weren't his only problem; Skip Fiscus from the National Art Council was breathing down his neck as well. He'd been in the middle of a video conference with the pain-in-the-ass representative, trying to explain Sophie's accusations in the restraining order as nothing more than a bitter end to their relationship and her attempt at malicious prosecution. Just as Skip was reassuring him that he would find a way to sway the council to give him more time to get the matter cleared up, Marlene knocked on his office door, letting in another cop to serve him with yet more papers. Skip had quickly ended the conversation, no longer promising anything at all.

He flexed his hands as the veins bulged in his neck, thinking of the injustice. If anyone on either council had been forced to put up with Sophie for two years they would have smacked her around too. They would never understand the type of rage she'd incited on a regular basis. But that was fine. Missy and Todd would have their own "serious and troubling matter" to deal with when he withdrew the funds for the generous scholarship program and Arts in the Park Festival he paid for every year. And Skip was going to be in a bad way when his wife found out about the little bimbo he'd taken to bed in Puerto Rico last summer. Neither Missy, Todd, nor Skip would soon forget whose side they should've taken from the beginning—and it definitely wasn't Sophie's.

He flipped on his computer screen, staring at her photo in the *Times* from last week's debut. She'd changed her appearance with makeup, fancy hairstyles, and inappropriate clothing, and she'd advanced her career with the help of Lily Thomas and Abigail Quinn, but she was still a screw up. David's final few reports documented her packing her bags and leaving Stone McCabe's house. From there she'd driven to an attorney's office on Wilshire Boulevard, then to her shop on Rodeo Drive where she'd resided at least until the time of David's arrest. The *idiot* wasn't capable of doing anything right. She couldn't even keep a marriage together for more than a month, which voided her trust. The money he'd had a right to was gone, his career in jeopardy, all thanks to her.

He rushed to his feet, fighting the need to chuck the monitor through the wall. Breath heaving, he walked to the window overlooking the main floor of his empty gallery. No one had come in at all today...or all week for that matter.

His phone rang and he went back to the desk to pick it up. "Yes, hello," he fought to smooth out his voice.

"Eric, this is Chavez."

"Hi, Chavez. I was just thinking about you," he lied, taking his seat again. "Marlene's set to ship my latest piece down to the gallery next week. It's a beauty if I do say so myself. The Big Apple's in for a treat."

"About that, Eric. Deidra and I have decided we're going to cancel next month's show."

He rushed to his feet. "*What*?"

"Please understand, Eric. I've just spoken with Skip about your suspension—"

"I haven't officially been suspended," he said through his teeth, starting to pace. "The council got their hands on some bad information. My lawyers are working on getting this cleared up as we speak." He tugged at his necktie that was suddenly too tight. "It's a huge misunderstanding."

"Regardless, this just doesn't seem like a good time to be showcasing your work. I'm afraid we can't take this on right now. We'll arrange shipment to have your pieces returned to you."

"No, wait—"

"I really must go. Goodbye, Eric."

"*Damn* it." He slammed the phone into the receiver and picked it up, intending to break it into several pieces, but set it gently back in place when he noticed Marlene standing in the doorway. "Yes, Marlene."

"Is everything okay?"

"Yes." He cleared his throat, reigning in the tatters of his temper, certain he might slap her ugly face if he didn't. "Yes, just fine."

"I thought you might like your afternoon espresso." She held up the small cup and saucer.

"That would be nice, thank you."

She brought the cup in, placed a napkin on the desk, and set down the fine bone china. "I think I might—" She looked over her shoulder as a blond with a dark tan walked down the hall. "Can I help you?"

"Yes. I'm Toni Terrell from the *Times*. I'd like to speak with Mr. Winthrop," she said, looking at him as she spoke.

"I'm afraid Mr. Winthrop has a full schedule." Marlene moved to the door, grabbing the knob, backing Toni up with her steps.

He measured the woman with the sharp, curious eyes, certain Ms. Terrell had the potential to be trouble. "It's fine, Marlene. I have a few minutes for Ms. Terrell. Please hold my calls."

"Yes. Of course. Can I bring you something to drink, Ms. Terrell? Mr. Winthrop is having an espresso."

"No. Thanks." She took the seat in front of his desk, pulling out paper and a pen from her bag.

"If you'll excuse me then." Marlene closed the door.

Eric sat as well, steepling his fingers, used to dealing with the press. "What can I do for you?"

"I'm working on an exposé on Sophie McCabe. My research shows you dated and were once engaged."

"Yes."

"I've been interviewing people here in Bangor. Many are saying Mrs. McCabe left due to a scandal."

He relaxed his shoulders some, sitting back. Ms. Terrell was looking for dirt on Sophie, and he was more than happy to oblige. "Yes. I guess she did."

"It's been reported that she stole from you."

"I'm not particularly comfortable getting into specifics, but I guess we could say she helped herself to money that didn't belong to her."

"So she did?"

He feigned hesitancy, looking away before meeting her intense stare again. "I'd really rather not say."

"If you were to say, would you be able to confirm that several thousand dollars were taken and a warrant was issued for Mrs. McCabe's arrest?"

Did it get any better than this? "Ms. Terrell..." He picked up his espresso, sipping.

"Some folks are saying she stole, but a few others have suggested she took the money to flee an abusive situation."

He set the cup down in its saucer with a smack. "That's ridiculous. I loved Sophie very much. I would never hurt a hair on her beautiful head."

"There are rumors floating around that there is photographic evidence to the contrary."

Pictures? He wanted to pull at his already loosened tie as sweat beaded, running down his back at the idea, but he laced his fingers once again. "I can tell you that couldn't possibly be true, because as I said before, I would never hurt the woman I had planned to spend the rest of my life with. Now if you'll excuse me—"

"Were you served papers Monday morning, Mr. Winthrop? Did Mrs. McCabe file a temporary restraining order against you?"

The viper had done her homework. "I'm all finished here." He buzzed Marlene.

"Is it true you've been suspended from the local art council and the National Art Council is considering doing the same?"

How the hell did she *know* all of this? He pressed the buzzer again. "Marlene, I'm going to need you to show Ms. Terrell out."

"What about today, Mr. Winthrop? Were you served papers by the state police an hour ago for harassing Mrs. McCabe?"

Marlene opened the door.

"Show her off the property. I expect you gone, Ms. Terrell."

"You didn't answer my questions."

"How could I possibly harass Sophie if I'm here in Maine and she's in California? Now please leave."

Ms. Terrell gathered her items, holding his gaze, leaving with Marlene following behind. He waited for the door to shut, then stood, watching Toni get into her vehicle.

"Bitch." He remembered the stir she'd caused with her article on Abigail Quinn earlier this year. She had the potential to be as much of a problem as Sophie. He turned away from the window, pulling at his tie, thinking of the pictures she'd mentioned. There were no photographs of Sophie other than the ones he'd allowed her to be in. There couldn't be.

Sitting again, he stared at the ball of paper he'd thrown, trying to dismiss the idea of photographic documentation as foolish gossip, but he couldn't banish the trickle of worry. How the hell could Sophie have taken pictures? She didn't own a camera, and she was either always at home or work. Where would she have... Dylan Matthers. "Shit." He picked up his phone, buzzing Marlene.

"Yes."

"I don't want to be disturbed for the remainder of the afternoon. Not by anyone."

"Certainly."

He stood, opening his door a crack, peeking out while Marlene typed on her computer with her back to him. Locking his door, he left his office, taking the rear staircase, moving out the back entrance into the thick of trees at the edge of the building, making his way through the forest toward the other side of town. He was going to get to the bottom of this potential fiasco before the day was out. If there were pictures of Sophie's bruises, Dylan Matthers was going to hand them over.

Forty minutes later, hot and sweaty in his black suit, he swatted at the branches of another pine tree as he studied the vile apartment complex he'd watched Dylan come out of several weeks ago. Most of the vehicles were gone from the parking lot and no one appeared to be looking out their windows. With the coast clear, he slipped around the corner closest to the putrid dumpster and into the building's front door, looking for the black bike Dylan rode to the mall the day he'd followed her to work, but it wasn't there.

Glancing around, he moved to the row of mailboxes, spotting *D. Matthers—3B*, and hurried up the two flights of stairs, peering over his shoulder from time to time. He knocked on her door but no one answered. Wiggling the knob, he shook his head when it opened.

"Idiot," he murmured as he walked into the tiny efficiency apartment, looking at the unmade bed, closet-sized bathroom, and messy galley kitchen that made up Dylan's home, keeping his eyes open for a camera. There was no sign of one on the counters or small table or anywhere else in the disheveled space, so he moved to the dresser drawers, pawing through the clothes, then the closet, finally finding the Nokia buried under the papers on the cheap TV stand. He powered it on, flipping through the images, finding nothing but shots of the woman with her friends at some campout. He scanned the place again, spotting the laptop on her mattress half hidden under a mound of blankets, and booted it up, swearing when he came to the password-protected screen. Crouching down, he entered her name, then her birth date, trying to gain access with no luck. "Damn it."

Footsteps started up the creaky steps and he stood, his gaze flying to the door as someone stopped in front of it, turning the knob. He rushed toward the bathroom, snagging the knife on the counter along the way, waiting for her to enter.

Dylan stepped in, swiping her long black hair off her shoulder as she closed the door with the sole of her sneaker and tossed her purse to the bed, gasping when he stepped out to greet her. "What are you doing here?"

"I want the pictures."

Her gaze darted to the computer as she swallowed. "What pictures?"

He narrowed his eyes, knowing Toni had been right. "*Where* are the pictures?"

She took a step backward, inching her way to the door. "I don't know what you're talking about. I don't have any pictures."

He stepped closer and grabbed her arm, anticipating her attempt to flee. "I know you took them," he bluffed. "I've heard all about it."

She shook her head. "I didn't."

He held up the knife. "Yes, you did."

"Oh god." Her breath heaved in and out as she eyed the blade. "I don't—I don't have them."

"How many are there?"

"A few—several," she corrected.

"Get them for me now."

"I really don't have them," she shuddered out, trembling.

"Who does?"

"They were on a thumb drive."

"Does Sophie have them?"

"Yes. Yes, she has them, but she probably threw them away."

He sent her a humorless smile. "I think we both know that's not true. What type of thumb drive?"

She licked her lips, still staring at the knife. "Uh, black."

"Black?"

"Yes. It's a black thumb drive. Please don't hurt me."

"Keep your mouth shut and I won't."

She nodded frantically.

"I know all about you, Dylan. I know where your mother and father live, where your sister and nephew are. You remember that."

A tear fell down her cheek. "I will."

He grabbed a towel off the floor and wiped the knife, then twisted the doorknob with the cheap fabric, looking into the hall. "Don't forget your family's safety rests in your hands."

"I won't."

Risking another moment, he stared at her, watching her tremble, almost certain she was afraid enough to do as he said. He hustled down the stairs and back out into the woods the way he came, swearing. Sophie had pictures. It was only a matter of time before she leaked them to the press. He yanked his cell phone from his pocket, ready to call the airlines and book a flight to Manhattan but thought better of it, dialing a different number instead.

"Yeah."

"It's me. I have a job for you."

"It'll cost you."

He rolled his eyes. "So you always say. I need you to go to Los Angeles and find a thumb drive. It has pictures of Sophie, my ex fiancé. She has a shop on Rodeo Drive, McCabe Jewelry. You'll probably find it there. It's black."

"That's easy enough."

"I'm not finished. I want you to take care of Johnston Sanders." The last thing he needed right now was the small-time thief he'd hired to play a few pranks on Sophie going to the cops or press with his story.

"How do you want him done?"

"However you want. Just make him disappear, and make sure it doesn't lead back to me."

"You got it."

"And I want her done too."

"Who?"

"Sophie. Make it look like an accident. You'll find plenty of pictures of her on the internet. Her last name's McCabe."

"Your tally's racking up."

"You just be sure to make it look like she met unfortunate circumstances. I've already got cops and some bitch reporter up my ass." And it was bound to get worse if he didn't deal with this now.

"I'll head out to LA tomorrow."

"Leave tonight. I expect something fast."

"I think half a million should have us both resting easy."

He paused mid-step. "Five hundred *thousand*?"

"Two bodies and a hunt for evidence. Sounds like a fair price to me."

He knew this man could and would deliver. "Fine. Just get it done."

"I want half delivered to my associate here in the city. I'll text you the address after you get yourself a new phone."

"I'll have one within the hour, and I'll be on the first flight I can get to New York."

"Then I'll have a body count in less than forty-eight, providing I get confirmation you've paid up."

"Let me know when it's done." He hung up, dialing the airlines next. Sophie should have been smart and kept herself hidden. He'd always told her she would die if she left. Now he would show her he'd meant it.

341

# CHAPTER THIRTY

SOPHIE SAT CROSS-LEGGED ON HER COUCH, DOODLING ideas for a bracelet in the sketchpad on her lap. She paused for a forkful of chicken, broccoli, and peapods from the to-go container at her side, glancing at the deadbolt she'd locked into place on the door, then returned her attention to the gift she was planning for Abby.

She scrutinized her potential new project, frowning at the twists of hammered silver and placement of bold red crystal beads, trying to figure out what on Earth she'd been thinking. Sighing, she slashed an "x" through the drawing and ripped it from the tablet, letting her latest attempt sail to the floor. *Nothing* she'd drawn tonight looked right. No matter how many times she put her pencil to paper, she couldn't translate the visions in her brain onto the sketchpad.

She rested her head against the back of the couch—her only piece of furniture—looking around her drab surroundings. curtain-less windows, bare hardwood floors, no lamps, tables, or flowers, not even freshly painted walls. The space was cozy enough and certainly had potential, but it didn't feel like home— not that she'd made any attempt to make it so over the last two and a half weeks.

She moved to twist the wedding band around her finger, dropping her hand, remembering the simple piece of silver was no longer there. Today had been the day. This morning she'd pulled off the ring, wiping at the steady stream of tears running down her cheeks as she put it away and hurried downstairs to work.

She'd caught herself more than a dozen times, trying to fiddle with the ring while she helped customers or sat in the backroom creating new product, which made taking it off all the more right. She and Stone were over. She hadn't seen or heard from him since the night she said goodbye on the cliffs.

She looked out the window into the bright lights of Beverly Hills, wondering what he was doing, pressing her palm to her heart, missing him terribly. Maybe he was with Amber at Smitty's shooting pool, or perhaps he had taken her to the mountain with the view. She closed her eyes, shaking her head, wanting to banish the idea of him bringing anyone to their place. "Why does this have to be so *hard*?"

Murphy looked up from his bed by her side, wagging his tail with a lazy flop.

"I can't keep doing this." She stood in a rush. "Let's get out of here, Murph. Let's go pick out a bedroom set." She scooped up the heavy puppy almost half as big as her, nuzzling his soft ears. "Maybe we should find a coffee table too, and a couple of plants. Let's make this place our home."

Murphy licked her face.

"Aw, you give the best sloppy kisses." She slipped on her strappy sandals, grabbed her purse and keys, sick of spending her time weighed down by sorrow and worry. Stone wasn't wasting his time thinking of her, and Eric would come after her whether she sat behind a bolted door or not.

She put Murphy on his leash and headed downstairs in denim shorts and a pink, sleeveless baby-doll top, opening the side entrance to the warm evening. "It's so *nice* out here," she said to the puppy as they stopped in front of her car parallel parked outside the building. Breathing in deep, she smiled, glancing up at the light in her apartment with a new sense of hope. Moving on was exactly what she needed to do.

Determined to take her first official step as a capable, single woman, she got in, started the car, and made her way through the impossible Friday night traffic, singing along with the radio. She belted out the refrain with Justin Timberlake as the Malcom's sign caught her attention, then the appliance store where she and Stone had spent an afternoon picking out the large majority of his kitchen, and her light mood plummeted. Stone's smile flashed through her mind, his face sweaty and his hair tucked beneath a kerchief as they bumped and brushed into each other, laughing while they played basketball. Then she remembered his intense stare as he moved inside of her, touching her face, showing her how it could be while they fell over the edge of ecstasy together.

Shaking her head, blinking, she realized she'd passed the furniture store and was merging on Highway One. "What am I doing, Murph?"

But even as she asked she kept going, eventually turning right, taking the road to Stone's cliffs. She pulled into her spot in the driveway, gripping the wheel tight, swallowing as she glanced from the basketball court to the empty spot where Stone usually parked his Mustang. Exhaling slowly, she stared at the darkened house she loved, frowning at the dead flowers she'd planted in the pretty pots. The lights should have been on, filling the beautiful picture windows with warmth. Stone's skillful hands and creative mind had brought this place to life, but tonight the charm was missing. His home seemed lonely and sad. Her gaze wandered to the house key still hanging on her ring, knowing she needed to mail it back. She wouldn't need it again. She didn't belong here anymore.

Murphy whined as the ocean breeze ruffled his fur.

"We shouldn't have come, but I'm glad we did. I needed to do this. I needed to see." She scratched him behind the ears. "Let's go pick out our furniture." She reversed and started down the hill. "Tomorrow we'll have to decide on paint—something nice and bright for the living room." Accelerating, she took advantage of the break in traffic and turned, heading away from the cliffs. She glanced back in the rearview mirror, blinking her tears away as her first home in Los Angeles faded in the distance then disappeared.

"Time to move forward," she murmured as the light ahead turned yellow. She tapped her brake, expecting to slow, but her foot pushed the petal to the floor. Gasping, she tried again, pressing over and over. "My brakes. I don't have any brakes!" She yanked up the emergency brake next, her heart thundering when she coasted closer to the juncture.

"God. Oh my god." She jerked the wheel to the right, attempting to avoid the oncoming cars in the intersection to her left, screaming as the screech of tires rung in her ears and headlights blinded her seconds before the car plowed into her side.

~~~~

Stone hit 'send' on his reply to Jackson and sat back, glancing at his watch before settling his hands behind his head—nine. It was definitely time to get the hell out of here. He'd been at the office since six thirty this morning.

"Knock, knock." Amber stood in his doorway in her black skirt and snug white top, showcasing her excellent figure.

"Hey."

"Hey." She stepped further into his office, her smile warming, holding a small cardboard box.

"All packed up?"

"Yeah. I'm sure Mia's looking forward to starting back on Monday now that her mother's moved in to help with the baby." She leaned against his desk. "There's still a bunch of cake in the conference room if you want some. I'd be happy to get you a piece."

"Nah. I'm all set." He'd avoided the goodbye cake deal they'd had for Amber earlier in the day, giving her a wide berth. The last thing he needed to do right now was get himself mixed up with the leggy temp. He was frustrated and miserable enough to do something stupid.

"So, I thought maybe... I was wondering if you might want to go shoot some pool."

Hell no. "I'm actually on my way home."

"Oh." She settled her butt on his desktop, not taking the hint. "Well, I heard about you and your wife—"

He sat up, no longer relaxed. "I'm not talking about that."

"No. Right." She stood up straight. "I was thinking I could leave my number with you." She grabbed a piece of paper and a pen, writing her phone number down. "If you ever need to talk—"

"Hey, Stone." Abby sailed into the room, wearing jeans and some fancy, trendy black top. "Hi, Amber." She glanced from the sheet of paper with the digits on it to Stone, then Amber. "If you'll excuse us, I need to talk to Stone." She backed Amber out of the room, shutting the door before Ethan's temp could say anything more.

Stone raised his brow in Abby's direction, leaning back again. "That was rude. I didn't know you had it in you."

Abby pulled up a chair next to his, facing him as she sat down. "How are you, Stone?"

He'd never been so unhappy—and he'd been pretty low before—but he shrugged anyway. "Fine."

"Good." She rested her elbow on the desk. "Now how are you really?

He sat up, recognizing the knowing glint in her eyes. "I'm fine. Just leave it alone."

"So, you're really just going to walk away?"

He stood, closing his laptop, and shoved it in the case. "I'm not talking about this."

"Sit." She pulled on his arm.

He held her gaze, debating whether or not he should walk out the door. She'd probably call him or come to the house if he did.

"Sit down, Stone. Please."

He sat with a huff. Might as well handle this right here and now and get it over with.

"I saw you two together. You *love* each other. Why aren't you doing anything about it?"

He dropped his face in his hands, rubbing at his forehead. "Because this is the way she wants it."

"Ask me how she is."

He glanced up, holding her gaze.

"Ask me how Sophie's doing."

He clenched his jaw. "How's Sophie, Abby?"

"She's more quiet than usual, her smiles are forced, and her eyes are sad, but she's hanging in there."

He swallowed, hating the idea of Sophie being unhappy.

"She's okay, Stone." Abby took his hand. "But she'd be so much better with you."

He let out a long breath through his nose. "There's nothing I can do."

"Or there's nothing you *will* do."

"What the hell do you want from me?" He rushed to his feet. "*She* had the papers drawn up." He slid a hand through his hair, recognizing the tinge of agony in his voice, still trying to deal with the hurt and anger.

"Can you blame her?"

His eyes flew to hers. "What's that supposed to mean?"

"You two start having problems, and suddenly Amber's everywhere."

"Bullshit. That's fucking bullshit."

"It's nine at night and the secretary's still here." She picked up the piece of paper Amber had written her number on.

He yanked the sheet from her hand. "It's just a number." One he had no intention of calling.

Abby huffed out an incredulous laugh. "Unbelievable."

"Take it easy. I'm not interested." He tossed it in the trash.

"Well I guess that's something."

He closed his eyes, leaning against the desk where Amber had sat minutes before. "Go away, Abby."

"We're doing a photo shoot together next week for *Trendy*. We're showcasing the *Escape* and *Freedom* lines together. She's shy, but the camera will eat her up. She's beautiful."

"Yeah." Abby wasn't telling him anything he didn't already know.

"This is huge for her. This is going to launch her career even higher. You could stop by and say hello."

"Or I can leave her alone. She has legs and a phone that works. She hasn't walked in here or the house, and

I haven't received any calls..." He'd hoped for either—both, but Sophie had done them both a favor. That still pissed him off.

"She got restraining orders against the PI and Eric. Jeremiah filed paperwork for a civil lawsuit yesterday."

"He did?"

Abby nodded.

"Is Winthrop still messing with her?"

"She hasn't said anything about it."

He scrubbed at his jaw, hoping the fucker was actually leaving her alone. "That's good I guess."

"Sophie's trying so hard to be brave, but she's afraid. This is a huge step. She needs you now more than ever. This is going to get so much harder as the court dates get near."

He didn't want her to go through this alone, but she'd kicked him out of her life. "I don't know what you want me to do."

Her eyes cooled as she shook her head—a look he'd never seen from Abby before. "I was pulling for you, Stone. I thought you were what she needed." She stood and walked to the door, opening it. "I guess I was wrong."

He clenched his jaw. "I didn't file the papers."

She turned. "Then what are you *waiting* for?" Her cellphone rang. "Hold on." She frowned, looking at the screen. "It's the hospital. LA General." She pressed "talk." "Hello? Yes, this is Abigail Quinn. Oh my—oh my god." Her terrified eyes held his. "How bad? Yes. Yes I'll be right there."

His stomach twisted into knots, already knowing it wasn't good. "What's wrong? Is Jerrod—"

"Sophie's been in a car accident. She's serious but stable."

His heart stopped beating as he reached for his

keys. "Let's go."

# Chapter Thirty-one

Stone rushed through the ER doors, hurrying to the receptionist's desk. "Sophie McCabe. Where is she?"

"Who are you, sir?" The woman blinked at him, her eyes magnified by coke-bottle glasses.

"Her husband. Stone McCabe."

"I'm Abigail Quinn." Abby stepped up to his side. "I was notified of her accident."

"Let's take a look." The woman typed on her keyboard. "Yes. Please go through those doors." She pointed to the thick, wooden double doors. "The nurse's station will be straight ahead."

"How is she? Is she okay?" He'd been sick with worry the entire forty-five minute drive through impossible traffic. What did "serious but stable" mean exactly?

"They'll be able to fill you in at the nurse's station, sir."

"Thank you." He pushed through the next set of doors with Abby following behind and stopped at the huge desk.

The nurse looked up from the paperwork she was filling out. "Yes, can I help you?"

"My wife, Sophie McCabe, was brought in—car accident."

She peeked at the large white assignment board over her shoulder. "She's down in room four. She just got back from being casted."

"*Casted*?" His stomach lurched. "How is she? How

bad?" he asked, desperate for answers.

"Why don't I take you down to see her?"

"Please." He hurried down the hall before the nurse made her way around the counter, stopping outside the glass door, looking in at Sophie laying against a pillow with her eyes closed and her neck in a brace. Cuts and scrapes covered the left side of her face, and her arm, the lower half casted in bright, white plaster, rested on the blankets pulled up to her waist. "Good Christ," he murmured, walking up to the side of her bed, brushing his hand gently through her hair as he leaned in close, breathing in her perfume. "Soph."

Her eyes flew open, staring into his. "Stone." She reached for his hand.

He smiled, lifting her arm gently, kissing her fingers peaking from her cast, weak with relief when she recognized him. He'd imagined amnesia, comas, breathing tubes, and all sorts of other horrible things on the drive over. "How are you feeling?"

Her lips trembled as a tear slid down her cheek. "I'm okay." Another tear fell. "I was in an accident."

"I know." He brushed his thumb over her soft skin, catching the drops, unable to stop touching her.

"I think the car's ruined." She sniffled. "I'm sorry."

"God, Soph, I don't care about that." He kissed her forehead, once, twice. "I'm just glad you're okay. That's the only thing that matters." He looked over his shoulder at the nurse. "She's okay?"

"Her tests came back normal. The MRI didn't show any signs of internal bleeding, but she does have significant bruising on her ribs, symptoms of whiplash, and a mild concussion, not to mention the fractured arm."

"But she should be fine? She'll make a full recovery?"

"She's very sore, which is normal. We're going to keep Sophie overnight for observation, but she should be good to go home tomorrow."

"Okay. Okay," he said again, exhaling a deep breath, relaxing his shoulders.

"We'll be moving Sophie to her room shortly," the nurse said, making notations on a paper before heading for the door. "Just buzz if you need anything."

"Thank you." He turned his attention to Sophie when the nurse left, sitting in the chair next to her, clutching her fingers in his hand. "So, it sounds like everything's going to be all right."

"What about Murphy? Is he okay? The doctor didn't know."

"I'll find out about Murphy," Abby said from the doorway.

"Abby," Sophie said, smiling. "Thank you so much for coming."

"Try and keep me away." She walked in, taking the space on the opposite side of the bed. "You're a little banged up, huh?"

"Yes, I guess so. I don't know if I'll be able to do the photo shoot next week."

"We'll get it worked out." She kissed Sophie's forehead, sliding a worried glance Stone's way. She fixed her smile as she stood straight. "I'll go see what I can find out about your baby boy."

"Thank you."

"I'll be right back." She walked out, disappearing down the hall.

"I hope he's okay." Sophie nibbled her lip, fisting her uninjured hand at her side.

"I'm sure he's fine." Scooting the chair closer, he brushed her hair away from the mess of scratches and bruises along her temple. "God, Soph, what happened?"

"I'm—I'm not sure. I don't really remember much. Murphy and I were on our way to buy furniture for the apartment. After that it's pretty foggy." She adjusted her position and winced.

"Hey." He settled his hand on her shoulder. "Try to stay still."

"My ribs are a little uncomfortable."

"Do you want me to call for the doctor?"

"No thanks."

Abby knocked on the door and came back in. "Murphy's at the animal hospital on Broadway—just a few blocks away. He has a couple of stitches by his eye and some bruising on his ribs, but he's going to be okay."

"Oh, he must be so scared." Sophie clutched at his hand. "Will you go get him?"

He wanted to tell her no. He didn't have any intentions of leaving her side, but how could he refuse when her eyes pleaded with him?

"They want to keep him overnight," Abby interjected. "The vet assured me he's being showered with tons of TLC."

"Sounds like Murphy's fine." Stone sent Abby a silent thank you.

"I don't want you worrying." Abby wiggled Sophie's foot beneath the blankets. "I'll stop by and see him on my way home. Jerrod will be here any minute."

"Thank you so much."

"Of course. I'll call you tomorrow and we'll figure out how we're springing you from this joint."

"I—" Sophie tried to move again and whimpered.

"Easy," Stone murmured, sliding his thumb along her fingers, hating that there was nothing he could do to take away her pain.

"I'm all right," she said shakily as she closed her

eyes, taking several breaths.

He stood. "Let me get the doctor."

"No. I'm fine. Truly." She gave him a small smile and turned her attention back to Abby. "I'm hoping you might be able to give me a ride to my apartment."

"It's already taken care of," Stone said before Abby could respond.

"Oh, that's—"

"I'm not leaving you," he interrupted, sitting again, sensing Sophie's refusal. "I'm staying right here, then you're coming home with me when the doctor releases you."

"But—"

"You're not going to be able to take care of yourself for a while," Abby reasoned.

Sophie looked from Abby to Stone and back. "The doctor said I'm going to be fine."

Abby's cell phone alerted her to a text. "That's Jerrod." She moved up the side of the bed, kissing Sophie's forehead. "We'll talk tomorrow. Try and get some rest."

The doctor entered as Abby left. "Mrs. McCabe, how are you feeling?"

"My ribs are a little achy, and I have a headache."

He walked to her side, shining the penlight in her eyes. "That's to be expected. The nurses are getting ready to bring you to your room."

"How is everything, Doc?" Stone asked.

The doctor looked from Sophie to Stone, his eyes stopping on the wedding band Stone hadn't taken off. "Sophie has an excellent prognosis. We're going to watch the concussion tonight, then she's free to go home, but you'll need to rest," he said to her.

"I'll be taking care of her."

"Good. She's going to need a little help getting

around. Lots of ice on the ribs and neck, then warm compresses to keep the neck relaxed after the first forty-eight hours, but we'll go over that more before you leave."

"Thank you." Stone stood, holding out his hand. "Thank you for taking such good care of her."

The doctor nodded, returning the shake. "I'll be in to check on you later, hopefully upstairs."

Stone turned back as the doctor left.

She smiled at him. "I appreciate you coming."

He smiled back. "Where else would I be?"

"It's getting late. I imagine you have to work tomorrow."

"I'm not worried about work right now."

"You're leaving for the concert tour soon. In a couple of days?"

"Yeah. Monday."

"You probably need to pack."

He clenched his jaw, understanding that she was trying to get rid of him. "I'm not going anywhere, Soph. I'm not leaving you, so get used to it." He looked at her pretty, graceful fingers, realizing for the first time since he arrived that she wasn't wearing her wedding band. He met her gaze, trying his best to ignore the punch of pain. "You're coming home with me to rest. Doctor's orders. I'm going to call Ethan and let him know I'll need my schedule rearranged for the next few days."

"No, Stone—"

"I'll be back." He walked off before she could say anything more. Sophie was coming to the cliffs with him whether she liked it or not. They were going to figure things out once and for all, and when she was all better, he wouldn't let her walk away again.

~~~~

Sophie stared at the ceiling in her private room, not daring to move. Every part of her body *hurt*. Her head throbbed, and each deep breath was agony, irritating her tender ribs. She was used to bumps and bruises. Eric had taught her to remember well, but even at his most vicious, he'd never delivered a beating that brought on a pain like this. She looked at the TV, trying to focus on the sitcom she'd turned on, but it was hard to concentrate on anything but the incessant ache.

The door opened, and her pulse kicked up a notch as Stone stepped in the room. He'd tucked his hair back with a kerchief, accentuating the dark stubble along his jaw, lending him a tough yet professional look in his slacks and polo.

"Hey." He smiled, walking up to her side, brushing his hand down her arm.

"Hi." She smiled back, wanting to take hold of his hand as she had earlier in the emergency room. The gentle slide of his fingers through her hair and tender kisses against her forehead had soothed her far better than any of the doctors or nurses had been able to. "You're still here." He'd walked out of her room in the ER almost an hour ago insisting he was rearranging his schedule with Ethan so he could take care of her. She'd figured he'd changed his mind and left, which would have been for the better. Now that the grips of vulnerability and initial shock of regaining consciousness in unfamiliar surroundings had lessened, she was better prepared to stand strong on her own.

"Of course I am." He tugged on the edge of her blanket, smoothing the starchy cotton around her waist. "It looks like they've got you all settled in. No neck brace anymore."

"No. They took it off."

"Good. How's the pain?"

"Okay."

"Liar."

She smiled. "I'm achy but I'm managing. I'm going to be okay."

"I'm glad to hear it." He sat on the edge of her bed.

"It's pretty late. You really don't have to stay." She wanted him to, so she needed him to leave. She'd just started getting used to him not being around. She'd finally come to grips with the fact that he wasn't going to be a part of her life anymore.

He took her hand. "I'm not going anywhere."

She suppressed a long sigh. This wasn't solving anything. What was the point of letting him spend the night or going home with him so he could play nursemaid? Why did he seem to want to drag out the agony of a hopeless situation?

"Look, Stone." She gave his fingers a squeeze. "I'm so thankful for everything you've done. You've been so kind, but you're under no obligation to spend an uncomfortable night sleeping in the chair."

"Are you blowing me off, Soph?"

"No." She huffed in frustration, regretting it instantly when her ribs screamed at the sudden movement. "I'm not trying to blow you off. I'm trying to make a difficult situation easier on both of us." She felt around for the call button at her side.

"What are you doing?"

"I need to use the restroom. The nurse said she doesn't want me standing up on my own."

"I can give you a hand. That's why I'm here. I want to help you."

She didn't *want* his help. Accepting his help was what got them into this mess in the first place. All of this was too much—their divorce, Eric, the business, the accident. She couldn't take much more turmoil in her life. "That's okay. I'll just—"

He pulled the button out of her grip. "Soph." He leaned in close, holding her gaze. "Let me help you." He brought his fingers to her cheek, stroking.

She closed her eyes in defense against the gentle words and gestures, breathing in his cologne, pressing her hand to his in a moment of weakness.

"Soph," he whispered, lacing their fingers.

She'd missed this—the sweet, tender side of Stone, but they weren't together anymore. Their marriage was over. She'd started their end with divorce papers, and he'd finished it by sending the documents back to Kevin for filing with the court. "I can't." She pulled his hand away, staring at his bare ring finger. "I can't do this."

"What?"

"Pretend that everything's the way it used to be."

"We're still friends, right?"

Being friends had worked weeks ago, but it didn't sit well now. "Yes, I guess we are."

"So then what's the problem?"

"I need to do this by myself. I need to stand on my own. I don't expect you to come to my rescue every time I have a problem. You have your own life," she finished, her eyes tearing up, betraying her.

"I'm not trying to rescue you."

"Good because I don't need you to."

"I couldn't agree more, but what about tomorrow?"

"Tomorrow's taken care of. Abby will bring me home."

"How are you going to take care of yourself and Murphy? You aren't going to be able to walk up those stairs to your apartment, let alone carry him."

She hadn't thought of that, but she needed to

figure it out, and she would. "I'll be okay."

The nurse walked in, heavyset and jolly, a big smile on her round face. "Hi, Ms. Sophie. How're you feeling?"

"Okay."

"We'll take 'okay.' Let me get a peek at those pretty eyeballs of yours and take a look at your ribs. Excuse me, Mr. McCabe."

"Sure." Stone stood, taking the chair at Sophie's side.

Nurse Karri came over, occupying the space Stone just abandoned, shining a light in Sophie's eyes, blinding her. "Looking good. Now for those ribs." She slid the hospital gown to the side, exposing the dark purple bruising along the entire left side of her ribcage.

Stone sucked in a breath through his teeth. "Jesus Christ."

"Mmmhm," the nurse agreed as she gently pressed her fingers against Sophie's ribs.

Sophie fisted her hand in the blankets, waiting for the torment to end.

"Definitely some nasty business, honey. Let's have you take a deep breath."

Sophie nibbled her lip, hating the idea of complying. "Are you sure I have to?"

"As sure as I know my name."

"Okay." She swallowed, slammed her eyes shut, and inhaled deeply, wincing, grabbing hold of the bed as her ribcage expanded.

"Easy, Soph." Stone took her hand, stroking, chasing away the worst of the agony with his gentle support.

"I know that's uncomfortable, but that's the best way to keep infections from settling in your chest." Karri patted Sophie's shoulder. "Can I get you anything?"

"Actually, I need to go to the bathroom."

"Well, who am I to keep you from the throne? Go ahead and stand, and I'll make sure you stay upright." The cheerful woman winked.

Sophie smiled, trying to be brave as she glanced at Stone, taking her hand from his so she could grip the bedrail and pull herself fully upright. She bit her lip, whimpering with the sharp, radiating throb. "Oh God."

"With bruising like that, you're going to be *very* sore, Ms. Sophie. I'd count on it for several days."

She held Stone's unblinking stare as she got to her feet, gritting her teeth with the torture, closing her eyes against a wave of dizziness.

"You okay, there?" Karri grabbed her arm, steadying her.

"Yes. Yes I'm doing just fine." She took several steps toward the bathroom, needing to show herself and Stone that she would be able to handle her injuries on her own. She made it halfway before she had to support herself against the wall, slightly winded and sweating. "See? I'm more than all right," she said to Stone as he sat back in his chair, his eyebrow raised and his ankles crossed. "Go on home and get some sleep." She gave him the best smile she could. "Thank you so much for everything."

His gaze turned hot. "Sophie—"

"I'm tired and ready for bed," she interrupted. "It's been a long day." She doubted she would be getting much sleep with the majority of her body throbbing, but it was time for Stone to go so they could head their separate ways.

"Sounds like the wife is kicking you out." Karri winked.

"Oh, no," Sophie started to correct the nurses

assumptions. "We're not—"

"I'll be back tomorrow." He got to his feet, walking to where she stood, pressing a kiss to her cheek. "I'll be back," he said again quietly, holding her gaze and giving her chin a gentle squeeze. Then he turned and walked out.

"That's a sweet husband you've got yourself there."

"Yes," she agreed, because it was easier pretending his gesture hadn't meant anything. Gathering her strength, she took another step, content that she was doing what was right for herself for once in her life. "I'm ready to keep going," she said to Karri and made her way to the bathroom.

~~~~

Eric shot up in bed as his new phone rang in the dark. "Yeah." He cleared his throat. "Hello?"

"It's me."

He switched on the light. "Is it done?"

"Johnston Sanders is fish bait."

"Good. What about Sophie? Did you find the thumb drive?"

"She's still alive."

"What the hell do you mean she's still alive?" He gripped the phone tight as he shoved his covers back and stood.

"Her brakes failed, but she managed to survive."

"Son of a bitch! I'm paying you to *end* her." He walked over to the dresser, smacking the antique brush and mirror set he'd given her for Christmas to the floor, finding no satisfaction when the glass splintered, smashing into small pieces.

"Hey, man, you said you want it to look like an accident. I put a slow leak in the brake lines. She crashed. She just didn't die. If you want her dead right now, I'll put a bullet in her head by morning."

He wanted her dead right this second, but if this wasn't done right the police would connect her death to him. "Stick to the original plan. The brakes, they don't look like they were tampered with?"

"Give me some credit. It'll look like wear and tear if anyone checks, but they shouldn't."

"Where's the thumb drive?"

"I can't find it. I searched her apartment this afternoon while she was downstairs. There's hardly anything in the place. It's not there."

"Damn." This wasn't working out the way he'd planned. "I'm paying you for results. Find the stupid thing and get rid of her. You'll have to search her ex-husband's piece-of-crap house. His name is Stone McCabe." He hung up, letting out another swear. How hard was it to kill one stupid woman? He walked downstairs to his bar and poured himself three fingers of whiskey, gulping the entire glass down in one go, reveling in the smooth flavor of the top-shelf beverage. He wouldn't rest until Sophie was dead. He glanced at his watch, anticipating the countdown until he got the call.

# CHAPTER THIRTY-TWO

SOPHIE SAT IN THE BACKSEAT OF THE CAB, MORE THAN ready for the ride to end. She'd been gritting her teeth, clutching the door's armrest for the last thirty minutes, waiting not so patiently for the car to pull up in front of her apartment. The bumps and numerous stops and accelerations were pure torture to her battered body. Two more blocks. Just two more blocks and the nightmare would finally be over.

She glanced down at her watch, fairly certain Stone had figured out by now that she wasn't waiting for him in the lobby as Karri told him she would be. He'd left a message at the nurse's station this morning, letting her nurse know he would be there to pick her up at ten thirty when she was set to be discharged. The doctor had let her go at nine twenty, and she'd wasted little time calling the cab company, with every intention of vacating LA General by nine forty-five at the latest. And she'd succeeded.

Perhaps her tactics were petty and ungracious, and Stone was going to be mad, but she needed to face this struggle on her own. She was a strong, self-reliant woman, and this was the perfect opportunity to show herself that she could face anything, even eye-crossing discomfort, without someone waiting in the wings to catch her should she fall. She'd come a long way since March. She had friends; knew the joys and sorrows of amazing sex, intimacy, and love; and had taken the first steps to stand up to Eric. She'd opened her own business, which she still needed to run...somehow, but never had she stood on her own. Mom had been her rock for most of her life, then she'd relied on Eric for too long, and now she depended on Abby and Stone for emotional support.

Taking care of herself and Murphy when Abby brought him by later this afternoon was going to be a bit of a challenge, but she could handle it. Maybe a little nap on her uncomfortable couch, then it would be time to clean up and get down to the shop, since Carolyn was away for the holiday weekend.

The cab *finally* pulled up in front of McCabe Jewelry, and she sighed her relief as she handed off her fare and gingerly slid to the door.

"Can I get the door for you?" The cabbie asked.

"Oh, no thank you."

"You're pretty banged up." He got out and opened her door anyway. "Here, let me give you a hand." He extended his hand and helped her out of the car.

"Thank you," she righted herself gingerly. "I really appreciate it."

"Get well soon."

"Thanks." She smiled and started toward McCabe Jewelry's entrance, taking her keys out of her purse. Just as she reached for the door, she dropped them. "That didn't just *happen*." Groaning, she closed her eyes, resting her tender forehead against the glass. "Come on, McCabe. Don't be a wimp. You can totally do this," she assured herself as she looked down at the sidewalk, devising her plan. If she bent at the knees and kept her trunk straight, she might not pass out from the pain. "Okay." She licked her lips. "Okay, here goes." She held on to the door handle, taking a deep breath, wincing, regretting the quick intake of air immediately as she bent at the knees, feeling around until her fingers connected with the metal. "*Yes.*"

Smiling her success, she fought to stand with her one good arm, moaned when she jerked her torso too quickly to the right, and gave up, putting the keys in her mouth to use both hands on the knob, finally making it to standing. Out of breath and weak from the effort, she leaned against the door. "You did it. You did it, Soph," she encouraged herself. Now she just had to tackle twelve steep stairs, unlock another door, and she was home free.

She swiped the hair back from her face, gasping when she spotted the Mustang in the reflection in the glass. "Oh no." She bit her lip, turning her whole body slowly, staring at Stone leaning against the hood of his car in ripped dark-wash jeans and a black t-shirt, his arms crossed at his chest, his eyes covered by the dark lenses of his glasses. "Crap," she muttered. How long had he been standing there? She slapped on a smile. "Hi."

He didn't smile back. "I left a message with your nurse."

"Yeah. They decided to let me go early."

"You should've called."

"I figured you'd need to get to work. I didn't want to bother you."

"It's not a bother if I offered."

She backed up, resting against the door when small black dots started dancing in front of her eyes and her pulse pounded in her head as the sun beat down, baking the area around her. God she needed to sit down. "Well, I made it. Thanks for—"

"Cut the bullshit, Sophie." He walked to where she stood and snagged the keys out of her hand. "You're about to fall over."

"I need to rest for just a minute. Then I'll be fine."

He unlocked the door, opening it for her. "Take a seat. You look like a ghost. I'm going up to get some of your stuff."

"No." She leaned against the counter, too fatigued to do anything more.

He slid his sunglasses on top of his head, revealing eyes hot with temper. "You're either going to Abby's or coming with me."

"I can't go to Abby's." She moved to the stool behind the cash register. "Abby and Jerrod are busy. They have plans tonight with Alexa and Jackson."

"I guess that means you're stuck with me. Which key is it?" He started toward the stairs, but she only stared at him. "Fine. I'll figure it out myself." He came down a few minutes later with a bag full of her stuff, more pissed off than when he went up. "Let's go," he snapped.

She stayed firmly planted on the cushioned stool. "I'm not going anywhere. I'm perfectly capable of taking care of myself."

"Let's *go*, Sophie."

"I said—" She stood faster than she should have, crying out with the sharp jolt.

"Soph." Stone dropped her bag and rushed to her side, gently wrapping his arm around her shoulders, taking some of her weight. "Are you okay? Do you need to sit back down?"

She swallowed, gripping his arm, leaning against him. "No. I'm okay." Who was she kidding? No matter how much she wanted to stay here and tough it out on her own, she couldn't. "I'm—I'm coming back here tomorrow."

"We'll worry about that tomorrow."

"We need to get Murphy." With little choice she accepted the support Stone offered and walked to his car.

~~~~

Stone slid Sophie a glance in the tense silence, watching her squeeze the armrest in a white-knuckle grip while she rested her head against the back of the seat, staring out the window. Clenching his jaw, he looked straight ahead, merging onto Highway One, trying to let go of the anger he hadn't been able to shake since he'd arrived at LA General and realized she'd skipped out on him mere minutes before he'd gotten there to pick her up.

What the hell was her problem? Why wouldn't she let him help her? Clearly she needed it, yet she'd kicked him out of her room last night, and today she blew him off for the second time. He shook his head, steaming out a breath, remembering her ridiculous attempt at unlocking her door to make it into her shop, growing more pissed off, thinking of her apartment. She was living out of Tupperware bins and had one stupid piece of furniture to her name, but she would rather stay in Beverly Hills alone than come home with him.

Abby had assured him he and Sophie were better together, that she was as miserable as he was, but as he looked her way again, he wasn't seeing it. He glanced at her naked ring finger exposed by her cast, as she stroked Murphy's side, then at his own. He'd pulled off the band, shoving it in his pocket after he left her temporary room in the ER last night. She hadn't noticed he'd been wearing it in the confusion, and he had no intention of wearing his damn heart on his sleeve when Sophie seemed to be handling their separation just fine.

He slowed, taking the turn toward the cliffs,

driving around the curves, careful not to jar Sophie any more than he could help. "Looks like we're here," he said as he pulled into his spot. "If you wait a minute I'll help you."

"Oh, I don't need any."

The cabbie could help her, but not him. "Whatever," he muttered, taking her purse and bag from the floor, then gently lifting one very drugged-up Murphy off the seat. "Come on, buddy. Let's get you inside."

Murphy licked his chin.

"Thanks." He got out, bringing Murphy into the house, settling him on the blankets where the puppy's bed used to be when he and Sophie still lived here. "There you go." He scratched behind Murphy's ears, happy to have the dog back in the house. "I'll go get your mom."

Murphy gave a halfhearted wag.

"I'll be right back." He stood, turning as Sophie walked inside.

"The flowers out front are dead." She moved to the plants that had withered by the window, frowning when crisp brown leaves disintegrated at her touch. "And the plants."

He shrugged. "I haven't been around much."

"I guess not." She ran a finger along the TV stand, creating a line in the dust as she looked at him.

"Work's been busy." He'd made sure of it.

"We'll have to get things cleaned up."

He shook his head. "Not today. Today you're going to rest."

She nodded. "I think I could use a little nap. They kept waking me up last night."

"Let's get you to bed."

"I can do it."

If she said that one more time he was going to lose it. She was driving him *crazy* with her insistence to do everything on her own, whether she could or not. "Are you planning to wear the scrubs?"

She looked down at the bulky light blue pants and top. "Mmm, did you happen to pack my pajamas?"

"They're in the bag." He lifted it, pulling out her pink tank top and striped shorts, handing them over.

"Thanks. I'll change."

"I'll get you some ice."

"I don't need any."

"*Yes* you do. The doctor said so last night, and so do your discharge instructions." He held up the yellow sheets of paper he'd had time to scan while she fought to buckle her seatbelt as they sat in front of her shop, asserting she could handle it by herself.

She nibbled her lip. "I hate the ice. It makes the pain worse."

"But it reduces the swelling. Get into your pajamas, and I'll take care of the compress and ibuprofen."

"I appreciate it."

He didn't want her to appreciate it; he just wanted her to let him take care of her. He walked to the freezer, opening the door with a yank, finding the ice pack she'd bought shortly after he got the black eye. He went to the bathroom, grabbed the bottle of ibuprofen, and walked into the bedroom, frowning as Sophie stood by the window still fully dressed in the scrubs. "I thought you were changing."

"I can't lift my arms over my head. It hurts my ribs."

"How did you get dressed this morning?"

"Karri helped me before the duty change."

"So what made you think you were going to get undressed by yourself?"

"I thought I could do it. I *want* to be able to do it. I *should* be able to take care of myself."

"Yeah, well sometimes you can't." He set her bag, purse, compress, and pill bottle down on the bedspread. "Come here."

She walked to where he stood.

"How do you want to do this?"

"Maybe you could help me lift it over my good arm and we'll slide it off from there. It's the stretching motion that hurts so much."

"All right. Let's do it." He moved closer, pulling the shirt up as she carefully lifted her arm, sucking in a breath with the movement.

"Stop." He couldn't stand seeing her in this much pain.

She froze. "What?"

"Are you attached to this top?"

"No. I was going to throw it away. It was either wear this or the gown."

"Hold on." He went to the kitchen and grabbed the scissors from the drawers Sophie had organized and came back. "I'll cut it off."

"Okay."

He started cutting up from the bottom hem, exposing her taut stomach, realizing she was braless as he went.

"Um, I'm not wearing a bra," she said, looking up from under her lashes the way he knew she did when she was feeling shy.

"I'm pretty sure I've seen you naked a few times before."

She smiled. "I know."

He smiled back. "It's no big deal, Soph."

"I didn't say it was. I just didn't want to surprise you or make you feel uncomfortable."

"I think I've got this. Ready?"

"Sure."

He pulled off her top one arm at a time, glancing at firm breasts and pink nipples before she covered herself with her casted arm. "How about a bra or something instead of the shirt?"

"If you packed one."

"You left this here." He walked to the dresser, holding up a black, front-close exercise bra.

"I didn't realize I had."

"You left several things here." And he'd left them where he found them, not ready to put them in a box and hand them off.

She met his gaze and looked down. "Oh."

Tension started creeping back into the room. "So, do you want the bra?"

"Yes, I guess that would work."

He stood before her again and slid it on one arm at a time, gently bringing the ends around her ribcage, the sides of his hands brushing the soft skin of her breasts as he fastened the clasp. "How's that?"

"Fine. Thank you."

"Go ahead and lose the pants, and we'll get you settled in."

"I tried." She swallowed. "The string's knotted. I can't bend my head far enough to see what I'm doing."

He fiddled with the knot, finally loosening it. "There." He stared into her eyes as he sent the pants down to pool at her feet.

"I, uh, they—they cut off my panties. They cut everything."

"Apparently." He turned, reaching into her bag, fishing out a pair of the silk scraps he used to love taking off of her, *wanting* her. In the two-and-a-half weeks they'd been apart he hadn't forgotten how easily he could make that beautiful body of hers respond with a touch of his tongue, brush of his lips, or slide of his fingers. The idea of never doing so again was almost more than he could stand. "Okay." He turned back. "Go ahead and step out."

She lifted her feet one at a time, and he gathered the clothes for the trash, then held out the pale pink panties. "Foot in."

She balanced herself with her hands on his shoulders and put her feet through the openings one at a time.

He slid the sexy underwear up her firm calves and thighs, trailing his thumbs over her smooth skin, settling the bands on her hips as he looked up into her gaze, thrilled as hell when he noticed her flushed cheeks and eyes hot with desire. "Do you want your shorts?"

"Yes please," she said, clearing her throat.

He took the pink-striped shorts from the bed and repeated the process, making certain to take his time, biting his cheek to prevent his grin of satisfaction when her breathing grew unsteady and she shivered. "Looks like you're all set."

"Uh, yes. Thank you."

Sophie certainly wasn't as indifferent as he'd feared. "Ready for bed?"

"Mmm. I'm tired."

He pulled back the covers. "Do you need help?"

"Maybe a little. If I can hold onto your arm while I lay myself back."

"Yeah, sure." *Finally*, she was letting him give her a hand. He helped her ease herself down to the pillow and leaned in closer than was necessary as he gently slid her hair out from beneath her neck the way he'd seen her do several times. "How's that?"

"Great." She sighed, smiling, closing her eyes with a small moan. "I miss this bed so *much*." Her eyes flew open as her smile vanished.

She missed their bed—now he just needed her to miss him too. "How about the compress?"

She wrinkled her nose. "Only if I have to."

"You definitely do." He pulled the covers up to her hips and grabbed a folded towel from the laundry basket that had been sitting in the corner since she left, wrapping it around the frozen pack. "I guess my black eye was good for something, or we wouldn't have this." He held her gaze, knowing she thought of the kiss in the kitchen as he did.

"Yes, I guess so."

He sat on the edge of the mattress, frowning as he stared at the dark-purple bloom of bruises. "Damn, Soph." He traced his fingers over her warm, battered skin.

"I couldn't stop. The light turned yellow, and I was in the intersection."

He continued sliding his fingers over her ribs, moving to her stomach, desperate to touch, trying to make up for the weeks he hadn't been able to. "You remember."

"Parts, I guess. It happened so fast. I dreamt about it last night when I was actually able to sleep—the blinding lights coming at me, and I think I screamed. Then when you and I were on our way here just now, we went through the intersection where the accident happened and I remembered that the light had been yellow."

"What do you mean you couldn't stop?"

"I pressed on the brake, but it didn't work."

His fingers paused on her skin. "They didn't work?"

"No, I pushed them all the way to the floor. I tried

my emergency brake, but I didn't slow down."

"Did the engine accelerate?"

She frowned, clearly trying to put herself back in the moment. "No, I don't think so."

"I had Ethan get me a copy of the police report. I was surprised to read that you were only a couple of miles from here. I thought you said you were buying furniture."

She shrugged and sucked in a breath.

He stroked again, automatically trying to soothe her.

"Murphy and I were on our way to do some shopping, but we ended up here at the house."

He tried to focus on the fact that something was off about her story, but he couldn't ignore the small stirring of pleasure that she'd come. "Why?"

"I—I don't know. I love it here. I love this house. I guess I needed to say goodbye."

The glimmer of pleasure vanished. "You don't have to say goodbye. You can come up here whenever you want."

"No." She shook her head carefully. "No, I can't. I can't move forward if I keep going back."

He looked away as her words stung. She was talking about moving on when he wasn't sure he ever could. "Yeah, I guess." He stood.

She grabbed his hand. "I'm sorry if that makes you upset."

He shrugged. "I'm not upset."

"Stone, I know you."

He wasn't about to admit that no one had ever crushed him the way she had when she left. "I just don't understand. We had a few disagreements. I contacted Jeremiah when I should have talked to you about it first. The next thing I know you're leaving and some cop's handing me papers for a divorce."

"It's the right thing."

"So you've said." He tried to pull away.

She gripped him tighter. "I just—"

"You'd rather suffer on your own in an apartment furnished with a *couch* than let me help you," he spewed, no longer able to hold back the anger.

Her eyes watered. "I'm sorry."

"Don't apologize. This is what you want. You're happy." He stared at her, wanting her to tell him she'd made a mistake and she was as miserable as he was.

"I don't know what else to do. I think this is for the best."

He clenched his jaw. "Yeah, you've said that too."

"I gave you back your life."

He pulled away, unable to take any more. "This is exactly the part I don't understand. You got mad at me for making decisions without talking to you first. When did you talk to me about this, Sophie? I didn't get a say one way or the other. You just walked away." Turning, he left as a tear trailed down her cheek. He didn't have time for this crap. He didn't want to care about her sad eyes when this was her damn fault. All he wanted to do was pick up a hammer and take out his frustrations on the guest room, but instead he grabbed his phone and dialed Ethan as he walked down the hall and sat on the couch.

"Cooke."

"Hey, it's Stone."

"How's Sophie?"

"Sore, but she'll make it."

"Good."

"Thanks for switching me up. I owe Jerrod and Hunter for splitting the concert tour."

"Family first,"

He grunted. He and Sophie were only family by a technicality at this point. "I'm hoping you can use your connections to look into something for me."

"What's up?"

"Sophie remembered bits and pieces of her accident last night and a little more today. She said she couldn't stop. She pressed the brake to the floor and even tried the emergency brake, but nothing happened."

"Huh," Ethan said.

"Exactly. I want someone to check the brake lines. I also want to know where Eric Winthrop is."

"You think it was him?"

"Absolutely. I took care of that car. There wasn't a damn thing wrong with those brakes. They were brand new. I changed them myself."

"Give me a couple hours to see what I can find out, and I'll get back to you."

"Thanks." He hung up, walking back to the bedroom when he should have gone to the trailer or basketball court or anywhere else but there. He glanced in at Sophie breathing deeply as she slept on her side of the bed. "Damn you, Soph," he murmured, clenching his jaw as he moved to stand next to her, staring at her gorgeous face despite the cuts and bruises, wishing he could turn his back as easily as she had. But he couldn't. He loved the hell out of her.

She'd come last night to say goodbye, but she was here now. He could give up and let her move on with her life, or he could fight for the woman lying in his bed. Sophie seemed more comfortable with the idea of being friends. If he needed to play the friend card for a while to win back what he wanted most, he would do it.

# CHAPTER THIRTY-THREE

SOPHIE OPENED HER EYES IN THE DIM LIGHT, SURPRISED BY how well rested she felt. She gave her shoulders a cautious wiggle, finding herself slightly less achy than she had been before she fell asleep. Frowning, she sniffed at the air, breathing in something spicy and delicious. Fried chicken maybe? Did Stone *cook*? She sat up slowly, taking several deep, agonizing breaths as she'd been directed to do in the hospital, and inched her way off the mattress, looking out the window at the sun sinking in the evening sky. How long had she been asleep? She glanced at the clock. "Seven *thirty*?" She'd slept for *hours*. Shadows replace bright sunlight, and the house was quiet. "Stone?"

He didn't answer.

She moved down the hall, treasuring the familiar surroundings she'd missed—the pretty living room. Even with dead plants and dust everywhere, it still felt like home.

She moved into the kitchen, stopping abruptly, taking in the transformation. "It's beautiful," she whispered, smiling sadly. The tile flooring, high-end white cabinetry, glossy granite counters, and intricate backsplash behind the range top was perfect. She walked to the shiny double ovens, brushing her fingers over the stainless steel handles. It was the dream kitchen she and Stone had designed together, and it wasn't hers to use.

Murphy yipped somewhere down the hall.

"Murph?" She turned, making her way back toward the bedrooms, giving a quiet tap on the closed guestroom door. "Murph? Stone?" She twisted the knob and stepped in, staring at Stone rolling a warm, sand-colored paint over the last exposed area of wall. "This looks great."

Stone whirled with the roller in hand, shirtless with his hair tucked behind a kerchief. "Jesus."

"Sorry." She moved further in, stepping on the cardboard protecting the new hardwood floors. "This is really nice, Stone."

He pulled the ear buds from his ears. "Thanks." He finished the spot, his muscles flexing with his movements, and set the roller in the bucket. "How are the ribs?"

She gently touched the bruising. "Not too bad." They were still awful, but complaining wouldn't fix it. "I feel like I have a little more energy."

"Good."

She wandered to the newly installed closet doors, glancing out the window toward the basketball court. "You've been busy. Everything's just about finished."

"Yeah. I wanted to get the last of it fixed up."

"The kitchen's amazing." She smiled. "It's everything I thought it would be."

"It'll be a good selling point. I'm putting the place on the market."

"What?" She stepped closer to him, her brows furrowed. "No. Why would you do that?"

He shrugged. "I wouldn't mind a change of scenery. Maybe I'll start flipping houses—live in them while I fix them up in my spare time, sell them, and move on to the next place."

That sounded awful. This was Stone's *home*. He belonged here. This secluded spot was perfect for him.

"You've worked so hard. I hope you'll change your mind."

He rubbed at the paint drop on his finger. "Probably not."

"Oh." Why did the idea of Stone not living on the cliffs make her want to cry?

"We should get you another pill, and I'll dish up some of the grub Sarah's mother dropped off."

"Aw, Janice cooked?"

"No, she said the lady at the gourmet store across from her shop made it, so it's guaranteed to be delicious."

She smiled. "That was very sweet for her to think of us."

"She dropped off a Caesar salad for tomorrow night from Sarah."

"I'll have to call them both and thank them."

"Your friends have spared us pizza deliveries and peanut butter and jelly for the next couple of nights."

"I'll go pull the stuff out of the fridge and get us drinks."

"Uh no." He moved to stand in her way. "You can go lay back down."

"I don't want to lay down." She hurt all over, but she would go stir crazy if she lay around endlessly. "Pulling a couple of containers out of the refrigerator isn't a big deal."

He blew out a deep breath, holding her gaze. "You know, Soph, for as sweet as you are you sure as hell have a stubborn streak."

She frowned. "I'm not stubborn. I can help out around here. I can't just stare at the ceiling forever."

"So sit on the couch and stare at the TV for a while. I'll bring you some dinner and a pill."

He was being so kind, and she'd upset him earlier.

"What if we eat at the table?" She'd missed their cozy evening meals. "Then I can admire all of the work you've done in the kitchen. The glass-fronted cabinets are so pretty."

"Why don't we save that for another night and eat on the couch so you can rest?"

Lying down would be better, whether she liked the idea or not. "Okay," she conceded. "Dinner in the living room it is."

His cell phone jingled with a text. He pulled the phone from his pocket, glanced at the readout, and cleared his screen.

A loud boom echoed down the road, and color filled the sky in the distance as the sun sank deeper. Today was the Fourth of July. What if Stone had plans he'd canceled because of her? "You know, now that I think of it, I'll probably have a quick bite to eat and head back to bed if you want to go out and enjoy the evening."

He shook his head. "I'm staying right here."

"It's a holiday, Stone. Ethan and Sarah are having a get-together. I'm sure Amber and Shane will be there. I know Abby and Jerrod were planning to go."

His gaze sharpened as he looked at her. "I'm not interested in seeing Amber tonight."

She still remembered how carefree his smile had been when he and Amber smiled at each other at Smitty's. "I'm really fine. I don't want to keep you from your life." She stepped around him on her way to the door. "In fact, I'm pretty tired again already."

He snagged her uninjured arm, stopping her. "You look wide awake to me."

"Nope." She looked away, aware that she wasn't a particularly good liar.

"I don't want to see Amber, Soph." He brushed his

thumb along her jaw. "I want to stay right here with you."

She stared at the floor, trying to ignore the way his touches sent her heart rate soaring, as they'd done when he helped her dress earlier.

"Let me put some food on plates for us while you relax and watch TV. Let someone take care of you for a change." He slid his palm down her arm.

She stepped back, needing her space. Being here was hard enough. Breathing him in and sleeping in their bed was almost more than she could handle. If he kept stroking her and staring into her eyes... "I've never done anything but let people take care of me."

He frowned. "That's bullshit."

"No. My mother took care of me, then Eric in his sick way, and you."

"Didn't you take care of your mother? And I'm pretty sure you kept this house running when we both lived here. If anyone took care of anyone, you took care of me." He took her hand, playing with her fingers. "I want to return the favor. Let me take care of you, Soph."

She had little resistance to Stone's sweet side. She pulled her hand from his, stopping his tender movements. "All right, but just for tonight. If you change your mind about going out—"

"I won't."

"But if you do—"

"I won't, Soph."

She nodded remembering a similar conversation the night he asked her to marry him. "Okay. I'll try to find something action-packed on TV."

"Sounds perfect."

~~~~

Stone set the last of the fixings Janice had brought by on the small table he'd made out of a piece of plywood and some two-by-fours. He put the napkins down, placing the silverware on top to keep the paper from blowing away in the wind, and stepped back, examining the bowls of fried chicken, potato salad, cantaloupe and watermelon balls, and plate of brownies for the makeshift picnic he'd put together on the fly. Nodding his approval, he lit the wood in the fire pit and sat down in the reclining lawn chair, adjusting the back for Sophie, making certain her view of the water in the distance would be nothing short of spectacular. "Awesome," he muttered. Good food, fireworks, and the ocean waves Sophie loved so much—the makings for a perfect evening for two.

And tonight would be perfect.

He sighed, rubbing at the back of his neck, remembering the conversation he and Sophie had in the guest bedroom just a few minutes ago. She thought he was interested in Amber. When Abby brought up the stupid idea at the office last night, he hadn't realized Sophie was the one who believed it. Ethan's former temp was hot and nice enough, but she wasn't Sophie, the only woman he wanted.

Sophie's abrupt departure was starting to make sense. More than once she'd told him she left to give him back his life. Apparently she thought she needed to move out of the way for Amber. And he couldn't necessarily blame her. He'd ignored Sophie at Ethan's party to talk ball with Amber, then the night at Smitty's when they won the pool game clearly left the wrong impression. Tonight he planned to set the record straight...subtly. He got to his feet, looking at Murphy konked out on the blanket from the meds the vet had given them to keep the puppy comfortable for the next couple of days, and walked inside through the French doors he'd installed in the kitchen. "Soph."

She struggled to sit up. "Yes? Do you need help?"

"Nope, but I want you to come with me." He took her hand, helping her to her feet, grabbing the pillow she'd been resting her head on.

"Come with you where?"

"You'll see." He snagged the flip-flops she'd forgotten in her rush to be gone all those nights ago. "Here. Put these on." He slipped one shoe on her foot then the next.

"Stone, what are we doing?"

"Enjoying the Fourth of July. Come on." He took her hand, leading her outside.

"*Wow.*" She smiled. "This looks so nice."

"We can eat and watch the fireworks if you want. They light them off on a barge not too far from here."

Her smile turned into a grin. "That sounds great."

He let loose a small sigh of relief. "Good. Let's get you settled on the chair."

She hesitated. "There's only one. What about you?"

"That's what the blanket's for." He carefully hooked his arm under her armpits, taking the brunt of her weight as he helped ease her down in the seat. "You doing okay?"

"Yes."

He settled the pillow behind her head. "You good?"

She nodded.

"So, do you want a little bit of everything? I didn't heat up the chicken. I guess it's good cold too."

"Cold friend chicken is delicious."

"All right then." He heaped a leg, breast, potato salad, and fruit on her plate. "Is that enough?"

Her eyes went huge and she chuckled. "That's more

than plenty."

"Too much?"

She shook her head slowly, looking at him the way she used to before everything changed. "It's perfect."

"Okay." He put a fork on her plate and handed it over.

"Thanks."

"You're welcome." He filled his own plate and dug in, groaning as he took a bite of crispy chicken that had just a hint of spicy heat.

"Good?"

"Delicious. Try." He picked up the chicken leg on her plate and held it to her lips, noting her struggle to balance her plate in her lap and eat.

She took a bite and rolled her eyes. "Mmm. Yum." She smiled, her lips shiny from the grease.

He grinned, relaxed in a way he hadn't been in too long. "You want more?"

"I can do it." She took the chicken piece from his hand, helping herself to a huge bite. "See?"

He chuckled. "I guess you showed me. Do you want your drink?"

She shook her head, still chewing.

"How about ice? Do you need another icepack for your ribs?"

"I need for you to eat your dinner and stop fussing over me." She reached out, touching his cheek.

"This is round-the-clock care, Soph. Your wish is my command."

"Such a good nurse." She grinned. "Maybe you could get me one of those bells."

He chuckled, loving that everything seemed right again. "I don't think so."

"I love the sound of the water," she sighed, staring out in the distance.

"It's nice."

The minutes passed in comfortable silence while they both ate their meals.

"I didn't realize I was so hungry." She wiped her hands and mouth on a napkin, "But now I'm stuffed."

"No brownie?"

She gave him a pained look. "Only if I want to be sick." A loud pop echoed in the air and she jumped, then laughed as the sky lit up with bright white sparkles. "I guess it's time for the fireworks."

"Here, let me have your plate." He set both on the table and moved closer to her side, leaning back on his hands as another burst of color filled the night.

"You look uncomfortable."

"Nah, I'm good."

"I can make room for you if you want."

She was offering to share. He wasn't about to miss an opportunity to be close to her. "Only if you're sure."

"Of course." She sat up, scooting forward carefully.

He snuck in behind her, settling her between his legs. "Here, lean back."

She rested her head in the crook of his neck, and he closed his eyes, savoring Sophie's warm body snuggled against him.

"Thank you."

"For what?"

"For taking such good care of me. This would be pretty awful if you weren't helping me."

"I'm happy to. I *like* taking care of you, Soph." He kissed her temple, wanting to wrap his arms around her, but took her hand instead, rubbing his thumb along her knuckles, watching the sky light up again and again as the breeze played with her hair, tickling his chest.

"This is a perfect way to spend the Fourth of July."

"Maybe next year we could give this a try without broken arms and bruised ribs."

She chuckled. "That would be nice."

He thought of her accident, knowing Eric was behind the whole thing, even though Ethan had yet to call him back with any new details. There were questions to be asked. Sophie had the answers he needed, but they would have to wait until tomorrow. Nothing was going to mess this up.

A large spray of fireworks, one after another, burst into life in a riot of colors as cheers erupted on the beach a hundred yards away. "I guess that's the end," he said.

"I guess so."

"Are you ready to go back in?"

She shook her head. "I miss this view. I don't think there's better for miles around. It breaks my heart to think you won't be here to enjoy it."

He couldn't stand the idea of staying here without her. He grunted, not willing to say anything else about the matter.

"Do you mind if we sit here for a while?"

The fire cast an orange glow against her soft skin as he held the woman he loved while the ocean waves crashed in the distance. "We can stay for as long as you like."

She settled her hand on top of his, and he laced their fingers, holding his breath, afraid he'd gone too far, but she didn't protest or pull away. He stared out into the night until the fire burnt down to embers, knowing Sophie had fallen asleep long ago. His cell phone rang, bursting his bubble of contentment. He answered before the first ring finished, not wanting to wake her. "Hello," he said quietly.

"Hey, Stone, it's Tucker."

"Hey, man, what's up?"

"Ethan contacted me earlier today about Sophie's brakes. I'm sorry I'm just getting back to you."

"It's fine."

"My buddy Detective Owens and I went down and took a look at Sophie's car before Wren and I headed over to Ethan and Sarah's."

"And?"

"Well, the car's a damn mess for starters. It took us a little while to make heads or tails out of what was what, but when we finally got in there we noticed a small tear in the line—must've created a slow leak."

His stomach roiled as he thought of how lucky Sophie was to be alive.

"Looks like wear and tear."

"Bullshit," he said, wincing, lowering his voice again. "I changed those lines not even a month ago. They're brand new. Eric Winthrop is behind Sophie's accident. Where the hell is he?"

"It's definitely not out of the question."

"Of course it's not. He's been messing with her for weeks—years. She filed for a restraining order, and then all hell breaks loose."

"I told Owens about the restraining order. He' looking into the situation closely, but he and Ethan have both confirmed Winthrop's in Bangor."

"You and I both know that doesn't mean jack shit."

"We *all* do. Owens was going to have Bangor PD bring Winthrop in for questioning."

"*Good.*"

"I'll have Owens get back to you with anything they find out."

"I appreciate it."

"Talk to you later."

"Bye." Sighing he put away his phone. Eric was in

Maine, but Sophie's brakes had been tampered with. If Eric didn't screw with the lines himself, he'd paid someone to. He glanced around in the dark surrounding them, not liking where this was going. He eased his way out from behind Sophie and picked her up, careful not to jar her ribs.

She opened her sleepy eyes. "Stone?"

"Shh. It's time for bed." He kissed her forehead.

"Okay." She closed her eyes again, snuggling her head on his shoulder.

He walked inside. "Come on, Murph."

Murphy followed.

He locked the door, scrutinizing the dark once again. Maybe pulling his gun from the lockbox wasn't such a bad idea.

~~~~

Eric opened his front door with a frown, looking at Clyde and Joe Burlington standing illuminated in the porch light. "Hello."

"Hi, Eric." Clyde shifted uncomfortably. "Uh, I hate to say it, but we're here on official business. We're going to need you to come down to the station with us."

"What the hell for?" But he already knew, and now Dylan Matthers was going to have to die.

"We have some questions we need to ask you."

He opened the door wider, ready to appeal to Clyde's deep sense of loyalty. "Come on in and ask them here. I'll pour you a drink or make you some coffee."

Clyde shook his head. "I'm afraid we can't. You'll need to come with us."

"What's this about?"

"The Los Angeles Police Department wanted us to bring you in and ask you a few questions about Sophie."

His heart kicked up to a wild beat. "Sophie?"

"She was in a pretty bad accident yesterday."

"Is she all right?"

"They say she is, but there were some problems with her car."

He struggled to bury the fear. Dylan Matthers was one thing, Sophie's accident and the LAPD another. How the hell had they tied the accident back to him? "I don't understand." He didn't bother to disguise the tremor in his voice. "Sophie has an accident and somehow I'm responsible?"

"It doesn't make much sense to me either." Clyde gave Eric's shoulder a solid pat of support. "Let's go get these questions out of the way, so we can get this off your plate."

"I need to call my attorney. First she accuses me of hitting her, and now murder? When is this going to stop?"

"We had no idea Sophie had it in her. We'll call Paul for you down at the station. Come on now."

"Okay." He stepped outside with Clyde and Joe, turning to lock the door, his hands shaking with waves of terror and fury as he twisted and pulled the key free. His "friend" had better call soon with good news. Sophie was ruining his life.

# Chapter Thirty-four

Sophie opened her eyes to the bright sunshine, staring out the window at the palm trees blowing in the ever-present ocean winds. She'd slept like a rock after spending the majority of the evening in the fresh air. Smiling, she remembered Stone's surprise Fourth of July picnic. He'd been so sweet to make their night on the cliffs special. She'd never enjoyed fireworks more with her head resting against his firm chest while they held hands in the dark.

She rolled to her back, letting out a small gasp of pain. She'd somehow ended up slightly on her side. Turning her head, she flinched, not expecting to see Stone lying next to her. She vaguely remembered him carrying her in from the lounge chair, laying her in the bed, and kissing her forehead as he covered her up. Then she'd fallen back into a deep sleep.

Her gaze traveled over his muscled shoulders and arms, his toned waist and black boxers uncovered. They'd woken together like this so many times, except he usually tucked her close in his arms and kissed her shoulder when he said good morning.

He stirred, opening his eyes, looking into hers. "Hey," he said, his voice rough with sleep and muffled by the pillow.

"Hi."

He repositioned his head. "How are your ribs?"

"They're okay." She stretched some, taking her required deep breaths, finding the pain bearable. "I feel like my mobility might be a bit better."

"That's good considering you fell asleep before we could get another pill in you." Yawning, he scooted closer, the warm skin of his stomach and chest pressing against her side as he rested his cheek on his hand, leaning on his elbow. "Do you want breakfast?" He slid his fingers along her ribcage, sending a rush of heat to her center with his teasing movements.

She needed to tell him to stop; she couldn't let him keep touching her like this, but she did nothing to move away, too weak with want for the man staring into her eyes. "Do you have any eggs?"

"If I do, they're the same eggs that've been here since you left."

She huffed out a laugh. "What have you been *eating*?"

"Stuff on the road mostly. I've been out of town more than I've been around, but when I *am* home Abby makes Jerrod bring me Tupperware containers with dinner in them."

She grinned, shaking her head. "She spoils you."

"You used to."

She shook her head again, her smile dimming. She didn't want to talk about "used to." "Making us a meal wasn't exactly five-star treatment."

His fingers moved to trace circles around her belly button. "You're a damn good cook, Soph."

She swallowed, wanting to shove his hand lower so he could touch her the way he did so expertly and put her out of her misery. "Thank you," she said, trying her best to focus on conversation instead of what Stone could be doing to her right here in this bed. "You should really take a couple of cooking classes. You have that beautiful new kitchen; it's a shame you're not using it."

"I didn't remodel the kitchen for me, Soph."

"This is your house isn't it?" She looked away, deliberately misunderstanding his meaning.

He took her chin between his fingers, forcing her gaze back to his. "It was ours for a little while."

But it wasn't any more. She pulled his hand away, attempting to sit up. "I should probably get Murphy his breakfast."

He rested his hand against her shoulder, holding her down. "I miss you, Soph. This place isn't the same without you and Murphy."

She shrugged away from his touch, no longer focused on her overactive libido. "I don't know what you want me to say."

"How about you miss me too."

"I—I do you miss you."

"So then why did you leave?"

She closed her eyes, sighing. "Because you have a right to your life."

"There was nothing *wrong* with my life. I liked my life just the way it was."

"Stone—" She rested her hand on his arm as her gaze wandered to the gun on the side table. "What are you doing with that?"

He looked over his shoulder. "Keeping it handy."

"Oh." She frowned. "Why?"

He sat up. "I've been wanting to ask you a couple of questions."

"Okay." She used his arm to pull herself up as quickly as her injuries would allow.

"Abby told me you've been working with Jeremiah lately."

"Yes," she hesitated. This was never a good subject for them.

"You've filed suit against Eric and have a

restraining order against him and the PI."

"Yes," she said again. "A temporary order."

"Good for you, Soph."

"Thanks."

"Has Eric given you any more trouble since the stuff he pulled a couple weeks ago?"

"No. He hasn't given me any more problems since David was arrested. He seems to have taken the hint—at least for now."

He huffed out a deep breath. "Maybe not."

Her brows furrowed again. "What do you mean?"

"Soph," he took her hand, pressing a kiss to her fingers in the way that always sent tingles rushing to her stomach. "Your accident... I don't think it was an accident."

She swallowed. "I'm not sure I understand."

"Your brake line had a small tear."

"Okay."

"That would allow the fluid to leak out slowly over time—probably a couple of days."

"Spell it out for me, Stone. I'm not a mechanic." Although she had an idea of what he was getting at, she didn't want to believe it.

"If you don't have brake fluid you can't stop. I think someone punctured your line. I replaced them myself before I gave you the car. They were solid."

She tucked her hair behind her ear. "Maybe—maybe they were just defective."

"Possibly, but it's interesting how they suddenly became defective after you filed for a restraining order."

She shook her head and rested her face in her hands as Eric's threats to kill her echoed through her head. "Why did I do this? Why did I start all of this?"

He eased her hands away. "Because you'll never be free of him until you finish it."

"Finish *it*, Stone, or is he going to finish *me*?" She pulled the covers back and got out of bed, staring out the window at the ebb and flow of ocean waves. "He told me this would happened. I never should've doubted he meant if for one second."

Stone walked around to where she stood, settling his hands on her shoulders. "We're going to figure this out. Tucker and his detective friend are working on it right now."

"Do you think that matters?" She turned to face him. "Eric thinks he's above the law. His money allows him to get away with far more than he should." She pulled away from him. "Why didn't I leave? I should have left. I should've gotten on the bus to Boise all those weeks ago."

"How would that be the solution, Soph?"

She crossed her arms at her chest. "He can't hurt me if he can't find me."

"You don't know that he wouldn't have."

"I was doing okay." She moved to sit on the edge of the bed. "I was making it."

"If hiding and sleeping in some disgusting motel in the ghetto are making it, sure."

"I was safer there than I am now. At least then I didn't have broken bones and bruises all over the place."

He sat next to her. "But look what you *do* have—friends, a job you love, your own shop. Murphy."

"I know." She sniffled back her tears. "I wouldn't trade any of it for anything. I just want to keep it." She brushed her wet cheek. "What are we going to do?"

"We're going to talk to Detective Owens. Bangor PD was going to look for Eric last night and bring him in for questioning."

"*Clyde* again?" She laughed incredulously. "Give me

a break."

"I know. Let's hear what Owens has to say, and we'll go from there." He took her face in his hands. "I'm right here, Soph. I told you I would be. You don't have to handle this on your own."

"Okay." She nodded, comforted by his reassurances until another thought occurred to her. "Wait, if Eric's in Maine, how did he mess with my brakes?"

"Let's talk to Owens."

~~~~

Stone walked closer to the bathroom door, making certain Sophie was still in the shower while he spoke with the detective.

"Unfortunately we're stuck," Owens said.

"That's bullshit," Stone spat, shoving his hand through his hair. "What happened with the interview?"

"Not much, but that shouldn't surprise you. Winthrop's got himself lawyered up. His attorney didn't let him say anything more than he had no idea what we were talking about."

"Fuck, man. I *know* he did this. I *know* it." He started back down the hall, trying to walk off the disgust. The bastard was going to get away with it.

"At this point it's impossible to prove, but I'm inclined to agree with you."

That didn't do them a damn bit of good. "So where does that leave us?"

"Not where I'd like. Bangor PD has agreed to keep Eric under surveillance, although I had to come down on Officer Clyde whoever-the-hell-he-is pretty hard to make that happen."

"Winthrop's got them in his back pocket."

"I noticed."

"Fuck." He sighed and bent down to pet Murphy, who stared up at him, wagging his tail.

"Look, there's no doubt physical abuse took place. We have the pictures you e-mailed over on file. And the stalking through his PI is inarguable, but Winthrop wasn't in Los Angeles when Sophie had her accident. What it comes down to is we have absolutely no proof tying him to a contract on her life."

Owens wasn't telling him anything he didn't know. He stood again, staring out the window as the detective continued on.

"Winthrop's attorneys are crying harassment. They're suggesting the tear in the brake line could've happened during the accident. Sophie's car is in such bad shape it would be hard for the prosecution to prove one way or the other."

Clenching his jaw, Stone closed his eyes. The waves of helpless anger left his head throbbing. "That's the most fucking stupid thing I've ever heard. The accident occurred *because* of the tear. She couldn't stop."

"I'm going to give it to you straight: We're dead in the water here. Sophie claims she couldn't stop, but Winthrop's defense team could easily argue inattentive driving. All they would have to suggest to a jury is she used faulty brakes as an excuse to cover her own ass. Your wife very well may be looking at a civil suit of her own. The driver of the other car's in just as bad a shape as Sophie is, if not worse. That's pretty much all the reasonable doubt a jury would have to hear to make them start to wonder."

This whole thing was a mess. "I took care of those brakes myself. There wasn't a damn thing wrong with them."

"Which strengthens their case even further until we can come up with proof otherwise."

The fucker had covered his tracks well. "This was a hit gone bad," he said with heat. "You and I both know it."

"But I need the evidence to back it up. We're talking attempted murder here. No one's going to touch this until there's something that'll make these charges stick. The State's not going to take on a case they're not going to win, especially with Winthrop's name attached to it."

"Subpoena his computers and phone."

"We already have. They were confiscated last night. Hopefully the lab boys find something."

"So we just sit back and wait in the meantime." He looked toward the bathroom when the water shut off.

"Pretty much. I'd suggest you keep your wife close for a while. We've got eyes on Winthrop. He'll make a mistake eventually. They all do."

Eric needed to mess up before Sophie was dead. "Let me know what happens with the lab."

"Will do."

"Thanks." He hung up, shaking his head. He'd never felt so powerless. Owens hadn't been any help. Basically he and Sophie were supposed to sit back and cross their fingers while Eric fucked with her life. His phone started ringing. Looking at the readout, he answered when Ethan's name popped up. "Yeah."

"Hey, it's Ethan."

"What's up?"

"How are things going with Owens?"

"They're not." He scratched at his jaw. "Winthrop did a hell of a job covering his tracks."

"How do you want to handle it?"

"I'll be sticking close to Sophie for a while until we see what's what. I don't know if the asshole's planning to back off now that the cops are on it or if he'll come after her again."

"You're pretty isolated up there. We could outfit the place with sensors and cameras for the time being. I can send Jackson and Collin over to set you up. It'll take a few hours."

"I won't turn it down."

"It's still pretty early. I'll send them over later this afternoon."

He looked at his watch, realizing it was only eight thirty. It felt like he'd been awake for hours. "Sounds good."

"If you want an extra set of eyes at night, Shane's pulling day duty for the next couple of weeks."

It was probably overkill, but he thought of Sophie's battered body. There wasn't anything he wouldn't do to guarantee her safety. "Sure, why the hell not?"

"Did you see the article?"

The muscle in his eye started twitching as he sighed, already knowing he didn't want to. "What article?"

"Toni Terrell took a slap at Sophie the way she did Abby."

He rested his head against the wall. The bitch reporter made a mess of Abby's life earlier in the year. Apparently now she was going to screw with Sophie's. "Fucking great."

"It's pretty rough."

"I'm looking forward to reading it." He sat down on the couch, opening his laptop.

"Let me know if there's anything else I can do to help."

"Thanks, man." He hung up, setting the phone on the cushion next to him and typed in the *Times* URL, immediately clicking on the fashion section. "Son of a bitch," he muttered, staring at the same picture he had seen of Sophie with Lily and Abby on the night of her debut, reading *Lily Brand's Freedom Line Disaster*.

Sophie's footsteps padded down the hall, the familiar scent of her soap and shampoo following her into the room.

He turned the laptop, angling the screen away from her view, looking at her as she stood before him with wet hair dripping on the soft fabric of her robe. "Hey. Did the shower help you relax any?"

She shrugged. "A little, I guess, although washing my hair one-handed was more challenging than I thought it would be."

"Maybe you'll let me help next time." He'd offered to hop in with her, but she'd turned him down.

She smiled. "I'll figure it out all by myself, I'm sure."

He smiled back. "I guess that's up to you."

She sat down next to him. "So what did the detective say?"

He turned the screen further away. "Not a whole lot. It's going to take some time to straighten all of this out."

She huffed out a breath. "What are we supposed to do in the meantime?"

"What we usually do. You'll get back to work when you're feeling up to it, and I'll tag along for a while until we know exactly what's going on."

"I'm going to have to go back to my apartment eventually."

He didn't want to think about that. "Eventually, but you need to stay with me for the time being."

She nodded. "Okay."

That was easier than he'd expected, but the next conversation wouldn't be. "Soph, Toni Terrell wrote an article about you in the *Times*."

"*What?*"

He turned the screen and she gasped, scooting closer.

"Lily Brand's *Freedom* line disaster?" Her shocked eyes met his. "I can't *believe* this." She moved closer, her leg and arm brushing his as they both read.

*Allegations of domestic violence against Eric Winthrop, famous painter and ex-fiancé...theft of thousands of dollars and warrant issued for her arrest...secret quickie wedding, marrying ex-mercenary...stalking private investigator...reckless driving almost causing a fatal accident.*

He continued scanning the shit article detailing Eric's suspensions and canceled art show, bringing up the restraining order, civil lawsuit, and pictures documenting brutal beatings, speculating their existence and whether or not they would be the end of Eric Winthrop's impressive career.

Sophie cleared her throat as she stood and started toward the bedroom.

"Soph." He followed her, capturing her wrist, turning her around.

She stared at him as tears rolled down her cheeks.

Damn it. He hated seeing that devastated look. "Come here." He pulled her into his arms.

She wrapped herself tightly around him as her breath shuddered in and out.

"I'm sorry, Soph." He kissed the top of her head, brushing his fingers through her hair.

"Why would she do that?" She eased back enough to meet his gaze.

"She's a terrible person."

"Doesn't she realize she's hurting the women and children Lily Brand is trying to help? If the public sees me as some irresponsible villain, they won't buy my jewelry, which means profits go down for Stowers

House."

He wiped away her tears. "Some people don't care. Clearly she doesn't."

"This is definitely going to damage my name, and possibly Lily and Abby's."

He stroked her cheeks. "Maybe for a little while, but I'm sure Lily's not going to put up with this. She knows your story, Soph. You're a survivor like Abby. You're just as strong."

Her lips trembled as her eyes softened. "Thank you."

"You, Lily, and Abby will turn this around. I have no doubt in my mind."

"He's going to see that article. Eric's going to see it and retaliate again."

He sighed. "Yeah."

She blew out a breath, pressing her forehead to his chest.

He lifted her chin. "But this time he'll have to come after both of us. We're going to fix this once and for all, Soph." He pressed a kiss to her lips and pulled her close again, holding on. He wouldn't stop until they did.

~~~~

Eric walked up his front steps, glancing over his shoulder at the unmarked police car down the road. He'd notice the black vehicle sitting by the curb this morning when he left to run errands, then he spotted it again at the library several minutes ago, and now here by his own place of residence. It was tempting to march over to the late model Chevy, pound on the glass, and demand the nosy bastards get the hell out of here, but his attorney warned him not to add any fuel to LAPD's fire.

Clyde had hinted that surveillance was a likely possibility, but he hadn't expected the men he played golf with to betray him. They'd turned tide, siding with Sophie, helping her try to build a case against him. He opened the door and shut himself inside, resting his body against the solid wood. His heart pounded and his breath puffed in and out with a deep rage and fear he hadn't been able to shake. His life was falling apart around him—videotaped interviews with the police, phone and computer confiscations here at the house and gallery, and the article Toni Terrell published this morning in the *Times* that the *Bangor Chronicle* picked up and printed. Everything he'd been able to keep carefully under wraps was now out in the open for everyone to see.

The town was treating him like a criminal. Few people shook his hand at the diner during the breakfast rush. He'd caught more than one person eyeing him while they cut into their eggs or French toast. No one was on his side, and it was all Sophie's fault.

Swearing, he hurried upstairs, walking into the closet, pulling the phone the cops hadn't known about from the pocket of one of his navy blue sports coats. He dialed the number he'd memorized, waiting through three rings.

"Yeah."

"I want that thumb drive, and I want it *now*."

"Not gonna happen. There are people swarming McCabe's place—putting in cameras and sensors."

He pounded his fist against the cedar shelving. "Goddammit!"

"This is starting to get a little more complicated than I want to deal with."

"I paid you."

"Half, which takes care of Sanders."

"You owe me Sophie and the thumb drive."

"I owed you the blond and thumb drive before the cops and reporters got involved. You shoulda let me put a bullet in her head."

"So do it. Fucking shoot her and make her disappear."

"Mmm, it's gonna cost you more."

He pulled the phone away and set it back against his ear. "*More*? I'm giving you half a million as it is."

"Another two-fifty and your ex won't be a problem by the end of the week."

"Tomorrow."

"It'll happen when I see the opportunity."

"As long as you find it before the week is out."

"Get me the money."

"I can't just fly off to New York." He glanced through the doorway of the large walk-in closet, through the windows in the bedroom. "I've got cops following my every move." And it wouldn't be long before the reporters started knocking on his door.

"Fine. I'll finish the deal, but if you even think about blowing me off, I'll take care of you next."

"You'll get your money. Just make Sophie vanish."

"You got it."

He hung up, shoved the phone back where he'd taken it from, and started downstairs toward the bar. *Never* had anyone told him what to do. He was always in control, but another quarter million was well worth Sophie's murder. He poured a drink, toasting the men in the black vehicle, deciding that having them close by wasn't such a bad idea after all. When Sophie turned up dead it would be all but impossible to pin it on him. The cops in Bangor and LA wouldn't be able to argue that he hadn't been right here.

# CHAPTER THIRTY-FIVE

SOPHIE PULLED THE ROAST FROM THE OVEN, MAKING certain she had an extra good grip on the pan with her casted arm jammed awkwardly in the oven mitt. She set the herb-crusted pork on the platter she'd readied, ignoring the sharp twinges plaguing her ribcage when she moved too quickly to turn off the burner under the steamed green beans.

Over the past couple of days her pain had lessened from excruciating to a constant annoying ache and her mobility had improved enough to allow her to tackle several light household chores and get back to McCabe Jewelry part-time, not that being there seemed to matter much. Few customers had walked through the doors since Toni Terrell created a media firestorm with her Sunday morning article. Both Lily and Abby had assured her the worst would blow over before long, but so far the press wasn't letting up. Journalists and photographers camped out in front of her shop then followed her and Stone wherever they went, whether it be the doctor's for her follow up examination or the grocery store to buy food for dinner.

The only place she and Stone were able to escape the constant scrutiny was here on the cliffs, where no trespassing signs were posted throughout his property. He'd borrowed Bear and Reece from Ethan Sunday afternoon and had no qualms about calling the cops and pressing charges against the first reporter who'd been foolish enough to knock on his front door. They hadn't had problems since—at least here. Stone's home had quickly become their oasis from the chaos of scandal.

The tabloid and entertainment rags had been relentless, posting daily speculations as to whether the talented, generous artist from the quaint New England town could possibly have abused UConn's former basketball superstar-turned-jewelry designer. More than one article had compared side-by-side pictures of her and Eric posing at his gallery events in stuffy, elegant clothing to present-day photos of her and Stone walking to his Mustang among the swarm of paparazzi, their arms wrapped around each other's waists with Stone in jeans, a polo, and sunglasses while she wore the trendy attire she'd grown accustomed to. The stark difference between Eric's snooty suits and ties and Stone's casual bad-boy looks fueled the flames of controversy higher.

More than one journalist had dug into Stone's past, shining a light on his troubled childhood and time in the Middle East. They vilified him as the selfish mercenary who'd cashed in on the war, suggesting that he was a harmful influence on Lily Brand's talented new darling, leading her down the wrong path to false accusations. Somehow Stone was getting more bad press than Eric, and Stone was the one who'd *helped* her.

She plopped garlic mashed potatoes into a serving dish, feeling a sudden rush of anger. Why did Eric constantly get away with everything? He'd had someone tamper with her brakes, and *she* was being cast as some irresponsible ditz who'd nearly caused a fatal accident. Was she not the one with the broken arm and bruised ribs?

She slapped the platter on the table and twisted at

the waist for the side dishes, wincing with the sharp pain. "Damn," she muttered, turning carefully, her eyes welling with frustrated tears as she glanced at the new shade blocking her view of the water beyond. Every window had been covered, preventing anyone from seeing in or she and Stone from looking out. Video equipment had been brought in, filling every available inch of free space with monitors and cables running across the floors so Stone and Shane could keep a lookout for the mystery man who still might be trying to kill her.

She closed her eyes, gripping the cool granite countertop, trying her best to pull herself together. The new life she'd built had quickly turned into the nightmare she thought she'd left behind. No matter the steps she'd taken to escape, Eric was still in charge. She was as afraid now as she had been the night she ran away, if not more. The constant need to look over her shoulder plagued her as much as it had months ago. She'd been gone several weeks, yet she walked on eggshells and was as alert to danger as if she turned her back on Bangor yesterday.

Taking a steadying breath, she faced the table and the cooling dinner she'd prepared, wanting to focus on what she had right this moment. She was safe for the time being. There was food on the table and a hungry man in the living room waiting to be called. "Time to eat."

She heard Stone's grunt of response and peeked in at him fiddling with one of the dozens of wires attached to the flat screen as she sat down, pretending she had an appetite for the meal she'd cooked.

~~~~

"Smells good," Stone said as he walked into the kitchen, checking out the spread Sophie had prepared. "Looks even better." He took his seat across from her.

"Thank you," she replied, sending him a small smile. "How about some mashed potatoes?" She reached for his plate and cringed as she stretched forward.

"How about I give you a hand instead." He grabbed her plate, putting sliced pork, mashed potatoes, and green beans on her dish.

"Thanks."

"You're welcome." He helped himself to huge portions, eagerly anticipating Sophie's latest meal. He'd eaten very well since she declared herself more than capable of cooking a few simple dinners. Taking a bite, he groaned, savoring the melt-in-your-mouth meat with a sensational rosemary and thyme flavor. "God, this is amazing, Soph." He cut another piece, scooping up fluffy potatoes to sample as well, pausing with the fork at his lips when he realized she had yet to start eating. "You gonna have some?"

"Sure." She picked up her silverware, stabbed a green bean, and put it in her mouth as she glanced at him with miserable eyes.

"What's up?"

"Nothing."

He raised his brow. They both knew that was bullshit.

She huffed out a breath. "I guess I'm just getting tired of everything that's going on."

She'd been a champ putting up with the assholes who'd followed them around constantly. Despite the smear campaign and backlash to her business, she went into work every day, and she had yet to complain about the equipment crowding their house. All in all she was handling the press and potential threat to her life incredibly well, but as he studied her closely, he realized the stress was starting to eat at her. "It sucks, but you're hanging in there."

"I just hate—I hate that the media has dragged you into this."

He shrugged. If he was taking some of the heat, they were leaving her alone.

"It's a big deal, Stone," she said, her voice riddled with frustration, pushing away from the table. "Eric's the bad guy here, and they've made you look like the problem."

He hooked his legs around the feet of her chair, pulling her back in. "I'm not ashamed of anything I did overseas. I had a job to do, did it well, and was paid accordingly. I know who I am. I don't give two shits about what they write or say about me."

"You saved me."

"And I'd do it again." He held her gaze, making sure she understood he meant it.

She blinked back tears as she took his hand and pressed his palm to her cheek. "I'm so lucky I have you. You're the best thing that's ever happened to me." Her eyes widened as she stared at him, immediately releasing him from her grip.

He swallowed, relieved by her clearly unintended confession, debating whether he should press his advantage. He picked up his fork instead and took another bite, now one hundred percent certain Sophie had left him because she thought he wanted Amber. When he fixed things between them once and for all she wouldn't be thinking of Eric or the media. He had every intention of reminding her she was the only woman he needed in his life. By the time he finished she would no longer doubt that they belonged together. "Eat, Soph. This is too good to throw away."

She picked up her fork, darting him a glance as she took a decent bite of pork and potatoes. Swallowing, she cleared her throat in the tense silence. "Is Shane coming over tonight?"

"Yeah. He should be here pretty soon."

She sipped her water. "We can't keep asking him to stay over."

"I'll ask for whatever I have to until we know for sure you're safe."

"That could take longer than a few nights, right? If there actually is someone trying to hurt me, he might be waiting for you to let your guard down."

He'd driven himself crazy with the same thoughts, so he decided to focus on each day as it came instead. "The cops are working on it."

"What about your job? You can't stay by my side forever. Ethan needs you."

"And so do you." He took another bite and swallowed. "We're going to wait and see what the police come up with. They're watching Eric in Bangor, and Owens is doing what he can on this end."

She pressed her lips together, releasing a long breath through her nose. "It doesn't seem like enough."

It sure as hell didn't. "But it's what we've got for now." He brushed the tips of her fingers with his, doing what he could to reassure her. "This is what I do for a living, Soph. You've gotta trust that me and the guys know how to keep you safe."

"I do."

"Good—" He stopped as the sensor started beeping on the central panel, alerting him to a breech on the property. Rushing to his feet, he hurried into the living room and activated the main switch on the keypad, immediately flooding the majority of his land with bright light from the fixtures Jackson and Collin had installed. He checked for any movements on the dozens of images filling the monitor.

"What is it?" Sophie followed. "What does the red light mean?"

"One of the motion sensors activated back by the canyons." He scrutinized the footage, backing up the pictures from the last five minutes. He spotted the hint of shadow at the edge of the screen. Someone was here, or had been. He glanced at his watch and grabbed his phone, dialing Owens when he realized Shane wasn't due for another twenty minutes.

"Detective Owens."

"Owens, it's Stone McCabe. I need a car out here to the house."

"What's going on?"

"We have potential activity along the back perimeter of my property by the canyons. The motion sensors activated, and I've picked up a shadow on the cameras."

Owens muttered something. "There's a patrol car in the area. They'll be right over."

"Thanks." He hung up and rewound the footage again, catching the quick, dark spot that vanished as soon as the lights glowed bright.

"Is he here?"

"There's an officer on the way," he muttered, sitting down. He focused on his job, zooming in on the movement.

"So he is?"

He glanced up, realizing Sophie stood at his side, pale, her arms crossed tightly over her chest. "Hey." He pulled her into his lap, brushing his fingers through her hair. "It's probably nothing. For all I know there's a wild animal running around, or some dumbass reporter trying to be sneaky. We're just checking to be on the safe side."

She nodded as his phone rang.

"Yeah."

"It's Shane. I'm turning up your road. Why am I following a cruiser?"

"One of the sensors activated."

"I'll go out with the officer and see what's up."

"I appreciate it." He hung up, relieved to know he had backup for the night. "That was Shane. The cops are pulling in, and so is he. We've got this, Soph. I'm not going to let anything happen to you."

She held herself tense. "I know."

His phone rang again as he pulled her closer against his chest, staying mindful of her still-tender body. "Yeah."

"It's Shane. We found a few footprints."

He clenched his jaw instead of swearing, not wanting to frighten Sophie. "Okay."

"We're going to look around and follow the tracks."

"Let me know when you start heading back."

"I will."

He stared at the monitor watching Shane and the officer disappear down into the canyons beyond his property. It would be interesting to see what they found. He'd told Sophie it was probably just a reporter, but what would someone searching for the next Sophie McCabe story be doing all the way out there?

# CHAPTER THIRTY-SIX

SOPHIE SENT THE FINAL SCREW INTO THE CLOSET WALL, securing the last of the shelves in place. She stepped back, examining her work with a critical eye, and nodded. "Not bad," she muttered to herself as she turned to Stone. "Okay. I'm finished."

Stone glanced over his shoulder from his perch on the stepladder, twisting the bulb into the pretty new fixture he'd installed. "Looks good."

"Thanks. This was fun."

"I'm glad you think so. Maybe I can get you to help me plan the gardens for the patio I'm going to put in off the master bedroom."

The idea of another creative challenge was very appealing. Somehow Stone had known she needed a distraction from the monotony of another night stuck behind drawn shades and locked doors. After dinner he'd taken her hand and pulled her down the hall to the guestroom, announcing that they had a project to take care of. He could have easily completed the job within minutes, but he'd let her help, patiently teaching her how to drill pilot holes and insert toggle bolts to mount the shelves. "I could do that."

He smiled as he secured the last of the three bulbs in place. "I have some rough sketches drawn up."

"You'll have to show me." She glanced toward the covered window, ignoring the claustrophobic sensation of late. Outside the stars twinkled and the quarter-moon shined bright, but she wasn't able to see it. The lack of fresh air and freedom to come and go as she pleased was starting to make her edgy. Ever since the light activated on the panel two nights ago, she'd been tense. Both Stone and Shane had assured her there was nothing to worry about, but she'd heard them muttering quietly on several occasions, and she couldn't help but notice that Stone wore his gun at all times—not just when they were out in public.

"There's one last thing to do," he said as he got down.

Frowning, she turned to the closet. "What's that?"

He grabbed the level and came up behind her, his chest bumping her back as he set the large piece of metal on the shelf and bent at the knees into a slight crouch. The green liquid in the center of the level stayed even between the two black lines. "Way to go, Soph," he said close to her ear, his warm breath tickling her skin, making her shiver.

"Thanks."

"It looks like we have a bonafide handywoman in the house." He stepped back.

"That's Ms. Fixit to you." She smiled as she turned, crashing into him. "Sorry."

He brushed his fingers down her bare arms, holding her gaze. "No problem."

She swallowed as heat rushed along the path his hands had taken. "Thanks again for letting me help." She smiled, trying to keep things casual. Stone's gentle touches and long stares were becoming harder to resist.

He slid his thumb along her knuckles. "It's nice having the company."

Her heart fluttered every time he *did* that. "I should probably..."

He lifted her hands, pressing his lips to her fingers. "You don't want to help with the cover plates?"

Her thoughts of escape disintegrated. "Uh, the what?"

He nuzzled her uncasted wrist, tickling sensitive skin with the scruff along his jaw as he held her other arm, nipping at the pads of her fingers with his teeth. "The cover plates for the light switches."

She exhaled a shaky breath, shuddering from his relentless assault.

"Soph." He closed the distance between them, touching his mouth to hers in a fleeting whisper, snagging her bottom lip, tugging.

She whimpered as he moved in for more, rubbing, teasing, coaxing her mouth into following his as he clutched at her hair. Her breathing grew ragged as she trailed her palms up the sides of his waist, waiting for him to finally take her under. For weeks she'd yearned for this, to be in his arms again...but this was wrong. This couldn't happen. "Stop." She stepped back. "I'm going to—I'm just—I need to..." She started toward the door.

"Wait." He snagged her by the elbow.

"I can't." She pulled free of his hold and hurried across the hall, closing herself in the bedroom, leaning against the door. This was *crazy*. All of this was too much—hit men, sensor panels, bodyguards, the media...*Stone*. She was weakening, caving into her wants at a time when she needed to stay strong. Spending every waking moment with him wasn't helping, nor did the fact that they shared a bed each night so Shane could have the couch.

But none of that mattered. Awkward sleeping arrangements and hours in Stone's presence didn't change the facts. They were divorced. Their marriage had ended because that made the most sense. If she hadn't been in an accident they wouldn't even be together right now. They lived separate lives—or typically did, and would again. She huffed out a breath as she paced the room, nibbling her nail, worrying that no matter how many times she reminded herself of their reality, she couldn't stop wanting him.

She glanced toward the window, craving a long walk on the beach, desperate to clear her crowded mind. Just ten minutes alone with her feet in the warm sand... But that wouldn't be happening anytime soon.

"Soph?" Stone called through the door, giving a quick knock before he walked in.

Whirling, she faced him. "I can't do this right now."

He shut the door behind him. "Soph—"

"Not right now, Stone," she said with a hint of panic, already knowing she had little resistance left against his searing looks and mind-numbing kisses. "I need a few minutes."

Clenching his jaw, he held her gaze. "Tell me you don't want this."

"I—I don't want this," she whispered, trying to convince herself as much as him.

"Tell me you don't want me."

She swallowed. "I don't want you."

"Why don't I believe you?"

She turned away. "I don't know."

He came up behind her, sliding his fingers through her hair. "I want this, Soph." He kissed the back of her neck. "I want you." He pressed his lips to her skin again as he wrapped his arms around her waist.

She clutched at his forearms. "We can't do this."

"Why?" He started on the bottom buttons of her pale-green shark-bite tank.

"Because Shane's just down the hall."

"He's watching TV."

"I'll be leaving when all of this is over." Even as she

spoke, she settled her head against his chest, her body a traitor to what she knew shouldn't be happening. "We'll both go back to our own lives."

"It doesn't have to be that way." He traced the lobe of her ear with his tongue while he parted her shirt, sliding teasing palms over her bra.

Trembling, she turned, staring into his deceptively lazy eyes. "This doesn't work. *We* don't work, Stone."

"We both know that's not true." His lips cruised over her temple and along her forehead. "God, Soph, I need you."

No matter how she tried to tell herself she didn't, she needed him too. She stepped closer instead of away as he cupped her face and kissed her, plundering as if he'd starved since the last time. She hooked her fingers into the top of his jeans, meeting his hungry demands as feverishly as he gave them.

He hummed in his throat, his muscles shuddering as she lifted his shirt, touching his stomach and pecs.

"Lay down with me, Soph," he murmured against her mouth, sending her top to the floor, walking with her to the bed, easing her down. "Are your ribs okay?"

She nodded, pulling his mouth back to hers as he settled himself on top of her.

"I need to touch you." He unfastened her bra, lowering his head to tease her nipples with wet, whispering slides of his tongue. "So soft."

She closed her eyes, sucking in a breath as sparks of anticipation started deep in her center.

He pulled at the snap on her denim capris and tugged down the zipper, getting to his knees, sliding off her pants and taking her panties with them.

She bit her lip and parted her legs, watching as he freed himself from his clothes, ready for him to enter her. Opening her arms, she invited him back.

He took his place on top of her, capturing her mouth while he pushed himself deep inside, swallowing her cries with the power of her climax. Before she could fall, he began moving slowly, lazily, bringing her up high with each thrust, taking her over again. He pressed his lips to her neck, her jaw, staring into her eyes as he brought his lips back to hers, kissing her endlessly until his breathing grew choppy and his movements jerky.

She cupped his face in her hands, holding his gaze as he gave into his own needs.

Filling her, he let out a raspy groan as he gasped for air, resting his forehead in the crook of her neck.

She'd missed this—what he could do to her, the connection. It was impossible to regret something she would happily repeat again. She slid her hands up and down his back, wondering where this left them.

~~~~

Stone lifted his head, kissing Sophie's shoulders, her neck, and jawline, staring into her eyes as he lay inside of her. Not ready to break their connection, he adjusted himself slightly, careful to keep his weight on his arms and off her bruises. "Every time, Soph. Every time you destroy me."

"I can easily say the same thing." She smiled, tracing her finger over his bottom lip. "Sometimes I wish I didn't know."

He frowned, nibbling the tip of her finger between his teeth. "Know what?"

"The way it is. How we are when we're together."

He captured her mouth once more, hungry for her flavor. "That doesn't have to change. I don't want this to be a one and done."

"We shouldn't have ended up here again."

"Why not?" He tried to keep the frustration out of his voice as he stroked his thumb along the side of her bicep. They *had* something. This was so much more than just sex and a business arrangement.

She shrugged. "I don't know. I thought we were both trying to move on. It's hard to do that if we're doing this."

"So that's what this was, blow off a little steam and go our separate ways? Is that all it has to be?"

She shook her head with another shrug. "I don't know how this works. I've never been in this situation before."

"Let's just lay it all out on the table." They would either figure this out once and for all, or he didn't know what they would do. "This thing between us, most relationships don't start out the way ours did."

"No. Our situation is pretty unique." She gave him a small smile.

"But somehow it worked. We were making it work." He tucked several strands of hair back behind her ear. "We had a couple of rough spots, but otherwise we were happy, weren't we? Or was that just me?"

"I was happy. I liked us until I realized maybe you didn't." Swallowing, she looked away. "I didn't have a right to hold you back from your life, Stone." She met his gaze again. "You were doing me a favor."

How did he make her understand that she *was* his life? "I stopped seeing our arrangement as a favor a long time ago. Were you happy being married to me, Soph?"

Her fingers paused against his back, then kept going. "Yes but it was foolish to continue the way we were.

"*Why*? What changed?"

419

"I think we needed different things."

"I think we let people—Eric and Amber—get in the way of what we had."

She evaded eye contact again.

He tilted her chin until she had no choice but to look at him. "Amber likes baseball, and she's nice enough, but she's not you. I love *you*, Soph. That's why I want to be married to you."

Surprise flickered in her eyes as they filled with tears.

"I love you, Sophie," he whispered, touching his lips to hers.

"I—I didn't know."

"I'm sorry I never told you." He kissed her. "Somewhere along the way I realized I've been crazy about you pretty much from the beginning." He kissed her, feeling her trembling lips. "All of this is new for me. I've never felt the way I do about you, for anyone."

"I love you too."

He smiled, relieved to hear the words. "That's a damn good thing."

She grinned. "I'm glad you think so."

He rested his forehead against hers, ready to confess the rest. "I, uh, I kind of need to tell you something."

"What is it?"

"I never sent the papers back to your attorney for filing." He held his breath as she blinked.

"You didn't?"

He shook his head. "I signed them, but I couldn't do it. I can't let you go, Soph."

"Kevin said everything was all set."

"I don't know what to tell you."

She chuckled. "All these weeks we've been apart..."

"I don't want to live my life without you. I want you

to marry me again."

She frowned. "But I thought you just said you didn't dissolve our marriage."

"I didn't. The courthouse deal was a quick fix for our pinch. The vows we took are real, but when I look in your eyes and say them this time, I want you to know I mean them. If you want, we can have a ceremony in front of our friends."

"How can I say no?" Laughing, she threw her arms around him. "Yes, of course."

"Stone, Sophie, I'm taking Murphy out," Shane hollered down the hall.

"Okay," they said at the same time.

Sophie grinned. "We should get up."

He grabbed her hand and kissed her fingers, not wanting the moment to end. "How about a movie?"

She nodded. "Sure. We should probably let Shane pick—"

Murphy's vicious barking carried through the window.

Stone pulled away from Sophie, rushing out of bed. Pulling on his pants, he grabbed his gun. "Stay here." He opened the bedroom door and hustled to the living room as Shane pulled a growling Murphy back into the house, locking up behind him. "What the hell's going on? Did you see something?"

"No." Shane moved to the monitors. "But Murphy did."

Stone joined him, bending close to the screens, studying the footage outside.

"I was watching TV when Murphy started whining. I figured he had to go to the bathroom. I gave the monitor a quick scan while I leashed him up. As soon as I opened the door he went ape shit and started pulling me toward the canyons.

Stone's eyes immediately moved to the footage back by the area where the footprints were found two nights ago. He rewound the tape, but there was no one there.

"Nothing's activated, but he's out there. He has to be," Shane muttered.

"Let's call Owens—" He turned when Murphy whined, wagging his tail. Sophie stood by the couch, her hands clasped and her face pale.

"What's going on?" She crouched down, petting Murphy as he nuzzled her cheek, leaning against her.

He hated seeing her afraid. "Murphy must've smelled something when he was outside."

"The man who caused my accident is out there."

"Not necessarily—"

She stood. "Yes he his."

He sighed, not bothering to argue when he would only be lying. "Shane's calling Detective Owens." He gestured to their friend, who'd turned his back to talk to the detective on the phone. "Nothing activated, so he's not on the property."

She crossed her arms. "What are we going to do?"

He walked to her, pulling her close, kissing the top of her head. "Wait and see how Owens wants to handle this."

"Okay. Thanks." Shane hung up and turned, facing them. "Owens will send a unit out to check the area, but that's all they can do without any confirmed activity."

He struggled to keep his frustration at bay, giving a quick nod of his head, not wanting to scare Sophie any more than she already was. "See? Even the cops aren't too worried about it." He took her hand. "Let's stick to the plan and start a movie while we wait to see what the cops find."

Shane nodded. "Sounds good to me. I'm pretty sure it's my turn to pick."

"We'll go make the popcorn," Stone added.

"I don't want popcorn," Sophie said.

"I do." He could care less about popcorn or the damn movie, but he wanted the fear to vanish from her eyes. Keeping her busy helped.

"I wouldn't mind popcorn—with real butter if you've got it," Shane chimed in. "Or maybe the caramel stuff you put on that one batch."

Sophie nodded, too polite to tell their guest no. "Sure."

He walked with her to the kitchen, helping her pop the kernels old-fashioned-style on the stovetop and melt butter and brown sugar together. As he did, he glanced at the monitor in the living room to see two officers moving toward the canyons in the right quadrant of the screen.

# CHAPTER THIRTY-SEVEN

RAIN POURED IN BLINDING SHEETS AS HE FOUGHT HIS WAY up the canyon pass. Sliding back a step, he caught himself on a sharp rock, swearing when he scraped his palm. He wiped the thick mud on his shirt and kept going, determined to finish this once and for all. He'd waited for days, holding out for the perfect opportunity to deal with Sophie McCabe, but she was never alone. Paparazzi loitered outside her jewelry store on a daily basis, and once she hunkered down in her ex's house for the night it was impossible to get a clear shot on her through the blackout shades.

Tonight, shades, surveillance cameras, and bodyguards wouldn't be getting in the way. The weather sucked, but he was going to use the downpour to his advantage. There would be no footprints to track, and his scent would be difficult if not impossible to follow when the cops realized they had a triple murder on their hands. The contract was for Sophie, but Eric would be getting a three-for-one deal.

The stupid bastard was crazy, calling everyday with threats, ranting his demands. If Winthrop kept it up he was going to get them both caught. It was bad enough he was dealing with security lights, barking dogs, and Los Angeles PD every time he came up here attempting to do his job. The last thing he needed to worry about was the lunatic artist with the big mouth. Eric Winthrop was a loose end he would have to deal with after he finished up and collected his cash.

Slightly winded, he made it to the top of the rise, hunkering low by one of the bushes, careful to avoid the cameras scattered around the property. He blinked rapidly as water dripped in his eyes, noting that the second vehicle belonging to the man who came to stay in the evenings wasn't there. "Perfect." Time to make this happen. He inched forward, stopping shy of the sensors he'd tripped the other night, lifted his weapon, aimed, fired, and hit the first video camera and floodlight, then the second set, third, and fourth. He sprinted forward, well aware that the clock was officially ticking. He came to a stop by the Mustang and fired on the front door's doorknob, rendering the lock useless, weakening the structure for a quick entrance.

Staring through his scope, he moved forward again, entering the dark, quiet house.

~~~~

Stone snuggled Sophie on the couch while he watched TV and she flipped through one of the hundred bridal magazines Abby had dropped off at McCabe Jewelry. Not even twenty-four hours had passed since he and Sophie decided to do the whole ceremony thing, and she and her pal were in full planning mode, calling each other at least every half hour with some random idea.

"What do you think of these hydrangeas?"

He glanced down at the deep pink flowers she pointed to on the page. "I think I like whatever you do."

Smiling, she rolled her eyes. "That's what you keep saying."

She'd wanted his thoughts on cream-colored candles versus white, traditional cake toppers or something a little more fun, invitations, and the little gift deals for their guests—and that was just in the last fifteen minutes. They were having a small ceremony on the beach and the after-party here on the cliffs in some rented tent. Why the hell they couldn't have burgers on the grill instead of a sit-down meal was still a mystery to him. He kissed the tip of her nose. "What's wrong with that?"

"It's not very helpful. You're allowed to have an opinion. This is your wedding too."

"Soph." He pulled her closer, wrapping his arm tighter around her. "You've got great taste. I know whatever you pick out is going to be beautiful."

"Thank you, but I want you to be happy as well."

"Are you my wife?"

"Yes."

"Do you love me?"

"You know I do."

"Then I'm happy."

"Aww, you're so sweet." She gripped his jaw gently, kissing him.

He pulled her back for more before she could ease away. "How sweet?"

She grinned. "I have three weeks to pull this wedding together. I'll show you how amazing I think you are later."

"Promise?"

She slid her tongue along his bottom lip. "Absolutely."

"I'm going to hold you to that."

"I hope you will." She resettled herself against his side, her smile dimming as she glanced toward the monitor before giving her attention back to the magazine.

He brushed his thumb along her wrist, wanting to soothe. He'd caught her looking at the screen more than once since they got home. He'd suggested dinner out to help chase away the tension, but she'd turned him down, wanting to get home and pour over all the stuff Abby gave her.

"Do you want me to check on the roast or something? It smells like it's ready."

"Mmm, no thanks." She shook her head as she bookmarked the page with the hydrangeas. "We've got at least another forty-five minutes before we eat."

He was looking forward to tender roast beef and vegetables on this raw, soggy night. "Okay." He settled back against the cushion, sighing, when his cell phone started ringing. Tipping the phone, he peeked at the readout. Shane. "Yeah," he answered.

"Hey, man. I'm running behind. The rain's pouring and the traffic's awful. I'm probably fifteen or twenty minutes out yet."

He glanced at his watch. "No problem. How'd the meeting go?"

"Looks like I've officially been assigned to the Appalachia Project."

He'd dodged a six-month stint in rural Western Kentucky, and he couldn't say he was sorry after the nightmare reports that had come back time and time again. "Should be fun."

"Can't wait. Sounds like it'll be...interesting."

"When do you leave?"

"Couple days after your wedding."

"That's right around the corner."

"Tell me about it. We'll talk when I get there. I can't see for shit. I just wanted to let you know I'm on my way."

"Thanks. See you soon." He looked at Sophie, who was staring at him with troubled eyes. He shoved his phone back into his holder, next to his gun.

"Is everything okay?"

"Yeah. Shane's running late. The rain's slowing him up a bit."

"Oh."

He pulled the magazine from her white-knuckle grip. "Soph, relax. Everything's fine." Despite the fun of wedding plans, she'd been on edge since the cops drove away last night. They hadn't found anything new, but reminding her so didn't seem to ease her mind.

"It's not fine, Stone. He was here."

"Maybe."

"We both know he was. Murphy's never barked like that before."

"Soph, they didn't spot any fresh tracks." But he had this morning when he went out for a look on his own. "And Murphy's not barking now."

They both looked over at the dog curled up and snoring in his bed.

"Yes, but—"

He shook his head. "No buts. Come here."

"I'm sitting right next to you."

"Closer." He grabbed her around the waist, careful not to hurt her ribs as he pulled her into his lap so she straddled him.

"Stone."

Ignoring her warning tone, he took her wrists, wrapping her arms around the back of his neck. "There. Much better."

She stared at him as he slid her skirt higher up her legs. "Stone," she said again.

He clutched her firm ass, bringing her closer. "What?"

"What are you doing?"

He raised his brow, moving his hand, rubbing his fingers over the crotch of her sexy purple panties. "I'll give you one guess." He nipped her chin.

Her pretty eyes went instantly dark with desire. "Shane will be here soon."

"He's not here yet." He pushed the barrier aside, invading silky fire.

She arched back, moaning.

He kissed her neck as she purred in her throat next to his ear. "Make out with me for a while, Soph."

She cupped his cheeks, her breathing ragged as she pulled his mouth to hers, teasing his tongue into a dance.

He groaned, following her lead, rubbing her with his thumb, bringing her up slowly.

"Let's go to bed," she panted out, gyrating against him, driving him crazy.

He didn't like being away from the monitors when Shane wasn't here. "What's wrong with the couch?" He moved in the rhythm he knew would get her off.

"You're trying to distract me," she shuddered out.

"So?"

She bit her bottom lip, whimpering, digging her nails into his shoulders. "You're going to make me cum."

"I know." He kept his pace steady, holding her gaze, watching as she stiffened on a long moan, pulsing against his hand. He brought her higher, not yet ready to bring her down, smiling his triumph when she clutched at him frantically, crying out loudly for the second time.

She sagged against him, her hot, steady breaths heating his neck. "I really like it when you do that."

He grinned.

She sat up, flushed and smiling, unbuttoning his pants. "Do you want a turn?"

"I'll never refuse a—" He stopped when he heard

the first pop, then the next and the one after that, recognizing the sound of muted gunfire. "Shit." He rushed up, setting Sophie on her feet, grabbing her hand as he shut off the living room light, watching the footage on the monitor go black with each gunshot "Fuck. Let's go. Come on, Murphy." He shielded Sophie's body, running with her and the dog down the hall while bullets penetrated the door, shattering vases and other fragile knick-knacks as they ricocheted through the room.

"Stay down! Stay down!" He shouted as Sophie screamed, covering her ears with trembling hands. "Get in the shower." He pushed her inside the bathroom and locked the door. "Come on. In the shower," he said quietly, crouching over her while Murphy barked and growled in her arms. "We need him quiet."

"Hush," Sophie commanded next to the puppy's ear.

Murphy stopped instantly, whimpering instead.

Sophie's heavy breathing echoed off the walls as rain pounded on the roof. He strained to hear, pulling his gun from its holster, taking aim when glass crunched on the hardwood floors of the hall.

"He's coming," she whispered, trembling.

He didn't have time to comfort her as he pushed her further behind the barrier of the marble stall, pulling his phone from the holder, hitting the button for Shane.

"Yeah," Shane said.

"He's in the house," Stone said quietly. "We're in the bathroom."

"Fuck, man, I'm turning up the drive right now."

"Get here." He set down the phone, squishing Sophie against the wall as the knob twisted in the glow of the nightlight. "Cover your ears," he said with deadly calm, ready to do what needed to be done.

Sophie did as he said.

He fired twice, around the chest and head range, and the man who wanted Sophie dead hollered out in a cry of pain.

Footsteps receded down the hall, and two rapid pops quickly followed along with the shatter of glass breaking in the master bedroom.

Stone kept his gun pointed for what felt like hours, his heart pounding, waiting, listening, his eyes glued to the door.

"McCabe, it's me," Shane yelled moments later, crunching his way down the hall. "I've called it in. Entering." He kicked open the bathroom door, aiming as Stone aimed at him. "Rooms are clear."

He rushed to his feet, a thousand weights lifting off his shoulders when he saw his soaking-wet friend standing in the doorway. "Stay with Sophie."

"Where are you going?" She stood, grabbing his shirt, her eyes wild with terror. "Stay here with me, Stone. Stay with me."

He couldn't. It was clear this wasn't going to stop until Sophie was dead. They were going to end this now, or Sophie *would* die. Next time the bastard might get off his shot, and he wasn't taking that chance.

"I'll be back." He yanked free of her grasp and shut the bathroom door, waiting to hear the lock click in place, and hustled into the bedroom. He noted the blood on the windowsill, catching sight of the man hunched and gripping his side as he hurried off into the shadows. "There you are you son of a bitch."

He hurtled his way outside, tucking himself into a roll as he hit the ground. Standing, instantly drenched by cold drops, he headed toward the canyons, following his prey into the brush and mud while blue lights flashed and police sirens wailed their way up his road. He wouldn't be waiting around for LAPD tonight.

Moving into the increasing darkness and staying close to the thick line of bushes, he squinted in the familiar surroundings of his land, trying to spot the bastard who wanted to murder his wife. His fears of the man getting away made him want to rush ahead, but getting shot wouldn't help Sophie. He paused, catching his breath as adrenaline coursed through his body, listening in the relentless rains for any sound that might give the hired gun away.

A twig snapped a few feet in front him, and he inched further forward, drawing his gun, finding the man hunkered low, peering through the sight of his rifle aimed at the house while muttering something into his cell phone.

The assassin turned his head in Stone's direction.

Stone raised his weapon. "Hands up, asshole, or you're dead."

"Fuck you." He whirled, launching himself at Stone.

Without hesitation, Stone fired. He hit the man in the shoulder but then fell back, losing his grip on his gun with the nasty thud of impact as the well-muscled killer landed on top of him. Stone reached behind him for his weapon, feeling nothing but open, empty air, and was forced into a roll over several unforgiving rocks toward the huge drop-off into the basin below. Stone used the momentum he gained to sit up and plow his fist into the fucker's face. "Who sent you?"

"You're going to die," the hit man replied, slamming the side of his hands into Stone's stomach, knocking the wind out of him. They rolled again, battling for leverage, bringing them closer to the ledge.

Stone struggled to move further onto solid ground, gripping the base of a bush as his right leg dangled and the man fought to push him to his death. Grabbing for anything next to him, he clutched a palm-sized rock, swinging, connecting with the man's temple. Using the moment of surprise to his advantage, he kicked out, shoving at the guy's chest, sending him over the edge as shouts and lights shined his way.

He lay where he was, gasping for each breath, wincing as the sickening smack of the body collided with the land below.

"McCabe," Detective Owens hollered as he ran, stopping next to him.

Stone rolled to all fours, shakily gaining his feet. "He's down there."

An officer hustled over, shining his flashlight over the edge. Stone followed the beam, staring at the gore, needing to see that the man wouldn't be getting back up to come after Sophie.

"Get somebody into the basin," Owens directed. "Are you okay? Do you need an ambulance?"

He shook his head. "No, I—"

"We've got a rifle and a phone over here," someone shouted.

"He was setting up again when I found him," Stone explained, following Owens to where another cop stood several inches from the evidence.

"Give me that pen." Owens took it from the officer and crouched down. "Let's figure out who's on the other end." He pressed redial with the tip of the ballpoint. The phone rang once.

"Is she dead? Did you finish it?"

Stone's gaze sharpened on Owens' as he recognized Eric's voice from their encounter in the Bangor Police Department hallway. He nodded his confirmation to the detective.

"We're wrapping this up right now."

"Who the hell—"

"Mr. Winthrop, this is Detective Aaron Owens from the Los Angeles Police Department." Owens pointed to a female officer with a phone at her ear.

"Go," she said, and within seconds a huge commotion filled the background of Eric's phone line.

"That should be Bangor PD taking him into custody," Owens said.

"It's about damn—"

"Stone! Stone!"

He looked up, watching Sophie break away from Shane and sprint forward. She launched herself into his arms, the force knocking him back a step.

"You're okay." She clutched his face in her hands, kissing him. "You're okay."

He moved further away from the scene the cops would want to process. "I'm fine." He kissed her again. "I'm fine, Soph." He hugged her, gripping her tight. "It's over. You don't have to worry anymore."

"Where's the man?" she asked as rain dripped down her face.

"He's dead, and Eric was just arrested."

"He's going to jail?"

He nodded. "For a long, long time. Let's get the hell out of here and dry off." He walked away, achy and relieved, still holding Sophie as he started toward the house.

# CHAPTER THIRTY-EIGHT

ERIC SAT ON THE BOTTOM BUNK IN HIS DISGUSTING CELL, waiting for the guard to tell him his attorney was here. He pulled at the uncomfortable, baggy blue jumpsuit as he looked down at the ridiculous sock-and-sandal combination he was forced to wear. For eighteen days he'd been stuck in insufferable conditions, waking at the crack of dawn to the shouts of the jail staff and groans of the dirty man above him. And he was expected to sweep and mop floors that were a hopeless cause and eat food that was little more than slop. He stood as an officer came to his metal and reinforced-glass door. "It's about time."

The portly man chuckled, shaking his head. "What's your rush? You're not going anywhere anytime soon." The guard let him out and walked him down to the visiting area. "Arms out and spread 'em."

Sighing, Eric complied, enduring the indignity of being patted down.

The guard buzzed open another door. "Go ahead in."

He walked into the sterile room where other men spoke with their public defenders or family members and took a seat across from the man who wasn't doing his *job*. "Why am I still here?"

Paul folded his hands, looking comfortable in the superior-quality threads of his Armani suit. "I'm working on it—"

"Not hard enough." He leaned in. "Do you know

what it's *like*? I shower once every two days. The 'milk' is powder and water, and there's no privacy when I need to use the bathroom. It's humiliating."

"I'm sure it is, but at this time I don't see the judge reversing his decision on your bail. The prosecution's case is solid, and they have enough evidence to consider you a threat to Mrs. McCabe's life."

*Mrs.* McCabe. He barely suppressed a scoff. She was still married to the longhaired fool. Sophie and her husband had ruined everything. She was supposed to be dead. He was going to sit in here and suffer while Stone McCabe took the money that rightfully belonged to him. "I never tried to hurt Sophie. I was set up. I want out of here."

His attorney held his gaze. "I'm going to fight for you in the courtroom, Eric, but you're looking at life. If we're lucky I'll get you a shot at parole."

"*Parole*? What happened to 'Eric, I'll take care of this?'"

Paul leaned in close. "I'm going to give it to you straight. I owe you that much. You're fucked. Prosecution is airtight. I haven't found any loopholes so far. The cops were real careful with this case—no mistakes that I've seen. We'll consider it a miracle if I can get you out in fifteen."

He wiped at the cold sweat blooming across his brow, barely able to tolerate the idea of staying incarcerated for another minute, let alone fifteen years to the rest of his life. Luckily the authorities hadn't linked him back to Johnston Sanders' death. He'd held his breath for days while the police investigated the moron he'd hired to kill Sophie. "You've already thrown in the towel. Maybe I need a new attorney."

"You'll have to make that decision, but they'll tell you the same thing."

His heart pounded and his hands shook. Why wasn't Paul scrambling to appease him the way he had for the last several years? When he issued threats people were supposed to *listen* and take action. "Find a way to get me out."

"I'll see what I can do, but as I said, the judge isn't going to reverse his decision on your bail. You need to prepare yourself for that." Paul stood.

"Wait." He scrambled up. "Where are you going?"

"My daughter has a school function in an hour. I'll contact the courts later this afternoon."

"Now. I want you to do it right this minute."

"I'll take care of it." Paul walked off, leaving him alone.

Sitting, he slammed his eyes shut, trying to gather himself as the guard called him. With little choice he got to his feet and went back to his cell, staring at the dirty, chipped walls and unsanitary toilet in the corner while his "roommate" hummed and did whatever it was that he did in his bunk.

He grew nauseous while the man above him grated on his nerves. This would be his life for months to come until he had his day in court. Paul had assured him he was doing everything he could to make sure he wouldn't go to prison, but the evidence against him was staggering—the dozens of pictures of Sophie's bruises, the reports David had compiled that the police had found on his computers, the sums of money he'd transferred out of his accounts around the time Sophie started having trouble in Los Angeles, and Dylan Matthers had decided to open her mouth and tell Clyde about the little incident in her apartment.

Everyone had turned against him. The newspapers were calling him a monster when he was the real victim. For once his money and influence didn't appear to matter. Everyone had written him off.

He jumped, startled by the loud buzz echoing through the cellblocks, and cringed when the door opened. Lunchtime. He hated leaving his cell.

"Let's go. Everyone out," the portly guard hollered.

Swallowing, Eric stepped from the cell, glancing toward the small slit of window in his room and the barbed wire keeping him from his freedom.

"Hey, artist." Someone bumped into him from behind.

He stood straight, sweating, as the disgusting, beefy man who'd been hitting on him since he arrived ran a hand over his butt. "You ready for me to make you my bride?"

Several men laughed.

Eric took another step forward. "Get away from me."

"I keep asking you for a date but you won't give me one. I'm about to take what I want." He grabbed Eric's crotch. "It's a little small, but I'm not picky. See you in the showers." He grinned and walked by.

Eric leaned against the wall, his legs buckling. Tomorrow was his shower day.

"Keep moving," the guard said.

"I—I need a minute."

"Keep moving."

He glanced back at the guard then at the man who would "date" him whether he liked it or not. He looked to the tall railing keeping him secure four stories up from the solid concrete floor, ran forward, and climbed.

"Get down!"

Shouts and jeers filled the hallway as he gasped for air, glancing around at the sea of blue jumpsuits. He made eye contact with his potential husband, turned, and let himself fly, closing his eyes, ready for the end.

~~~~

Sophie stood in her shop, smiling as she handed off her latest sale. "Thank you."

"You're welcome, honey."

Business was booming now that she was back in the press's good graces. She was once again Lily Brand's sweetheart and latest survivor instead of the irresponsible woman who fled from arrest warrants and caused life-threatening accidents with her carelessness, as they'd painted her to be just weeks ago. "I hope you'll come again," she said as the older woman walked out and Stone stepped in, wearing carpenter shorts and a white t-shirt, his hair tied back in a kerchief. Her stomach tightened with the rush of tingles as she grinned. "Hi."

He walked up to the counter, leaning over to kiss her lips. "Hey."

"How's the day off?"

"Not too shabby. Murphy and I just about have all the pavers down. He's home napping."

It had taken them almost three weeks to repair the house after the fiasco on the cliffs. Now that doors, windows, and flooring had been replaced, they were moving on to the bedroom patio. Stone had been starting on their latest project as she walked out the door this morning. "Sounds like you've been busy."

"A little." He pulled her back for another kiss. "You look good, Soph." He slid an appreciative glance up and down the slim-fit, side-slit, black-ruched maxi-dress. "Can you get away for lunch?"

She shook her head. "Carolyn left early today. I wanted her to relax since she'll be here tomorrow and Saturday morning by herself."

He frowned. "Is something going on Saturday?"

"Mmhm." She smiled, taking his hand, playing with his fingers.

"Oh, yeah? What?"

"I'm going to a wedding."

Eyes playful, he pulled her hand to his mouth, nibbling her knuckles. "Maybe I could be your date."

"Definitely."

"I need to talk to you about something." He nipped again.

"Okay. What's going on?"

"Come here." Gesturing with his head, he tugged her out from behind the glass counters and hooked his arms around her waist. "So, I got some news."

She swallowed, not sure she was going to like it. "Is everything okay?"

"Yeah."

Unease started weighing on her shoulders. "Stone, what is it?"

He sighed. "Soph, Eric killed himself this afternoon."

She blinked, surprised, trying to feel something. "Oh."

"I thought you would want to know. I'm sure it's only a matter of time before the press starts in again."

"I don't know what to say or...think...or feel."

"You don't have to say anything, and you'll think and feel whatever you want when you're ready."

"I imagine I should be relieved or maybe a little sad or maybe even happy, but I'm just glad he's out of my life." She kissed him. "How do you feel?"

"He was a disgusting human being who hurt you. If there's a hell, I'm sure he's burning in it."

She nodded. "I guess that sums it up."

He locked his arms tighter around her. "I don't

want to talk about him. He doesn't have anything to do with you and me anymore."

She smiled and snagged his lip. "Consider the topic dropped."

"I love you, Soph."

"I love you too." She straightened the hem along the neck of his shirt. "Do you want to pick something up for dinner tonight?"

"Sure."

"What do you want?"

"You."

She grinned. He always said that. "I was thinking we could grill—maybe salmon."

"Sounds good to me. Then I'll have you for dessert." He nibbled her ear. "Maybe for an appetizer too."

She shivered with the anticipation. "I could handle that, especially since I won't see you tomorrow night."

He shook his head. "Nope. Can't have the bride and groom seeing each other before the wedding."

"Even though we're already married."

"Don't piss on tradition, Soph."

She laughed, and he grinned. "Got it." She brushed her fingers along the back of his neck. "So I talked to Lily this morning about the donation we want to make to the *Escape* and *Freedom* lines next year. Are you sure you're okay with that?"

"As far as I'm concerned it can't happen soon enough. That trust has bad juju connected to it. Let's make good things happen with the money."

"Do you know how lucky I am?"

"About as lucky as me."

She smiled, loving her husband desperately. "Lily wants us to meet her at her office at five to sign some paperwork."

"I'll be there."

"She said she wants to grab a picture of us too."

He frowned. "Why?"

She shrugged. "She didn't say, but I'm assuming it won't be a big deal."

"If you're not worried, I won't be either."

She smiled. "I'm not."

The shop door opened, and she pulled away as two women came in, staring at Stone with naked lust shining bright in their eyes. She smiled again, so thankful that he was hers. "Good afternoon, Ladies. Welcome to McCabe Jewelry."

"I'll let you get back to it. See you in a couple hours." He kissed her again with a bit of heat. "My wife will take good care of you," he said to the women and walked out the door.

# Chapter Thirty-nine

Stone's white shirt and khakis billowed in the warm winds as the parade of pretty little girls started down the sand path in their flower girl dresses. Emma, Kylee, and Olivia held hands, except for when they stopped occasionally to toss petals from the baskets hanging on their arms as they passed chunky cream-colored candles lit in delicate glass vases along the way. Abby came next in a pale-blue, sleeveless, above-the-knee getup, stopping at the flower-filled arbor facing the waves. He looked down at Murphy by his side when the pup's tail started to wag and lost his breath when Sophie appeared by the last row of chairs in her simple, open-back, A-line gown. She was stunning, walking his way, smiling as small wisps escaped her fancy up-do and her dangled earrings caught the light of the setting sun. She stopped next to him, handing off her pink hydrangea bouquet with one yellow tulip nestled among the blooms to her Matron of Honor.

"You look beautiful, Soph," he murmured.

"Thank you."

"Stone. Sophie. Please join hands," the judge who married them at the courthouse said, leading them through their vows for the second time as they stared in each other's eyes. Turning to Shane standing next to him, Stone took the ring he originally put on Sophie's finger and slid the simple silver back in place. She did the same, swearing the identical promises they had only months ago, but this time when he spoke to her he meant what he said, knowing he would love her for all the days of his life.

"I now pronounce you man and wife...again. Stone, you may kiss your bride."

He stepped closer, sliding his thumb along her cheek, stroking her soft skin while the surf pounded on the coast. "I love you, Soph. So much."

She smiled, blinking back tears. "I love you too."

He captured her mouth in a long, warm kiss as their friends clapped. Easing away, he laced their fingers. "Looks like you're mine for good."

"I wouldn't want it any other way."

"Should we go party?"

She grinned. "Absolutely."

They walked arm in arm past their guests, making their way over the walking bridge to the tent on the cliffs above.

~~~~

Delicious meals had been eaten and cake served. Sophie rested her head against Stone's shoulder as he turned her around the dance floor, surrounded by the people they loved most. Everything about the night had been perfect. The stars and moon shone bright, and the lights in their house glowed warm while the man she adored held her close.

"Are you ready for Hawaii?" He said quietly next to her ear.

"Mmm." She lifted her cheek from his chest. "I wish we could've taken the whole two weeks Ethan offered you."

He shrugged. "Ten days is good enough for me. I know how important the fashion show is."

"Not as important as you."

"Yeah, but I think I'm going to like watching my wife walk the runway from the front row."

She grinned. "It is pretty fun."

He wrapped his arms tighter around her, pulling her closer. "I'm just glad things will finally start settling down around here after you, Abby, and Lily finish up with this final round of publicity. With Shane heading off to the mountains and a few of the newer guys handling the out-of-town duties, I won't have to travel as much."

"Mmm." She was thrilled with the idea of having Stone here in LA most of the time. "It'll be nice getting back to the way things used to be...sort of." She smiled. "I'm pretty sure I forgot to tell you Carolyn's willing to take on a few more hours, and I'm thinking about bringing on another sales person part-time, which means I can work from home more often."

"Sounds like a perfect time to think about starting our family." He kissed her. "I want to make a baby with you, Soph."

She looked across the tent at Sarah's large belly while she and Ethan danced, then at Hailey and Austin cooing and smiling down at their growing son. There was nothing she wanted more than to carry Stone's child. "We could try tonight."

He grinned. "You've got a deal."

She laughed. "You're going to be such a great daddy."

The song ended and Lily approached. "Hey, guys. I'm sorry to interrupt, but I have to head out."

Sophie broke away from Stone to hug her boss. "Thank you so much for coming."

"I wouldn't have missed it." Lily handed over a thin box. "I wanted you to see this now. I had them put a rush on it."

"Oh. Sure." Sophie took the box, tearing at the paper when Stone nodded for her to go ahead. She pulled free next month's issue of *Trendy*, gasping. "Lily, *look* at this. It's *beautiful*." She touched the gorgeous image of Stone staring into her eyes, kissing her knuckles among the headlines on the cover.

Lily had convinced them to pose for several shots after their meeting Thursday evening, saying she and the fashion editor of *Trendy* wanted to pull something together for an upcoming article.

"I thought so too. You're both stunning."

But that wasn't it. The page exuded love and tenderness.

"The media seems to be fascinated with you right now, so we're capitalizing on it." Lily took the issue from Sophie and flipped to a two-page spread showcasing half a dozen pictures of the worst of her bruises Dylan had captured with her camera. Next to it was an article discussing the statistics of domestic violence, then on the opposite page, she and Stone walked together in the ocean surf, snuggled close while they talked and smiled. The crazy photographer had yelled and demanded for over an hour, but he'd also captured a photograph of genuine affection and kindness in the aftermath of a nightmare.

"Thank you so much, Lily."

Stone stepped closer, angling the page his way. "I wasn't thrilled with Zenn or whatever the hell his name is, but this is actually great."

"I want women to see this. Everyone deserves what you two have." Lily kissed Sophie's cheek, then Stone's "Have fun on your trip. I'll see you next week. Stone, take good care of her."

"You know I will."

"I love this," she said as Lily walked off, still

admiring the page. "I love that everyone will get a chance to see the way you love me."

"It's nice."

She shook her head, touching his cheek. "It's amazing. You're amazing, Stone. You gave me a chance to escape and find myself again."

He closed the magazine and pulled her against him. "I decided a long time ago that the night you missed your bus and got into my car was the best thing that ever happened to me."

A fork tinged against glass, then another and another.

He smiled. "I guess I should probably kiss you."

She grinned. "I definitely think you should."

He pulled her closer, and she happily closed her eyes, accepting the warmth of his embrace.

# ABOUT THE AUTHOR

Cate Beauman is the author of the best selling series, The Bodyguards of L.A. County. She currently lives in North Carolina with her husband, two boys, and their St. Bernards, Bear and Jack.

www.catebeauman.com
www.facebook.com/CateBeauman
www.goodreads.com/catebeauman
Follow Cate on Twitter: @CateBeauman

# THE BODYGUARDS OF L.A. COUNTY

**Morgan's Hunter**
Book One: The story of Morgan and Hunter
ISBN: 978-0989569606

**Falling For Sarah**
Book Two: The story of Sarah and Ethan
ISBN: 978-0989569613

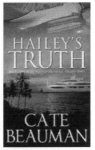

**Hailey's Truth**
Book Three: The story of Hailey and Austin
ISBN: 978-0989569620

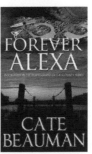

**Forever Alexa**
Book Four: The story of Alexa and Jackson
ISBN: 978-0989569637

**Waiting For Wren**
Book Five: The story of Wren and Tucker
ISBN: 978-0989569644

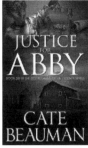

**Justice For Abby**
Book Six: The story of Abby and Jared
ISBN: 978-0989569651

**Saving Sophie**
Book Seven: The story of Sophie and Stone
ISBN: 978-0989569668

# Coming Spring of 2015

**Reagan's Redemption**
Book Eight: The story of Reagan and Shane
ISBN: 978-0989569675

7000051Π00204

Printed in Great Britain
by Amazon.co.uk, Ltd.,
Marston Gate.